A FERRY OF BONES & GOLD

SOULBOUND I

HAILEY TURNER

Cover design by AngstyG.
Professional Beta Reading by Leslie Copeland: lcopelandwrites@gmail.com
Edited by Sandra at One Love Editing
Proofing by Lori Parks: lp.nerdproblems@gmail.com

A Ferry of Bones & Gold is dedicated to
Nora Sakavic
You were there at the beginning of this journey.
I've promised you this story for years, and it's as much yours as it is mine.
Thank you for all the years of friendship and sarcasm.

1

Special Agent Patrick Collins was not supposed to be here.

New York City was not the beaches of Maui, where he should have been enjoying a long-delayed and much-needed vacation with as many tropical drinks as he could suck down. Instead, he was back on duty for the Supernatural Operations Agency, tasked with investigating a pair of emergency cases he was certain someone else could have handled.

"Out fifteen hundred dollars and no chance of reimbursement," Patrick muttered angrily as he navigated the midday traffic to find a parking spot on a block close to his destination.

This was what he got for answering his phone right as he arrived at Washington Dulles International Airport to start his vacation.

Never again.

"I should've just gone to Maui," he said, thinking wistfully of all the drinks with little umbrellas he wouldn't get to enjoy.

Patrick had been wanting to try them for years, if he were honest.

After nine years as a combat mage in the Mage Corps under the

1

direction of the US Department of the Preternatural, Patrick had walked away from frontline fighting at the age of twenty-six with habits not necessarily suited for civilian life. The SOA, a National Intelligence Service under the supervision of the Department of Defense, had immediately recruited him. Which meant Patrick continued doing what he'd been trained to do in the military, just on domestic soil rather than foreign, with a little less ordnance thrown into the mix.

Three years on and over a hundred cases later, his job mostly amounted to getting dropped into cities both large and small where monsters and demons hid in the shadows of the preternatural world. Being assigned to the Rapid Response Division within the SOA meant Patrick never got the easy jobs. He got paid to get his hands and soul dirty eviscerating demons, human or otherwise. Hazard bonuses made up a good chunk of his paycheck, but on a day like this? The money was never enough.

"When this is all over, you can go wherever you want. Just get the job done first," Supernatural Operations Agency Director Setsuna Abuku told him over the Bluetooth connection in the car. "Preferably without any collateral damage this time."

"It's like you don't know me at all," Patrick retorted.

Setsuna let out a sigh that sounded like static through the speakers. Patrick's former childhood guardian and current boss had an attitude problem. Namely, she didn't like his on every day that ended in 'y' and he didn't like hers.

There were reasons for that.

"The SOA isn't the military with a multibillion-dollar budget and the ability to write off your destructive tendencies with a mere warning."

Patrick rolled his eyes as he twisted the steering wheel and shifted the car into reverse. Parking in a red zone behind a police car wasn't ideal, but right now it was his only option. "That's a shame. You might want to look into changing your budget."

"Please stop complaining, Patrick."

"If you ever gave me a day off, maybe I would."

"I have. You didn't. Where are you?"

"About to head into a crime scene."

"You should have reported to the New York office before going into the field."

"I'd rather suffer through a migraine. Knowing my luck, this case might give me one within the first twenty-four hours."

"Patrick."

"They got another body, Setsuna. What was I supposed to say? No, I can't make it? This is what I came here for. This is why *you* sent me, remember? Dead bodies and missing people. I won't get any work done holed up in meetings all day."

Patrick put the car into park and took the key out of the ignition. The call reverted back to his cell phone as the engine and power died. The June heat hit him hard as he got out, phone pressed to his ear.

New York City was hotter and muggier than Washington, DC, and he already missed the car's air-conditioning. Sweat trickled down the back of his neck, and Patrick ran a hand through his messy dark red hair. The sides were trimmed short, but it was a little long on top. The style had grown out of his military buzz cut from three years ago and wouldn't pass regulations these days.

Getting spoiled, Patrick thought to himself. Here he was complaining about air-conditioning when he'd spent years living without it.

Setsuna's annoyed voice cut his musings short. "*Patrick.*"

"What?"

"Check in with Special Agent in Charge Rachel Andrita at the New York office after you finish processing the body."

"Is that really necessary? This case is being handled through DC by way of me. It's no longer her problem," he said.

"If you want a roof over your head instead of sleeping in your rental car, then yes, it's necessary."

Patrick scoffed at that. "You forget my bed consisted of a cot, a hard bunk, or the ground for years. Come up with a better threat."

"Take the meeting, Patrick. That wasn't a request. And try not to make this situation with the NYPD worse than it already is."

"You know I hate dog and pony shows, Setsuna. If you wanted ass kissing, you should've sent someone else."

"You were the only one I could send."

Patrick paused in opening up the trunk of the car, fingers tightening on his cell phone. "Was I?"

Setsuna's silence reminded him too much of a childhood where answers were never forthcoming. Patrick angrily shook his head and yanked the trunk open. A blast of hot air rose up from the space, making him wince at the heat. He unzipped his messenger bag, pulling out the travel lockbox that contained his semiautomatic HK USP 9mm tactical pistol.

"Are we done?" he wanted to know.

"We're done."

Patrick hung up without saying goodbye and tucked his phone into the back pocket of his black jeans. He was never going to win employee of the month at this rate.

Patrick entered the code to unlock the box and flipped open the lid, revealing the handgun inside. He pried it out of the foam interior and slid the magazine home, keeping his hands out of sight of anyone passing by. Not that there were many at the moment. Everyone seemed more interested in the police presence farther down the street.

He attached the holster to his belt and slid the handgun home, the weight of it familiar. Patrick let his right arm drop down to his side, fingers brushing over the warded leather sheath strapped to his thigh. The double-edged, ten-inch dagger was an artifact he'd been gifted with three years ago during the Thirty-Day War in the Middle East. He never went anywhere without it these days, but if he could give it up, he would.

"Fucking hell," he said, letting out a heavy sigh.

Orders from his superiors could be annoying, but those of the godly persuasion were usually worse.

Patrick grabbed his secondary gold SOA badge attached to a black leather backing from his messenger bag and hung it around his neck. It tangled with the dog tags he still wore, the metal chains warm against his skin. Shrugging on the black nylon jacket with its gold agency lettering on the back, Patrick closed the trunk and headed up the street for the crime scene.

Curious onlookers had gathered near the apartment building in question. Patrick squinted through his aviator sunglasses at the crowd and the news van situated front and center right outside the police line.

The NYPD's Preternatural Crimes Bureau held jurisdiction over the murders that had drawn Patrick to New York City. When he'd called the PCB upon landing at LaGuardia, the assistant to Giovanni Casale, the PCB's Chief of Preternatural Crimes, had requested he keep out of sight of the media. They weren't ready to announce the feds were taking over the case. With the cameras camped outside the cordoned-off area, Patrick only had one real option to stay out of sight.

"Time to get to work," he muttered.

Patrick spun his index finger in a lazy circle while he walked, reaching for that presence deep inside his soul he'd always been aware of, even as a young child.

Magic.

Roughly a quarter of the world's population could manipulate their soul's energy into magic. Children were tested young, with magic running through a range of types and affiliations, from various kinds of elemental magic to the more sinister calling of necromancy. Magic was only as strong as a person's soul, and a soul still needed to keep a body alive. Evading magical burnout was impossible some days, but the risk for mages was lower compared to other magic users.

Mages were the only ones on record who could open up their

souls to the rivers and lakes of metaphysical energy running through the earth in the form of ley lines and nexuses. That external, wild magic acted as a booster, giving them a reach most magic users could never attain on the basis of their soul alone. Mages were highly sought after by governments and militaries alike the world over for their ability to tap into that magic, though in some countries they were little more than slaves.

Patrick hadn't been conscripted into joining the US Department of the Preternatural, but the pressure he'd felt at seventeen to sign those recruitment forms with Setsuna's permission had felt a lot like he didn't have a choice.

Maybe if he hadn't been orphaned at the age of eight, things would be different. Maybe if he hadn't been magically crippled during the Thirty-Day War—that clusterfuck the Dominion Sect almost won on behalf of all the hells three years ago—he wouldn't be so fucking bitter. Patrick knew better than to deal in *what-if* scenarios, but it didn't stop him from occasionally diving down that rabbit hole.

Patrick flexed his fingers, feeling a knuckle pop as he shook out his hand.

"Focus," he told himself.

Magic, willed out from his tainted soul, spun itself into a pale, glowing blue sphere no bigger than a golf ball. It nestled against the curve of his hand, mostly hidden from sight. The mageglobe acted as an anchor point for whatever spell or ward Patrick needed to call up. The color used to be brighter, but the once vibrant shade had faded to a washed-out hue. The mageglobe's dullness was a visual clue to the internal damage he'd suffered at the end of that month of literal hell on earth.

Patrick might have lost the reach and strength necessary to tap into a ley line and cast high-level spells and wards, but he could cast a look-away ward in his sleep. The mageglobe pulsed softly with magic, the spell within its pattern creeping into his aura, that extension of a human soul.

He pushed his magic outward, the invisible force spreading through nearby auras in the crowd with no one the wiser. The look-away ward didn't make him invisible; it simply kept people's attention from wandering his way until after he ducked under the yellow Do Not Cross police tape and entered the apartment building unhindered.

Patrick let the ward drop once he was out of sight of the media, the mageglobe fading away. He slipped quietly through the lobby filled with numerous police officers. He pulled off his sunglasses and hooked them over the collar of his dark blue T-shirt. Blinking to adjust his sight, he took a quick look around.

While most of the uniformed officers came and went like they had places to be, a few men and women in plain clothes gravitated around a tall man in a suit giving out orders. Patrick headed in that direction, figuring he was in charge by sheer presence alone, because Bureau Chief Giovanni Casale had a voice that would do any drill sergeant proud.

"...can't clean it up until we get it secured," Casale was saying. "Ramirez, get somebody to watch out for that damn SOA special agent. Paula said he should be here soon."

The dark-haired woman in a neat pantsuit with a gold shield on her belt arched an eyebrow and jerked her thumb in Patrick's direction. "Found him, Chief."

Casale's attention zeroed in on Patrick, who wasn't intimidated at all by the intensity of it. He stuck out his hand, meeting Casale's gaze with unblinking green eyes. "Special Agent Patrick Collins. I'm with the Rapid Response Division based out of the SOA's DC office. The director sent me your way."

Casale shook his hand, grip firm. "Tell me you're someone with expertise in demons and that Rachel didn't sabotage our request for new help."

Patrick arched an eyebrow, curious about the rancor in Casale's voice that he didn't bother to hide. "I'm a mage. Demons are my specialty. The SOA should've contacted you about that."

Casale gave him a sharp, measuring look. "I've been on-site for the better part of half a day dealing with this mess. I haven't had a chance to check my email."

Patrick glanced up at the ceiling. "Heard you got another body."

"Eighth this year. Third in the past goddamn month and a half. The time between murders is getting shorter; we've got no leads and very messy crime scenes. The SOA's local field office wasn't worth the headache they were giving us, so we appealed. And now you're here." Casale jerked his thumb at the two people standing closest to him. "Detective Specialists Allison Ramirez and Dwayne Guthrie. They're lead on this whole mess and reporting directly to me. People, this is our latest SOA liaison."

Tall and black, Dwayne nodded a hello but didn't offer his hand. His partner, Allison, was about Patrick's height and appeared younger than Dwayne, her curly, dark hair pulled back in a tight french braid. She eyed him with frank professional curiosity. "Never worked with a mage before. Our last liaison was a witch."

Patrick shrugged. "Just feed me more often. Where's the body?"

"Third floor. Let's get you up there," Casale said.

The elevator they took was on the small side, and everyone had to squeeze together to fit. Patrick noted the space the other three left around him with mild disinterest. That didn't stop him from striking up a conversation.

"So, what's the buy-in?" he asked.

"What buy-in?" Dwayne repeated with just enough confusion in his tone that anyone other than an SOA agent would fall for it.

"Oh, come on. We all know the NYPD hates partnering with the SOA. It's all right if you don't want to talk about the pool on how long the new guy will last in front of your boss. Just let the bookie know I'm good for a hundred to see this through."

Allison shook her head. "You're that sure of yourself?"

Patrick flashed her a smile as the elevator came to a shaky stop and the doors opened. "I can always use the extra cash."

As soon as they stepped out of the elevator, the smile on Patrick's face disappeared. His magic responded to the faint traces of hell in the vicinity as it always did. The discordant recognition cut against the protective wards that made up his personal shields to contain the taint of his magic. Layered in skin, locked inside his bones, his shields weren't enough to keep his damaged magic from recognizing when something from any of the hells past the veil had leaked through. Nothing left a stain in the metaphysical energies of the world quite like that.

"I think you're right about demons. The whole floor is contaminated with a hellish taint derived from black magic," Patrick said, looking over his shoulder at Casale.

Casale clenched his jaw hard enough the tendons in his neck stood out before he let out an explosive sigh. "The witch we have monitoring the crime scene hasn't notified me of a risk like that."

Patrick started walking, dodging past a couple of uniformed cops standing guard in the hallway. "She's not a mage. The taint is barely noticeable, but I can still sense it. Someone without my reach would probably miss it."

"Everyone working at the PCB carries protective charms. Are those enough to keep our souls safe?"

"Depends on what I find at the crime scene."

Patrick had a feeling he'd be stripping a lot of souls of lingering stains caused by black magic before he left. That was never fun for anyone.

Black magic was illegal for a lot of reasons, not the least being most victims of those spells ended up dead. Patrick knew that better than most. He'd survived a premeditated attack and still carried the scars—physical, mental, magical—from when he was a child and a demon nearly clawed out his heart.

Patrick's ability to track and kill demons and monsters with ties to the preternatural world was a side effect of that childhood trauma. That little quirk in his magic had made him an asset to the Mage Corps and was the reason he had been assigned to a Special

Operations Forces team. His hunting skills meant the Hellraisers' mission success rate looked good on paper, but it did shit-all for Patrick's personal health.

Someone had propped the apartment door open with a potted plant. Patrick stepped inside, moving past the tiny kitchen to the living room and its bloody center of attraction. He was mindful of the numbered evidence tags scattered over the floor, making sure not to knock any over. He stopped near the once pristine white couch, staring down at the victim's remains.

Patrick wasn't looking at a whole body, just pieces of it. The ceiling resembled a bloody Pollack painting, courtesy of the dead man's eviscerated torso. The rib cage had been pried open like meaty butterfly wings, revealing a half-empty cavity that was missing a heart and three-quarters of the lungs. The soft skin of the abdomen was nothing but shreds, intestines spilling out of the lower part of the large, jagged hole in ropey, pinkish-gray knots.

Strings of muscle clung to the raggedly broken bones jutting out of what remained of each arm. The victim's legs were gnawed through at the thigh, the femur bones bitten clean through. Blood saturated the carpet and the nearby couch cushions, as if he'd been dragged off the couch to the floor. Fat bits of flesh were scattered across the floor around the body, but Patrick didn't see any sign of the missing limbs or organs.

Patrick would bet his entire next paycheck the guy had been eaten alive.

Members of the Crime Scene Unit and a representative from the medical examiner's office were carefully working around the body. The state of the victim made their job slightly more difficult than usual.

"You told the next of kin they're getting ashes back and not a body for a viewing, right? Did you burn all the other ones as well?" Patrick asked.

"They all got cremated. Standard procedure for homicide cases under our purview. We're not new at this," Dwayne said, sounding vaguely irritated.

Patrick knew most police forces didn't like a federal agency coming in and stepping on their toes. The defensiveness wasn't unusual. But he needed to play nice if he was going to get anywhere with this case. So he bit back the retort sitting on the tip of his tongue, mindful of Setsuna's request, and focused on the dead instead of the living.

"Anyone have a spare set of gloves?" he asked.

"In the case," a woman with CSU on the back of her jacket said.

Patrick followed where she pointed and went to dig up a pair of latex gloves. Pulling them on, he approached the body and crouched down for a closer look at the victim's face. The report he'd read on his MacBook during the short flight to New York had contained details about the dead that weren't showing up in the press—yet.

The waxy skin of the mutilated face was cold to the touch. He pulled down an eyelid to get a better look at what linked this murder to all the others. The astrological sign sliced into delicate skin had been done with such precision that Patrick doubted it was the work of the demon who had ripped the body apart.

He touched a finger to the sign that represented the immortal god Ares, an uneasy feeling settling in his gut. In his experience, nothing good ever came from magic that called to the gods.

Patrick couldn't sense any magic left behind in the body itself. Whatever spell the signs had been a catalyst for, it was nearly gone now. The only trace of it left was the residual of hellish taint.

"Are the signs the only things connecting the murders?" Patrick asked.

"The current MO is half-eaten bodies and the signs. There aren't any links we can find between the victims. There's no consistency between their economic, religious, racial, or social backgrounds. We've only found bodies in Manhattan though," Dwayne said.

"Can you be certain they've only been found in Manhattan? Are they all locals?"

"The PCB has jurisdiction in the five boroughs. We've looped in our affiliates outside New York City, but we haven't received any calls from other departments, and we haven't released critical details to the public," Casale said.

"Any sign of forced entry?"

"None. Door was locked and so were all the windows except the one running the air-conditioning unit, but there's no sign it was tampered with," Allison said.

"Poor guy's wife is a nurse and came home after an overnight shift at New York-Presbyterian in Lower Manhattan. Found him like this," Dwayne added. "She had a nervous breakdown, and EMTs removed her from the premises."

Patrick settled his weight back on his heels, still studying the body. "Hopefully not far. I'll need to make sure she's clean of magical residue before she can be let go. You said you ran off the local SOA agents previously working with you. What was their conclusion?"

"Nothing helpful," Casale said with a snort. "One witch suggested looking into hellhounds and maybe getting animal control to help with it."

Patrick rolled his eyes. "On a scale of one to bullshit, I call bullshit. Body looks like it got hit by a magical IED, not a rabid dog."

"You think that's what happened? A magical IED?"

"No. I guarantee the ME report for this victim will be the same as all the others in this case. No forced entry into the home. Body half eaten, and signs carved on their eyes." Patrick stood up and stripped off his gloves, depositing them in a biohazard bin nearby before heading to where the other three stood. "Killings like this, especially with the signs, means these people were targeted for a specific reason."

Casale studied him with an unreadable look in his eyes. "You're talking assassination."

Patrick shrugged. "Assassination, murder—both get you dead."

"That's more than the other SOA agents gave us, Chief," Allison said quietly.

Which shouldn't be the case, but Patrick was familiar with the rot hiding deep within the SOA that Setsuna and her predecessors hadn't been able to completely carve out.

Patrick crossed his arms over his chest, the jacket pulling against his shoulders with the motion. "I'll need to see the full file on this case, not just the encrypted report you emailed my boss. I also need to make sure no one else is leaving with residual black magic in their souls. Who else has been in contact with the body?"

"We'll get you names," Casale said with a grimace. He waved a hand at the crime scene and everything in it. "Give me your take on all of this."

"I don't know what the signs relate to, but the chewing and rending and the magic? At the very least, you have a demon problem."

"Mayor will be thrilled," Dwayne muttered.

Casale let out a heavy sigh and pointed a finger at the two detectives. "Both of you are in charge until everyone clears out. I'm going downstairs to feed the press. That should give Special Agent Collins enough time to make sure everyone here won't need to call a priest for last rites. Collins? You're coming with me after my presser. We're meeting with my favorite pair of eyes."

Dwayne glanced at Casale in surprise. "I thought your meeting with him was next week?"

"I'm moving it up."

Patrick frowned. "Who are we visiting?"

"Someone who might be able to shed some light on this mess, if we're lucky."

"If you have local help outside the SOA, why haven't you gone to them before this?"

Casale gave him a hard smile before turning his back on the group and heading for the door. "The SOA is technically the cheaper option, and the City gets pissed when we go over budget with our overtime. Make sure my people are safe, Collins. Any of them get hurt, the next thing I'm sending your agency is a complaint."

Patrick barely refrained from rolling his eyes. Looked like the animosity between state and federal agencies was still alive and kicking.

"Right," Patrick said, eyeing Allison and Dwayne. "Who wants me to check their soul first? I have to warn you, that spell hurts like a son of a bitch."

In unison, the two pointed at each other, silently volunteering their partner to go first.

2

PATRICK SPENT AN HOUR STRIPPING SOULS OF HELLISH TAINT. HE knew what to look for, but his magic didn't make the process easy on the recipient. The NYPD officers were more stoic about the process than the handful of neighboring tenants on the floor.

What Patrick desperately needed—once he finished—was a cigarette to ease his nerves. He'd spent the drive from LaGuardia into Manhattan avidly hating the No Smoking sticker mocking him on the driver's-side window. Patrick had carried more than one bad habit home with him from the front lines and hadn't broken any of them yet. Truth be told, he hadn't really tried. His VA-assigned therapist despaired of him ever making real progress some days.

"You'll need to get names of everyone living in the apartment building and get them cleansed later," Patrick warned the PCB witch on duty.

"We'll handle it," the officer replied. Etched onto her badge beneath her last name and badge number was a small pentacle, denoting her rank as a witch. What kind, Patrick had no idea, but she had magic, and that was all that mattered.

With nothing more he could do, Patrick left the crime scene in favor of tailing Casale through the Manhattan streets. They ended up near the Flatiron Building, though their destination wasn't that iconic structure.

Patrick parked behind Casale's unmarked police car in a loading zone outside an office building a few blocks south on Broadway. Its entrance was actually located on E. 21st Street, the building's powerful protective wards glittering at the very edge of his vision. Patrick got out of his car, curious about a place that would spend a lot of money to set mage-level defensive wards on a public threshold.

Casale looked over at him as he was about to shut the car door and shook his head. "Leave your jacket behind and hide your badge."

Patrick raised an eyebrow at that but did as he was told. He tossed his SOA jacket and sunglasses back in the car before tucking his badge underneath his T-shirt where it couldn't be seen. He wasn't leaving his sidearm or dagger behind.

"Let's go," Casale said, already halfway to the building entrance.

Patrick hurried to catch up. Crossing the warded threshold made his fingertips tingle, but the wards didn't flare in warning to his presence. Patrick's personal shields did what they were supposed to do and kept his tainted magic contained.

He was glad to get out of the midday heat and into the cool, air-conditioned lobby though. Casale flashed his badge at the security guards on duty up front and spoke briefly with them to gain access to the building while Patrick skimmed the directory of companies residing at the address. There weren't many.

Casale headed for the elevator bank. When one of the security guards attempted to wave Patrick away from getting buzzed through the scan-card security gates, Casale said, "He's with me."

The few people coming and going into the building were on the younger side, dressed casually like Patrick in jeans and T-shirts. He wasn't wearing any of their expensive sneakers or designer wingtips, so his black, well-worn combat boots stood out a little more than usual. A security guard directed them to the appropriate elevator, keeping back a few stragglers who looked more curious than irritated about the delay.

"Twenty-fifth floor," Patrick said as the elevator doors closed, and it started to rise at a quick pace. "PreterWorld?"

"We're in the old heart of Silicon Alley. The company owns the building and rents out a couple of lower levels to other companies," Casale explained.

"Why are we here?"

"Like I said. Meeting my favorite pair of eyes."

The elevator came to a stop and the doors opened up on a huge, mostly open-plan work floor. Sunlight streamed through the windows encircling all sides of the building, competing with the lights overhead. Long tables instead of cubicles offered up shared workspaces in conjunction with randomly placed coffee tables and comfortable chairs where people worked diligently on their MacBooks.

Half the people working had headphones on as they listened to music, a few heads bobbing here and there to a beat no one else could hear. Patrick could see a pool table in one interior room that was clearly a gaming area, along with multiple flat-screen televisions. Despite the hour, a first-person shooting game competition was happening. A snack station full of junk food and healthy food in equal proportions, as well as coffee and beer, was being ransacked for an afternoon pick-me-up by no less than ten people.

PreterWorld was the largest tech company originally catering to the social media habits of those born with magic or who belonged to the preternatural world and weren't shy about sharing their identities. The social media platform, which incorporated status updates, photos, and video on a feed, initially had a cultlike following before more and more mundane users began wanting access.

Patrick wasn't a fan of social media. His hatred of sharing every last little detail stemmed from living a life of secrets. PreterWorld, and the notoriety and fame one could conceivably gain from it, had never been something he wanted. He had to give the tech CEO credit though. Patrick's magic recognized most of the employees as magic users or someone who hailed from the preternatural world, which was a much higher percentage than most people ever hired.

Casale ignored the curious eyes and strode forward. They bypassed a multimedia capable conference room on the way toward the corner office situated behind partially frosted glass walls that screamed CEO.

Patrick tried to remember anything he could about the company's owner and founder. Young, as most tech entrepreneurs were, and stupidly rich after the IPO went public. But it was Casale's mention about eyes that finally triggered Patrick's memory from a long-ago meeting with Setsuna during one of his shore leaves.

There were a handful of god-touched people in the world he needed to steer clear of. Setsuna kept him updated on their whereabouts when she could. The general public might not know the CEO of PreterWorld was a seer, but the federal government did, and apparently so did Casale.

Shit, Patrick thought.

He kept his expression neutral, despite the desire to *run* beating at the back of his mind. He was aware of all the eyes on them as they walked the length of the company floor to Marek Taylor's office. The whispers in the background weren't as quiet as the gossipers thought they were.

The tall, strikingly handsome Latino man who opened the office door wasn't Marek, but someone, or rather, some*thing* else. Recognition burned briefly through Patrick's magic beneath his shields with the specific spark that meant *werecreature*; he just didn't know which kind.

Werecreatures were native to Earth. They weren't like demons who had to cross over from the many hells in existence or the fae who called the fringes of the veil home in a different plane. Way back in the murky annals of history, werecreatures used to be humans who changed into the sort of predatory animal you'd see in the wild—normal, fuzzy, liked to eat rabbits kind of werecreatures. They were feared and ostracized even worse back then when discovered by society, but those in power had seen an opportunity.

A Roman mage had been ordered by his emperor to create an army of werewolves. Calling on the power of Lupa, the she-wolf who suckled Romulus and Remus, he tried to subvert what nature had wrought. His attempt at magical control backfired and resulted in the werevirus, one of the first recorded instances of magically created biological warfare introduced into society.

The werevirus was an incurable disease made up of two substrains that caused those who were infected to change into monstrous beasts. Over time, the magic that still powered the werevirus allowed it to jump species, and the world had more than werewolves on its hands now. Born or bitten, werecreatures didn't have easy lives.

Patrick didn't know what beast the guy carried beneath his skin, but he knew the stranger had preternaturally enhanced strength and senses. Patrick's personal shields kept the taint in his soul under control, with a side effect of dampening his power to the point most people could never tell he was a magic user. If they did, they never figured him for a mage. Werecreatures were always hit or miss though. Their sense of smell was just too damned good.

"Leon," Casale said in greeting.

"Casale."

Leon carried himself with a confident manner that didn't promise violence but did promise he'd end any fight someone else started. Patrick's gaze flicked up and down Leon's body, automatically checking for weapons and finding none. Not like the man needed one since he was a werecreature.

Leon was handsome though, dark-haired and dark-eyed. He

was the kind of guy Patrick had hoped to pick up in Maui while on vacation, someone who would be able to fuck him into oblivion. Pity his week of debauchery in paradise wasn't happening.

Leon's gaze jumped from Casale to Patrick, brown eyes narrowing. "Who's he?"

"He's new," Casale said easily enough, coming to a stop in front of the doorway Leon was blocking.

"What happened to Ramirez and Guthrie?"

"Not your business. You mind letting us through?"

Leon looked like he minded very much, but a voice from inside the office spoke up. "Let them in, Leon."

Leon scowled and stepped out of the way, allowing the pair to enter the spacious modern office. Marek Taylor—CEO, billionaire, and one of the United States' few true god-touched seers—was in his late twenties, with stylishly cut brown hair and sharp hazel eyes that watched them with an eerie intensity.

Patrick didn't envy Marek's position. Mages, especially combat mages, had a higher risk of dying on the job than other kinds of magic users based solely on the types of missions and cases they handled. Seers on the other hand, they went blind, their power increasing in strength with every color they lost until the only thing they could see was the future. Most went crazy after their slow slide into darkness and ended up dead, usually by way of suicide.

Patrick had done the slow dying thing once before. He'd rather eat his gun than go through it again.

His magic had easily recognized Leon's true status, but recognition of Marek's was slow to seep through his awareness. Patrick sensed a depth of power that reminded him of those blue holes in the ocean, the marine sinkholes that hid so much below the surface. Marek carried power in his soul, the likes of which Patrick knew he shouldn't mess with.

The Fates always got so fucking *pissed* when he broke their favored mouthpieces.

"Close the door on your way out, Leon," Marek said after a moment of tense silence.

Leon never took his eyes off Patrick. "You sure?"

"It's fine."

"I'll be right outside."

"Don't listen in," Casale told him. "What we need to discuss is classified."

"No promises," Leon sneered.

He stepped out of the office and yanked the door shut. Casale looked over at Patrick. "Can you keep him from eavesdropping?"

Patrick nodded. Rather than focus his magic through a mage-globe for a simple silence ward, he stepped closer to the wall at his back. Raising his hand, he sketched out a sigil on the glass wall. Magic followed his finger like ink. He pressed his hand over the softly glowing lines and forced his power outward. Static washed through the room, creating a barrier of magically created white noise that would keep anyone from listening in on their conversation.

Marek pushed his office chair away from the desk and stood up. His outfit was casual, in keeping with the no formal dress code theme of the company, but Patrick had a feeling all of Marek's clothes were brand-name. One of Patrick's few friends had grown up in Paris and had tried to school him on fashion when she found out he was clueless. They'd had to find ways to pass the time in the field somehow, but Patrick hadn't cared about civilian clothes when he was wearing a uniform.

Marek came around the desk and didn't offer anyone a seat on the handful of chairs or the leather couch taking up space in his office. He came to a stop a few feet from them, hands on his hips.

"I saw our meeting for next week," Marek said, staring at Casale.

"I know, but something came up. We need to talk," Casale replied.

"I saw our meeting for next week," Marek repeated slowly. "But I didn't see you coming here today."

Casale stared at him in surprise. "You always see my visits."

Marek's gaze slid away to pin Patrick like a bug in an entomologist's collection. "Which means I didn't see you."

Patrick kept his heartbeat steady from long practice. A good lie held up through a good story told with both voice and body. With a werecreature not present to smell truth from a lie, Patrick could keep his secrets safe—he hoped.

"Or you didn't see the problem that Casale came here to ask you about," Patrick countered.

Marek glanced at Casale before his attention returned to Patrick. "I'm assuming you mean the murders that have been in the news lately. I don't need to be a seer to know which case requiring a chief's attention in the field is the immediate problem. Besides, if I spent every waking hour looking into what people were doing, I'd be locked up in Bellevue."

"I'm not here about what you do in your free time," Casale said.

"No, you're just here to buy the future."

"I'm prepared to pay whatever price you set for your vision."

"Is the City?" Marek asked caustically.

"We got another body today, Marek. A good man died for no reason we can discern, just like all the others. I've got a brand-new missing person case with one of Wall Street's premier hedge fund managers about to blow up in the news. Dealing with Malcolm Cirillo's wife every day isn't easy for me, you know that. I wouldn't be here if I didn't think you could help."

"And him?"

Patrick raised an eyebrow at the finger Marek pointed at him before smiling lazily at the seer. "The latest person assigned to the case."

"You got a name?"

"Why don't you answer Casale's question?"

"Why don't you answer mine?"

Patrick shrugged and didn't open his mouth.

"Marek," Casale said, trying to redirect the conversation. "Will you help?"

Marek stared at Patrick for a few seconds longer before huffing out an irritated sigh. "I have a meeting in ten minutes. Make it quick. What do you want to know?"

"Who or what is killing people in Manhattan and leaving astrological signs on the eyes of the dead?"

Marek's hazel eyes washed out to a silvery gray. His aura cracked wide open and magic—invisible, ancient, *primordial* magic—ran up hard against Patrick's shields before rebounding right back at the seer. Marek let out a strangled cry, hunching over on shaky legs, the brightness of his aura dimming. Patrick caught one of his arms before he could face-plant on the floor and hauled him over to the nearest chair.

Marek put his head between his legs and took in heaving breaths of air. His reaction told Patrick all he needed to know about this case—that it was, as always, *complicated* as fuck when Patrick was brought into the mix.

While Casale checked Marek over, Patrick deactivated his silence ward. Between one breath and the next, Leon barreled into the office, a growl coming from deep in his throat.

"Bad vision," Patrick told him. "Don't worry, we're leaving."

Leon curled his lip at him, teeth far sharper than they had been earlier. "What did you ask him?"

The way Leon put his body between them and Marek, the way he touched and scent-marked the other man in the way of pack, told Patrick they were more than just coworkers. Lovers, maybe; at the very least, friends.

"I'm sorry this is the outcome, but you don't have the clearance to know, Leon," Casale said as he stepped aside to let Leon take his place. "He may need a hospital. I've never seen Marek react like this before."

"We know what to do for him when this happens. You don't. Just get the hell out of here, Casale," Leon growled.

Casale didn't try to press his case. Instead, he jerked his head at the door, and Patrick followed him out of the office to the elevator, excruciatingly aware of the dark looks the werecreatures in the workforce were sending their way. Patrick could feel eyes follow their every move, and the weight of all that attention didn't lift until the elevator doors closed on PreterWorld's headquarters.

"That was a waste of time," Patrick said, breaking the silence on the ride down.

"Marek has never not seen the future before," Casale said, a deep frown on his face.

"First time for everything."

"Not for him."

"Whether his sight works for you or not, I don't think his pack will like you coming around after this." At Casale's sharp look, Patrick rolled his eyes. "What? I may not see the future, but I'm not fucking blind."

"Outside," Casale ordered tersely as the elevator doors opened on the lobby.

They left the building, and Casale directed Patrick into his unmarked police car. Patrick slid into the front passenger seat and sighed in relief when Casale started the engine and turned on the air-conditioning.

"Ward us," Casale said.

Patrick sketched out another silence ward on the dashboard, filling the car with static. "Talk."

The look Casale shot him came from a man who was used to giving orders, not obeying them. Patrick held Casale's gaze, refusing to back down.

"Marek's status within the werecreature community isn't common knowledge. How did you know Leon was a werecreature?" Casale asked.

"I'm a mage. It's a handy trick we get taught," Patrick lied easily enough. "What's Marek's relationship with Leon?"

"What Marek does with his personal life isn't the government's business, as he likes to remind me."

"Do I look like I give a fuck? I'm not some xenophobic asshole, despite my job."

"Your agency doesn't really inspire a lot of faith in most people, Collins."

"I'm aware of the problems in the SOA. But those problems aren't this one. You're the one who asked for help from my agency, and I'm what you're getting. But I can't do my job if you don't share what information you have."

Casale studied him silently for a long minute before abruptly changing the subject. "You're a mage. Why aren't you working with the PIA?"

The Preternatural Intelligence Agency was the traditional choice for most mages who left the Mage Corps when they declined to re-up with the military. That agency's intelligence operations extended beyond combat zones, specializing in the collection and analysis of preternatural-sourced intelligence by way of aboveboard channels and clandestine endeavors. The PIA had all but begged Patrick to join them, but he'd chosen the SOA instead.

It'd been a form of rebellion at the time that hadn't really changed anything. Patrick was still weighed down by obligations he couldn't escape.

"I've seen enough of the world on the government's say-so. I didn't need to see any more of it. Figured I'd come back home to the States instead," Patrick retorted. "Stop changing the subject."

"Marek is a seer. He can do what he likes."

"Leon wasn't god pack. He didn't have their eyes. Maybe he's an employee for PreterWorld. I'll give you that, but employees don't normally look like they want to murder you for harming one of their coworkers. If Leon considers Marek pack, that gives them a status I'm sure the local god pack isn't too happy about."

"You're not wrong," Casale grudgingly admitted.

Patrick didn't have a great track record with werecreatures, especially those of the god pack persuasion—mostly because he didn't get on with their animal-god patrons.

God packs were werecreatures infected with a super strain of the werevirus, called the god strain within scientific communities. A side effect permanently altered their eye color to that of a wolf's bright, bright blue or near-metallic amber, making it impossible to hide in plain sight like Leon could. As visible scapegoats, god packs had formed to take the punches from a society that still, to this day, hated and feared their kind. Doing so allowed people infected with the lesser strain of the werevirus to keep leading seminormal lives.

In the past, god packs had been named so for the mantle they carried in honor of their chosen animal-god patrons. These days it was rare to find a god pack that still had a connection to those immortals. But magical favor or not, their lot in life made them arrogant and difficult to work with.

Kind of like Patrick, but he liked to pretend otherwise.

"You didn't get a chance to ask Marek about Malcolm Cirillo," Patrick said. The missing person case was important, but he didn't feel it took priority over the murders right now. That didn't mean he could ignore it.

"As much as I'd like to give Isadora Cirillo an update, we aren't getting anything else out of Marek today."

"I can follow up with Marek at his home tonight. We need answers."

Patrick doubted they'd get any out of Marek, but he had to cover all his bases. They had ritualistic murders going on and a missing hedge fund manager, whose case wasn't related except for how his wife insisted it was during her initial interview with the police. Apparently, when the husband of Manhattan's most powerful high priestess witch of an old coven went missing, people paid attention. The case reading he'd done on the flight over made it obvious Isadora thought she had clout within the City, and maybe she did.

Patrick would worry about that later.

"Marek has the money to have a healer on call to take care of the migraine his sight gave him, which means he'll probably be at his preferred bar tonight. Emma Zhang and Leon Hernandez own Tempest here in Manhattan. Local werecreature spot, but you didn't hear that from me," Casale said.

Patrick wondered if Marek's relationship with his employees was strictly work related or something deeper. "Sounds right up my alley."

"They won't see it that way, but if you want to risk getting bitten, be my guest. Don't come crying to me when it happens."

"I won't be turning furry anytime soon. What's the address?"

Casale rattled it off before saying, "I'd like to keep my working relationship with Marek on the up and up, so remind him we're still willing to pay."

Patrick waved off his request and reached for the door handle. "Yeah, yeah. I'll tell him he's owed a hundred grand. Not like the guy is hurting for money or anything."

"Keep me in the loop," Casale told him as he got out of the car.

"I'll do my best."

He was a federal agent, and this was his case now. Patrick was within his rights to keep it within his jurisdiction, but he'd found over the last three years it was easier to rely on local law enforcement for support. Patrick didn't have a partner—his damaged magic was too distracting, according to the few people he'd worked with in the beginning before running solo—and he needed to find backup where he could.

Patrick closed the door and headed for his rental car, fingers itching to hold a cigarette. He really needed a smoke to help calm the stress he could feel starting to settle tight over his shoulders.

But instead of hanging around in territory he knew he wasn't welcome in, Patrick got behind the wheel and got back on the road.

The SOA's New York City field office was located in a Lower Manhattan high-rise building covered in protective wards. Patrick ignored the adjacent parking garage that was just as heavily warded in favor of pulling up right in front of the entrance and turning on his hazard lights.

He had no intention of walking into the building and dealing with SAIC Rachel Andrita until he absolutely had to. Casale's distrust of the woman was enough for Patrick to tread carefully. Patrick might work for the SOA, but he didn't trust a lot of the agents in high positions.

Patrick pulled out his phone and called Setsuna's executive assistant in DC. "Hey, Brianna. It's me. Can you patch me through to whoever handles transient employee housing in New York City? I'm in the middle of a case, and I don't have time for a meeting."

"The boss won't like that," Brianna warned. He could hear her typing away on her side of the line.

"I run my cases how I like. You know that."

"I know you do. I deal with your paperwork regarding damages the most. Transferring your call now."

Patrick ended up talking to a woman out of Human Resources here in New York City who was reluctant to hand over the keys to an apartment without him meeting with Rachel first. Patrick may or may not have used his working relationship with Setsuna to get the woman to override Rachel's request and deliver the keys to him in person.

"Thank you," Patrick said as she passed the keys and a manila envelope with housing information to him through the open passenger-side window after checking his ID.

"You were supposed to meet with the SAIC first. She won't be happy that you didn't," the woman warned him.

"Tell her to talk to the director."

"Oh, believe me. I will. I'd like to keep my job. Sign the form, please."

Patrick did as asked, scrawling his name where he needed to on the three-page form. He passed back the paperwork but kept the sheet describing the temporary residence assigned to him. The SOA had discounted rates with certain hotel chains, but they also held a small number of leases on apartments and houses in several major cities since it was sometimes cheaper to put up agents in housing rather than in hotels.

Patrick had been given an apartment instead of a hotel this time around, making it a lot easier to ward. Hotels were public space, which meant good luck finding a viable threshold to lay down wards and lock out everything that went bump in the night. Patrick had a bad habit of bringing work home with him. He'd learned over the years that demons had ingrained stalker tendencies and would never understand the concept of personal space.

The newer-looking apartment building that was Patrick's temporary home for this case was located in the Turtle Bay neighborhood, several blocks southwest of the Queensboro Bridge. Patrick didn't sense anyone except mundane humans on any of the floors during his ride on the elevator. His borrowed fifth-floor, one-bedroom apartment had a view of the street and not much else. It came furnished though, and the highlight of the place was the queen-sized bed. Second place went to the central air running through the building.

Patrick dumped his suitcase and messenger bag in the bedroom, grabbed a clean set of clothes and some toiletries, then headed to the bathroom. He wanted a shower to wash off the stink of travel and any lingering smell of death, even if it was only in his head.

He stripped out of his clothes, the claw-mark scars on his chest pulling a little when he yanked off his T-shirt. He'd had the scars for so long the scar tissue had faded to a milky white instead of the vivid pink they'd been for the first few years of their existence. Patrick rubbed at his chest as he stepped into the shower, trying to ease some of the tightness there.

Patrick got clean and got dressed, trying to sort out his thoughts on the case so far. He needed some time to absorb the details and wanted to get his hands on Casale's case files. That likely wouldn't happen today since he had somewhere else he needed to be.

He grabbed his phone and googled the bar Casale had mentioned. Tempest looked to be a place serving up craft beers and cocktails instead of the swanky club lounge Patrick would've pegged Marek to prefer, though it did have a lower-level event room. Which meant the dark blue jeans and black T-shirt he wore would be passable attire. Patrick tossed his phone back on the bed and turned his attention to the bottle of Macallan 15 Year Old whiskey he'd packed for Maui.

Patrick had plans to use it to help settle his thoughts, a form of self-medication that involved a glass filled to the brim with whiskey. He'd learned a trick or two when it came to his drinking habits over the years. Patrick measured how far gone he was by how well he poured.

He'd barely wrapped his fingers around the neck of the bottle when his plans changed in the blink of an eye.

Patrick let go of the whiskey bottle and reached for his handgun instead, clicking the safety off. The weak threshold wrapped around the apartment hadn't been tripped, but someone else was in here with him now. The second he acknowledged that fact, Patrick heard the television in the living room turn on.

"Fuck," he said under his breath.

Patrick got unwanted visitors that were not of the demonic variety from time to time. Nothing ever stopped them from showing up, but it never hurt to be prepared. Magazine locked in place and a spelled bullet in the chamber worked for him. Patrick walked out of the bedroom, weapon in hand, and the moment he saw who was sprawled on the couch, he seriously thought about pulling the trigger, lack of suppressor be damned.

"What the hell are you doing here?" Patrick demanded.

"Watching baseball, what does it look like? We don't get cable past the veil," Hermes said, not taking his eyes off the flat-screen television mounted on the wall. "Do you know you've got something like eight hundred channels? At least one hundred of those have to be porn."

Patrick scrubbed a hand over his face, thinking longingly of his whiskey and the fact he had hours to kill before needing to be at Tempest. "I'm way too fucking sober to deal with you."

"Still traveling with alcohol? You really shouldn't—"

"Touch my whiskey, get shot."

Hermes flipped him off. "Wouldn't kill me. Sit down, Patty-cakes. We've things to discuss."

Patrick glanced down at his weapon and sighed. Hermes was right. Not even spelled bullets could kill an immortal. "I hate that name."

Hermes just smiled. It didn't reach his gold-brown eyes.

"You're still fucking creepy," Patrick told him.

He clicked the safety back on and set the handgun on the small round dining table situated near the kitchen on the living room side of the kitchen's pass-through. He pulled out one of the two chairs and sat down backward on it, resting his arms over the top. Patrick ran a hand through his damp, dark red hair, never taking his eyes off Hermes.

"What do you want?" he asked.

The immortal turned off the television before stretching out his arms along the back of the couch. His aura was dimmed so much he seemed human. Hermes looked young, with the fit body of a mid-twentysomething male and the modern fashion sense of a punk on acid. His curly brown hair was bleached and dyed a washed-out blue up top, dark roots showing there and on the shaved sides of his head. Black skinny jeans with a multitude of holes in them were tucked into old Doc Martens and the band T-shirt he wore listed out tour dates from forty years ago.

Patrick was certain Hermes had gone to at least one of those concerts.

"I want what I always want." Hermes tilted his head in an arrogant way, gaze half-lidded but always, always sharp. "To talk."

"Should've gone somewhere else, then. I'm not known for talking. Just ask my old SERE instructors. Or my therapist."

"It was either you come to me or I come to you, and it's not like you can easily cross the veil between worlds. Besides, I'm enjoying this modern age. Interesting things are happening."

Patrick scowled. "Why are you *here?*"

Because crossing the veil was a difficult journey even when you were born with that inherent power. Immortals were once worshipped as gods over thousands and thousands of years, the slavish attention of their followers feeding their primordial power. Stories of their exploits were written down as history before fading into legend and finally turning into myth when their followers died out and the world changed as magic fell to the wayside for long years.

While the world forgot about them and their temples fell to ruin, that didn't mean immortals had died; they simply faded away to a shadow of their once former powerful selves.

That changed in the last one thousand years or so, when magic began showing up in the human population at a rate higher than a few paltry percentage points. People rediscovered the old myths as living truth and began to worship immortals as gods again. Their power began to return, breathing life into old lives once more.

Then there were those who wanted to own them, as if a god could be owned.

The Dominion Sect had formed hundreds of years ago, drawing together mundane humans and magic users who believed in a better way of life. That their belief required the world to be subjugated through magic, and gods from the hells didn't bother the group's founders, nor their descendants. The Dominion Sect had gained followers across the world, though it was only within the last century or so that loyal magic users had come to see a godhead as their divine right. It didn't matter that a human soul alone couldn't possibly carry the power of a god—they still wanted it. Greed wasn't rational, especially when it came to power.

Patrick touched a hand to his chest, his mind skittering away from old memories.

Immortals could find safety beyond the veil, but that was no longer a guarantee, not after the Thirty-Day War. They could find strength in new worshippers, and while science was all the current rage, religion was a quiet, powerful force not to be discounted.

One of those forces was looking at Patrick like he was a problem to be fixed or destroyed.

Preferably destroyed.

"I have a message for you," Hermes said.

Patrick froze. "The last time you gave me a message, we nearly lost an entire city."

"Ashanti still saved you."

"Don't," Patrick ground out, mouth twisting. He curled his hands into white-knuckled fists. "Just...*don't*, Hermes."

Patrick's past was riddled with painful moments, and certain parts were a goddamn minefield of emotions. The Thirty-Day War, and everything he'd lost in that fight, was still an open wound, even now.

Hermes didn't care. He never did.

The immortal pinned Patrick with a hard look, the fire in his gaze bright like the sun. "You still owe us, so stop running."

Patrick didn't promise anything, as always. Immortals hadn't earned his trust, the same way he hadn't earned their faith. That enmity wouldn't change the fact that the immortals siding with all the heavens had endeavored to blackmail him into a soul debt when he was a child and didn't know what he was agreeing to.

They'd done so in order to use him as a weapon in a war his family had started, but which Patrick wanted no part of, even now.

Hermes stood in a sinuous motion before walking over to where Patrick sat. He grabbed one of Patrick's hands and pressed an ancient Greek obol into his palm. "This is for you."

Patrick curled his fingers around the roughly hewn gold circle. "You know, we invented these little plastic things called credit cards. You can even pay with a phone app these days."

Hermes' mouth curved in a cold smile. "I know. As convenient as both options are, my money is better. I'll bring you more when Artemis and I find the rest. Dionysus lost them in some poker game in Atlantic City. We're still tracking them down."

"Greek coins? I'm in the middle of a case, Hermes. What the hell am I supposed to do with Greek coins?"

"Save us."

Hermes left the same way he arrived—disappearing through the veil as only an immortal god could. Patrick let his head fall against his bent arms, rolling the coin between his fingers. He could feel the familiar throb of a tension headache coming on.

"Fuck," he said tiredly. "*Fuck.*"

The dagger strapped to his right thigh pulsed with a warmth Patrick could feel through the leather sheath. He wondered if all the prayers of its blessed making would be enough to get him through this latest mess.

He fucking hoped so.

3

Tempest was located somewhere on Avenue B, near a park Patrick didn't know the name of. He did know better than to try driving in a major city for a night out unless he absolutely had to. Parking would be nonexistent, and besides, he wanted a drink. Patrick called for an Uber and arrived in the neighborhood a little before 2000.

The area was more up-and-coming than worn-down, even if the buildings were older than most people walking down the street. Patrick slipped out of the car a few doors down from the bar since traffic was temporarily backed up almost to the corner.

The night was muggy, but the weather was slightly cooler than it had been during the day. The Greek coin was a strangely heavy weight in his pocket. Patrick brushed his fingers over the leather sheath on his right thigh, activating the look-away ward burned into the leather with a tiny push from his magic. It twined around his body in an unobtrusive way.

No one would notice his dagger, just like no one would notice the handgun holstered at the small of his back. The spell came in handy when Patrick needed a weapon or two but didn't want anyone to know he was carrying. He expanded his personal shields just enough to hide the feel of the active ward and nothing else right as he approached the bar.

Some werecreatures were gathered around a couple of small tables outside. Two people were vaping, the smoke smelling like caramel and strawberries when it hit Patrick's nose. Pushing past the desire to stop and light up his own cigarette, Patrick headed for the door instead. The cacophony of sound coming from inside Tempest told him the bar would be crowded.

Patrick was immediately stopped at the entrance by two things: the bouncer checking IDs and the searching spell that ran fingers of magic up and down his body, looking for any metaphysical threat. The spell was low grade, but well maintained. Nothing Patrick couldn't easily hide from at his level of training, but he made a mental note to keep an eye out for any other surprises.

"ID," the bouncer demanded.

Patrick left the thin leather case with his agency ID and badge in his pocket. He pulled out his regular wallet instead and slid free his Washington, DC, driver's license, holding it out for the bouncer to check. One casual glance at the license and an indelicate sniff of his person later, Patrick was past the guarded door with a low warning of "This isn't a tourist trap."

Patrick ignored the warning.

He gave his eyes a moment to adjust once inside. The long bar on his left had a crowd three people deep waiting for drinks. The space behind them was standing-room only right up until the crowd hit the few tables hugging the wall on his right. Conversation was loud, the music louder. Gaining preternatural hearing from the werevirus meant most of the bar patrons didn't need to yell to be heard.

Despite the crowd, the place wasn't overwhelmingly hot. Marek, or whoever owned the bar, had apparently splurged on air-conditioning, which Patrick silently appreciated. He carefully maneuvered around people to get a better look at what the bar had to offer by way of alcohol.

The place was nice in that made-to-look-old kind of way. Beer on tap was more microbrew and craft than commercial, and the wooden shelves that went up to the ceiling behind the bar were filled with bottles of brand-name liquor to better serve up the cocktails Tempest was also known for. A metal rod was bolted to the wall in between two of the higher shelves and ran the length of the workspace. Patrick could see a skinny metal sliding ladder pushed out of the way for the moment at the very end of the workspace.

Recessed lights in the ceiling and the bare bulbs mounted on the walls were surrounded by thin iron cages. The light burned with a dim, almost amber hue. The crowd fluctuated more at the rear of the space than anywhere else. It took Patrick a moment to see part of the reason was due to the line down a short hallway for the restrooms and a set of stairs that led to a basement housing the bar's event room.

It took nearly ten minutes for Patrick to finally reach the bar itself after waiting while others received their drinks. Two of the three bartenders were women and busy with other orders. The third was a man Patrick couldn't bring himself to look away from, desire uncoiling in his gut with a sudden spike of heat.

Fuck me, he thought only a little desperately. *Please.*

For once, not being in Maui wasn't a bad thing.

The man was taller than Patrick by a good few inches, with broad shoulders that filled out his black, short-sleeve button-down shirt nicely. The almost too-tight shirt accentuated his solid physique, and Patrick honestly wouldn't mind seeing the muscles hidden under his clothes. The guy looked like he knew how to manhandle a person in the best way, and Patrick's cock twitched in his jeans at that thought.

Patrick's gaze did a slow up and down of what he could see before coming back to rest on the man's handsome face, with its strong jawline, sharp cheekbones shadowed by the hint of a beard coming in, straight nose, and expressive mouth. Casually messy black hair was trimmed shorter on the sides and faded into a slightly longer length up top, falling across his forehead in soft waves. He wasn't the only person sporting that hairstyle in the bar, but he wore it the best.

The man's hair still wasn't long enough to hide his eyes. Even in the low light, Patrick could see they were a wolf-bright, intense blue that almost seemed to glow. He stared at Patrick with an unblinking intensity that would make most mundane humans duck their head and werecreatures want to bare their throat. Patrick held the man's gaze defiantly, refusing to look away.

Werewolves—god pack or otherwise—had never frightened him. In Patrick's experience, plain old flesh-and-blood humans were worse.

The man's nostrils flared a little as he scented the air, probably taking in the burst of Patrick's sudden arousal. Patrick had a fleeting thought to lock down his shields a little more to hide his scent completely, but decided not to. He'd left his scent unencumbered, because walking into a bar catering to werecreatures smelling like nothing was a good way to get tagged as a problem.

The man's biceps flexed in a distracting way when he leaned his weight against the counter, the preternatural strength in his body unmistakable. His hands were long-fingered where they rested against his work area, tapping out a rhythm against metal. The coiled strength in his body, paired with those eyes of his, would make it difficult for most people to miss he wasn't completely human.

"What can I get you?" he asked, his London accent easy to pick out through the chatter around them.

Definitely European god pack, but what he was doing here in New York City, Patrick didn't know. The bartender flashed him a polite smile, gaze falling to Patrick's mouth for a split second in a tell Patrick had long ago learned to read.

Patrick licked his full bottom lip, watching those bright eyes flick downward again. "If I said you?"

"Wouldn't be the first time I've heard that," he drawled around a smirk. "But I'm on the clock."

It was a fucking shame Patrick was working a case right now. "Johnnie Walker Blue. Neat."

One dark brow arched upward. "Coming right up."

Since no crafting was involved in Patrick's drink, just a straight pour into an empty glass, it took him less than a minute to receive it. The bartender set the glass of whiskey on the bar, sliding it over.

"Forty dollars," he said. "You want to open a tab?"

Patrick dug out his wallet and pulled out a fifty-dollar bill, handing it over. "No, but keep the change."

He took the money and gave Patrick a contemplative look. "Cheers, mate. Name's Jono. Come back to me when you want another round, yeah?"

Patrick raised his glass slightly in answer to that statement before slipping away so the next person could order. He took a sip of the whiskey, the flavor exploding over his tongue. It tasted delicious, though Patrick couldn't help but wonder what it would taste like on Jono's lips.

Can't have everything you want, Patrick told himself.

If he could, he wouldn't be in this situation.

Patrick slipped through the crowd toward the back of the bar, scanning the faces around him until he caught sight of a familiar one from earlier that day. Leon had a seat at the back corner table taken over by a group of people headed up by just the man Patrick was looking for.

Marek seemed far more at ease now than when they'd left him hunched over in pain in his office. The tech CEO sat beside a pretty Chinese American woman wearing a little black dress and gesturing with one hand while the other held a pint glass steady on the table. The people surrounding them were pressed in close, drinks in hand and empties shoved to the middle. The conversation looked friendly, the vibe open and relaxed.

That ended the moment Leon got eyes on Patrick.

Patrick drank down his whiskey in one long swallow as Leon stood up and headed his way, a scowl on his face and anger in his eyes. No sense in wasting good whiskey.

Leon slid through the crowd with deadly focus, and people instinctively pulled away. He came to a stop directly in front of Patrick, standing toe-to-toe with him, forcing Patrick to tilt his head back in order to look him in the eye.

"What the hell are you doing here?" Leon demanded.

Patrick held up his empty glass and wiggled it from side to side, ignoring the curious looks directed their way. "I thought it was obvious."

"Get out."

"Oh, you know I can't do that." Patrick smiled, showing his teeth in a challenge any werecreature would recognize. "A mutual acquaintance owes your boss some money for an answer. I'm here to discuss payment and trade."

"There a problem, Leon?" Jono asked.

Patrick watched out of the corner of his eye as Jono slipped free of the crowd to stand at Leon's right in an obvious show of support. Patrick inwardly sighed. Pack solidarity was in full force. Patrick doubted he'd ever get the chance to find out what Jono was like in bed now that they were standing on opposite sides.

"Nothing I can't handle," Leon replied.

"I guarantee you can't handle me, Leon. But I'm not here to fight. I'm here to do my job," Patrick said.

His gaze flickered around the bar, tracking the movements of the crowd and picking out people taking position to act as further backup. They weren't being subtle about it. The noise level had quieted some as their little group became the focus of everyone in the bar.

"Your job gave me a migraine that cost me a thousand dollars to get rid of," Marek said as he came up behind Leon and Jono.

"You can afford it."

"What's going on?" the Chinese American woman asked with a weight of authority to her voice that had Patrick reassessing the power balance in the group.

She was an alpha, and the only person in their small group who didn't shift to give ground to her was Jono.

"This is the guy who came by with Casale this afternoon, Emma," Leon said.

Dark brown eyes glared at Patrick angrily, but he let everyone's animosity slide off him like water.

"You're not welcome. Get the fuck out," Emma said to Patrick.

Patrick ignored her and looked over her shoulder at where Marek stood behind the three. "You mind calling off your guard dogs?"

Leon's hand shot out and grabbed the front of Patrick's T-shirt, hauling him up on the balls of his feet in a sudden move that made Patrick's teeth clack together. "That's fucking it—"

"Leon," Marek said sharply, grabbing at his shoulder. "Let him go. He's a fucking cop."

Patrick didn't fight to break Leon's hold, just smirked up at the taller man. He flipped the empty glass up in the air close to Leon's head, forcing Leon to grab it with his free hand to keep from getting hit in the face with it. Patrick thought he heard the glass crack when he caught it.

"You heard him," Patrick said. "Hands off."

For a second, Leon didn't move. Then he abruptly let Patrick go with a hard shove. Patrick stumbled backward a step but caught himself before he went too far. As he turned his head to look at Marek, something caught his eye.

Caught his magic.

A man was walking toward them from the rear of the bar with a single-minded focus that screamed *wrong*. Patrick's war-trained instincts rarely failed him when it mattered, and he moved without thinking.

Patrick lunged around Leon for Marek, getting a hand around the seer's arm even as he unholstered his sidearm with the other. Patrick felt Leon's hand come down with bruising strength on his shoulder right as the minor scanning spell wrapped around the bar *shattered*, the sound of its destruction like distant ringing bells in his ears.

Patrick's magic screamed a warning, recognition searing right through him in a momentary burn that set his nerves on fire. Even as Leon hauled him backward, Patrick yanked Marek forward, getting him out of the way of his weapon.

Patrick got two shots off at his target before Leon grabbed his wrist and wrenched his arm toward the ceiling. He hissed at the painful pull of muscles and lifted his finger off the trigger, eyes still on the man who was still *coming at them*.

"What the *fuck*?" Jono exclaimed in disbelief, teeth suddenly sharper in his mouth, muscles shifting against his bones.

The crowd panicked, scrambling away from the threat in their midst. Leon's grip loosened just a little in surprise; that was all Patrick needed to get free. He twisted out of Leon's hold, shifted his grip on Marek, and shoved the seer in Jono's direction.

"Watch him," Patrick snarled before bringing up his sidearm in a two-handed grip.

The spelled bullets hadn't stopped the man—because he wasn't a man.

Wasn't even close to being human.

Gray light twisted away from the tears the bullet impacts on the body had caused, peeling back the glamour wrapped around what was hidden beneath. Its clothes disintegrated into smoke, revealing mottled, leathery gray skin split open around the joints, black bone sticking outward and tethered in place by slick muscle and knotted tendons. Razor-sharp claws jutted out from the stumps of its palms, clicking together as it moved.

The demon was humanoid in shape, a hunched-over bipedal that made Patrick's heart crawl up his throat as the glamour fell away completely. He couldn't look away from the stumpy torso with skin split over a thick ribcage and a head that had no eyes, no nose, nothing but a wide, gaping maw filled with rows of jagged teeth. A long, pointed tongue whipped out of its mouth with sickening prehensile strength.

Soultakers were hell's version of a walking bottomless pit of hunger. They fed on souls and magic, eating a person alive to sustain their own presence on the mortal plane. Patrick had only ever fought them during the Thirty-Day War, and they were a goddamn *nightmare* to kill.

People screamed as they became aware of the demon's presence. Everyone behind Patrick stampeded for the door, but there were plenty of people trapped behind where the demon stood.

"Emma!" Marek yelled, sounding frantic. "The pack!"

Patrick never took his eyes off the soultaker as he holstered his handgun. It wouldn't do anything against a demon of this caliber. He'd learned that the hard way three years ago. Instead, he wrapped his fingers around the hilt of his dagger, yanking it free of its magicked sheath. The double-edged blade was pitch-black in color, a familiar weight in his hand that settled Patrick's focus.

He dropped his shields, every last one of them, dragging his magic out of his soul in a crackling, fearsome rush the soultaker couldn't resist. Patrick made a cutting motion with his left hand through the air. Half a dozen mageglobes exploded into existence, his magic burning fiery bright like the lure it was.

The soultaker opened its mouth and *screamed*.

The sound was like breaking metal, making Patrick's teeth vibrate in his jaw. The soultaker charged forward—but not at Patrick.

It went for Marek and Jono.

Patrick put himself in the demon's path without a second thought because that's what he'd been trained to do. He led with a searing blast of raw metaphysical energy tailored for close quarters that knocked the soultaker off its feet for a few seconds and charred a stool. He grunted as the soultaker snapped at the lingering traces of the blast, sucking down Patrick's magic.

He spun up the next spell, magic burning bright through a mageglobe as he sent it careening to the floor. It exploded in a wave of magic that Patrick built up into a shield ward he knew wouldn't be strong enough to imprison a soultaker. But something was better than nothing right now.

"Everyone get the fuck out!" he yelled, pitching his voice loud as if it were a battlefield and not a bar on a Thursday night in Manhattan. "Right fucking now!"

Even as he spoke, the soultaker was already eating a hole through his shield.

Patrick was a combat mage, not a witch, warlock, sorcerer, wizard, or any other kind of magic user. He'd been assigned to the Mage Corps and not the Caster Corps for a reason. His repertoire of spells and wards were heavy on the offense, whittled and honed to vicious precision in a long-running guerrilla war against the monsters hell and the Dominion Sect sent against the mundane world.

For all his skill and strength, his magic was only as strong as his soul—and *only* his soul. According to some people, Patrick was a mage in name only these days. He'd lost the ability to tap into the ley lines running deep in the earth and channel their external power through his soul. That soul wound was a crippling one, but he'd learned to work around the damage it had inflicted with grinding stubbornness.

Patrick sacrificed another mageglobe to the shield, building up another layer as the soultaker ate its way through the first, pulling magic out of his soul with unrelenting bites.

Around him, everyone rushed for the door in a panic, most moving with preternatural speed. Emma and Leon were the only ones who moved *away* from the exit, which made Patrick swear violently.

"What part of *get out* don't you understand?" he yelled at them.

"We're not leaving until our pack is safe," Marek snapped from behind him.

People from the event room below were scrambling away from the stairs in the back, racing around the dome of magic Patrick had the soultaker temporarily trapped inside. While Leon and Emma frantically tried to herd their people out of the bar, Patrick's attention remained locked on the demon.

He could see the tears in his magic as the soultaker greedily chomped its way through the ward. A sharp ache cut through his middle from the inside out. The pain was all the warning Patrick got before the second shield collapsed, eaten away by the soultaker.

The demon charged at him, mouth open, its tongue snapping through the air with a strength that could break bone. Patrick was only distantly aware of people yelling behind him as he stood his ground. The mageglobe he flung between them was a distraction that got swallowed whole. Another spike of pain snaked its way through Patrick's body as he dragged his shields back up, but he ignored it, meeting the demon's charge halfway.

It wasn't the best idea to get drawn into close quarters with a demon without tactical body armor and no backup—he could practically hear his old captain screaming in his head about the *stupid fucking stunts* he pulled—but Patrick didn't care.

Couldn't care.

Patrick *could not* let the soultaker out of the bar to feast on innocent bystanders.

He knew what would happen if he did.

He flung his last two mageglobes at the demon, the combined explosion sending it reeling backward. Patrick dodged underneath the demon's arms and twisted around behind it as quick as he could, trailing raw magic from his fingertips as an enticement. The soul-taker went after him instead of the last few people racing out the bar door, following the taste of magic on the air, in Patrick's soul.

Patrick poured his magic into another mageglobe, exploding it at the demon's back. The soultaker crashed to the floor, its body unharmed from the attack. Even as Patrick watched, shreds of his magic were sucked into the demon's snapping mouth, blue wisps disappearing between sharp teeth. The soultaker would keep coming after him until it ate every last bit of magic he had—then it would move on to his soul.

Losing pieces of his soul always fucking *hurt*.

Here goes nothing, Patrick thought right before he threw himself on top of the demon before it got back on its feet.

While his magic couldn't stop the soultaker, he carried something else that could. What Patrick didn't have until the waning days of the Thirty-Day War, but which he had now, was the dagger in his hand.

Between one heartbeat and the next, ghostly, silvery words rose up from the depths of the black blade. All the languages spoken by the immortals who'd prayed over its making to imbue it with sparks of their power flowed across the gods-forged steel. The temporary magical strength of a multitude of gods was a crutch Patrick was more than happy to use when the situation called for it.

The black blade cut through the dense bone of the demon's rib cage like butter, searching for a heart it didn't have. Thick, tarry fluid flowed out of the wound as the soultaker tried to pull itself off the dagger, screaming in what might have been agony if it were capable of feeling pain.

Bright, shining light burst around the dagger in a flash more reminiscent of lightning than fire. The soultaker's maw stretched wide on a death scream that made Patrick want to plug his ears as white-hot, heavenly magic seared it from the inside out until the only thing that remained of it was ashes. The dagger point scraped across the cement floor, the silvery prayers fading once again into the void. The matte black of the blade lost its internal shine, the magic it carried within going dormant once more.

Patrick lifted the dagger away from the ashes scattered on the floor. The ugly stench of sulfur hit his nose, making him cough. Patrick turned his face into his shoulder so he wouldn't blow ashes everywhere.

The ache behind his ribs still lingered, a physical reminder of the magic and shreds of his soul he'd lost to the soultaker. It wasn't critical damage by any means, but Patrick had limited reach with his magic these days, and waiting for it to replenish took time. Any loss, no matter how small, put him at a disadvantage, and his job was one where disadvantages could get a guy killed.

Like it almost had tonight.

Getting to his feet, Patrick took a wide step out of the soultaker's ashes, wincing as he did so. His bones ached, a reminder that his personal shields had held up. The anchor points of the shield ward had been magically carved into his bones by a goddess who had done so out of purely selfish reasons. They weren't easy to carry, but they were useful.

Patrick looked down at the dagger in his hand, inspecting it with a critical eye. No nicks on the blade from the fight—not that any ever showed up—and the soultaker's blood had sloughed off like water. He slid it back into its sheath, not bothering to activate the look-away ward again.

The nerve behind his right eye throbbed, the tightness from his earlier tension headache threatening to return. Patrick knuckled his eye hard enough that bright spots exploded across his vision. Shaking his head, Patrick opened his eyes and stared at the empty, damaged bar.

He was about to head downstairs to make sure everyone had made it out alive when a sound from behind him had Patrick reacting instantly. He spun around, magic twisting through a mageglobe in his hand, ready to fight, but managed to restrain his *kill first, ask questions later* instincts when he saw who stood there.

"You're alive," Marek said, staring at Patrick in surprise.

Jono stood behind Marek in the doorway, his wolf-bright blue eyes locked on Patrick. He stayed close to Marek, acting almost like a bodyguard, exactly how Leon had done at PreterWorld earlier in the day. The protectiveness wasn't lost on Patrick.

Patrick clenched his fingers into a fist, extinguishing the mageglobe. "I'd be terrible at my job if I wasn't."

Marek glared at him, but the anger quickly faded. "You never said you were a mage. I thought you were a cop."

"You thought wrong," Patrick replied. "Special Agent Patrick Collins, at your service, though I wish I wasn't. I'm with the SOA and was assigned to the latest case the PCB is handling. I flew in this afternoon."

Marek tried to step closer but was held back by Jono's firm grip on his shoulder. Marek's gaze was riveted on the ashes spread across the bar floor, his lips pressed into a hard white line. When he finally raised his eyes to meet Patrick's gaze, a hint of otherworldly light flashed across them.

"We need to talk," Marek said.

In the distance, Patrick could hear sirens growing louder as the police drew closer. Patrick knew his night wouldn't be over for hours after this mess, and all he wanted to do was go back to his borrowed apartment and drown himself in his bottle of whiskey. Instead, he took out his phone to send a message to Setsuna.

"Yeah, we do."

4

"What the hell happened?" Allison asked as she walked into the bar. Dwayne was hot on her heels, and behind him came two members of CSU with gear in hand.

Patrick waved them over, not moving from his spot halfway between where Marek and Jono stood near the bar and the uniformed officers who had responded from the local station to a call of shots fired. They'd quickly learned it wasn't a problem they could handle.

The matter with the dead demon was preternatural in nature, which meant jurisdiction was automatically conferred to the Preternatural Crimes Bureau. That didn't stop the officers from trying to take witness statements from a known werecreature in a hostile manner. Patrick hadn't much cared for their attitude since their arrival and had promptly pulled the federal card on them when he pulled out his badge. Police hated that tactic, but Patrick wasn't here to make friends.

"That case you called me in for? I know what kind of demon it is," Patrick told her when she drew close.

"Are you serious?" Dwayne asked flatly. "Six months we've been running this case, and you waltz in and break it wide open in less than twenty-four hours? Unbelievable."

"You wouldn't have wanted to be the person dealing with the damned thing at the time. Trust me on that."

"You obviously did."

"And I'm very grateful for that since he's the only reason we're all alive tonight," Marek interrupted sharply from where he was slouched against the bar, tapping away at his phone. "Where's Casale?"

"On his way back to the PCB according to Dispatch," Allison answered.

Marek grunted but didn't look up from his phone. "Special Agent Collins? I need to talk to Casale."

"Give me five minutes," Patrick replied. He turned to face Dwayne and Allison, lowering his voice. "The demon is dead. You're not getting anything but ashes. I'll give Casale my report. You can read it when you get back to the station."

"It's Thursday night. This place is always packed. Where are all the witnesses?"

"Gone. I'm not going to guess how many were werecreatures, but they won't want to be identified since none of them were god pack. Besides, you have witnesses. I'm bringing them back to the station with me."

Allison frowned. "This doesn't make any sense. This attack doesn't follow the MO at all. A bar? It's a public space. Everyone else was home alone behind a threshold when they died. Who was the demon after?"

Patrick tilted his head at where Marek was still typing away on his phone. Jono hadn't said a word yet but was watching them with undisguised interest. More to the fact, he was watching Patrick, and the weight of Jono's attention made Patrick very, *very* aware of his presence.

"My money's on Marek. Which means I need to get him behind

some stronger wards for the next couple of hours while we sort everything out," Patrick said.

Marek's head finally lifted. "A couple of *hours?*"

Patrick ignored him. "Scene is yours now."

Dwayne and Allison shared a long look that Patrick couldn't read. Finally, Allison pursed her lips before nodding. "We'll tell the chief you're on the way downtown while we handle everything here."

Marek put his phone away and approached their small group. He thrust his hand out at Dwayne, looking more than a little annoyed. "Here. I made a copy of the security feed for you guys. Don't go messing around with the computers back there without a warrant because I'm not giving you permission to take anything else."

Dwayne took the flash drive from him with careful fingers. "Thanks."

Marek looked as if he was ready to crawl out of his skin if he stayed there any longer. Patrick jerked his thumb at the entrance in a clear signal to leave. "We'll talk later, Detectives."

"Bye," Allison replied, already turning her attention to the crime scene.

"You said your car is outside earlier," Patrick said. "How far away is it?"

Marek would've led the way out of the bar if Jono hadn't overtaken him. "I bought the parking spot from the City when I financed the bar for Emma and Leon. It's out front."

"I keep saying you should've just bought the whole bloody lot of them. Leon would quit whinging about parking if you did," Jono said as they walked outside.

The vehicle parked right outside the bar was a glossy black Maserati GranTurismo that Patrick wouldn't be averse to opening up on a long stretch of highway if he owned it. He wallowed in a serious case of car envy for a second or two as he took in the expensive vehicle.

Pays to be rich, he thought tiredly.

Marek unlocked the car with a beep from the electronic key fob. Patrick let Marek get behind the wheel without argument. Jono waited on the sidewalk expectantly, and Patrick reached down to move the front passenger seat forward before gesturing at Jono to get in the back.

"I'm taller than you," Jono pointed out.

"That's nice," Patrick drawled. And it probably would be in any other situation. "But I'm the federal agent with a weapon. Unless you want me to shoot through you at a threat, get in the fucking back seat."

Jono stared at him for a second or two, a slow-growing smirk curving his mouth upward at the corner. "Sure thing, mate."

Jono got into the back seat—but not before making a point to get into Patrick's personal space and brush against him. Patrick bit his lip, refusing to give ground, and told his traitorous dick that now was *not* the time to be interested. Judging by Jono's knowing look, Patrick had failed to keep his attraction to himself.

His shields were hiding his magic, but not his scent, and Patrick belatedly fixed that with a thought as he climbed into the car. He closed the door and buckled up.

"Get us to the PCB station," Patrick said.

"I'm not a taxi driver," Marek replied as he pulled into the street.

"Be happy I'm letting you drive at all and we're not taking the subway."

"Why would we take the subway after what just happened? That's not quick, and you seem to want quick."

"Because of the wards. We have them in the London Underground," Jono said.

Patrick glanced over his shoulder at the other man, mildly surprised at the correct answer. "Yeah."

New York City's subway was a lot like the London Underground or the Paris Metro. Hell, it was like any other rail system in the world that cut through the earth. They were old, extensive, and crammed full of people. Beyond that, they were built from the rails up by both mundane and magical means. The protective wards kept the trains and people safe while running through fringes of the preternatural world below that sometimes broke through the veil.

The subway was probably the safest public place in the City against demons right now. Patrick couldn't say anything about pickpockets.

The drive downtown was a mostly tense, silent affair, broken only by the ringing of Patrick's cell phone. He noted the name on the screen and didn't hesitate to answer it.

"Collins. Line and location are not secure," he said.

"Soultaker," Setsuna stated flatly in greeting, ignoring Patrick's warning.

"I see you got my message. It's dead."

"Any identifying trace signature?"

"No." Which hadn't been a surprise. Patrick rubbed his thumb against his temple, but the temporary pressure didn't do anything to stop his headache. "I'm going to need backup."

"I'll put a task force together."

"Who?"

"You'll know when they arrive," Setsuna said cryptically before hanging up.

Patrick pulled his phone away from his ear and scowled down at the dark screen. "Fucking hate when she does that."

"What's a soultaker?" Jono asked from the back seat.

"Keep your ears to yourself."

"No promises."

"Fucking *werewolves*," Patrick muttered as he slouched in the seat.

Less than five minutes later, they reached their destination. The Preternatural Crimes Bureau took up an entire block downtown on Centre Street. The square building was five stories high, with a small adjacent parking garage that Marek pulled into. The officer on watch duty at the entrance seemed ready to read them the riot act for trying to park in a restricted area. One look at Patrick's SOA badge got them buzzed through.

"Guest parking is next level up. You'll need to exit the garage and enter the building from the street," the officer said.

"Thanks," Marek replied.

Marek drove where directed and found a spot, squeezing his car carefully between a cement pillar and an older Toyota. They got out and headed for the exit, taking the stairs down to the street. Before they even reached the PCB's main entrance, Patrick could sense the buzz of protective wards built into its walls and foundation knock against his shields.

Shaking his head to clear it, Patrick led the way inside. The sergeant on desk duty sitting behind bulletproof and warded glass eyed their approach curiously. He wasn't the only one.

"Sage," Marek said, sounding relieved.

He brushed past Patrick and hurried through the lobby, making a beeline for the woman who'd stood up from one of the hard plastic chairs along the wall at their arrival. She was petite, though her high heels more than made up the difference between herself and Marek. The blue office sheath dress she wore showed off her tanned skin. Thick, straight black hair was tied back in a low, sleek ponytail, framing a face with distinct Native American features.

Patrick's attention zeroed in on the necklace she wore as he walked closer. The turquoise pendant gave off a cool wash of magic that had a specific feel to it he only ever sensed when the fae were involved. The artifact, a portable object capable of holding magic that non-magic users could wield, was well made. Sage didn't look like a fae, but then again, glamour could hide anything.

"I got your message," Sage said, searching Marek's face. "Are you all right?"

"I'm fine. I thought you were going to wait for me at home?"

Sage rolled her eyes in exasperation. "You said you were being questioned by the police. I wasn't going to let you face that alone."

"I told you I was okay."

"Stupid isn't a good look on you."

Marek wrapped his arms around Sage and gave her a soft, welcoming kiss on the mouth. She huffed in irritation, but Patrick didn't miss the way her hands shook ever so slightly as she pulled him closer. Marek murmured something too low for Patrick to hear before turning them around to face him and Jono.

"This is Sage Beacot, my partner. I texted her earlier about what happened tonight and where I'd be," Marek explained without apology.

"I'm also a lawyer, specifically his," Sage added coolly. "I'm a senior associate at Gentry & Thyme."

Patrick's headache throbbed a little harder at that bit of news. He hated dealing with lawyers, but he hated dealing with fae lawyers even more. Whether Seelie or Unseelie, they all gave him a migraine.

"If you're bringing in the fae, I'm gonna have to call in someone from legal on my end," Patrick warned.

While the fae couldn't legally lie, they traded in half-truths and misleading language all the damn time. They were required to follow the letter—but not the spirit—of the law. Most fae outside Underhill were lawyers for a reason. Patrick wasn't up to playing word games with one tonight.

"I'm not fae," Sage said.

"Your artifact says otherwise."

"Bit rude asking what everyone is," Jono said directly behind him in a low voice that sent an unexpected shiver down his spine.

Werecreatures all had higher body temperatures than humans of any persuasion. The heat emanating from Jono's body distracted Patrick for a second or two as he thought about how Jono would feel against him in bed. Patrick was glad his shields could hide his scent, but they couldn't hide the way his heart skipped a beat.

"Special Agent Collins?" the sergeant asked through the speaker.

"Yeah," Patrick said, ridiculously thankful for the interruption. He dug up the thinner wallet containing his agency ID and badge, holding it up for the sergeant to see.

"The chief is expecting you. Fifth floor. Take the first bank of elevators right past the door."

A buzzer sounded and the door that accessed the rest of the building unlocked. Patrick eyed the way Sage stood defiantly beside Marek, expression seemingly carved from stone, and figured he had a better chance at disarming a bomb than convincing her to stay behind. He waved at them to follow him through the door.

"Come on," he said.

They followed the sergeant's directions and took the elevators up to the fifth floor, the doors opening onto a hallway. The open plan from Marek's company wasn't in practice here, and it took being escorted by a detective working late to find the conference room where Casale was waiting for them.

Casale was in a different suit than the one he'd been wearing earlier in the day. This one was a bit wrinkled, as if he'd thrown it on in a hurry. The clock hanging on the conference room wall read 2256, so that was likely the case.

"I'm thinking I should've appealed months ago if these are the results you get me in less than twenty-four hours," Casale said.

"You're entirely too happy about me fighting a demon in a bar tonight," Patrick replied irritably.

"You got us a break in the case. I'll take that." He waved them to the nearest available seats even as he got out of his. "Give me a minute."

Casale left the conference room. Patrick shrugged and chose the nearest chair to sit down in. The other three glanced at each other before sitting down on the other side of the conference table in an us-versus-them arrangement. No one spoke until

Casale returned five minutes later carrying a large carton of what smelled like Chinese food, a bottle of Gatorade, and an industrial-sized bottle of Tylenol. He set all three in front of Patrick.

"Eat," Casale ordered.

Patrick stared at the food. "Did you just steal someone's dinner?"

"Of course not. I gave him money to go buy more and extra time on the clock for his break. Now eat."

In the field, Patrick had always carried extra ration bars hidden away in his pockets and field pack because using magic used up energy, and he required calories to replenish both. A *lot* of calories. His old team knew he'd be an irritable son of a bitch until they got food in him after any fighting. They'd taken to carrying extra rations along with their own to keep him fed.

It'd been a long time since Patrick had worked with a mundane human who understood what it took to keep a magic user healthy.

Patrick grabbed the plastic fork sticking out of the carton and stabbed a piece of General Tso's chicken. He popped the piece into his mouth and started chewing, watching as Casale took the seat at the head of the table. Casale turned his formidable attention on the other three first.

"Jonothon de Vere," Casale said in greeting. "Do Estelle and Youssef know you're here?"

Jono leaned back in his chair and crossed his arms over his broad chest, giving Casale a thoughtful look. "I'm not acting on the god pack's behalf, if that's what you're asking."

"Then you should go."

"He's a witness," Sage countered.

"Ms. Beacot, so nice to see you again. This case really doesn't need your presence," Casale said.

"I'm Marek's counsel of record for when his sight is requested. You shouldn't have even seen him today without me present," Sage replied coolly.

"The situation required some immediate answers, which we still haven't received."

"The City knows the cost of requesting his sight. Until such payment is made—"

"It's all right, Sage," Marek interrupted, settling his hand on hers, which were clasped together on the table. "Just this once, they don't have to pay the fee."

Sage gave him an incredulous look. "Marek—"

"No. Don't argue. This situation is different."

"Because it concerned you personally?" Casale asked, his voice dry as a desert.

"Because I didn't see it coming, okay?" Marek snapped.

Casale stared at Marek with an unreadable look in his eyes. "I don't care that Jono is a witness, and I don't care about your counsel. What we need to discuss regarding your sight and this case is restricted."

Marek shook his head. "Jono and Sage are staying."

"This isn't a negotiation, Marek."

"They *stay.*"

Patrick paused in midbite, looking across the table at Marek. The seer had lost a bit of color in his face, eyes a little too wide as he argued with Casale. Maybe the situation was out of the ordinary, maybe it was the hint of fear in his eyes; either way, Casale caved.

"What is discussed in this room stays here," Casale said in a hard voice. "There's too much at stake regarding this case if information is leaked. The usual paperwork is being drawn up regarding your sight, Marek. It will apply to all of you."

"We're not signing anything until I see what contract you're giving us," Sage replied.

Patrick kept eating his stolen Chinese food, watching the conversation be punted across the table like a tennis match. The chicken was actually pretty good, as far as greasy takeout was concerned. The Gatorade left an artificial aftertaste in his mouth he could've done without though.

Someone knocked on the door ten minutes later before opening it. The uniformed officer handed Casale a manila folder and a couple of pens before leaving without a word. He thumbed through the papers before sliding it across the table to Sage.

"Take a look and sign it," Casale said.

Marek reached over and plucked the folder out of Sage's hands, grabbing a pen while he was at it. "We're signing."

"Marek," Sage said exasperatedly.

He turned and looked at her, and whatever she could see in his eyes that Patrick couldn't, it was enough to get Sage to stop arguing.

"Casale asked me about the murders on the news earlier today. I saw the demon in the bar, but I didn't see it *tonight*. Sign the contract, Sage," he said in a tight voice.

"Okay," she said quietly.

"Wow," Patrick said. "I think that's a first."

"First what?" Casale asked.

"First time a lawyer is signing something without reading it. What if there's a clause in there that says you have to give up your firstborn to the PCB?"

Sage shot him a withering look. "You're not funny."

"It's happened before. The giving up the child part, not the lawyer signing without reading. Although on second thought, I'm sure that's happened before." Patrick pointed his fork at Marek. "Where did you see the demon?"

"You mean the soultaker?" Jono asked pointedly.

Patrick internally sighed when Casale's head snapped around to look at him. "Just couldn't keep your ears to yourself, could you?"

Jono smiled lazily at him and didn't say a word.

"The demon is a *what*?" Casale bit out in a tight voice.

Patrick reached for the bottle of Tylenol and twisted off the cap. He shook out five of the 200 mg pills and swallowed them with the last of the Gatorade.

"You're gonna give yourself an ulcer," Jono warned.

"Blame the job, not the medication," Patrick said.

"Was what you killed tonight a soultaker?" Casale demanded.

Patrick thought about lying, but something told him the Fates seeing through Marek's eyes wouldn't appreciate it. "Yes."

"An explanation for those of us who aren't versed in demonology would be nice," Sage said.

"Soultakers are shock troop demons. They're used in war if they're used at all because they're as difficult to control as they are to fight against."

Unless one had an alliance with immortals, but that was neither here nor there. Patrick shoved those thoughts aside to deal with later, preferably with a bottle of whiskey at hand.

"They're almost always summoned by Dominion Sect magic users," Casale stated flatly. "Are you telling me we might have an active cell in New York City?"

"You got eight bodies carrying eight signs for the gods in death. I'd bet all the stock Marek owns in his company that soultakers are the murder weapons. Who is pulling the trigger? Your guess is as good as mine, and mine would be the Dominion Sect," Patrick said.

Casale was quiet for a long moment, his expression unreadable. When he did speak, he directed his words to Marek. "Where did you see the soultaker in your vision?"

Marek chewed on his bottom lip before letting out an explosive sigh. "There were trees around me in the vision, but I could see buildings, so I don't know, a park? New York City has a lot of those, so good luck figuring out which one it is."

"Anything else?"

"I could see the demon crouching over someone on the ground, but I couldn't see who it was. I don't know if I knew them."

"Or if it was you," Casale said.

Marek flinched at his words, and Patrick wondered if the Fates he served had ever showed him his own future. Sage wrapped her hand around his and gave him a gentle squeeze. Marek turned his hand in hers, threading their fingers together.

"I see the future, Casale. I see it at the whims of the gods I'm at the mercy of. It's not always what any of us want to see," Marek said.

Sage looked away from Marek and met Patrick's gaze. "You seem to know how to handle this kind of demon."

"I'm a mage. It's my job," Patrick replied.

Except it wasn't something all mages were taught, because they didn't carry damage in their souls the way Patrick did. All magic users were taught according to what their magic had an affinity for. Some practitioners handled the elements. Other practitioners healed. Still others tried to raise and enslave the dead—something frowned upon in pretty much every country now, no matter how many hits those videos got on YouTube.

Patrick had a tendency to put out fires with gasoline.

The overkill method was not the SOA's favorite, but when push came to shove, he got the job done.

"Then why don't you explain why it targeted Marek? You have eight bodies, and now they're going after a seer. We have a right to know why so we can protect him and ourselves," Jono said.

The look Jono gave Patrick was challenging but not unexpected from a god pack werewolf. Casale's greeting earlier and Jono's answer had piqued his curiosity about Jono's position here in New York City. Most major metropolitan cities only had one god pack, and rivalries meant war no humans liked to see. Jono taking the lead due to his status wasn't unusual, and Marek seemed fine with him doing so, but it might be a problem later down the road.

Patrick met Jono's gaze across the table, refusing to give ground. "Soultakers will eat anyone's soul, but they like the clean ones best and ones with magic even more. Marek? He's a seer. On a scale of one to ten when it comes to power, he's an eleven. If the

Dominion Sect wants a power source to anchor whatever spell they need these souls for, then Marek would be it."

Casale drummed his fingers against the table a couple of times before he pointed a finger at Patrick. "Ward Marek's home tonight."

"That's not necessary," Marek tried to protest.

"I think it is. I won't put a security detail on you out of respect for your pack, but I don't think your people will be enough to keep you safe." Casale looked at Patrick. "Can the SOA field a witch?"

Marek shook his head. "I don't want a government agent living with me around my pack. I won't risk their privacy like that."

"Then I'll ask my wife, unless you have any objections about that?"

"No, we don't," Sage answered quickly for the both of them when it looked like Marek might continue to argue.

At Patrick's questioning look, Casale said, "My wife is a priestess in a coven here in Manhattan. She can get Marek set up with someone his pack won't mind."

Patrick would've preferred a witch from the SOA, but he didn't feel like arguing. Judging by Marek's immediate refusal of the first offer, they'd be fighting all night about it if Patrick pushed.

"I'll ward his home tonight. Send your witch over as soon as you can," Patrick said.

"I'll call my wife and get the ball rolling." Casale pushed himself to his feet, a frown on his face. "It goes without saying if you see anything else, you tell us, Marek. Please. We'll pay the cost, and gladly."

"If I see anything else for this case, I won't even charge you," Marek said grimly.

Casale nodded. "Collins, I'd like to speak with you in private. The rest of you can wait here until I'm done with him. We won't be long."

Patrick left the conference room with Casale, trailing after him down a long hallway filled with small offices until they came to

Casale's. His assistant's desk outside was covered in papers and files sorted into neat stacks. Casale's office was large and meticulously warded with such care he doubted it was done by anyone in uniform.

"Your wife ward your office?" Patrick asked as he sat down in one of the two leather chairs in front of Casale's wide wooden desk. The space was double the size of the offices they'd walked past, as befitting the rank Casale held.

"If Angelina could ward my life to keep me safe, I think she would." Casale waved vaguely in the direction of the closed door. "The silence ward activates automatically. They can't hear us no matter how hard Jono and Sage try."

Patrick blinked at that bit of information Casale had unexpectedly given him. "Sage is a werecreature? I thought she was fae?"

"She didn't tell you?" Casale asked.

"She carries fae magic in an artifact. I thought it helped anchor a glamour."

Casale sighed, rubbing at his temple. "That's on me for assuming you'd figured out her status, like you've figured out everything else tonight. She's a werecreature but works for the fae. I'd feel bad about disclosing her status, but you'd have found out anyway if you're hanging around Marek for the duration of the case."

"Probably."

"What happened tonight, Collins?"

"I went to the bar to ask Marek about what he saw this afternoon. Didn't take very long for the soultaker to show up."

"How?"

"The demon wore glamour. Only a mage could cast that spell strong enough to completely hide a demon's presence from a bar full of werecreatures."

"So an active cell of the Dominion Sect is a strong possibility."

Considering Patrick's past history with soultakers and the people who favored using them the most, he thought it was less

63

a strong possibility and more an actuality. "Probably our only one."

Casale nodded, seeming unsurprised at that assessment as he stared at Patrick. "You handled the one tonight. I've heard not even tanks could dent them during the Thirty-Day War."

"Aerial strikes or spelled tank shells worked best. Those with ties to the preternatural world, like werecreatures, had better luck getting in close and killing the demons than mundane humans did, but it was still risky," Patrick replied.

If Casale's wife was a priestess in a prominent coven, notwithstanding his own rank, it was unsurprising Casale knew a bit more than the average person about the demons who'd been the backbone of the Dominion Sect's fighters in the Middle East.

"Then how did you kill it tonight?"

Patrick rubbed at his mouth before shrugging. "That's classified."

"Really?" Casale asked flatly.

Patrick blinked, his mind swelling with disjointed memories of the Thirty-Day War that had broken him in ways that could never be fixed. It had started with a torn veil in the Giza Plateau, spread through the cradle of civilization, before ending in Cairo. The public still didn't know everything that had happened during that time, despite the numerous war correspondents embedded with the military and civilian videos uploaded onto the internet during the fighting.

The truth, buried beneath a mountain of bureaucratic red tape and classified Top Secret, Eyes Only across a dozen countries, was worse. Patrick knew it only because he'd lived through it.

Hidden beneath the chaos of hell reigning on Earth for almost a month was the attempt by a Dominion Sect mage to capture a god. Bolstered by the strength of the nexus beneath Cairo that now no longer existed, the mage had almost succeeded in stealing a godhead.

It wasn't the first time they'd tried it.

In the end, it took the sacrifice of a different god to put an end to that madness when Patrick couldn't finish the job. The official report of how the Thirty-Day War ended didn't include his name, and Patrick was fine with that. He didn't want to go down in history as the guy who fucked up even as the world declared victory. If he'd done what he was supposed to do back then, if he'd done what the immortals who sided with heaven had ordered him to do, he wouldn't be in this situation now, watching history repeat itself.

Patrick took a deep, silent breath and tried to steady his thoughts. Hindsight was always so fucking perfect and so fucking *useless*.

"I was trained at the Citadel and spent nine years with the US Department of the Preternatural in the Mage Corps before leaving for the SOA. So, yeah, Casale. The missions I've been assigned and the cases I've worked are classified at a level you can't reach. I've seen things and done things your average witch will never have experienced," Patrick said.

"Regardless of the appeal I sent through, I don't trust the SOA," Casale told him. "Your last few directors have been self-serving, and the one before all of them was a traitor. Tell me why I should trust *you*?"

"Because I'm all you've got," Patrick said simply, meeting Casale's gaze and not looking away. "So give me a week, Casale. One week to see if I can't stop whatever is happening around these murders. I'll keep you in the loop and work with you."

The silence weighed heavily between them for a long minute before Casale finally relented.

"One week," Casale agreed in a low voice. "And I want your word as binding that you'll keep the PCB updated. I don't care that the case is now under federal jurisdiction. This is my City, and it's my job to help keep it safe."

Promises, contracts, oaths, agreements—they were all binding in ways even the gods respected. Whether written down or spoken out loud, tying a person's soul to their words bound them to a commitment they could not escape.

Patrick should know.

He'd *tried*.

"One week," Patrick echoed. "Thanks for your understanding."

"Christ, don't thank me for this. Get out of my office. We're done for tonight."

"I'll send you my report later for your files."

Casale waved a hand in irritation. "Do what you have to do. Just make sure the City is still standing at the end."

Considering the ruins that parts of Cairo ended up in, as well as other cities in the Middle East, it was a reasonable request. Patrick just wasn't sure he could meet it.

5

Sage tailed them all the way to Marek's Fifth Avenue penthouse apartment overlooking Central Park on the Upper East Side. Marek hadn't gone the obvious nouveau riche path and bought a brownstone or space in a luxury tower. No, he'd gone straight for blue blood territory, buying up an entire Art Deco building. Patrick was vaguely jealous. If he'd come into that much wealth at a young age, he probably would've bought a tropical island somewhere and never told anyone the location.

They parked in the basement amongst a fleet of other vehicles. Patrick climbed out of the car and was the odd man out on the way up to the apartment. Sage and Marek were in deep conversation, with Jono chiming in every now and then. Patrick's headache had eased enough that their chatter didn't make the receding pain worse.

He'd have preferred going to his borrowed apartment to sleep off the day, but the time on his phone said it was 2346 and his night wasn't done yet.

When the elevator doors opened with a soft ping onto a small foyer, the mahogany apartment door on the other side was already open. Leon stood behind Emma in the doorway, both of them waiting impatiently for their arrival. Patrick hoped no one else was in the apartment. He was so done with people right now.

"Marek," Emma said in relief as she rushed forward to hug him. "You're safe."

"Relatively speaking," Marek muttered as he hugged her back.

Emma let him go but not before scent-marking him on the throat with a swipe of her hand and wrist. Marek didn't fidget beneath her touch, as if he was used to her forwardness. Her actions spoke louder than words at Marek's place in their pack.

He was *pack*—period.

Leon hadn't moved from his spot in the door, glaring at Patrick. "You're not welcome here."

"Patrick is here to ward Marek's home," Jono said easily enough. "Casale's orders."

"Marek's home is already warded, by a mage no less. We don't need his help."

Jono shrugged. "Let him in, Leon."

Leon scowled. Patrick thought he'd have another fight on his hands, but Jono was god pack, no matter what his personal rank in New York City might be. Leon stepped aside without argument, still looking annoyed, but the doorway was cleared.

Emma pried herself away from scent-marking Marek and Sage with the focus of a mother hen and hustled them inside the apartment. Patrick noticed she still wore those impossibly high heels from the bar earlier and barely came up to Marek's nose. The woman was tiny but bossy, and Marek didn't even try to fight her.

"After you," Jono said.

Patrick felt too boxed in when he stepped inside the apartment. The threshold wrapped around the home practically sang in his ears, making the nerves in his teeth tingle. Patrick shook his head to clear it, taking in the apartment with a quick look.

Crown molding lined the ceiling, a holdover from another design period, but that was the only hint of age in the home. What walls he could see were white and decorated with framed photographs instead of art. A wall of windows facing Central Park probably provided a lot of sunlight for the sleek kitchen with its modern appliances and the wide, open-plan living area. A hallway led to other rooms, and a staircase led up to a second level, housing who knew what up there.

Patrick peeled away from the small reunion going on and headed for the windows. He stared down at the street and the hazy, dimly lit darkness that made up Central Park in the center of Manhattan at night. His gaze skipped over the swath of inky urban greenery to the tall buildings on the Upper West Side. The distance was a length Patrick knew any decent sniper could easily handle when finding their target.

He reached out and touched his fingertips to the cool glass, sensing the pulse of the threshold against his shields. It was strong —as strong as Patrick could probably have made back when he could tap a ley line. But that wasn't the case any longer. Throw in a demon that could chew its way through the veil, and Patrick knew his magic wouldn't be enough to ward this place.

The magic in the Greek coin he carried was another matter entirely.

He dug out the obal Hermes had given him that afternoon. The magic embedded in the gold coin wasn't too dissimilar to the sort lying dormant in his dagger. An immortal's primordial magic, even just a spark, always felt different to his sense. More wild and dangerous than what humans could produce in their souls, reminiscent of the metaphysical power running beneath the earth.

Patrick had learned to manipulate ley lines before he was thirteen years old. The military had honed that ability in the Citadel before he lost it to a soul wound he'd carry to his grave. Some things, however, the body would never forget. He might not be able to channel external magic through his soul anymore, but manipulating embedded magic in something closely resembling an artifact was still possible.

Patrick pressed the coin against the glass, holding it there against the flat of his palm. A golden glow filtered out between his fingers as he coaxed the foreign magic free, shaping it into the form of a barrier ward. That particular ward was the strongest form of defensive magic a mage could cast, and one which he'd never had much luck in holding up for very long with his own magic.

But this wasn't his magic.

No mageglobe, just a mind full of *command*, of *will*, as Patrick shaped magic into what he needed. He was careful to keep his own magic free and clear of the power he held in his hand. No sense in tainting the defense he was constructing by creating a hole a demon could waltz right through.

Lines of light crawled away from the coin and his spread fingers, cutting over the glass like a brilliant glowing spider web. It moved as fast as lightning, wrapping itself around the entirety of the apartment building, sinking into the threshold already laid down. The threshold bent beneath the weight of magic but didn't break, absorbing the barrier ward that now encased the apartment with power borrowed from an immortal.

When the ward came full circle, locking into place inside the coin, Patrick let it go. The rough-hewn circle of gold glinted in the window, having sunk into the glass, anchoring the magic.

Patrick turned around to face Marek and the others, jerking a thumb over his shoulder at the Greek coin. "Don't remove it."

"Do I want to know what you just did?" Marek asked.

"Yes," Sage answered as she crossed her arms over her chest. "Yes, we do. That didn't smell like normal magic."

Emma groaned before making a beeline for the kitchen. "God-damn it. We didn't conduct hospitality with you first."

Patrick rolled his eyes. "I'm a federal agent. You don't need to do that."

Leon pointed a finger at him. "You're breaking bread and having wine before you leave."

"Water," Jono corrected. "The bloke ate five paracetamols at the station. Alcohol isn't a good chaser."

"I'll take wine," Patrick said, because he was never going to say no to free alcohol.

Jono gave him a *look*, which Patrick ignored. The god pack alpha might be used to giving out orders, but he wasn't Patrick's boss, so he didn't have to listen.

Emma came back with the heel of a slightly stale French bread loaf in one hand and a glass of water in the other, which was just unfair. Patrick would've preferred the wine. She thrust both at him with a defiant look in her brown eyes.

"Be welcome," she gritted out, very obviously not meaning the words, even if it was the act itself that mattered.

Patrick tore off a piece of the bread and popped it into his mouth, washing it down with a mouthful of water. It left a gummy film on his teeth. At the edge of his senses, Patrick could feel the threshold react to the casually done ceremony. The faint, almost antagonistic bite of foreign magic eased.

Hospitality greetings were binding welcomes that ensured no harm would be done to the hearth and home while a magic user was present, and vice versa. Breaking the welcome meant suffering through an annoying headache for the next day or so, and the threshold forever banning the person in question from entering the home again. It made things awkward when it was the owner who screwed up.

Patrick handed back the water glass. "Happy?"

"No," Emma retorted.

"The magic?" Sage pressed, like a dog with a bone, as most lawyers were.

Patrick wiped his fingers on his jeans to get rid of the bread crumbs. "I used the artifact to set a barrier ward. I'm hoping it will be enough to keep the soultaker out, but there's no guarantee. It would be best if you stayed inside for the next few days."

"I have a job," Marek reminded him.

"You're the owner. Take the time off so you aren't lunch for a demon," Patrick shot back.

"The demon was after Marek?" Emma asked sharply, spinning around to look at the seer.

Marek winced. "No?"

"*Marek.*"

"I mean, maybe? Yes? It's complicated, Emma! And I can't exactly talk about it."

"Oh, we're talking about it," Emma growled.

"The details of the case aren't available to the public," Sage said, rubbing a finger against her temple.

"Marek is pack and under my protection. I have a right to know."

"*We* have a right to know," Leon added.

Marek threw his hands up in the air and turned to Patrick. "Are you done?" he asked, very unsubtly.

Patrick wasn't going to stick around longer than he needed to. If Marek was going to break the NDA against Sage's advice, then he could deal with the consequences, whatever they might be. Far be it from Patrick to police a seer.

"Yeah, I'm done. Call me if you see anything," Patrick said.

He was halfway to the door when he heard multiple people cry out Marek's name. Patrick snapped his head around, hand reaching for his dagger, ready to fight. No signs of a demon hit his senses, and the barrier ward was quiet around them.

Marek had fallen to his knees, clutching his head, expression twisted in pain. Emma and Leon were on their knees beside him, holding him up with preternatural strength. Sage crouched in front of him, her hands on Marek's face, grounding him. Jono had stepped closer, a troubled look in his eerie, bright blue eyes, but he didn't reach for Marek.

"Ngh, someone dim the lights," Marek ground out through clenched teeth.

Sage shot to her feet and hurried over to the nearest light

switch, plunging the floor into near darkness. Emma and Leon gently coaxed Marek to his feet, guiding him over to the couch. The pair tucked themselves on either side of Marek, watching him worriedly. Sage came back and knelt in front of him again, one hand resting on his knee.

Marek sucked in a breath, then another, sounding like he was trying not to get sick. He still hadn't opened his eyes. "Patrick? I'm gonna call you Patrick. Special Agent seems too formal after tonight."

Patrick froze, not liking where this was going. "I was leaving."

Marek let out a low, pained laugh. "Yeah, you were. But Jono is going with you."

"What?" Jono said, taking a step closer.

Patrick's gaze cut to Jono before returning to Marek. "No."

Marek gingerly leaned back against the couch, as if he didn't want to jar his head too much. Patrick knew that feeling. "You need to take Jono with you."

"I'm not the one who needs a bodyguard. That's you."

"The wolf stays with you."

The hairs on the back of Patrick's neck stood on end, nerves singing at the ethereal, echoing, *female*-sounding voice that came out of Marek's mouth. His eyes were open now, a pure, unblemished white, different from the silver earlier that afternoon. They seemed to glow with a soft luminescence that no human eyes should ever hold.

"Fucking *hell*," Jono swore.

Marek pushed himself to his feet with a lithe grace that didn't belong to him. Emma and Leon remained frozen where they sat, watching their friend with wide, worried eyes. Sage tracked his movements with a pained expression on her face. Patrick had to lock his body in place at Marek's approach, ignoring the desire to *run* because he refused to retreat from the immortal currently in control of the seer's body.

The crackle of power pouring off Marek made Patrick fight

back a flinch. He didn't want to think about what it was doing to Marek. He met that otherworldly gaze in a human face without blinking.

"Get out of your vessel before he burns through another shade of color," Patrick warned in a low voice.

"Then do as you have been told."

"You're going to have to be more specific than that," Patrick bit out, knowing whichever Fate currently hijacking Marek's body was likely to do the opposite and double down on vagueness instead.

Marek's body leaned into his personal space, mere millimeters separating them. When he spoke, his breath ghosted over Patrick's ear in a chilly puff. *"The wolf stays with you."*

Patrick glared straight ahead, clenching his teeth so hard his jaw ached. "Fine."

The amount of vitriol he managed to pour into that one word was more reminiscent of a *fuck you* than an agreement, but this Fate could take it or leave it for all he cared.

Apparently, she took it.

Marek suddenly slumped against him, and Patrick's arms automatically came up to catch him, staggering under the other man's weight. With a grunt, he guided Marek to the floor when it became apparent the seer's legs would no longer hold him up.

"You all right?" Patrick asked, keeping his voice low.

Marek clenched his hands around the fabric of Patrick's T-shirt with surprising strength, face buried against Patrick's chest as he simply breathed.

"So long as you don't piss off the Norns anymore, then yeah," Marek rasped.

Leon came over to them, carefully prying Marek out of Patrick's arms with easy strength. Marek kept his eyes closed, face drawn tight with pain. Patrick shoved himself to his feet and looked over at Jono, who only had eyes for him. For a moment, it felt like they were the only ones in the room. Then Patrick blinked and jerked his attention back to Marek.

"I think this situation is why I asked you to come here, Jono," Marek muttered.

Jono stiffened, mouth pressed into a hard line. He didn't say anything, merely stared at Marek before roughly shaking his head. "You look knackered, mate. You should get some rest."

"Don't leave him, Jono."

"Marek—"

"*Don't.*"

Jono's shoulders sagged a little. "I won't. I swear."

"Okay." Marek pressed a hand to his forehead, mouth twisting in pain. "Bye."

Jono seemed to take that as the cue to leave. He headed for the door, waving his hand at Patrick. "Come on. We'll have to stop by my flat first. I need clothes if I'm staying with you."

The traitorous part of Patrick's brain wanted to answer with *you really don't.* Instead, he focused on the logistics of their travel. "I'll call an Uber."

Jono snorted. "No one is going to stop for someone with my eyes."

"I'll drive you," Sage offered. She grabbed her purse and paused just long enough to brush a gentle kiss against Marek's cheek and drag her hand against the side of his throat to scent-mark him. "Do not wait up."

"I don't plan to," Marek said weakly.

"Good. You need to rest."

"We'll keep an eye on him until you get back," Leon promised.

Sage nodded before following Jono out of the apartment. Patrick gave Marek one last, lingering look before leaving. The three of them took the elevator down to the garage.

"Will he be safe?" Sage asked, not looking anywhere but straight ahead.

"I don't know. If his patrons can keep him out of a demon's reach, then maybe," Patrick said, opting for the truth over a lie.

Sage nodded silently before squaring her shoulders and leaving the elevator when they reached the garage. She unlocked her car with the press of a button on the key fob. Patrick ceded the front seat of the BMW to Jono this time around and climbed into the back. He closed his eyes, still feeling as if the Fates could see him, despite leaving Marek behind.

Sometime later, the car braked to a stop and Patrick opened his eyes. Jono got out and hurried toward the front door of a four-story walkup. Patrick had no idea where they were. Sage hadn't bothered looking for parking, merely turned on her hazard lights and pulled up the emergency brake.

Patrick stared out the window at the door Jono had disappeared through. "What did Marek mean about Jono coming here?"

"That's not my story to tell," Sage said.

"He's god pack."

"Yes, but he's not ours."

"Did you learn obfuscation from Marek or law school, because I have to tell you, it's not helpful."

Sage calmly pulled up the GPS map function on her phone. "I need your address."

Patrick rolled his eyes and gave it to her. The sooner he got to his apartment, the sooner he could sleep. Luckily for him, Jono didn't take forever.

Less than ten minutes later, Jono returned to the car, carrying an overnight bag in one hand. He climbed back into the passenger seat, and Sage took the car out of park. She followed the quiet instructions of the GPS app to Patrick's apartment. Like at Jono's place, she didn't bother looking for parking when they arrived.

Putting the car into park and turning on the hazard lights again, Sage watched them get out. "Be safe."

"Keep an eye on the pack, yeah?" Jono said.

"Always."

Sage drove off. Patrick dug out his keys from his pocket and headed for the front door of the apartment building. Jono stayed right on his heels, the heat at his back something Patrick couldn't ignore.

"I don't have a spare bedroom," Patrick said on the elevator ride up. "You can sleep on the couch."

"Rather be sleeping in my own bed," Jono said.

"You want to disobey the Fates, then be my guest. They can't get pissed at me if you walk out of here."

"Seems you know quite a bit about how they work. Seems they know *you*."

Patrick refused to rise to the bait in Jono's words, wanting more than anything to dive into his whiskey bottle. If Hermes had come back and stolen it, they were going to have a short conversation over the barrel of his handgun.

The elevator doors opened, and Patrick stepped out, walking down the short hallway to the apartment. He let them inside, waving a hand in the direction of the couch as he unholstered his handgun and set it on the dining table.

"That's yours," Patrick said.

Jono set his overnight bag by the couch, taking in the small apartment with curious eyes. "Could do with an upgrade."

"The SOA doesn't pay for maid service or home delivery of a second bed."

Jono turned to look at him, studying him with that too-bright gaze of his. "Pity, that."

"House rule number one. Keep your eyes, ears, and nose to yourself."

Jono arched an eyebrow, mouth curving in a faint smile that was more mocking than anything else. "And if I don't?"

"Then I guess I'm casting silence wards every time I need to have a conversation with someone that isn't you."

Jono stalked forward, the single-minded intensity in his gaze pinning Patrick where he stood. He refused to back down from that powerful regard, which meant when Jono reached for him, Patrick thought about putting himself out of reach.

He didn't.

Jono deliberately pushed Patrick backward until his back hit the wall. Patrick had to tilt his head up to look him in the eye, forcing his heartbeat to remain steady. Jono removed his hands and planted them against the wall, bracketing Patrick in. This close, Patrick could feel the heat in Jono's powerful body, could smell the faint hint of cologne mixed with sweat as the werewolf leaned down to speak into his ear.

"What was it you asked for at the bar?" Jono murmured, his breath blowing softly over Patrick's left ear.

The shiver that slid down his spine made Patrick bite his tongue. "I'm working."

"I'm not." Jono pulled back just enough that Patrick could see his eyes again, the brightness of the blue otherworldly in his handsome face. "I can't smell you anymore, not like at the bar. Drop your shields."

"No."

Jono stepped closer, his head dipping down, lips hovering over Patrick's mouth as he pitched his voice low and deep. "Drop your shields, Patrick."

The words were spoken with the powerful authority of a god pack alpha werewolf who wasn't used to being told *no*. Patrick had stood his ground against more dangerous creatures in his life. Hell, he'd run from the demands of the gods themselves. Refusing Jono's demands was easy.

The problem?

Patrick didn't want to.

New York City wasn't Maui, not by a long shot, but if Jono was offering, then Patrick wasn't going to say no. He knew Jono wanted his scent for an ulterior motive—*tracking*, a voice in the back of his mind whispered—because he wasn't stupid. But

Patrick's shields could hide him from anything, even a werecreature's powerful sense of smell.

There wasn't a demon overriding Patrick's scent this time when he dropped his shields, just his own damaged magic with its black taint scarred deep. Jono drew in a deep breath through his mouth, and when he let it out, Patrick swallowed it whole.

Jono's mouth was warm on his, heat bleeding between them as Jono crowded him against the wall. Patrick let him, let Jono slide one leg between his, one hard thigh riding up high to rub against Patrick's cock. He ground down against the pressure, cock hardening almost instantly, ignoring the discomfort of his empty holster digging into the small of his back.

It'd been *months* since the last time he'd had sex, and Patrick gasped against Jono's mouth when warm fingers yanked at his belt buckle, tugging him up a little on the balls of his feet. He got his own hands on Jono's belt, and between the two of them, they got their jeans undone as Patrick rode Jono's thigh without shame. The grinding pressure was exquisite and everything Patrick wanted right at that moment.

Touch. Heat. Someone else in his arms to make him feel *good*.

One big, warm hand slipped beneath his underwear, and Patrick arched into the touch shamelessly, letting his head thunk against the wall with a moan. "Fucking hell, just get me off right here."

Jono chuckled against his ear, mouth dragging down his throat to suck at the delicate skin there, breathing in whatever scent he was after. Patrick turned his head a little to give him better access, arching into Jono's touch.

"Is that what you want?" Jono asked.

Patrick wanted a lot of things he never got, but he'd take tonight because he could.

He shoved his hand down Jono's pants and squeezed that thick, heavy cock, licking his lips. "Can you hear my heartbeat?"

"Like a bloody drum," Jono growled as he lifted his head, pushing into Patrick's touch.

Patrick turned his head, staring into Jono's eyes. "I want this."

The truth in his words was one Patrick didn't mind giving up.

With a groan, Jono pulled his hand off Patrick's cock and grabbed him by the ass, hauling Patrick into his arms. He wrapped his legs around Jono's waist, dropping a hand between their bodies to pull Jono's cock free of his underwear. Jono was *big*, and the thought of getting fucked by him made Patrick's mouth water even though he knew he wouldn't get that tonight.

This, right here, was a one-off of mutual using.

Jono lined their cocks up together and started to stroke them off. The first drag of those warm, tight fingers made Patrick groan. He canted his hips up into the circle of Jono's fingers, wanting more. Precum pearled at the tips of their cocks, and Patrick reached down to spread it around with his thumb. Their fingers tangled together, getting a little slicker, but the dry friction was almost too much at times.

"Gods," Patrick moaned on a particularly hard stroke. He dug his heels into the small of Jono's back, urging him closer. "How long can you hold me up?"

"However long I like."

Patrick couldn't help but laugh a little breathlessly, pleasure zinging through his nerves. "Show-off."

Jono didn't reply, merely distracted Patrick by kissing him hard and deep, stealing the air from his lungs. Patrick tightened his legs around Jono's waist, urging him closer, and Jono obliged. Trapped between the cold wall at his back and the heat of Jono's body, that warm hand which wasn't his own stroking him off, Patrick wasn't going to last. Too long spent doing this alone meant the edge was getting closer and closer.

Patrick smacked one hand against the wall above his head, fingernails digging into the paint as he pushed into Jono's grip. "Faster."

Jono looked at him with those wolf-bright eyes, strands of hair sticking to his skin. Patrick was pinned in place by desire and Jono, and he gave in to both willingly enough. Jono jacked them both off, their cocks sliding against each other as Patrick writhed in Jono's arms.

When Patrick came, it was with Jono's hand on his cock, Jono's mouth on his, muffling his cry with hard lips. Patrick shuddered as his orgasm rolled through him, body going almost languid for a few seconds, held up by Jono's easy strength.

"You smell good," Jono muttered against his mouth.

And that, Patrick knew, was a lie. He didn't need preternatural senses to know that.

"Bet I'd smell better with your cum on me," Patrick muttered, not ready yet to lose the rapidly diminishing afterglow. He knew that was a thing with werecreatures—scent and scent-marking in all its varied forms.

Jono nipped at his bottom lip. "Let's find out."

Jono used Patrick's cum to slick up his own cock. Patrick could feel the motion of Jono's hand against his body as he worked himself over before coming with a groan, face tucked against the curve of Patrick's throat, the scent of sex thick between them.

Jono lifted his head, and Patrick watched as he raised his cum-covered hand to his mouth, licking the mingled taste of both of them off his thumb. Patrick's cock gave a valiant twitch at the sight, and while he would be up for another round under any other circumstances, he'd given Jono what the other man wanted.

A way to keep track of Patrick whenever his shields were down.

Which would be never.

"Put me down," Patrick said, unwrapping his legs from Jono's waist.

Jono kept his hands on Patrick's ass until he got his feet on the floor. Patrick wiped his hand on his T-shirt before grabbing at his jeans, hauling them back over his hips. He didn't bother tucking his cock back inside his underwear.

"You wanted my scent, you got it," Patrick said, sliding away from Jono. "I'm going to bed. There are extra blankets in the hall closet."

Jono said nothing as Patrick left him behind in favor of going to the bathroom to wipe himself clean. Still holding his jeans up, Patrick crossed the hallway to his bedroom and closed the door behind him. He pressed his forehead against the cool wood, sighing quietly.

That was probably one of his shittier decisions, having sex with someone the gods threw in his path. Still, getting off in Jono's arms had been the only good thing to happen to him today, as fleeting as it was.

"Focus on the case," Patrick muttered under his breath.

Because the murders needed his attention more than the hot as fuck werewolf sleeping on his couch.

6

PATRICK'S CELL PHONE GOING OFF JARRED HIM OUT OF A LIGHT sleep. He automatically reached for his handgun where it rested on the nightstand near the bedside lamp before he was even fully awake. The knee-jerk reaction of get up, grab your weapon, and go had yet to fully leave him even three years out of the Mage Corps.

Picking up his phone instead of his handgun, Patrick squinted at the screen. The time read 0729. The incoming call was a New York City area code, with no name attached.

"Collins. Line and location are not secured," Patrick said when he answered, voice rough from sleep.

A crisp, decidedly annoyed female voice came through the speaker, not familiar to Patrick at all. "Special Agent Collins? This is Special Agent in Charge Rachel Andrita."

Patrick winced, flopping onto his back. "Ma'am."

"I understand you stopped by yesterday to pick up keys to your housing assignment and didn't bother to let me know you were on the premises."

"Something came up."

Rachel paused, as if waiting for him to continue. She let out an annoyed huff when she realized he had nothing else to add. "I expect to see you at my office at nine o'clock sharp."

Patrick wondered if it was too tactless to hope another body would turn up within the next hour and give him an excuse to miss the meeting.

Probably, he mused. "Understood, ma'am."

"Good."

Rachel hung up and Patrick tossed his phone on the bed, the charger cord nearly pulling it to the floor. Scrubbing a hand over his face, he winced at the tightness in his neck and the faint ache in his chest. His headache was gone, but the reminder of last night's dance with a demon still hadn't faded completely.

Patrick got out of bed, grabbed some clothes from his suitcase, and headed for the bathroom. If pressed, he could get ready in ninety seconds or less, but he wasn't in a hurry this morning, mostly because of Rachel's ultimatum. So he took his time under the shower spray, letting the warm water loosen his knotted muscles.

What he wouldn't give to be waking up on a resort beach in paradise. The apartment didn't even have coffee. Patrick wasn't doing anything work related until he had some coffee.

He scrubbed himself clean, soaping off any last lingering traces of Jono he carried on his skin. Thinking about last night was dangerous territory, so he didn't, refusing to indulge in a morning jack-off session because he knew what he'd be missing. It made for a nice memory though, despite the situation.

Patrick finished up and got out of the shower, drying off with a white towel that looked and felt like it belonged in a cheap hotel. He got dressed in a pair of dark blue jeans and a wrinkled button-down shirt that he immediately rolled up the sleeves on.

The agency dress code was supposed to be business suits, but field agents were known to ignore it more often than not. Patrick wasn't all that interested in running after a preternatural suspect in a suit and smooth-soled Oxfords in ninety-degree heat. He left the towel on the bathroom floor and went back to the bedroom to pull on his boots and strap on his tactical handgun and dagger.

When Patrick came into the living room, he found Jono lying on the floor instead of the couch, shirtless, with one arm thrown over his eyes. The extra blanket from the closet was tangled around his waist, putting his chiseled abs on display. Patrick stopped staring at his phone in favor of staring at Jono, idly wondering if Jono's muscle definition was as hard as it looked and if he could maybe check using his tongue.

For scientific reasons, of course.

It's a fucking shame we didn't get out of our clothes last night, Patrick thought.

Too bad it wasn't happening again.

"What was wrong with the couch?" Patrick asked.

"Hard as a bloody rock," Jono mumbled, not moving.

"You need to get ready. I got someplace to be, but I need coffee first."

"Nine o'clock meeting, yeah, I heard."

Patrick kicked Jono's bare foot sticking out from the blanket, earning him a sleepy-eyed glare. "Remember house rule number one? You keep your eyes, ears, and nose to yourself."

Jono very obviously let his gaze travel up and down Patrick's body. "I'd rather break the rules like last night."

"Last night was a onetime-only thing."

"Of course it was," Jono drawled.

Patrick refused to acknowledge the way Jono's deep voice affected him, opting instead to lock down his shields as tight as he could. Judging by Jono's sudden frown, whatever he'd been picking up from Patrick's scent, it was gone now.

As much as Patrick wanted to take Jono to bed, it would be unprofessional and possibly dangerous. He didn't trust the gods and their unknown reasoning for wanting Jono to stay. Whether or not he could trust Jono remained to be seen.

Jono rolled to his feet in a smooth motion, the blanket falling away from his naked body. Patrick's eyes drifted downward, getting an eyeful of Jono's gorgeous cock. He resolutely didn't think about how this morning could have gone if he didn't have a SAIC riding his ass. He had a feeling he'd enjoy it more if it was Jono.

Blowing off Rachel to blow Jono would earn him zero points with Setsuna. Sometimes his job was the ultimate cockblock.

"I can't smell you," Jono said, stepping into his personal space.

Patrick lifted his phone, pressing the power button so they could both see the time on the lock screen. "Five minutes, then I'm leaving without you."

"The Fates that Marek sees for wouldn't like that."

"I don't fucking care."

The words came out harsh, falling between them like heavy stones. Jono blinked, taking a step back in the face of Patrick's sudden and intense fury that he couldn't contain. Taking a deep breath, Patrick reined in his anger as much as he could, but he'd never reacted well to orders given by gods.

They always ended up fucking him over, and not in the good way.

Jono looked at him for a moment before tipping his head in the direction of his overnight bag. "Five minutes, you said? Don't leave without me."

Patrick didn't dignify that with a response, too annoyed at himself for not policing his emotions. He was a better agent than that, but this case was getting under his skin. The hints Patrick could see in the evidence, the presence of gods—none of it was good.

Almost exactly five minutes later, Jono came out of the bathroom in jeans, a gray T-shirt, Chukka boots, and his black hair gelled into some semblance of style. Patrick let himself look for a second or two because he damn well wanted to.

"Very Euro trash," Patrick said.

Jono slipped on his Ray-Bans to hide his distinctive eyes and headed for the door. "You're one to talk. Aren't you feds supposed to wear suits?"

"The last time I wore a suit I ended up running through a forest after a wendigo and ripped my clothes to shreds when I took a header down a hill. I stopped doing suits after that."

That had happened during his second case with the SOA. Patrick had reverted to his current style of dress after that, and Setsuna had let his choice in clothing slide without comment. Patrick took what wins he could get with her and was happy.

He locked the door on his way out and raised the strengthened threshold wrapped around the apartment. He rubbed away the twinge of pain in his chest, the physical ache an echo of the magical one in his soul.

Patrick had googled the nearest place providing food and coffee while Jono got ready. The little coffee shop half a block away looked like a local chain dedicated to the art of coffee, but no one was taking time to sit at any of the small tables. Morning rush hour on a Friday meant it was grab and go. When Patrick reached the counter, the woman taking his order didn't look up from the iPad doubling as the register.

"Whaddya want?" she asked.

"Large coffee with two shots of espresso and an everything bagel," Patrick said. He looked over his shoulder at Jono. "What do you want?"

"Double espresso and two chocolate croissants."

The woman punched in his order on the screen. "For here or to go?"

Patrick dug out his wallet. "For here, but make the drinks to go."

He paid with his card, getting an emailed receipt for reimbursement purposes, then stepped aside to wait for their order. When it came, their drinks were in paper to-go cups, though they'd served Jono's free shot of sparkling water to go with his espresso as a palate cleanser in a small glass. Their food was in small plastic baskets, and they carried everything over to the empty table in the corner.

Patrick sat down with his food and coffee, freeing up one hand long enough to cast a silence ward. He discreetly drew the sigil on the underside of the table, pushing his magic through the air around them.

"Sweet tooth?" Patrick asked, eyeing Jono's breakfast.

"I'm usually asleep right now. Figured I could use the sugar," Jono said.

Patrick took a sip of his coffee, then another. The caffeine went a long way toward making him slightly less homicidal. "How long?"

"How long have I been a bartender?"

Patrick gestured with his coffee cup at Jono's face. "Since you were infected."

The espresso cup stilled halfway to Jono's mouth. "Bit of a personal question, innit?"

"I warded our area. No one can hear us." At Jono's disbelieving look, Patrick craned his head around and yelled, "Hey!"

No one paid them any attention. Patrick picked up half his bagel and took a bite, eyeing Jono expectantly.

"Magic doesn't guarantee privacy," Jono replied.

"Gets pretty close. You're god pack, even if you weren't acting in that capacity at the PCB last night. You lost the right to privacy the second your eyes changed color. I know paperwork for immigration anywhere sucks, but it's especially crappy for those with your kind of ties to the preternatural world. Did Marek pull strings to bring you over?"

"What makes you think it was Marek?"

"What he said last night about the reason you're here. If it's this case, and if his patrons want me to keep an eye on you, I need some background on you."

"Why don't you run one of your agency's fancy background checks and find out on your own?"

"You're sitting right in front of me, and we're stuck together for who knows how long because immortals don't know when to mind their own fucking business. This way is quicker, but only if you talk."

"I'll talk if you will."

"So long as you don't ask me about anything classified, then sure," Patrick replied blandly.

Which was, oh, nearly his entire life.

Jono drank down his double espresso in one long, searing gulp before following it up with the sparkling water. He set the glass down with a sigh. "I got infected when I was seventeen. I'm thirty now. Bad blood transfusion at a hospital after a car accident on the M1 while coming back from hols. The mistake shouldn't have happened."

"No shit," Patrick said. "Blood is supposed to be screened."

Jono's lip curled. "Their supplier was a bit dodgy. Turns out the company was doing a healthy side business with the Edgware Night Court."

Patrick made a face. "Fucking vampires."

"Too right. My mum and dad kicked me out after the whole mess even with the court case going on. Couldn't stand having a bloody werewolf staying with them, and the Tottenham estate we lived in at the time almost rioted when I tried to come home. Never saw so much as a quid from the settlement either. Bunch of bollocks, that was."

"Money is a great divider."

Jono nodded agreement. "The London god pack allowed me to stay in their territory, but they never accepted me into their pack. I didn't get on with the lot of them, and the alphas didn't want me around after a while. When Marek showed up in London three years ago with a job offer to manage his friends' bar, I didn't say no. When I left, the London god pack exiled me."

"Marek offered you a job and a place with the New York City god pack? Didn't think he had that kind of pull."

"No. The god pack here wanted nothing to do with me."

Patrick stared at Jono, thinking about all the ways rival god packs could make life a living hell for the citizens of the cities they claimed. "And they haven't run you out of town yet?"

"Marek won't let them."

"More like the fucking Fates won't let them," Patrick muttered.

Jono shrugged expansively at that. "I'm here, even if Estelle and Youssef wish I weren't. I don't care much for the way they do business with the packs under their protection, but it's not my place to argue."

Patrick snorted, gulping down a mouthful of coffee. "You don't strike me as the kind of guy who's willing to be walked over."

"Yes, well, I'm an independent. Can't form a pack because that was part of the agreement I made with the god pack here, and it'd be a sodding territory fight if I tried. So I don't."

Independent werecreatures were people who either hadn't found the right fit in a pack yet, or they'd been exiled from ones who wanted nothing to do with them anymore. Independents were the least powerful in any territory werecreatures held beneath the watchful eyes of their local god pack. It was a lonely sort of existence.

That Jono, a god pack alpha, had yet to form his own pack when his instincts had to be screaming at him to do so, made Patrick question just what future the Fates had seen for the Brit.

"What about you?" Jono asked, forcefully steering the conversation away from himself.

Patrick took another bite of his bagel. "What about me?"

"Nah, Pat. Don't be like that. Fair's fair. You asked, I answered. Now it's your turn. How long have you been with the SOA?"

Patrick wasn't fond of nicknames outside the Hellraisers, his old Special Operations Forces team with a preternatural bent to it. Right now, he didn't feel like arguing with Jono about it. At least it was better than Pattycakes.

"Three years," Patrick said, because that was technically public record and it wasn't a lie.

"And before that?"

"Classified."

"Bollocks."

Patrick slouched in his chair and shook his head. "Nope."

"Are you taking the piss?"

"Does it smell like I'm joking?"

"I can't smell a bloody thing about you," Jono said, sounding deeply annoyed about that fact.

Patrick drained his coffee before getting to his feet, leaning across the table a little. "Good."

He could see the brightness of Jono's eyes, even through the dark sunglasses. Jono glared at him but didn't demand answers Patrick wouldn't—and in some cases, *couldn't*—give. Instead, he followed Patrick out of the little coffee shop. They headed to where Patrick had parked the car on the street and got in. Patrick let Jono mess with the radio until he found a station playing alternative music in between what felt like thirty minutes of commercials and radio DJ conversation. Patrick hadn't splurged for satellite radio when he got the rental, and he wasn't going to drain his phone battery to use Spotify.

"I'm not taking you into the SOA building," Patrick said when the GPS on his phone showed they were halfway there. "You can wait for me at the Starbucks a block away."

"What am I? Your dirty little secret?" Jono asked, sounding surprisingly not bitter.

Patrick jerked the steering wheel to the left and cut off a taxi so he didn't get stuck behind a bus. He ignored the loud sound of an aggressively honked horn behind them. "No. The agency office here doesn't need to know about you. It's not their business what a seer dictates me to do."

"You work for the Supernatural Operations Agency. How is Marek's vision not their business?"

"It's not," Patrick said cuttingly.

Jono dropped the subject, but the tense silence from his side of the car didn't go away. When Patrick pulled over quickly in a bus stop zone near the Starbucks, Jono didn't immediately get out.

"I'm supposed to stay with you," he said.

"If a soultaker eats its way through the veil in the middle of an SOA building, it won't just have to deal with me, but everyone else who wears the badge and is magically inclined."

"And if it comes after me?"

"Run."

Jono shook his head before getting out of the car. "In that case, I could've had a lie-in back at your flat."

The car door slammed shut with enough force to shake the entire vehicle. Patrick watched Jono walk away for a few seconds, gaze lingering on his ass, before he hit the gas pedal again and pulled into traffic.

It didn't take long to reach the SOA building. This time he parked in the adjacent garage and went inside, getting cleared by security through both machine and magical means. Patrick was waved over to the front desk beyond the security gates. It was manned by a couple of secretarial staff members who handled the flow of visitors who weren't employed by the federal government and those just passing through.

"I'm here to see Rachel Andrita," Patrick said in greeting.

The woman didn't look away from her computer screen. "ID, please."

Patrick handed over his badge in the folded wallet. Her eyes flicked from the picture on his ID card and agent number on the metal badge itself to his face twice before she seemed satisfied. "Thirtieth floor. Her assistant will be waiting to receive you."

Patrick took the designated elevator up with a group of people in suits and skirt ensembles, all of them barely giving him a second glance. Several stops later, Patrick got off on the thirtieth floor and made his way to Rachel's corner office after getting directions from the floor receptionist. A woman in her early thirties was sitting outside Rachel's corner office at a desk that was surprisingly clear of clutter, typing away on a keyboard with fast strokes and wearing a hands-free phone headset.

"Sit," she said, without looking up. "Ms. Andrita knows you're here."

Patrick arched an eyebrow at the curtness but didn't argue. If this woman was anything like Brianna, Setsuna's executive assistant, she wouldn't let anyone into her boss' inner sanctum without permission no matter their status. So he took a seat outside on a chair and waited.

At exactly nine o'clock, Rachel's assistant got up to open the office door. "She'll see you now."

Patrick stood up and went to meet the SOA's Special Agent in Charge of New York City.

The corner office overlooked the street instead of the side of a neighboring building. The wards wrapped around the space reminded him of the ones in Casale's office, only stronger. Patrick cased the room automatically, checking out the commendations and degrees hanging on the wall and the bookshelves that actually held books rather than decorative knickknacks.

The space had that monotone feel to it all the government alphabet agencies seemed to have these days: all the furniture matched in dull colors, walls were painted white or beige, and halogen lighting made people's eyes twitch by the end of the workday. Not a place Patrick wanted to work.

Rachel didn't stand up or offer her hand in greeting when Patrick approached her desk. She merely took in his appearance with cool brown eyes. "Your outfit leaves something to be desired."

"The director has never had a problem with how I dress for the field, ma'am," Patrick replied mildly.

Since she hadn't offered him a seat, he took one anyway. The narrow-eyed look she shot him told Patrick this meeting was going to go terribly.

Fucking politics, man.

Rachel leaned forward in her leather seat, all business. Her honey-blonde hair was pinned away from her face in a loose chignon that brushed the collar of her silk blouse. In her midforties, but looking at least ten years younger, Rachel was a career-oriented witch who had made climbing the SOA ranks her life's goal. That she wasn't yet riding a desk in DC with a title that carried more weight didn't mean she wasn't angling for a promotion.

Patrick knew this case would look good on her resume, if only it had stayed in her office. So he wasn't surprised when the first thing Rachel addressed was the transfer.

"I understand Director Abuku felt it necessary to send someone from the Rapid Response Division, but this case has spanned six months already, and the PCB was mostly handling it with our help. I'll be frank, Collins. I really don't think your presence is necessary, and I informed the director as such last night," Rachel said.

"I'm sure the director took your suggestion under advisement," Patrick replied in the neutral voice he'd perfected in the military when dealing with incompetent—from his perspective—superior officers.

"I understand there was an altercation at a bar last night. What happened?"

"I really can't say, ma'am."

Rachel tapped her perfectly manicured fingernails against the hard oak of her desk. "That answer is unacceptable. We're all on the same team here, Collins."

"It's an active investigation, and I report to the director, not to you. If you want to be read into the case going forward, you'll need clearance from Director Abuku."

Rachel didn't show her irritation about her request being denied, a testament to her ability to read a room. Patrick wondered why a SAIC was so interested in a case formally assigned to a lower-level witch that Rachel hadn't looked twice at. Only when it got taken out of her hands, metaphorically speaking, did she start to raise a fuss.

"I understand Chief Casale had plans to seek answers from a seer. Has that meeting occurred yet?"

Warning bells rang loud and clear through Patrick's mind at that question. As far as he knew, Casale's meeting with Marek hadn't been telegraphed.

So he lied.

"I'm not sure."

"We both know the bar you were at last night is affiliated with Marek Taylor, a seer the government keeps tabs on. Did he have a vision or not?" Rachel asked.

"Again, you'll need to discuss that with the director."

Rachel sat back and touched a few keys on her keyboard, staring at her monitor. "If the City is willing to spend that much money on a seer, then I really think my office should be more thoroughly involved. When this is over, you'll be on your way again and we agents here in New York City will be left to pick up the pieces. You have a tendency toward collateral damage in the field. I'm not comfortable having you be my office's representative. I want to assign you a partner."

Patrick fought back a grimace. "No."

"Excuse me?" Rachel said sharply.

"Ma'am, the case is no longer under the purview of your office. It's now being handled through DC, which means it's mine. I don't do partners, and you don't have the authority to change the parameters of how I run things."

"I see." Rachel clasped her hands together over the desk and stared him down. "Is stonewalling how you normally run things? Is that standard operating procedure for your division?"

Patrick didn't move an inch under her gaze. "This isn't stonewalling. This is me following my orders, which come from the director we both serve under. If you have a problem with that, take it up with her."

The impasse lasted at least a minute before Rachel broke the staring contest with a ploy at faux concern. "Every field agent is required to have a partner. The fact that you don't is worrisome."

"I don't need one."

Patrick could be a team player and had been in the Mage Corps, surrounded by people who'd been trained like he had been to deal with magic and demons in a war zone. He missed his old team more than his therapist knew, but those who were left were running dark right now and he hadn't heard from them in months. Coming into the SOA when initially recruited, he'd tried working with a partner or two those first weeks after clawing his way out of the bottom of a bottle and suicidal thoughts.

It didn't end well.

Setsuna had been the one to transfer his last partner and affirm his solo status in the records. Patrick worked his cases alone because of the gods he could never outrun. He didn't need to subject someone else to his shitty life.

"I'll bring up my concern with the director again. I want to be kept apprised of any new leads in the case as they come up," Rachel said.

"I'll keep that request in mind."

The faint tic at the corner of Rachel's mouth told him she knew he was only spouting lip service. "We'll talk later, Collins. This meeting is over."

Patrick tipped his head her way. "Ma'am."

He left her office feeling like he had a target on his back. Patrick couldn't get out of the building and to his car fast enough. Throwing himself behind the steering wheel, he slapped his hand against the roof of the car, warding the vehicle for silence despite the sting that came with using his magic right now.

He pulled out his phone and unlocked it, swiping into his contacts. His thumb hovered over Setsuna's name before he sighed and tapped back to the keypad. Patrick entered a string of numbers instead, letting the call ring through three times before hanging up. He repeated that two more times before waiting thirty seconds and calling once more.

Setsuna picked up on the first ring.

"Line and location are secure" were the first words out of her mouth.

"I got voluntold to keep Rachel updated on the case," Patrick said.

"Don't."

"I wasn't planning on it before, and I'm definitely not planning on it now. What is going on, Setsuna?"

"I wanted you to form your own opinion without mine influencing yours."

Patrick froze, staring at the empty seats in the car parked nose to nose with his. It felt like someone had poured ice water down his spine. "You don't trust her."

"I don't trust a lot of people, and we are still cleaning house."

"You've been cleaning house since I was a child."

"You know why."

Patrick swore, closing his eyes. Yeah, he did, and that was the problem. He leaned forward and rested his forehead against the steering wheel. "You think Rachel belongs to the Dominion Sect."

"I think this case has been purposefully delayed from reaching my desk for six months. It was luck the DC office received the appeal from the New York City PCB at all."

Patrick thought about Marek and his inability to have clear visions at the moment. He thought about the Fates who saw fit to saddle Patrick with a werewolf. He thought about the signs carved on the dead, Hermes' sinister warning, and the too-sharp attention of a witch who should have been on their side.

The next words out of his mouth felt like glass, slicing deep. "You think it's Ethan."

Setsuna's silence spoke volumes.

The Dominion Sect had gone by many names throughout the centuries, but their number one priority always remained the same: the subjugation of the gods and removal of the veil between worlds. Rogue magic users of every creed who belonged to the shadowy group all lived double lives, as did their many human followers. Ferreting any of them out was difficult. The higher-ups rarely made mistakes, but when they did, those mistakes were brutal for everyone involved.

Patrick's mother had never really known the true nature of the family she married into. That blindness cost Clara Patterson her life when Patrick was eight years old and Ethan Greene had murdered her.

It cost Patrick more.

He leaned over the front-seat divider and opened the glove compartment, pulling out the pack of cigarettes he'd stashed there yesterday. Screw the no smoking policy on the rental; he'd pay for the damn cleaning fee.

Prying a cigarette out with his teeth, he lit the end with a bit of mage fire burning from his fingertip. He stuck the key in the ignition and turned it just enough to get power so he could crack the window open and flick ash through that thin gap.

"Handle this case how you normally would," Setsuna finally said, breaking the silence after he'd smoked down half his cigarette. "I'll send Rachel another email about her interference."

"Make it a phone call," Patrick said.

"It will be handled."

His lip curled at that, knowing full well how Setsuna handled shit like this—by sending Patrick in. Only this time, she couldn't use him. "And my backup?"

"On their way."

"Who's coming?"

Setsuna hung up without answering. Patrick wondered just who she'd chosen to send as help if she wouldn't risk saying their names out loud, even on a burner phone. None of the choices he could think of were good ones.

"I hear smoking will kill you."

Patrick had a mageglobe in hand, burning with raw magic, before his brain recognized the bored sound of Hermes' voice coming from the passenger seat.

"God *fucking* damn it," Patrick ground out, glaring at the immortal. "Do you really have to keep showing up like this?"

"Aww, Pattycakes. Did I scare you?" Hermes drawled, a nasty smirk on his mouth. "You should watch your back."

Patrick snuffed out his mageglobe and stuck his cigarette back between his lips, drawing in a lungful of smoke. "You got anything worthwhile to tell me, or did you just show up to mock me because you're bored?"

Hermes lifted one foot and put it on the dash, his dirty Doc Martens scuffing up the black interior. His knee poked out of the hole in his black skinny jeans, showing off a scab or two. "I have a message for you."

"Next time, why don't you just call?"

"So you can ignore me? Where's the fun in that, Pattycakes?"

Patrick arched an eyebrow, as if the answer wasn't obvious. "What do you want?"

Hermes' hand darted out cat-quick, plucking the nearly finished cigarette out of Patrick's mouth. He slipped it between his own lips, breathing in deep to burn it down to the filter. Smoke drifted out of his nose and from between his teeth. Hermes stubbed it out on the console between them, smearing ash around the cup holder.

"Isadora Cirillo wants to meet with you. Make time for her," Hermes told him.

"How do you know the missing hedge fund manager's wife?"

Hermes' gold-brown eyes turned molten. "How do you think?"

The immortal disappeared, leaving only smoke behind. Patrick stared at the empty passenger seat, Hermes' words ringing in his ears, the threat unmistakable.

"Fucking gods and their fucking games," Patrick muttered, reaching for his pack of cigarettes again.

One of these days, they'd be the death of him.

7

JONO DUG OUT HIS MOBILE, ONLY HALF LISTENING AS PATRICK DROVE off behind him. Swearing under his breath, he speed-dialed Marek while standing outside the Starbucks. The line rang a couple of times before Marek finally picked up.

"Yeah?" Marek answered, sounding worried. "Jono? Why aren't you asleep?"

"The sodding mage left me at a Starbucks," Jono growled.

"What?"

"He's got a meeting at the SOA. Wouldn't take me with him."

"Man, I *don't* want another migraine. Are you safe?"

Jono scanned the immediate area through his sunglasses, picking out all the office workers easily enough by sight and scent. He couldn't smell anything out of the ordinary, but magic was always a tricky thing to defend against.

"Can't bloody tell."

The demon at the bar last night had seemed human right up until it wasn't. Standing out in the open like this set Jono's teeth on edge, but hiding inside the Starbucks wouldn't be much better. At least out here, if he had to run like Patrick had suggested, he wouldn't be boxed in.

"Why don't you call an Uber and come have breakfast with us?"

"Patrick told me to wait."

Marek snorted. "Since when do you listen to anyone, much less a mage?"

Jono sighed heavily, nostrils flaring with the remembered bitter scent of the mage in question. Patrick's interest had been there at the bar and continued in the flat. Before Jono even knew what the other man was, he'd liked what he'd seen standing on the other side of the bar counter.

Patrick was all lean muscles and callused hands, with a cocky tilt to his head, and ginger hair that Jono ached to get his fingers in and give a good yank to. Getting eyes on Patrick in the bar last night had made Jono wish he wasn't working, because he wouldn't have minded taking Patrick home and absolutely *wrecking* him.

Then the demon had showed up, and Patrick had shown what he really was, and Jono had expected that whiff of desire in the bar to have been false. Magic users, he'd come to learn over the years, were a hard read, but scents never lied. It's why Jono had tried to seduce Patrick a little last night—because he wanted to, but mostly so he would know Patrick anywhere through smell alone.

Jono wouldn't have pushed for sex like that if he didn't believe what he offered wouldn't be reciprocated. He wasn't one to force himself on people, or force obedience out of them, not like some god pack members he could name. But then the bloody bastard had gone and shielded like no other magic user he'd ever encountered before, and Jono couldn't smell him at fucking all.

Drove him mad, and he couldn't even say why.

"Since your bloody patrons ordered me to stay with him," Jono finally said.

If it had been anyone else giving the order, Jono would've told them to fuck off and done what he liked. His rank as a god pack alpha—which was bloody ridiculous some days considering he had no pack—meant there were few things in the world that could make him obey.

But gods?

Jono knew a thing or two about gods and the punishments they could mete out for disobedience. If they wanted him to follow after Patrick like a mindless puppet, then he would, no matter how much it grated, if only to save his own skin.

That didn't mean he had to like it.

Marek sighed. "I'm sorry, Jono. I really am."

"Is he why you brought me here?" Jono asked the question again because he couldn't help himself. He stared blankly at the street and the cars driving past. "To the States?"

"I want to say yes, but I don't know" was Marek's honest reply, as it always was when Jono searched for answers. "I wish I could see that for you."

He'd never been able to, which Jono had always thought was strange. Marek's offer of employment three years ago and a promise of something more in the future had been the lifeline Jono needed at the time. Leaving London had been painful—it was home and always would be—but it was no longer welcoming. *He* had no longer been welcome.

New York City hadn't been much better, what with Estelle and Youssef looking for an excuse to exile him from their territory. Only Marek's rank as a seer, driven by the Fates, kept the god pack alphas in check. They'd still denied Jono a place in their pack and forbidden him from forming his own in their territory.

Being an independent-ranked werecreature was fucking *terrible*.

Jono squeezed his eyes shut for a second, rubbing at his mouth. "You promised me—"

He broke off, unwilling to voice the one desire he'd been wishing for since waking up in hospital in London on the operating table, veins on fire, screaming as his body twisted itself into something new.

He wanted a family. A home.

Pack.

"I know what I promised you," Marek said quietly. "I wish I could say this whole mess is your answer, but the mage isn't a werecreature."

"Neither are you, mate."

"Yeah, but you trust me. I wouldn't trust a mage working for the SOA if my life depended on it."

Jono rolled his eyes. "It does, remember?"

Marek made an annoyed sound. "He's an asshole."

"True, but the bloke does have a nice arse."

"Did you fuck him?" he heard Emma yell in the background, easily picking out her voice with his preternaturally enhanced hearing.

"I got his scent, if that's what you're asking."

Marek let out a surprised squawk before there was a scuffle and Emma's voice came more clearly through the mobile. "Really, Jono? *Really?*"

Jono shrugged, even though she couldn't see it. "Would've done it anyway before I even knew he was a mage."

"Ugh," she groaned. "No picking up customers. That's a *rule.*"

"That's your rule, love. Not mine."

They both knew it was a rule in name only. Emma would never tell him what to do, and hadn't over the course of his employment at the bar as their manager. She and her pack almost felt like his own some days, except they weren't.

They couldn't be.

That didn't stop her from being his friend.

"Come have breakfast with us. Leon is making chilaquiles."

Jono's stomach growled at the thought of food, especially if Leon was cooking. "I should stay."

"If he leaves you high and dry, I'll kick his ass for you."

"I can do my own arse kicking, Em."

"Let her have some fun," Leon yelled in the background.

Jono chuckled. "I'll bring the bail money."

"Marek has it covered," Emma retorted. "Perks of being best friends with a billionaire."

She failed to acknowledge the fact that both she and Leon were multimillionaires now that PreterWorld was a publicly traded company. They might not live like they were filthy rich, but they had money. They owned a floor in Marek's building though, and Jono liked spending time there with the lot of them.

"Are you reopening the bar tonight? Need me on shift to manage?" Jono asked.

"Depends if we can get it cleansed in time. The PCB finished processing the scene sometime early this morning, and we have access again. Casale assigned Marek a sorcerer for protection. We're gonna swing by Tempest after breakfast and check out the damage, see if the kid can do anything about it."

"Is he really a kid?"

"Baby sorcerer, and he's Casale's son."

Jono winced. "Bloody hell."

"Yeah. We'll keep an eye on him. Wouldn't be good for any of us if Tyler died."

"Too right." Jono fought back a yawn. "I'm going to get some coffee. I'll ring you later."

"You better."

Emma hung up and Jono tucked his mobile into his back pocket before heading inside the Starbucks. He didn't know how long Patrick's meeting would take, but if he didn't get more caffeine in him, Jono wouldn't be fit for human *or* preternatural company.

Jono sat at one of the tables near the window to keep an eye on the street for Patrick's car once he had his coffee. In the craziness of last night and the annoyed mood Patrick had woken up in, neither had remembered to exchange numbers. So Jono drank his coffee slowly and kept his attention on the street. He was almost finished with his Venti coffee when he saw the black car from earlier pull up to the curb.

Downing the dregs of his drink, Jono tossed it in the bin on his way out. He pulled open the car door and climbed inside, nose twitching at the smell of smoke and nicotine, and an underlying electric burn reminiscent of the sort that sometimes emanated from Marek. He wondered about that, especially in the absence of Patrick's own bitter scent.

"Thought you weren't supposed to smoke in here? Meeting go that poorly?" Jono asked.

"It went" was Patrick's short reply as he pulled into the street.

Jono eyed him over the rims of his sunglasses. "I can see that."

Patrick's mouth curled in a scowl, and Jono's attention lingered on his plush lips. He wouldn't mind seeing them wrapped around his cock. As fun as last night was, it had ended too soon for Jono's liking.

Patrick gunned it across the intersection on a yellow light. "Can you get me into Tempest?"

"I have keys," Jono said slowly. "Why?"

"I need to see the crime scene."

"Police already finished their cleanup."

"I'm not the police. Can you get me in or not?"

"Yeah, Pat. I can let you in."

"Good. Means I don't have to pick the lock."

Jono lifted his hips enough to pull his mobile free of his pocket and tapped in his passcode. He went into his text messages and pulled up Marek's name, typing out a message.

HEADING TO TEMPEST WITH PATRICK.

The response from Marek was immediate. MR. HOT ASS BETTER NOT MAKE A MESS LIKE LAST NIGHT.

Jono snorted quietly and would've responded except he got a notification in the status bar of another message. He tapped back into the queue and accessed the group chat between himself, Emma, Leon, Marek, and Sage.

ESTELLE AND YOUSSEF CALLED. THEY WANT TO SEE THE BAR, SO WE'RE MEETING THEM THERE, Emma had texted.

WHEN? Jono texted back.

THIRTY MINUTES.

"Shit," he muttered.

"What now?" Patrick asked.

"The god pack alphas are coming by."

"To the bar?"

"Yeah."

"When?"

Jono checked the time. "Close to half past."

Patrick made an aggrieved sound in the back of his throat and proceeded to drive like a Formula One driver all the way to the bar. By the time he parked in Marek's reserved spot outside Tempest, Jono had to pry his hand off the dash.

"You drive like a bloody maniac," Jono told him.

Patrick yanked the keys out of the ignition and got out. "Let's go."

Jono climbed out of the car and led the way to the front door. The bar's name was spelled out in a wooden sign across the front façade, the letters purposefully aged. Tempest was named after Emma's pack, a point of pride with them. Marek had bankrolled its opening some years back, but Emma and Leon owned the place despite also working for PreterWorld. The only time Marek had made a hiring decision was when it came to Jono. Neither Emma nor Leon had protested Marek offering Jono the bar manager position three years ago.

Jono unlocked the front door, letting them both into the bar. Overriding the usual lingering smell of alcohol and sweat was a sulfuric smell that Jono could almost taste in the back of his throat. It made his nose twitch. Aside from that smell, the bar was a mess, both from the attack and the police presence afterwards.

"You mind if I get things cleaned up a bit?" Jono asked.

Patrick waved him off. "It's fine."

Jono nodded and walked to the rear of the bar where the cleaning supply closet was located near the bathroom. He picked up a couple of rags and a spray bottle of cleaner from a metal shelf and began the process of wiping down tables and the bar counter. Jono kept one eye on Patrick, watching as he slowly paced around the site where the demon's ashes had been scattered.

When Patrick called up a mageglobe, the hairs on the back of Jono's neck stood on end. That bitter scent he'd smelled last night hit Jono's nose, the taste of it blooming across his tongue for a split second.

Magic, Jono thought, even if it didn't smell like any magic he was used to.

He paused in his cleaning to watch Patrick work, having only seen a mage cast magic a handful of times before. No words were spoken, no circles drawn, no artifacts used—just pure stubbornness and the raw power of a soul fueled by magic bending power to his will.

Jono honestly couldn't look away.

The fiery mageglobe cast pale, blue-tinted light across Patrick's face as it hovered near his shoulder. The color wasn't as deep as Jono was used to seeing in magic, and he wondered about that. Patrick caught the mageglobe in his fingers and tossed it to the floor where the soultaker had died. Magic crawled over the floor to recreate the outline where ash had settled last night. Patrick seemed to stare through it all, through Jono, at things only he could see.

"What are you looking for?" Jono asked.

"Answers."

When nothing else came out of his mouth, Jono got busy setting the bar to rights again. Patrick did his thing, whatever it was, while Jono did his job. He was halfway finished cleaning up the work areas behind the bar when his preternaturally enhanced hearing caught the sound of familiar voices out on the street. He'd been keeping an ear open for when the others would arrive, so he set the dirty glass he was holding into the wash bin.

"Marek and the others are here," Jono said.

Patrick, who'd mostly been ignoring him, snapped his head around. "Marek is here? That fucking idiot was supposed to stay home behind the barrier ward I built him."

He looked pissed, like the scraggly wet kitten Jono had found one time huddled in a stairwell in the block he'd grown up in. Jono didn't think soothing Patrick was an option the way he had with the kitten and a saucer of milk, but he still tried.

"You want a pint?" Jono asked, gesturing at the array of beers on tap.

"Only if I can throw it at Marek's head."

There went that idea.

Patrick passed his hand through the air, and the magic he'd been controlling disappeared as if it had never been. Jono stepped out from behind the bar right as someone unlocked the front door and pushed it open.

Marek came inside first, holding open the door for everyone else. Jono's eyes tracked over the small group, jumping from Emma, Leon, and Tyler to the god pack alphas and their dire. Jono forced back the scowl he badly wanted to greet them with. Ever since arriving in the United States, he'd been at odds with the New York City god pack for more reasons than just their purposeful refusal to let him join their pack.

Nicholas Kavanaugh stepped aside, ceding space to his alphas. The god pack's dire, essentially a rank held by a loyal pack member who enforced their alphas' orders, was a traditional role usually filled by arseholes in Jono's experience. The look Nicholas gave him was filled with contempt, but Jono let it slide off like water, turning his attention to the god pack alphas.

Estelle Walker was thirty-five years old and was a born god pack werewolf. Her bright amber wolf eyes were set in a heart-shaped face, wavy brown hair skimmed her shoulders, and her lean body moved with a lithe grace that wasn't human. Youssef Khan was her forty-year-old husband of five years, though the pair of them had been together for several years before that. Jono rather thought it was due to power maneuvering—they'd fought to take over the god pack six years ago in a challenge and were successful—but the pair had affection for each other.

Caring for each other didn't mean they cared about the packs under their guardianship. Jono didn't like the hard line they'd set down for pack tithes, nor how high they'd raised those tithes to begin with at the start of their rule. That sort of financial abuse had ensured most packs didn't try to fight back, though they'd had little luck with the Tempest pack. Emma, backed by Marek's billions, her own wealth, and Sage's legal expertise, had carved out a spot of quiet, stubborn rebellion the god pack couldn't outright counter for fear of bringing the federal government down on them.

Marek's position as a seer gave Emma leverage no one else had, and she used it ruthlessly to care for those she could within the werecreature community. Jono had always admired her for that, even as he chaffed at his own restrictions beneath the pack agreement that enabled him to remain in New York City.

Jono made his way to Patrick's side as the god pack alphas approached, refusing to show his throat in the traditional act of greeting and deference. His refusal was noted, as always.

"I understand you're taking liberties with a rank you don't have," Estelle told him in an icy voice.

Jono met her antagonistic attitude with a hard smile, feeling the heavy shift of his teeth along his gums as they sharpened. "I was a witness, and Marek needed pack support."

"You should have called us."

"Wasn't my decision."

"Casale knows you aren't one of ours. He exceeded his authority."

"I'm sorry, do you have a badge?" Patrick asked, sounding

annoyed. "Because Casale didn't exceed anything, and this problem doesn't concern you."

"The PCB knows to call us as representatives for those who are pack to ensure their anonymity. Your boss isn't doing his job," Youssef retorted.

Patrick pulled his badge out of his back pocket and flipped it open. "I'm not with the PCB."

Estelle and Youssef went still in the way only preternatural creatures could. Jono watched their bright amber eyes lock on to the identification and he could practically *see* the moment they realized they weren't dealing with the NYPD.

Patrick snapped the thin leather wallet closed and tucked it back into his pocket. "You can make demands all you want, but your supposed authority doesn't exist with me or the SOA. This case isn't your business, so back the fuck off."

Youssef shook off his surprise, eyes narrowing. "We weren't informed the SOA had taken over the case."

"What part of not your business did you not understand?"

"It's our business when it involves werecreatures under our protection."

Patrick jerked his thumb in Jono's direction. "From what I understand, Jono doesn't have a pack and he isn't part of yours. Which means he's not your concern, the same way Marek isn't because of his status. They're the only two I'm dealing with as witnesses right now, so your argument is still a bunch of bullshit."

Youssef took a step forward but was restrained from going further than that by Estelle's hand on his arm. She studied Patrick for a few seconds before shifting her attention to Jono.

"You do not speak for us or for the packs in our territory," she said coolly.

"I know," Jono said, trying to keep the frustration out of his voice.

"Nicholas will stay with the Tempest pack to act as liaison with the authorities during this case. You are to refrain from communicating with any pack involved in the attack that happened last night, Jono."

"It's like you're deaf, when I know you've got preternatural hearing. You aren't calling the shots, Estelle. Which means the god pack isn't going to embed anyone with any pack, least of all the one Marek belongs to," Patrick said.

"You can't—"

Patrick cut her off, eyes locked on her face. "Federal law trumps your pack laws in a situation like this. If I hear of you trying to interfere again, you can expect a knock on your door from the SOA."

Jono could have warned Patrick that Estelle and Youssef didn't like being told what to do. Their rank meant everything to them, and having it taken away by an SOA special agent wasn't going to douse their temper any.

When Youssef pulled free of Estelle and took a threatening step forward, Patrick flexed his fingers and conjured up a mageglobe that stopped Youssef in his tracks. The fiery blue magic spun in his hand, a threatening gesture the god pack couldn't ignore.

"This conversation is over," Patrick said in a low, hard voice.

Jono couldn't smell Patrick's emotional state, couldn't get a read on the other man, but the scent of his magic was still just as bitter as before. Jono had spent half his life navigating the world with enhanced senses, but he didn't need them in this moment. He didn't doubt for a second that, if Youssef took one more step, Patrick would take him down hard.

"We'd like to be contacted in the event you need to speak with anyone who is pack," Estelle said after a tense moment of silence.

"You aren't being read into the case." Patrick pointed at the exit. "Door's that way. Get the fuck out."

It was a dismissal they had no choice but to obey. Jono watched as Youssef spun on his heel and stalked out of the bar, Estelle and Nicholas right behind him. The door slammed shut with a loud *bang* that made Jono wince.

Patrick made a fist, snuffing out his magic before he turned to glare at Marek. "You're supposed to be home behind the barrier ward I built you."

"I have a minder," Marek retorted, gesturing at the sorcerer. "Tyler Casale here is my own personal guard, courtesy of the Crescent Coven."

"Hi," Tyler said, lifting one hand in a wave.

"Casale," Patrick echoed. "Any relation to the chief of the PCB?"

"He's my dad."

Patrick pinched the bridge of his nose, aggravation in every line of his body. Jono knew he was staring but didn't care. Patrick intrigued him the way few people did these days.

"Marek, if you get eaten by a soultaker, your patrons better not blame me," Patrick said.

"I'll be fine," Marek protested.

Patrick shook his head and waved a hand at Jono. "Let's go."

"Where are we going?" Jono wanted to know.

"Back to the PCB. Marek? Go home."

"We're cleansing the bar first," Marek replied, a hint of defiance in his voice.

Patrick just shook his head at that answer, already halfway to the door. Jono looked over his shoulder as he hurried after Patrick. "Be safe."

Emma nodded, already tying up her thick black hair into a ponytail, ready to get to work. "We got this."

Jono flashed back to the demon from last night and wasn't so sure about that. Leaving the bar behind him, he made it to the car right as Patrick started the engine.

"Is it safe to leave Marek alone?" Jono asked as he buckled up.

"If the gods want his ass saved, they'll tell me," Patrick said cryptically.

Jono didn't know what Patrick meant by that. "Did you find what you were looking for back there?"

Patrick pulled into the street, staring straight ahead. "No."

Jono couldn't tell if he was lying or not. The lack of scent was strange, forcing Jono to rely on his other senses. He dialed up his hearing and listened to Patrick's heart beating just a touch off rhythm.

Liar, liar, Jono thought to himself.

Whatever answers Patrick had found in the bar, Jono wasn't privy to them.

"You sure about that, mate?" Jono asked quietly.

Patrick stared straight ahead and didn't speak, his heartbeat strong and even in Jono's ears—except when it skipped a beat.

8

PATRICK SPENT TWO HOURS AT THE PCB BRINGING HIMSELF UP TO speed on the case files, all the while trying not to think about what his magic had pried out of Tempest's walls. The residual hellish taint that had been at the other crime scene was barely present in the bar, but his magic had still caught on what remained.

He'd still found where the soultaker had most likely stepped through the veil: at the rear of the bar, in the short hallway where the bathrooms were. Traces of a look-away ward had been buried beneath the taint, the remains too degraded for him to locate any magical signature. Patrick was certain the perpetrator hadn't been in the bar at the time of the attack.

Patrick didn't have time the other night to go over the crime scene with his magic, too worried about getting Marek somewhere safe. Knowing that the soultaker had ripped its way through the veil with outside help reinforced Setsuna's silent implications during their phone call.

Third time's the charm, Patrick thought grimly as he pressed a hand to his chest, T-shirt rubbing over his scars.

He reached for another case folder, flipping it open and sorting through the stack of reports and crime scene photographs. Patrick had taken over a small conference room since no desks were free out in the bull pen, utilizing every last bit of space on the table to sort through everything. For the most part, PCB officers left him alone, but there was no hiding from their chief.

"I got an angry phone call from the god pack alphas this morning," was the first thing out of Casale's mouth when he entered the conference room sometime later.

"I told them to stay out of the case," Patrick said as he drew a silence ward on the table, pushing static through the room with his magic. "Maybe I should have them arrested since they're incapable of listening."

"That's a media mess we don't need right now."

Patrick shrugged. "Wouldn't be me dealing with them."

"DCPI has enough problems killing media rumors about this case. Let's not make their job harder," Casale told him.

Patrick set down the stack of photographs depicting mangled bodies and looked over at where Casale stood. "Your wife sent your son to guard Marek."

"I know. I'm rethinking my appeal to Washington right about now."

"It's a little late for regrets."

"I'm aware of that. You should know Rachel called me this morning as well."

Patrick frowned. "Let me guess. She wants you to keep her updated on the case."

"Right on the money. Of course, this is the first I've heard of her being interested after brushing off my concerns for the past few months when she wasn't making it difficult to appeal. I'm not inclined to play nice."

"You don't need to. SOA Director Abuku instructed me to handle the case, not any local agents. You're not required to keep Rachel updated, and I'd rather you didn't."

"I have no desire to be in the middle of a federal intra-agency tug-of-war. Besides, your boss said to only work through you, so I will." He didn't exactly sound happy about that, but Casale was nothing if not dedicated to his job and doing it right to the best of his abilities. "Now, you want to tell me what a god pack werewolf is doing following you around?"

Patrick glanced out the interior frosted windows that looked onto the hallway. He could see Jono's shadowed form where he sat outside the door, still in the spot Patrick had left him.

"Marek wants Jono to stay with me."

Casale crossed his arms over his chest, arching one thick eyebrow. "Does he, now?"

"He had another vision after I warded his apartment."

Casale's gaze sharpened. "He had another vision? Of what?"

"Don't worry. He's not charging you for it. I was told to keep Jono close."

"Why?"

"I don't know."

Patrick tried not to let his frustration bleed into his voice. Orders from the gods always complicated everything.

"Werecreatures don't have magic. It doesn't make sense that you'd need to protect Jono from a demon who wants to eat magic."

"They don't have magic, but the werevirus was made from magic. It alters their soul for the physical change. They still die like everyone else who gets trapped in a soultaker's teeth."

"You think he might be a target?"

Patrick shrugged. "At this rate, who the fuck knows? But I'm not going to ignore what a seer tells me, so Jono stays."

The situation wasn't all bad. Jono was definitely easy on the eyes, even if Patrick needed to keep his hands to himself.

"You got anything else for me?" Casale asked.

Patrick reached out and picked up a photocopied page from an online investors website, the power couple standing in front of a desk unfamiliar to his eyes. Hermes' warning hovered at the back of his mind, and Patrick's eyes traced over the classically Grecian faces of the dark-haired woman and her husband.

"I need to set up a meeting with Isadora Cirillo," Patrick said.

"Her contact information should be in the file. You got six days left. Don't waste them."

Casale let himself out. Patrick dragged his fingers through the sigil on the table, breaking up the silence ward. The static faded away. Before the door could shut all the way behind Casale, Jono slipped inside on quick feet, looking vaguely irritated.

"I told you to wait out in the hall," Patrick said.

Jono dragged a chair out and sat down in it. "Piss off. Every cop out there is eyeing me like I need to be in handcuffs."

Patrick had a split-second mental image of Jono naked and handcuffed to his bed. He bit back a groan and discreetly shifted on his chair. He seriously needed to get laid. Last night's fun had woken up his dick in the worst way. Having Jono around testing his *don't touch* resolve was proving distracting.

Patrick cleared his throat. "The case files are classified."

Jono held up his phone and waved it from side to side. "I'll keep myself busy."

Patrick doubted Jono would keep his eyes to himself, but he didn't want to argue. With the Fates having glued Jono to his side, it would be impossible to keep the werewolf out of the loop entirely. So Patrick put Jono out of his mind in favor of finishing his review of the case file, taking his own notes on a borrowed tablet of yellow legal paper.

An hour and a half later, he finished reviewing every single case file for each murder and absorbed the information found within. The clock on his phone said it was a little after 1400, and his stomach was reminding him he needed to eat something. Patrick started putting the case files back in order. It took him two trips to the bull pen to return them to the secured filing cabinet they were being stored in.

Returning to the conference room, Patrick retrieved Jono.

Picking up his messenger bag from the chair, he jerked his head at the door. "Come on. You can have that lie-in back at the apartment."

Jono closed the game app he was playing on his phone and stood up, stretching his arms over his head. His shirt rode up a little, pulling tight across his broad chest. Patrick thought he heard a bone pop in Jono's spine, but he was too busy staring at the hint of chiseled abs to really pay attention.

Jono noticed and gave Patrick a lazy smile. "All right. You can join me if you want."

"Not interested," Patrick said, lying through his teeth.

If anything, Jono's smile got wider. "Keep telling yourself that, love."

Patrick did, every second of the drive back to the apartment. They left the PCB in the early afternoon, the ride made with the music on low, which Jono drowned out with questions after the second block disappeared in the rearview mirror.

"What was that at the bar?" Jono asked.

Patrick braked for a red light and took a moment to check his phone. Setsuna still hadn't responded to his texts and emails. "You're going to have to be more specific."

"Your magic smells wrong."

"You don't need to worry about my magic."

"I think I should if you're supposed to stand between me and a soultaker."

The light turned green, and Patrick stepped on the gas. "Are you really going to complain about that now after last night when I saved your life?"

Jono stared at him and didn't speak for five blocks. Only when Patrick braked to a halt for another red light did Jono move, preternatural quick, fingers brushing against Patrick's throat. He reacted instantly even as Jono's fingers snagged on the stainless steel chain half-hidden beneath his T-shirt.

Patrick twisted against the seat belt in the confined space

without taking his foot off the brake pedal. Between one breath and the next, he had his right hand wrapped around Jono's throat, fingers and thumb digging in hard. His left hand grabbed Jono's wrist with enough pressure on the tendons there to make Jono's fingers twitch.

Jono's wolf-bright eyes narrowed to slits, but he was looking at the dog tags, not the near-murderous expression on Patrick's face. Patrick had to throttle back the instinctive urge to *kill* at the unexpected breach of his personal space.

"Military before SOA," Jono said around Patrick's tight grip, the words nearly bitten off. "Is that how you got a soul wound?"

Patrick bared his teeth in a silent snarl, fingers tightening a fraction more before he let Jono go. He yanked the dog tags out of Jono's grip, stuffing them back under his shirt. The light turned green, and he slammed his foot down on the gas pedal.

"You do that again and I will shoot you," Patrick promised.

The faint bruises Patrick had pressed into Jono's skin were already fading, the werewolf's accelerated healing taking care of the minor injuries in less than a minute.

"So you're Mage Corps."

Patrick tightened his hands on the steering wheel and pretended it was Jono's neck all over again. "Not anymore."

He'd walked away from the military and his team to save his sanity. But Patrick still missed it some days: the uniform, the missions, the regimented way soldiers lived their lives, his *team*. The way he'd been able to delay the soul debt he owed immortals by paying his service to his country instead. For all the battles he'd been in, Patrick had been safe there on the front lines from something exponentially worse, as fucked-up as that truth was.

"Sorry," Jono said a few blocks later.

"My life is not your business," Patrick ground out.

"Then why do the Fates want me in it?"

Patrick didn't answer him and kept not answering him for the rest of the drive back to the apartment. He managed to find parking a block away and paid the meter to the limit with his card. Patrick ignored Jono on the walk back to the apartment. Once inside and past the threshold, Patrick set up his MacBook on the dining room table and got to work.

The first thing he did was access the SOA's archives through an encrypted employee web portal. Patrick had his notes from the case file, but he needed copies of reports from the Thirty-Day War the SOA had on file. His personal experience fighting soultakers was useful, but he needed more than memories right now.

The rest of the afternoon was a tunnel vision of research, so much so that he didn't know how much time had passed until Jono was snapping his fingers in front of Patrick's eyes to get his attention.

Patrick blinked, turning to look at him and trying not to wince at the stiffness in his neck and shoulders. "What?"

"Your fridge is empty. What do you want for dinner? I'm paying," Jono asked.

"Is this an apology meal?"

"I'd cook, but you've nothing for me to cook with."

The last time someone had apologized with food, his team's sniper had given Patrick the last candy bar out of his care package. That was in the middle of an FOB after a long few days outside the wire. Tonight, he was in New York City with an abundance of choices.

So he went with the obvious one.

"Pepperoni pizza," Patrick said.

Jono nodded at his request and pulled out his phone, tapping away at the screen. Patrick cracked his neck, wincing at the noise it made. Outside the living room windows, the world was drifting into twilight. He'd spent so long in the throes of research that he'd lost track of time. No wonder his entire back felt as if it were made of knots.

Patrick saved what he had compiled from his research using an encryption program. He signed off on his report for the PCB and emailed that to Casale, then sent another email to Setsuna in their personal code with the subject line of *Still Not in Hawaii*. He'd see if she finally answered that one, which was him basically asking—yet again—where the hell his backup was.

"Pizza will be here in an hour," Jono said a couple of minutes later as he put his phone away.

"How many did you get?" Patrick asked as he closed his MacBook.

"I could murder a whole one by myself, so I got two."

That meant Patrick wouldn't have to share. He'd grudgingly accept Jono's apology if it meant he got free food. He got up from the table, stretching out the kinks that came from sitting for hours on end in a hard chair. Jono had returned to the couch to continue watching television, having settled on a channel showing the highlights of what had happened in American sports that day.

"Didn't think you liked baseball, what with you being English and all," Patrick said. He sprawled out on the other end of the couch, kicking one foot up on the coffee table.

"You Yanks hardly show any proper football. Better something than nothing, even if baseball is the most boring sport in existence."

Patrick really couldn't disagree. He found baseball tolerable only when he was at a game getting drunk and eating too many hot dogs. Still, Patrick was content enough to spend the next forty-five minutes listening to commentators talk stats and show replays of today's game highlights, if only to give his mind a rest. When Jono's phone rang, Patrick watched him leave to go retrieve the delivery from downstairs since they couldn't buzz the guy in. Jono returned a couple of minutes later carrying two large pizza boxes and a six-pack of beer.

Patrick ate straight out of the box, folding the greasy slices of pizza in half and devouring them one by one. Jono opened their beers by prying off the bottle caps with his hands, passing one to Patrick first before taking a sip of his. Patrick would say dinner was almost nice, if it didn't feel like an extension of Jono's apology in the car.

Dinner wasn't enough to make him forget that incident, and Jono didn't try to broach the subject again that night. The quiet between them felt strained, ushering Patrick to bed at a decent hour for once rather than waiting out the tension.

Patrick woke up at the ass crack of dark before dawn to his phone ringing. He fumbled it out from beneath his pillow and answered it without looking. "Someone better be dead."

"So you're psychic now as well as a mage. I'm not paying extra for that. We got another body," Casale said, sounding entirely too awake for the stupidly early hour.

Patrick double-checked the time and swore under his breath. "It's not even oh-four hundred."

"Murder waits for no man."

Patrick kicked the blanket off and sat up, rubbing hard at his eyes. "Where?"

Casale rattled off the address, then hung up. Patrick hauled himself out of bed and dressed in record time, holstering his sidearm on his right hip and strapping his dagger onto his right thigh. He came out of the bedroom to see Jono half-awake and pulling on his shoes, already dressed.

"What did I say about keeping your ears to yourself?" Patrick said through a yawn.

"How else am I supposed to keep up if I don't know what's going on?" Jono asked as he stood up and headed for the door.

Patrick pointed a finger at Jono. "Ears to yourself."

As he passed by, Jono leaned down and snapped his teeth at the tip of Patrick's fingers. "Sure thing, Pat."

Patrick reflexively yanked his hand back and scowled at Jono, who only laughed in a way he refused to find sexy.

They left the building and retrieved the car. Despite the hour, a lot of other vehicles and taxis were on the streets, ferrying home late-night drunks and taking hard-core revelers to their next destination.

Patrick followed the GPS on his phone, taking a crosstown route before swinging a right onto Amsterdam Avenue. The address Casale had provided was in the Upper West Side, Morningside Heights, right smack next to Columbia University. Which meant instant media coverage they couldn't afford. People equated most college students with kids who didn't know any better, and the public always had a bleeding-heart complex when it came to kids.

He parked behind an unmarked police car and grabbed his agency jacket from the back seat. Patrick pulled it on despite the still-muggy weather, making sure his badge hung prominently around his neck. He didn't want to keep taking out the one in his pocket every time someone needed to check his ID.

Jono stuck close to his side, sunglasses on despite the hour. He looked ridiculous, but better to hide what he was within view of the media cameras than to give the impression the werecreature community might be linked to the murders when they weren't involved.

"Stay close and do what I tell you," Patrick said as he flashed his badge to a cop manning the perimeter. He ducked under the Police Line – Do Not Cross tape, then held it up for Jono to duck under. "And if you have to get sick, don't get sick near the evidence."

"Right. I'll just ask for the loo," Jono muttered. "Not my first time seeing a dead body."

Considering how werecreatures sometimes handled territory disputes and other problems, Patrick wasn't surprised to hear that. "I guarantee you've never seen one like this."

Patrick and Jono entered the building, getting directed to the tenth floor where an apartment at the very end of the hallway was a hive of late-night activity. Recognition punched through his shields when they stepped off the elevator, sliding through the new damage in his soul.

What was it Casale said? Three bodies in a month and a half? Patrick thought to himself as they passed a pair of uniformed police officers. *This brings the total up to nine.*

This murder was far too close timing-wise to the last one. The perpetrator, whoever they were, was ramping up their killings. While Patrick had a pretty good idea why, he just didn't know when anything would come of the attacks.

Casale was waiting for them in the living room, wearing a suit as if it were body armor. He nodded a greeting before pointing at Jono. "You stay out here and keep out of the way."

Jono, who made a quiet gagging sound behind Patrick—most likely from the smell—was all for it. "Too right I will."

"Bathroom is over there if you were stupid and ate breakfast."

"At this hour it'd be more like a midnight snack," Patrick said.

He approached one of the two bedrooms and paused in the entrance for a minute, taking in the crime scene with sharp eyes. Whoever she had once been, it was hard to see in the mutilated mess she'd become on her ruined bed. Her torso had been cracked open like a bloody butterfly, organs ripped out of the gaping hole and body chewed on like the last one.

Her left arm was missing up to her elbow with pieces of flesh scattered around the stump. Half her face had been eaten away, along with a good portion of her neck as well. Patrick could see the white vertebrae of her spine through the mess. Her legs were half-gone, stripped down to the bone in areas, as if the soultaker had peeled away flesh and muscle one layer at a time. Blood stained the bedding, having congealed beneath the body where it wasn't splattered across the white wall and wooden frame of her bed.

CSU was already hard at work processing the scene. The room felt crowded even though only two of them were inside it. Patrick had a feeling it was the hellish taint pressing against his shields that made him uncomfortable.

Allison handed him a pair of latex gloves before he stepped

inside the bedroom. She looked tired, and Patrick wondered if she'd even gone home last night. Dwayne appeared marginally better, but he had at least ten years on Allison of working shifts like this. He could probably power through on nothing more than a couple of coffees at this point in his career.

Patrick pulled on the gloves and carefully stepped around numbered evidence tags on the floor to reach the body. He prodded at the victim's ruined face, pulling at her lashes to get a better look at the sign carved into her eyelids. Taurus this time, which called to Dionysus. Patrick had a feeling that god wouldn't be playing poker in Atlantic City any time soon. If he was smart, Dionysus would have gotten the hell away from the Eastern Seaboard.

Wonder if Hermes has found the rest of the coins yet, Patrick thought.

"Time of death?" he asked.

"We're still waiting on the ME," Dwayne said.

"Who found her?"

"The roommate came home from a club and found the victim like this. She's being seen to by EMS."

"I'll check her soul for any taint and let your on-call witch know. The residual is the same here as with the last body."

Casale heaved out a sigh. "I'll warn everyone they're getting their souls scoured again."

"Always fun," Allison muttered from her spot by the door.

Patrick retreated from the body, carefully making his way out of the bedroom. He stripped off his gloves and deposited them in the portable biohazard bin CSU had put next to the door. "I'll stick around until processing is done just in case."

"You think the demon might make a reappearance?" Casale asked.

"The bar could be an outlier attack, but who knows. Better safe than sorry."

Patrick spent the next two hours or so monitoring the scene

and quietly tagging the people who would need to have their souls scrubbed of the taint by himself or one of the witches employed by the PCB. Jono stayed out of the way on the living room couch, attention on his phone. He did let Patrick know Marek was home and that nothing had tripped the barrier ward during a lull moment.

"That's good, innit?" Jono asked, looking up from the string of text messages.

Patrick shrugged. "We'll see."

He wouldn't put anything past Ethan and whoever else was aligned with the Dominion Sect helping to commit murder in this city. Patrick stayed until the body was wheeled out on a gurney in a black body bag, overseen by a PCB-affiliated witch. The body would be taken on a one-way trip to the ME's warded incinerator. People who died by way of demons or black magic were always burned. Fire permanently cleansed anything, even the dead. There could be no burial for a body ruined by hell.

"This won't look good in the press," Casale said before they left the apartment.

"I know. Just keep them at bay," Patrick replied.

"That's going to be difficult after today considering we have two more bodies in less than a week. Talk of a serial killer is making everyone uneasy and the commissioner wants answers. So find me some."

"He does know I took the case over, right? I'm not at his beck and call."

Casale nodded. "He knows. That doesn't change the fact we're doing all the legwork for you."

Patrick didn't say anything to that, attributing Casale's annoyance to the early-morning wake-up call they'd all been subjected to. He waved at Jono to follow him to the elevator while Casale coordinated with the PR representative out of DCPI on how best to handle the press down on the street. Jono kept his sunglasses on as they left the building. Outside, the sky was lightening from the encroaching sunrise.

Patrick pulled out his phone as they walked down the pavement toward his car. He scrolled through his contacts for Setsuna's cell phone number, not her direct office line, and called her. It rang five times, but she didn't pick up, the call going to voicemail.

His message was short and to the point. "Ninth body. Call me."

"You're going to get more bodies, won't you?" Jono asked quietly as they ducked under the police tape.

"Yeah," Patrick said, mouth twisting at that admission.

"How many more, you think?"

"I don't know."

He didn't; not really. The number of people the Dominion Sect had sacrificed to the hells in order to call forth enough soultakers to rip open the veil at the start of the Thirty-Day War had never been finalized. A spell like that required a range of different magic, and the mages who had performed it were wanted all over the world.

That spell was finding its bones in New York City.

Somehow, Patrick needed to stop what was happening.

He pulled out his keys and unlocked the car with a push of a button when they were only a few feet away. Before he even lifted his thumb off the key fob, the car exploded.

Patrick felt it spark at the very edge of his awareness, a quicksilver heat that jerked him out of the calm city street to the uncertainty of the front lines he thought he'd left by the wayside three years ago. He grabbed blindly for a weapon he no longer carried, the weight of his rifle an absence only replaced in his nightmares. Patrick's instinct to fight would never die.

You could take a soldier out of war, but you couldn't take the war out of the soldier.

Even as he ripped his shields out of his body, hands grabbed him by the shoulders and hauled him backward with preternatural strength and speed. Patrick's feet left the ground, partly from

Jono's efforts to get them clear and partly from the concussive force of the explosion ripping through the air. The scorching heat of hellfire burst outward from the car, licking at his shields as it sent a plume of toxic smoke into the sun-kissed sky. Glass and metal cut through the air like deadly shrapnel.

Jono's preternatural speed got them meters away, just not completely in the clear. They crashed to the pavement two cars away from the epicenter of someone's attempt to murder Patrick. Strong arms wrapped around his body as he landed on top of Jono rather than hard concrete. Jono grunted in his ear from the impact, holding him tightly as the leading edge of the hellfire explosion burned against Patrick's shields.

Patrick thrust both his arms into the air, a mageglobe spinning rapidly in the space between his hands. In war, even seconds could be too long to guarantee survival, but the shield ward had already formed in his mind the moment his subconscious recognized what was happening. His personal shields would keep them safe, but everyone else on the street needed cover.

Patrick poured his magic into a tall, curved shield between the street and the hellfire raining down like metaphysical napalm. This defensive ward wasn't one that came easily to him, but it formed and it held, and that was all that mattered.

Screams filled the air, cutting through the ringing in his ears. Jono shoved them both to a sitting position, one of his hands having slipped underneath Patrick's shirt during their mad scramble to get clear. The heat emanating from Jono's touch seared through Patrick even as all his concentration focused on the shield ward.

He dragged his magic higher, wider, covering the street around them and forcing it up the sides of buildings. Patrick put his magic between everyone and the terrifying destruction of a hellfire bomb usually only found in a war zone. He spread his fingers, palms pressed flat against the distant sky as he shored up the structure of the shield with as much magic as he could spare.

The shield wavered, not nearly as strong as he needed it to be, and he could feel his magic leaving his soul faster than usual. Patrick gritted his teeth and concentrated on holding it up the way he'd done countless times on the front lines—by ignoring the pain and pushing through his limitations as much as he could.

Because he had no other choice.

Patrick stared up at the sky around the rapidly spinning mage-globe framed between his hands as sizzling splatters of hellfire rained down on his shield ward. He drew back his own personal shields, letting it sink back beneath his skin. Jono made a sound in the back of his throat, his warm breath blowing across Patrick's ear when he spoke.

"You carry your shields in your bones," Jono said, making it a statement, not a question.

Patrick didn't respond, too focused on the once clear sky now marred by black smoke rising high above the street. The acrid smell of it was something even his shields couldn't keep out. He clenched his hands into fists, manipulating his magic to fold the edges of his shield over the burning, destroyed vehicles to contain the hellfire. Shields weren't his strong suit, even back when he could tap a ley line, but he refused to let this one break.

"Collins!" Casale yelled, his voice cutting through the cries filling the air.

For a split second, Patrick could smell desert sand and the cloying scent of death. He could hear the steady burst of suppressive fire trying to clear him a way to the center of that death spell, Ashanti's ashes still hot under his fingernails.

Patrick wrenched his mind out of memory and focused on the here and now.

"Clear!" he shouted back, forgetting that no one had called for his status, that this wasn't a war zone, except for how it was.

Jono shifted behind him, and suddenly Patrick was being hauled to his feet by strong arms, held close against Jono's solid body. He was reminded of the other night, how easily Jono had manhandled him so they could both get off. It was nice to know the other man could use his strength to keep them safe as well.

"What the fucking hell was that?" Jono asked.

Patrick dropped his arms a little, the mageglobe following his hands. He couldn't quite choke back the ugly laughter that escaped his mouth. "Hell is right."

Casale was suddenly by their sides, expression equal parts fearful and furious. Patrick belatedly realized he was still wrapped up in Jono's arms and reluctantly stepped away from the taller man.

"Was that your car?" Casale demanded.

"Yeah. Something tells me we're on their radar."

"You think?" Casale said, staring at the vehicles the hellfire bomb had destroyed, still burning away behind Patrick's shield covering the street. "Are you all right?"

No, Patrick thought. What he ended up saying was "Yes."

He couldn't afford to be anything else right now.

Jono stared at Patrick like he didn't believe him at all, but he didn't question Patrick's state of mind. Which was fine with Patrick, because the only person he didn't argue about his mental health with was his VA-assigned therapist. After today, Patrick figured he owed the man a call.

"Anyone else hurt?" Patrick asked.

"We're clearing the area, but I don't think so. You got your shield up in time," Casale replied.

Patrick nodded, most of his attention still on the hellfire burning itself out beneath his shield, the warning as clear as sunlight.

The Dominion Sect knew he was in town.

9

"You can't take me off the case," Patrick argued. "I'm running it now."

Casale pointed at the smoldering remains of the rental car and two squad cars. The vehicles were currently being doused by a witch with an affinity for water magic instead of the FDNY for security purposes. Casale had dispatched a couple of other PCB witches whose affinity with defensive wards were strong to work with the bomb squad on clearing the area.

"Someone just tried to kill you," Casale said.

"They did a shitty job of it since I'm still breathing."

Jono made a strangled noise in the back of his throat that both Patrick and Casale ignored.

"I take personal offense to someone targeting the people working my cases. I know I can't take you off the case; I just need you *safe*. You're no good to me dead, Collins."

Casale had a point, even if Patrick didn't like it. "This isn't the first time I've survived a bomb scare."

"That doesn't make this situation better," Jono interjected.

"I need you alive to finish this job, not dead in the street from another bomb. You are *not* handling the processing of this crime scene and are getting the hell out of sight of the media," Casale told him.

Patrick resisted the urge to look over his shoulder at the cluster of news vans parked at the far end of the street, the cameras pointed their way.

"Fucking rats," he muttered under his breath.

He really, truly hated dealing with the media.

Casale jerked his thumb over his shoulder. "Ramirez and Guthrie will drive you back to the PCB or wherever you're staying."

"PCB," Patrick said. "I'm not done working."

Just because someone had tried to murder him didn't mean Patrick had time to take a break.

Minutes later, Patrick and Jono climbed into the back of Allison and Dwayne's unmarked police car. He slouched in the seat after buckling up, leaning his head back. He ached, right down to his bones, a gritty, low-grade pain that stemmed from the shredded pieces of his soul and partially drained magic, courtesy of the soultaker. He needed a couple of days of uninterrupted rest to heal both problems, but at this rate, Patrick doubted he'd get any.

"Where's Marek?" Patrick asked when they were halfway to the PCB.

"Home. He's watching the morning news about the murder and the attack. Nothing has tripped your ward," Jono said, looking up from his phone and the text messages on the screen.

Patrick closed his eyes. "He better stay there."

Jono kept quiet in the face of that statement. The other man couldn't speak for Marek, and Marek seemed to do whatever the hell he liked, no matter Patrick's warnings. If Patrick had been born a seer, he wouldn't have any faith in an immortal to keep himself safe and always one step ahead of danger.

Allison and Dwayne didn't try to engage either of their passengers with conversation on the drive back to the PCB. This morning's double whammy of murder and attempted murder had put people on edge. Patrick was thankful for the quiet, if only so he could *think*. The case was racking up bodies like a bookie accrued debts, and he'd almost been added to the mix.

What am I missing? Patrick thought.

The Dominion Sect had stolen souls in sacrifices to the gods. While New York City had a nexus pooled beneath its streets and subways, it didn't have a relic of an altar to hold the structure of the spell in place. No pyramids, no shrine, no temple, no anything from the old world and the even older religions which shored up the lives of the immortals.

Patrick couldn't get ahead of what he didn't know, and he *needed* to.

"Come on," Jono said when Allison and Dwayne dropped them off in front of the PCB. "Let's find you some food."

Patrick thought about arguing, but the sound of his stomach growling ended that fight before it began. "Fine."

Midmorning on a Saturday downtown meant the usual weekday crowds had disappeared. Jono steered him to a deli that was still open one block away that served thick sandwiches, soups, and salads. The building it resided in was one of the older ones taking up space in the Manhattan skyline.

Patrick ordered a roast beef sandwich with all the fixings, a bag of chips, and a Gatorade. Jono got double the amount Patrick ordered, and they returned to the PCB with their lunch. The sergeant on desk duty buzzed them through without comment. Patrick led Jono to the same conference room he'd worked out of yesterday.

The room was thankfully empty, and they spread their food out on the table. Jono took off his sunglasses and set them down nearby, along with his cell phone. Patrick unwrapped his sandwich and took a hearty bite, hoping the faint headache he had would go away if he fed it.

Patrick was halfway through his sandwich before he finally asked the question that had been swirling around his head for a while now. "How did you know the explosion was about to happen?"

Because Jono had grabbed him before the sound of the explosion even reached Patrick's ears. Even now, what stood out in sharp relief in Patrick's memories was the heat of Jono's touch.

"I smelled it when the spell ignited," Jono said.

Patrick knew hellfire had a distinctive smell, so it was no surprise Jono was able to react so quickly. The werevirus altered their souls and bodies, making their enhanced senses highly sought after by the US Department of the Preternatural. Patrick had worked with a handful of out werecreatures who weren't god pack in the Preternatural Infantry during his time in the military. Teams relied on werecreatures to clear hot areas of land mines, spell traps, and embedded enemy fighters. The threats could be metaphysical or human-made, but werecreatures were adept at sniffing them out.

Patrick popped a potato chip into his mouth and crunched his way through the cheesy flavor. "Thank you."

"You don't have to thank me for saving your arse, Pat."

"All the same. If I didn't have my shields up, I would've been dead. So the gesture is appreciated."

Jono looked up from unwrapping his second sandwich. "I don't know many magic users who carry their shields in their bones."

It was a careful, curious statement, but it still made Patrick's shoulders tighten. He kept his gaze trained on the chips he'd poured out on the paper wrapper. He thought about giving Jono the cold shoulder, but doing so would make their time together during the case more stressful. Patrick didn't need any more stress in his life.

Most magic users didn't power permanent personal shields. It took too much energy, too much magic, even at a low-grade level. Patrick's personal shields hadn't been set by him, but by a goddess to help hide the taint in his soul from prying eyes. Since the Thirty-Day War, they'd also hidden the damage his soul had accrued in that fight.

They hid *him*, in all the ways that mattered, but a part of Patrick didn't want to hide from Jono. He blamed wanting to get laid—*badly*—but Patrick owed the other man, even if a soul debt wasn't in the cards between them.

"I was Mage Corps, like you guessed in the car," Patrick said, not blinking. "Metaphysical wounds are just as bad as the physical ones. I'd argue worse, in some ways. You can't see damage to a person's soul like you can to their body."

Jono's wolf-bright eyes never left his. "Your magic smells odd. Not bad, just odd. Suppose that's due to a soul wound?"

Patrick shrugged, mouth dry, but he got the words out anyway. "I took a hit three years ago in a fight. It was bad. I lost the ability to tap a ley line or a nexus."

Some of his detractors within the SOA considered Patrick a mage in name only. It didn't matter that he had more magic in his soul than the strongest practitioner who couldn't tap a ley line. Since he couldn't access external magic, some people argued he should no longer carry the rank of a mage within the agency. A title didn't make a person though, and Patrick had a lifetime of magical training under his belt only another mage would understand.

In the end, Patrick kept his rank, kept his job, even if it felt like he was missing an arm some days.

"Can you alter your shields a bit? Make it so I can smell you?" Jono asked.

"My magic isn't the easiest to be around," Patrick said. He knew how his magic felt to others—knew no one liked it.

Jono never looked away when he said, "It doesn't bother me."

Patrick paused in reaching for his sandwich again, pinned by Jono's steady gaze. "I doubt that."

"Your magic has a bitter scent to it, but that's loads better than half the things I smell walking down the street at any given hour. Enhanced senses aren't always easy to live with. I smelled the hellfire bomb, but I couldn't smell you until you lifted your shields. In a fight, I want to know where you are."

Patrick let out a dry bark of laughter. "Sounds like you want to watch my six."

"If that's what they call it these days, then yes."

Patrick picked up his sandwich and took a bite, not trusting his immediate response to Jono's answer. Three years ago he'd left the Mage Corps and his team behind because he couldn't protect them the way he needed to anymore. Since joining the SOA, he'd worked alone, with no partner to watch his back. If he was honest, it got tiring. Hunting a serial killer with a werewolf would be a lot easier than trying to do it alone.

Patrick mentally shifted his personal shields, feeling magic ripple through his skin in a tingling sensation. The layers became porous enough to allow scent through and nothing else. Jono took a deep breath, the sound loud in the room, despite the bull pen beyond the closed door.

"Cheers, mate," Jono said quietly.

"You realize I'm gone at the end of this case, right?" Patrick said.

"I don't think the Fates will be pleased about that."

Patrick made a face. "Yeah, well, fuck the Fates. Fuck this entire day."

Jono laughed, the sound going straight to Patrick's dick. Jono gave him a knowing look, and Patrick resigned himself to Jono attempting to read his emotions through scent until he got on a plane out of there.

They finished their lunch, and Patrick went to retrieve the case files containing the murders and the missing person case to review again. The Cirillo file was thinner than all the rest, but the missing person report itself was fairly detailed. Patrick's attention kept drifting back to the photo of the couple. They weren't familiar, but they were a problem.

Gods always were.

He pulled out his cell phone and dialed the number on the business card in the file. It rang twice before a young-sounding woman picked up. "Isadora Cirillo's line."

Patrick assumed he got her assistant. "Is Mrs. Cirillo available?"

"Can I ask who's calling?"

"This is Special Agent Patrick Collins with the Supernatural Operations Agency. I'm working with the NYPD on her husband's missing person case."

"One moment."

The line went blank in the way of being put on hold. Patrick waited maybe thirty seconds before the call picked up again and a different, richer voice filtered through the speaker. Patrick tightened his grip on his phone.

"Patrick," Isadora said, with far too much familiarity in her voice.

He thought about Hermes' message in his now-destroyed car, and the implications of the relationship Hermes had with the woman speaking on the other line.

"Mrs. Cirillo, I presume," Patrick said carefully.

"I expected the SOA to get involved. I didn't think they would send you."

Patrick rubbed at his eyes until spots burst across his the back of his eyelids. "I don't know you."

"Then I suppose it's time we were introduced. My office is closed tomorrow. You'll meet me at my hearth and home instead."

"Will I?" Patrick asked, glaring down at the business card and a name he doubted was real.

"It is the least you owe me and mine."

He tried not to flinch at her words, but it was hard. Patrick had an idea of who he would be meeting when he knocked on her door. Either way, he wasn't looking forward to it. "What's your address?"

Isadora gave it to him, then hung up. Patrick set his phone on the table and tossed the business card aside. It landed on a photograph of a body, hiding the carved-open chest cavity.

People were dying with signs carved into their eyelids for a reason. The reason wouldn't be found in the case files at the PCB. It could only be found in Patrick's past. It was his job to tie it all together, but he really didn't fucking want to.

Doing so would make the nightmare real.

When he dragged his gaze away from the files scattered over the table, he found Jono staring at him with a quiet intensity that made him tense up.

"What?" Patrick asked defensively.

"Hope you don't plan on going alone," Jono said.

Patrick wondered what the Fates would do if he left Jono by the wayside. "I'll decide in the morning."

Jono wasn't impressed with that answer, but he let the argument drop. Patrick went back to digging through the case files, because some days the dead were easier to deal with than the living.

Setsuna called him in the late afternoon, her name on his cell phone's screen breaking his concentration. Patrick abandoned the detailed photos of dead bodies in favor of answering. Across from him, Jono looked up from his phone, head tilting to the side.

"A car bomb? Really?" Setsuna asked in lieu of the traditional hello.

"Military grade. Ruined my rental and two other nearby vehicles. The hellfire caused a small fire on the roof of the building, but the wards kept it from burning anything critical."

"Nothing you couldn't handle since you're still breathing."

"I told Casale that. He didn't take it too well."

"He doesn't know you like I do."

"Sometimes I wish you didn't know me at all."

"We can't change the past, Patrick. The future is what we need to worry about. I'm calling to tell you one out of two of your task force is in town. They'll meet with you tonight."

Some of the tension in Patrick's shoulders eased, but only a little. "Where?"

"They'll find you, so make yourself available. And Patrick?"

"Yes?"

"Stay alive."

Setsuna hung up. Patrick pulled his phone away from his ear and scowled at it.

"She sounds like a right lovely lady," Jono drawled.

Patrick snorted and put his phone away. "A lovely pain in my ass, that's for sure."

He started putting the files back together so he could put them away. Jono watched him curiously. "Are we leaving?"

"She said make myself available. I can't be available inside the PCB, so yeah, we're leaving."

"Where?"

Patrick ran through his options and discarded most of them in seconds. He didn't know who might be watching the apartment, the SOA office downtown was out of the question, and Marek's apartment was impossible to reach because of the barrier ward. Setsuna's order to make himself available gave Patrick an idea on who was coming.

And if he was right, he'd rather they meet in public.

"Is Tempest open tonight?" Patrick asked.

Jono nodded. "Tyler managed to cleanse the bar. It's back open for business. I usually work weekend nights, but Emma is giving me paid time off until this is all over."

"Then let's go. After what happened this morning, I need a goddamn drink."

Patrick put away the files in their assigned cabinet before they left the PCB, a look-away ward burning through a mageglobe in Patrick's hand.

"Bit paranoid, aren't you?" Jono asked as they started walking.

"Keeps me alive."

Patrick didn't drop his look-away ward until they were two blocks away. It faded between one step and the next, everyone's awareness of their presence sliding through them, as if they'd been there all along.

"Want me to get an Uber?" Jono asked. "It'll be a quick ride to Tempest from here."

Patrick shook his head. "We don't want quick. We want to get lost."

Someone had gotten past the heavy police presence in Morningside Heights to set the hellfire bomb on his car. Patrick wouldn't put it past the Dominion Sect to sic some of their acolytes on him. If anyone had eyes on the two of them, it would be difficult to keep watch in a crowd.

As they turned a corner, a heavy gust of wind smacked Patrick in the face. He glanced up at the now-cloudy sky, a marked difference from the clear blue that morning. The air had a muggy feel to it, like the lead-up to a storm.

Patrick put the change in weather and the warning it could be out of his mind in favor of leading Jono two blocks north to the Spring Street subway station. Patrick picked up a single-ride subway ticket to get through the fare gates while Jono used his MetroCard. They blended in with the crowd waiting on the platform and took the next 6 train running north, riding it all the way up to Grand Central Station.

Even before they arrived at that transit hub, Patrick could sense the magic emanating from it. The famous station contained the anchoring circle of protective wards that ran through the entire subway system. Power bled out in all directions, a faint buzz to his senses that was easy to ignore.

The train came to a stop and the doors opened automatically. As they exited the train car, Jono slipped his hand into Patrick's and tugged him through the crush of people ready to get their

Saturday night started. Jono's hand was warm in his, the strength in the hold impossible to miss. Patrick let him take point, Jono's presence as a predator something human instinct couldn't ignore. People got out of his way without even realizing it.

"Where to now?" Jono asked.

"Anywhere," Patrick told him.

Jono took him on a circuitous route through the station to catch the 7 train going west. They took it crosstown, getting off at Times Square. Rather than get on another train, they went topside into the summer crowds of tourists filling the Great White Way. The famous intersection burned bright with the neon lights of dozens of electronic billboards, familiar store-brand logos, and the famous advertising screens attached to the One Times Square building.

Patrick still carried his handgun and his dagger, the look-away ward set in the leather of his holster and sheath keeping curious eyes at bay. Patrick pulled his hand free of Jono's grip and reached for his phone. No messages and no calls.

"Let's keep moving," he said.

They walked through the crowd and didn't stop until Patrick found the first bus line going south. They squeezed their way onto a bus carrying more tourists than locals. Patrick ended up pressed against Jono's front, one hand gripping a hand strap while he kept the other to himself. That lasted as long as it took for a taxi to cut the bus off and the driver to slam on the brakes. Patrick swayed hard with everyone else, staying upright with the help of Jono's hand that suddenly found its way to his hip.

This close, and all Patrick could think about was their fleeting time together the other night and the way Jono wouldn't stop looking at him, even now.

"We staying aboveground?" Jono asked, his thumb stroking distractingly against Patrick's waist beneath his shirt.

"Down to the Financial District. We'll catch a taxi there."

"All right."

Jono never let go of Patrick, and he couldn't find it within himself to ask Jono to give him space. Touch for the sake of it wasn't something Patrick got to indulge in often, while werecreatures thrived on it.

Maybe we both miss this, he thought.

It wasn't a question he would ever ask.

Patrick hailed a taxi rather than an Uber when they finally made it off the bus. The yellow vehicle blended in with traffic more. They'd spent an hour and a half backtracking through the streets of Manhattan to lose a tail that may or may not have even existed. Patrick preferred being cautious over being dead.

When the taxi arrived at Tempest, a familiar Maserati was parked out front. Patrick scowled as he paid for the ride.

"I'm going to kill him," Patrick said.

"Defeats the purpose of keeping him safe, yeah?" Jono replied.

"He'd be safe in a grave."

Jono threw back his head and laughed as he stepped onto the pavement. Patrick enjoyed the view, eyes lingering on Jono's ass. He thought about fully raising his shields again, but the flashback to the hellfire bomb stayed his hand. Patrick kept his shields at the level they currently were—strong but porous enough to let scent through. Walking into a bar full of werecreatures capable of smelling truth from a lie wouldn't be comfortable, but he wouldn't be staying long.

The bouncer waved them inside, keeping his attention on the street and guarding the door. The tingle of the searching spell someone had recast slid over Patrick's shields before falling away. Recognition filtered through his magic as they stepped inside, the overwhelming sense of *werecreature* just as strong as the first time he'd visited.

The bar was half-full, conversation held to quiet bubbles that didn't drift far from huddled groups. The sound system was turned on low, a marked difference from the noise of Thursday night. The metaphysical feel of the place was calmer, lighter, the cleansing done yesterday having cleared the bar of any hint that hell had trespassed on the premises.

Patrick followed Jono up to the bar where Emma, Leon, and Sage had made room for them. Tyler had taken a spot at the far end and was ignoring everyone in favor of his phone.

Patrick claimed the seat next to Sage, pretending he wasn't aware of the line of heat from Jono's body on his other side. He glared across the bar counter at where Marek was mixing a drink in a shaker. "I told you to stay fucking *put*. Did you not see the news this morning?"

"Yes," Marek said.

"Do you like tempting fate?"

Marek rolled his eyes as he poured out the mixture into a coupe glass and garnished it with a thinly shaved orange peel. He passed it over to Sage before turning around to open a small cupboard with a glass door. He pulled out a bottle of Glenlivet 25 Year Old single malt scotch and flipped over a glass to pour out an ounce of the good stuff. He placed the drink in front of Patrick like a peace offering.

Patrick really didn't want to take it, but fuck, that was some *good whiskey* right there.

"On the house," Marek said.

"This doesn't mean you're off the hook for disobeying orders," Patrick retorted.

He picked up the glass anyway and took a sip, relishing the taste of it. Patrick had no plans to get drunk tonight, but he wasn't saying no to free alcohol. Besides, he did most of his drinking behind a locked door in a room that housed no one else but him for a reason.

Marek braced himself against the work counter behind the bar. "Just so we're clear, I'm not one of your little soldiers you can boss around."

Patrick turned his head and gave Jono a *look*. Jono shook his head and rested his elbows on the bar. "Nah, Pat. I didn't say nothing."

Marek rapped his knuckles against the wood, dragging Patrick's attention back to him. "An unnamed source told the news the hellfire bomb was military grade and so was the defense. Your name might not be in the news yet, but the rank you have to be to pull off that kind of save is. The media is pressing the PCB for answers on who they hired."

Patrick made a face and took another sip of the whiskey, not admitting to anything.

Emma peered around Sage at him, tucking some of her hair behind one delicate ear. "Who did it target? You or Jono?"

Patrick paused with his glass halfway to his mouth. He finished the motion because he wasn't going to waste good whiskey, but Patrick suddenly wished he could tighten his shields. A warm hand settled on his thigh. He turned to stare at Jono, meeting those wolf-bright eyes and seeing nothing but concern in the older man's gaze.

"You're supposed to stay with me," Patrick said slowly. "They never said why."

He didn't have to elaborate on who *they* were. He thought back to Thursday night, to when the soultaker attacked. The demon had gone after Marek—but Marek hadn't been the only one in that vicinity.

Jono had been standing right beside him.

"You said Marek was the target," Jono told him.

Patrick downed the rest of the whiskey, needing the burn to steady himself. He wished he could enjoy it, but it felt like acid in his mouth. "Marek might not be the only one."

"I don't have a clean soul. Why would they want me?"

Patrick couldn't answer that, and even if he knew something, he wouldn't talk about it in Tempest. Too many ears and eyes that didn't need to know the inner workings of his mind, or the details of this case.

"You want another?" Marek asked.

Patrick shook his head. "No."

Marek served him a glass of water instead. Patrick pulled it closer and ignored the conversation around him in favor of his phone. Still no missed calls or messages. He accessed his email but didn't see any new ones that mattered.

All the while Jono's hand stayed on his thigh, and Patrick was acutely aware of the heat in the touch.

Tempest didn't get much busier than when they arrived, which was odd for a Saturday night. Patrick didn't know if it was because of gossip about the attack or if the doorman had orders to keep anyone human out. Still, he didn't leave his spot except to use the restroom, even if Jono left him to take over for Marek behind the bar. Patrick told himself he didn't miss Jono's touch.

It was close to 2130 when the first of Setsuna's promised backup finally arrived.

Patrick was nursing his second glass of water when a commotion at the front door had him jerking his head around. One hand automatically strayed to his sidearm without even thinking about it, magic flickering against the palm of his other hand. When he saw who walked inside, Patrick stopped reaching for both.

Fuck my life, he thought resignedly.

The newcomer was undead, the sucking emptiness where a soul once resided in human flesh a familiar recognition that pulled at Patrick's magic, even through his shields. The vampire was as tall as Jono, who was at least three inches over six feet. Blond hair was cut short, the icy blue of his eyes standing out against too-pale skin. The vampire's gaze swept the room, taking in everything with a quick glance, before finally settling on Patrick. Thin lips lifted in a slight snarl, revealing jagged teeth that always reminded Patrick of a piranha.

Emma was on her feet in an instant, Leon right by her side. They planted themselves between the vampire and those in the bar, refusing to give ground. Everyone else had gone still and quiet, the music the only noise in the place for several tense seconds.

"This is pack territory. We have treaties with Tremaine's Night Court and the other master vampires in this city that require your kind to stay the hell away," Leon growled.

The vampire didn't move, gaze still riveted on Patrick like a predator ready to pounce. "Not my Night Court."

His answer didn't seem to sit well with Emma and Leon. Patrick slid off the stool and approached where they stood. He managed to get a step past the two when a strong hand gripped his arm, holding him back. Patrick rocked back on his heels as he looked over his shoulder at Jono.

"Remember how I said I needed to make myself available?" Patrick asked.

Jono's eyes weren't on him, but on the vampire. "Didn't think you meant like this."

Patrick didn't try to get free of Jono's grip, merely faced forward again, meeting the vampire's piercing gaze. "Einar. Were you the only one he sent?"

The vampire didn't say a word.

Someone else answered for him.

"No," a sultry voice said. "Our master sent me."

High heels clacked sharply against the floor as someone else walked inside the bar. She brought with her a sexual energy that made Patrick's dick twitch in his jeans, despite not being attracted to women at all.

Carmen always did have that effect on people and monsters alike.

She sauntered forward on five-inch stiletto heels, wearing a burgundy corset minidress that clung to every curve of her body. The neckline plunged indecently low between her full breasts while the hemline was scandalously short. Gold and pearl necklaces hung from her throat at varying lengths, swaying with every step she took. The outfit as a whole was a modern-day look that teased her Venetian courtesan roots.

The color of Carmen's dress brought out the bronzed undertone to her tanned olive skin, giving her a sun-kissed look Einar would forever lack. Her long black hair fell to her waist in a riot of curls. She looked human, but between one step and the next, the glamour she wore like a second skin sloughed off, revealing her true form.

Curled horns twisted away from her hairline over her skull, her hair parting around them. Gold and diamond hoops were pierced through each ear from lobe to pointed tip. The pupils of her dark brown eyes weren't black, but a deep, dark red. The sexual energy emanating from her grew stronger, thickening the air with people's arousal. Her heart-shaped face hadn't changed at all since the last time Patrick had seen her, and neither had the icy crimson smile she bestowed upon him, her eyes locked with his.

Patrick did himself a favor and adjusted his shields, blocking out the sexual aggression Carmen thrived in.

"*Ciao, bastardo*," Carmen said, the succubus' voice tinged with her native Italian accent even these hundreds of years later.

Jono's grip became almost bruising for a second or two before loosening enough that Patrick could pull free. He took that step forward and put himself between the two groups, keeping his eyes on Carmen.

"I see that necrophilia thing is still working out for you," Patrick said.

"I see your manners haven't improved."

"I save them for the living."

Carmen's smile grew wider, though Einar looked like he was contemplating murder.

Then again, the vampire always looked like he was contemplating murder.

Patrick barely paid him any attention. Einar was here for Carmen's protection, but they all knew Patrick wouldn't lay a finger on her. As the favored lover to one of the world's most notorious vampires, any attack against Carmen was an attack against Lucien. Patrick didn't know how old Carmen truly was, but her first recorded appearance hit the history books about five hundred years ago. Still nearly half a millennia younger than Lucien, but that didn't make her any less dangerous.

Thinking about Ashanti's favorite child, Patrick wondered what the hell Setsuna had offered to get Lucien to agree to watch his six. Not that Patrick trusted the vampire *at fucking all*.

No wonder Setsuna wouldn't tell me who she was sending, he thought to himself.

Lucien was a public relations nightmare just waiting to happen, not to mention illegal on so many fronts it wasn't even funny. Patrick's fingers twitched with the need for a cigarette to calm his already frayed nerves.

"Did he come to the bar?" Patrick asked.

Carmen clucked her tongue at Patrick in a sharp *tsk*. "He does not come to you. You go to him."

Patrick thought about keeping his ass right where it was, but he didn't have that option. Setsuna had given up who knew how many favors, cashed in an unknown number of debts, to bring Lucien and his Night Court to the United States on such short notice. Patrick couldn't trust any help coming from the SOA right now. His only option had been reduced to a vampire who absolutely hated his guts and would rather Patrick be dead.

Except Lucien had made a promise to Ashanti, one that began and ended with Patrick. Lucien didn't give a shit about honor, but he believed in obeying his mother. That was the only reason he hadn't stabbed Patrick in the back since the end of the Thirty-Day War.

"You'll need to give us a ride. My car died a violent death this morning," Patrick said.

Carmen arched one perfectly plucked eyebrow. "Us? He is not in the mood to play with wolves."

"I can't leave Jono behind. Seer's orders."

Carmen's intense gaze shifted from Patrick to Jono, before sliding away to settle on Marek, who had come out from behind the bar to stand in solidarity with Emma and Leon. Neither of them appreciated the attention directed Marek's way, and they put themselves in front of him in a protective manner. The anger on their faces warred with the lust Carmen was drawing out of everyone, no matter their sexual orientation.

Carmen tilted her head to the side, her curly hair shifting around the horns on her head. "Far be it for me to ignore the will of a mouthpiece. Bring the wolf."

"You sure about this?" Jono asked in a low voice.

Patrick shrugged. "I need the backup."

"Not sure you need what's on offer from her."

"We're going with you," Marek announced.

"Oh, hell no," Patrick said, turning to face Marek. "You are marching your ass back home and getting behind that barrier ward."

Marek gave Patrick an unimpressed look. "Remember what I said about not being one of your little soldiers?"

Patrick would have argued the point, except Carmen's amused laughter interrupted him. Her smile was now tempered into something mocking and cold, sharp teeth a gleaming line between the vibrant red of her lipstick.

"Let them come," she said. "You are backed too far into a corner to ignore a weapon when you find one, Patrick."

She had a point. That didn't mean Patrick had to like it.

Carmen spun on her heel, the glamour wrapping itself around her body, hiding her true self once again. The horns disappeared, the otherworldly shape of her melting back into her human form. The red center of her eyes darkened to black. Despite his shields, Patrick doubted she'd reined in the sexual energy she exuded. It was the way of her kind, after all, no matter the form they took.

"Uh," Tyler said from behind them. "Should I come with you?"

Patrick figured it would be a really, *really* bad idea if the police found out who had come to New York City. He shook his head and gestured vaguely at the door. "Go back to Marek's home and wait for him there."

Tyler seemed relieved at the order, even if he was a little red in the face and subtly shifting on his barstool. Getting an erection in public with no way to get relief was never fun. In fact, the only person who didn't seem affected by Carmen's presence was Jono.

Patrick wondered about that as he followed Carmen out of the bar, letting Einar take point. A black SUV was double-parked on the street with its hazard lights on, every window tinted black. Einar opened the side passenger door for Carmen to get in before claiming the front seat. Patrick got a glimpse of another vampire behind the wheel before Carmen gestured impatiently at him.

"Well?" she demanded. "Are you coming or not?"

Patrick and Jono climbed into the far rear seats of the SUV without argument. The second the door shut, the driver took the vehicle out of park and slammed his foot on the gas. Patrick looked over his shoulder in time to see Marek, Emma, Sage, and Leon scrambling into his Maserati, intent on not getting left behind.

"You never could stay out of trouble, Patrick," Carmen said as she tapped away at her phone, shooting off a text message.

Patrick wanted to tell her this whole mess wasn't his fault, but he'd be lying if he did.

"YOU HAVE GOT TO BE FUCKING KIDDING ME," PATRICK SAID.

Carmen smirked over her shoulder as she wriggled a key into an old iron lock on the door and twisted it. Delicate wards burned over the iron, spreading outward to cover the warehouse door before fading away. The lock clicked loudly in the little alleyway they were all crowded in.

"We made a deal. It's been in our Night Court for decades," Carmen replied.

Patrick knew she wasn't talking about just the building.

The abandoned warehouse in the Meatpacking District was one of the last few buildings not bought up by real estate conglomerates and turned into trendy nightclubs and luxury condos. It had definitely seen better days, what with its boarded-up windows near the roof and layered graffiti stretching across the entire side of the building not facing the street.

The front of the building was surprisingly inaccessible, with the only way inside being the side door located down the alley. Carmen stepped aside and let Einar push open the old, heavy door.

The wards seemed to have kept trespassers at bay, though Patrick doubted that faded magic had really done much considering the power emanating from the building's threshold once a person got close enough to sense it.

If the building didn't want you there, then you wouldn't stay.

The name of the place said it all, and names still held power, even in this modern age. An old, corroded brass sign still hung on the door bearing the name Ginnungagap on its plating. Patrick had to ignore the urge to run battering away at his lizard hindbrain. He chewed on the inside of his bottom lip, trying to get his nerves under control. He'd closed his shields up tight, so none of the werecreatures with him could smell his fear, but they could still hear his heartbeat going a mile a minute.

Patrick would blame it on the alcohol he'd drunk, except he hadn't had nearly enough to infuse him with much-needed liquid courage. In all honesty, he knew there wasn't enough alcohol in the world to get him through this reunion intact.

"When did she name it?" Patrick wanted to know.

Carmen stepped into the darkness beyond the doorway. "It named itself and goes where it likes. This city is one of its homes."

Ginnungagap, the yawning abyss.

"Fucking immortals," he muttered under his breath.

Jono shot him a sharp, appraising look that Patrick tried to ignore.

"Move," Einar ordered as he followed Carmen inside.

Given the choice, Patrick wouldn't set one foot on their claimed territory. But he didn't have a choice, and that was why he was here. Patrick ground his teeth together and stepped over the threshold, fully expecting to be swallowed whole by the reality behind the myth.

He wasn't.

The others slowly came in after him. The threshold they crossed was powerful, ancient, and surprisingly malleable in the way it filled every last inch of the building's structure, blocking out the world. The dead zone inside the warehouse made Patrick's skin crawl, all sounds from outside muffled inside the walls.

Patrick pulled out his cell phone to check if it still worked and found he had no signal. The dead zone blocked electronics the same way he had a feeling it would block any unwanted magic. If he still had the ability to tap a ley line, Patrick doubted he'd be able to do it past Ginnungagap's threshold.

He tried anyway, conjuring up a couple of weak witchlights, tiny sparks of magic that could be used to light the way. Casting them felt like pulling teeth, but Patrick held the spell in his mind, making it clear his intentions weren't anything but benign to the building and what lived inside its structure.

I mean you no harm, Patrick thought.

It felt like an age before the pressure eased and he could breathe again. A warm hand brushed against his, and he turned his head to look at Jono. The taller man was staring into the darkness with a tense expression on his face.

"We shouldn't be here," Jono said in a low voice. "This doesn't feel right."

"You can wait outside," Patrick told him.

Jono shot him an aggravated look. "You're off your bloody head if you think I'm leaving you in here alone."

"Then shut up and let me do the talking."

They started forward again, Patrick's magic barely pushing back the dark. Musty, sour air hit his nose as everyone carefully worked their way through years and years of debris to the center of the building.

Someone hidden in the dark flipped a switch. The humming whine of a generator powering up reached Patrick's ears. Several floodlights came on, the light almost too bright in the dark, enclosed space. Patrick vanished his witchlights, squinting to try to save his night vision, but it was a lost cause. He couldn't see much beyond the ring of light they stood in, but the back of his neck prickled from too many eyes on them he couldn't see.

Emma, Leon, and Sage moved to surround Marek, their backs to him in a small protective circle. Jono stood so close to Patrick he could feel the heat in the other man's body. It was a nice reminder that he wasn't alone, even if things might be easier if he was.

"I'm rethinking not listening to you for once," Marek said in a hushed voice.

"Maybe you should've thought of that before you decided to tag along," Patrick retorted.

"Still not your little soldier."

"Shut. Up," Sage told her lover through gritted teeth.

Movement caught Patrick's eye, and he looked at where Carmen seemed to suddenly appear out of the shadows, her glamour gone once more. Her red pupils seemed to expand, burning like embers in her face. Einar stood beside her at the light's edge, still her ever-attentive guard dog. Shadows moved in the dark behind them both, Patrick hard-pressed to track them.

"Where is he?" Patrick finally asked.

Carmen smiled, sharp teeth flashing in the light, and didn't say a word. Patrick dropped his shields to find out for himself. Recognition of the undead was almost overwhelming, not because of the multitude of vampires he could sense surrounding them, but because of how deeply he knew their master.

Lucien was familiar in a way an infected wound was—weeping, rotten, and in danger of becoming gangrenous.

A figure slid free of the surrounding darkness, stepping into the light on cat-quiet feet. Tall, built lean under the heavy leather jacket he wore and hidden weaponry he never went anywhere without, Lucien hadn't changed at all. Patrick could see that even from where he stood. The same brown hair, the same black eyes, the same ugly hatred in the snarl of his mouth—all of it familiar.

I really fucking hate reunions, Patrick thought to himself.

"Oh, shit," Emma whispered behind him, the *we are going to die* tone easy for Patrick to pick out.

Lucien had that effect on people.

Those who'd come with Patrick tonight might not know who they faced, but their instincts knew the monster wrapped in pale, pale skin standing before them.

A thousand years ago, Lucien had lived the life of a soldier beneath William the Conqueror's banner. He died on the battlefield and was born again by the mother of all vampires. He'd gone by many names over the centuries, but the one he carried now he'd favored for two hundred years or so.

Lucien was still riding high on everyone's Top Ten Most Wanted Lists, no matter what name he went by. His notoriety these days came more from murder and mayhem, a weapons- and magic-trafficking empire, and money laundering rather than the fact he was an undead bloodsucking bastard.

"I didn't ask Setsuna to call you," Patrick said, breaking the heavy silence.

"I wouldn't have come if she was the only one who begged," Lucien replied. His accent was a flat thing ground down by time. He took on the inflections of the country he traveled in as easily as people changed clothes.

Lucien stalked forward with all the grace of a tiger hunting prey. The sheer, overwhelming sense of his presence made Patrick's bones ache. Patrick stared Lucien down, because he'd never learned how not to, no matter how many bruises he ended up with at the end of their meetings. Running wasn't an option.

It never had been with Lucien.

"Setsuna doesn't beg."

Lucien flashed his teeth in a disdainful snarl. It was met by a warning growl from Jono as the werewolf put himself between the master vampire and Patrick. For a second, Patrick could only stare at Jono's back, too surprised to do anything but gape.

"Back off," Jono warned Lucien.

"I don't take orders from your kind," Lucien said in a low voice. "This isn't your territory. It's not even your country. You are a long way from your home, wolf."

Patrick grabbed Jono by the arm as he stepped around the other man. "What the hell, Jono? Didn't I say let me do the talking?"

Jono never took his eyes off Lucien. "Tell me this vampire isn't who I think he is."

"Let's go with yes, judging by the expression on your face."

Patrick put himself between Jono and Lucien with barely a second to spare before Lucien went toe-to-toe with him. At five feet ten, Lucien was an inch taller than Patrick and stronger and faster in all the ways that mattered outside magic. Patrick tilted his head back just enough to meet Lucien's gaze, ignoring how his heart raced uncomfortably fast in his scarred chest.

Warm hands settled on his hips, strong fingers holding on tight. Jono pressed himself against Patrick's back, a powerful presence that shouldn't have made his dick twitch like it did, but Jono was fucking *distracting*.

Patrick really couldn't afford to be distracted right now.

"Running with wolves these days. That's new," Lucien said.

His breath was cold where it blew over Patrick's face, the smell of it like old copper. Patrick kept his hands at his side and resisted the urge to reach for his dagger.

"Not by choice," Patrick replied.

"That's *not* new. Neither is the fact your current case will kill you."

"Gonna dig me a grave?"

Lucien smiled, chapped lips cracking at the motion, but he didn't bleed. "I don't break my promises. Not like you."

Patrick opened his mouth to argue, but the words never made it past his teeth. A cold hand wrapped around his throat the same instant the muzzle of a pistol pressed beneath his chin. Vampires had a speed matched by no one else in the preternatural world, a speed that gave birth to the stories that said they could fly.

A speed not even a werewolf could match.

"I wouldn't," Lucien said when Jono surged against Patrick's body, reaching for the vampire. The shove of the weapon against Patrick's jaw was enough to make Jono go immediately still. His wordless snarl was loud in Patrick's ear, a heavy vibration through his ribs.

"Let him go," Jono growled, his hands holding on to Patrick tight enough to bruise.

Lucien's black eyes never blinked as he stared at Patrick. "No."

Patrick swallowed against Lucien's hard grip, still capable of breathing. That bit of leniency didn't come out of the goodness of a heart that didn't beat, but from a promise Lucien had made to Ashanti to keep Patrick alive.

Because of Ashanti, Lucien was still dogging Patrick's steps when needed, even in sunlight. As one of the first immortals and a goddess in her own right, Ashanti's rare ability to walk in sunlight and not be burned to ashes had manifested itself in only a handful of her direct descendants.

Ashanti had always been fiercely loved by her children. Most people didn't know the mother of all vampires was dead because legends weren't supposed to die. Funny how you could keep a story alive even after the subject was gone.

Patrick leaned into Lucien's grip and the pistol, the pressure almost choking him. "I'm trying this new thing where I keep all my blood inside my body. Don't ruin my winning streak, Lucien."

Patrick was dimly aware of someone who wasn't Jono swearing behind him, but most of his attention was focused on the vampire who literally held Patrick's life in his hands.

Lucien's grip tightened ever so slightly, and Patrick tried not to gag. "I haven't missed working with you," Lucien said in a low, hateful voice.

"You could've stayed where you were when Setsuna called, but you didn't. You know what that tells me?" Patrick swallowed against the weight of the pistol against his body and the murderous promise in Lucien's black eyes. "You're going to fight with me, just like last time."

"And is it like last time?"

Patrick didn't blink. "No. Because we know what's coming."

"Just because you see it doesn't mean you can stop it. Remember what it cost us when you couldn't stand your fucking ground?"

Patrick flinched, thinking about Ashanti. About her Asanbosam stature that instilled so much fear in people. About her iron teeth and the bone hooks sheathed in steel caps that she'd walked the earth on for thousands and thousands of years. About the way she looked when she died, swallowed up by dry desert sand in an impossible sunburned heat, sacrificed to magic. How her body collapsed into ashes in the face of heavenly magic poured into the gods-made dagger she'd literally walked through hell to deliver to Patrick.

He hadn't been able to save her, and Lucien would always, *always* blame Patrick for his mother's death.

"I'm sorry," Patrick said for what felt like the thousandth time.

Apologies were meaningless to the dead and undead alike.

"One of these days, I will kill you," Lucien promised, shoving the pistol harder against the underside of Patrick's jaw.

"Fuck you, mate," Jono said, the fury in his voice vibrating through his chest and into Patrick's back. "Let him go before I rip your fucking face off."

Patrick would've told him to shut up if he'd had the breath to spare.

"Does the wolf speak for you now?"

Patrick raised a hand and made a seesaw motion with it. "More like the Fates do. Couldn't leave their favorite wolf behind."

It wasn't a threat, nor a warning, merely a fact Patrick didn't mind sharing. However Lucien took it, it was enough to get him to finally back off.

Lucien's fingers lifted off his throat one by one. The muzzle of the pistol skimmed up over his jaw to kiss his lips in a deadly promise before lifting away entirely. Patrick managed to draw in a single ragged breath before Jono was hauling him away from Lucien, putting space between them. Jono's arms were strong around his body, holding him close as Patrick gingerly touched his throat with one hand.

"That's gonna leave a bruise," he muttered, voice coming out a little raspy.

When Patrick glanced up, Lucien was back by Carmen's side, looking off into the darkness of the warehouse.

"Naheed, I require your presence," Lucien called out.

Patrick tried taking a step forward, but Jono's arms tightened, refusing to let him go. Patrick shot him an exasperated look. "You're not helping, Jono."

"You nearly got your head blown off by that fucker and you didn't even fight him. You and your suicidal tendencies can sod off with me letting you go," Jono retorted.

Patrick sighed in annoyance but figured this was one fight he clearly wouldn't win without some effort. He focused instead on the woman with thick dark hair who came tottering into the light on wedge-heeled sandals, her summery sundress clean despite the filthy location. She led someone familiar by the hand, and Patrick made a strangled sound in the back of his throat.

"What the fuck are you doing here?" Patrick demanded.

"What does it look like, Pattycakes? I'm delivering a message," Hermes said as he sauntered forward.

Naheed let go of Hermes' hand with a smile and picked her way daintily over to where Carmen stood. Her large blue-green eyes were curious, but she didn't speak. Naheed was human, the neck-lace of scars on her throat proof of her status as a willing feeder to vampires. She was Lucien's favorite meal, had been ever since Patrick first met her years ago.

Lucien had been given Naheed when she was a toddler as payment from a subjugated village in Afghanistan whose rulers didn't want to become vampire fodder. She'd been hooked on opium at the age of three, along with her entire family, and had never known anything but addiction until Lucien claimed her. He'd cleaned her up because he had never liked the way drugs tasted in the blood of the humans he kept within his Night Court.

Marek pushed his way past Emma, an inner light glittering in the depths of his eyes. Emma grabbed him by the wrist and kept him from going any farther, but it seemed to take more strength than normal.

"Oh," Marek said, not quite sounding like himself. "It's you."

Hermes placed one hand on his chest and bowed in Marek's direction, the gesture surprisingly genuine. "Good evening, Skuld."

Marek's eyes washed out white, the shift in his voice frightening. "*Cousin.*"

Emma and Sage shared a bleak look while Leon's expression remained unreadable. Patrick figured the three of them were well aware of what it meant when Fate took control of Marek's life so thoroughly. Patrick really hoped the seer wouldn't lose an entire color by the time this case was finished. He hated to think he'd be responsible for Marek getting that much closer to madness. All the money in the world couldn't buy the seer sanity after a certain point.

Jono's arms tightened around Patrick, warm hands skimming over his ribs through the T-shirt he wore. Patrick tried not to squirm.

"You don't smell human, mate," Jono said to Hermes.

Hermes winked at him, but there wasn't any humor in the immortal's face. "That's because I'm not."

"Then what are you?" Emma asked in a low voice. She still had hold of Marek, and the Fate inhabiting his body didn't seem to mind.

Hermes ignored her in favor of wandering into Patrick's personal space, not intimidated by Jono's presence at all. He eyed the bruises Patrick could feel coming up on his throat and shook his head.

"You never learn, do you?" Hermes said.

Patrick dug in his heels when it felt like Jono was about to haul them both out of reach. Jono's entire body went tense as Hermes leaned in and pressed his mouth to Patrick's. Patrick could feel Jono growl more than hear it.

The kiss felt like static, an electric burn that crackled through his skin from lips to toes. Patrick would have gasped, but he didn't want to give Hermes the satisfaction. Hermes kept up the pressure for a second or two but didn't try to take anything more than a touch. When the immortal pulled away, he left behind healed skin and the ability for Patrick to swallow without feeling as if his throat was about to cave in.

"We need you in one piece," Hermes told him.

Patrick touched his throat, the heat of bruises gone. "Knew it wasn't because you cared."

"Dionysus was in Atlantic City when he felt the call from the spell. He's left the country to escape it. So has Artemis."

"Not surprised. We cleaned up the focus of his sacrifice this morning. Who's left?"

Hermes studied the chipped black polish on his nails, picking at a few of the ragged, bitten-down edges. "Does it matter? You have a job to do, Pattycakes."

"Your misplaced faith will ruin you, Hermes," Lucien said.

Hermes casually flipped the vampire off with one hand while making a lazy circle in the air with the other. The sound of coins clattering on the floor at Patrick's feet reminded him of a Vegas casino's slot machine cashing out a win.

Hermes pointed at the coins. "These are for you."

Patrick toed one of the old Greek coins with the tip of his boot, the rough-hewn gold circle shining in the floodlights. "What are they for?"

"Payment for the dead."

Patrick winced at the sound of Skuld's voice coming out of Marek's mouth. "Immortals don't die."

"We can be broken. We can be forgotten."

"We can be used," Hermes said in a low, vicious voice, eyes snapping with a fury that burned. "I don't want to lose what belongs to me the same way Macaria did. Neither do I wish to become a conduit for power-hungry mortals the way Ra did."

Patrick drew in a sharp breath at the sound of that goddess' name, wishing his shields could hide the sound of how hard his heart was beating.

"Might I remind you the Dominion Sect used the pyramids in Giza to try to enslave him. We are nowhere near Greece and its relics for them to use you and your pantheon like that," Carmen pointed out.

Hermes' expression twisted into something monstrous for a split second before it smoothed away into the visage of a man once again. "You don't need to be in our homeland here on the mortal plane for this spell to come to fruition."

"Then what do they need?" Patrick asked.

Hermes spread his hands, his smile as sharp as knives. "Wonderful thing about America. People came from all over the world to build this country. They carried their beliefs and their gods with them to these shores. This city was built with hands that prayed to hundreds of deities. The Dominion Sect doesn't need a several-thousand-year-old monument when they have skyscrapers."

Patrick shrugged out of Jono's arms with a little effort. He knelt and gathered up the coins, counting up an even twenty-four, two for each of the sacrifices tied to the zodiac spell. All the dead needed to pay the ferryman. He filled his pockets with the coins before straightening up.

Stepping around Hermes, Patrick headed for Marek and the immortal who would never let the seer go. She watched him come with a secretive twist to Marek's mouth, the power drifting out of his aura deep and fathomless and entirely inhuman.

And yet, Emma still had not let go of him, as if Fate didn't scare her one goddamn bit.

"Can you see the end?" Patrick asked Skuld bluntly once he stood in front of her and her vessel. "Can you see the future?"

Skuld didn't blink, her eerie attention never wavering. *"Not here. Not anymore. There are too many possibilities now that you are standing in the way, and my sight is not the only one searching for a new reality."*

The warning fell heavily between them, but Patrick refused to let it weigh him down.

"Then let Marek go. This isn't his fight, it's mine. That's what all of you wanted, isn't it? For me to fight?"

"Your acceptance doesn't clear your soul debt."

Patrick barked out a sound that in no way resembled laughter. "I'm well aware of what your side thinks I owe it. Let Marek go. It's not him you want, it's me, and *you've got me.*"

Skuld closed Marek's eyes, and when they opened again, they were hazel once more—human eyes in a human face. Marek's knees buckled, but Emma moved fast to catch him, holding him up with preternatural strength.

"I have him," Emma said, her gaze shifting over Patrick's shoulder for a quick moment. "Hurry it up, will you?"

Honestly, Patrick was so fucking done with tonight.

"We're leaving," he said loudly.

"You have until summer solstice," Hermes warned. "Find a way to stop them."

When Patrick turned around, Hermes was gone, having disappeared through the veil. The sudden quiet in the warehouse made his skin crawl. He stared across the lit-up space at where Lucien stood.

"Are we done?" Patrick asked.

Lucien turned his back dismissively on the group. "For now. I'll contact you when the rest of the weapon shipments arrive. You and your magic aren't enough to deal with this problem. You never have been."

Patrick's mouth twisted bitterly. "Right."

Taking a trip down memory lane was never fun. If Patrick could bury his ghosts, he would. They just never stayed dead.

Patrick moved to sling Marek's other arm over his shoulders, and all of them got the hell out of there. Jono and Leon guarded their retreat while Sage cleared them a path in the face of Lucien's Night Court with a fearlessness that impressed Patrick.

They reached the exit and crossed the threshold. Patrick felt as if he could breathe again once they were outside Ginnungagap.

"I have such a headache," Marek moaned.

Leon came up to take Patrick's place, helping Emma carry Marek's weight between them. Patrick pointed at the mouth of the alley. "Let's go. I don't trust what lives in the walls of this place."

"You talk as if it's alive," Sage said.

"It's something," he muttered.

"*Lucien* is something," Leon retorted, looking a little wild around the eyes. "*Madre de Dios*, Patrick. How the hell do you know that psychotic bastard?"

"Long story, highly classified. If I told you, I'd have to kill you."

They cut down the alley for the street, huddling on the sidewalk amidst a nightlife that seemed out of place now. All the unsuspecting people out to have a good time were completely unaware of the monsters that had settled in their midst.

"We shouldn't have asked for his help," Sage said when they were half a block away.

"*We* are doing nothing," Patrick retorted. "*I* am dealing with Lucien, not you."

Marek flapped a hand at him, head tilted back, eyes closed. He looked drunk, providing the perfect cover for why the group was in the area. "Not alone."

"I'm not getting rid of Jono, if that's what you mean."

"No." Marek breathed in carefully through his nose, gritting his teeth against whatever pain was pounding through his head and body from channeling an immortal. "That's not what I meant. You're not fighting alone."

"I have backup now."

"Fucking illegal backup, is what it is," Jono snapped. He reached for Patrick and carefully tilted his head back to get a better look at the now-healed skin on his throat. "That arsehole wanted to kill you."

Patrick blinked up at him, trying not to lean into Jono's touch, and failing just a little. "Lucien always wants to kill me. That's nothing new."

Everyone stared at Patrick with disbelieving looks on their faces. Well, everyone except Marek, who tipped forward and promptly got sick all over the pavement.

"We need to get Marek home. That shitshow in there gave him a migraine and probably caused him to lose another shade of color," Leon said angrily.

"Think it affected red this time," Marek slurred. "Your hair looks a little lighter, Patrick."

Patrick ran a hand through his dark red hair. "I'm sorry."

"Not your fault I was born like this."

Sage reached out and touched Marek's shoulder. "Let's go. You need to relax for the rest of the weekend."

"Aw, no. We'll call Victoria. She's gotta heal this. Your birthday party is tomorrow."

"We can have it another weekend."

Emma relinquished her spot beside Marek to Sage. Leon and Sage walked Marek a few cars down to his Maserati. Emma stayed put, a tiny, practically impenetrable wall between Patrick and her pack.

"What do you want?" Patrick asked tiredly.

Emma pursed her lips. "What's really going on? And don't give me some bullshit classified answer, Patrick. This isn't the military. This is New York City. It's our *home*. So tell me the truth."

Emma was a force to be reckoned with. All stubborn fierceness, ready to attack any threat aimed at those she claimed as hers. Emma *cared*. In Patrick's experience, that was always dangerous.

Patrick grimaced. "The truth is I can't tell you. I can't, Emma. But I need you to know I'm doing everything I can to make sure what I think is going to happen won't."

"By partnering with Lucien?"

"By using whatever methods I have to, no matter how illegal they are, to make sure this city is still standing at the end. I promised Casale that. I'll promise you the same thing."

"And if you break that promise?"

"Then it won't matter, because we'll all be dead."

Emma stared at him for a long moment before letting out a heavy sigh. She ran a hand through her thick black hair, messing up some of the loose curls she had it styled in. "Youssef and Estelle don't want us to have any contact with you."

"Okay? And?"

"You kept Marek safe," she said quietly. "He's mine and Leon's best friend, the only family we have left after we got bitten. You didn't think twice about throwing yourself between him and that demon the other night. You didn't hesitate. I know a lot of people who would have."

"Youssef and Estelle, to name a few," Jono said, sounding irritated.

Emma didn't protest that accusation. Patrick wondered just how many cracks existed in the werecreature community here that Jono could say that and Emma wouldn't come to the god pack's defense in the face of a rival god pack alpha.

"You don't owe me this, Emma," Patrick told her.

"This isn't a debt," she said. "This isn't anything like whatever those immortals are holding over your head to get you to do their bidding. I'm offering because it's the right thing to do. Because Marek is in deep already, and I'm not letting both of you drown in the problems that keep coming our way, no matter what Youssef and Estelle say. That's what pack does, Patrick. That's what pack *is*."

The fierceness in her words had Patrick wishing he could believe what she offered came with no strings attached. But he knew nothing in life was free.

"I'm not pack," he reminded her.

Emma glanced over at Jono. "I have a feeling that might be changing. Give me your phone number."

Out of everything she could have asked for, it was the easiest thing to give up. They swapped phone numbers, and then Emma gave him an apologetic look. "I'd offer you a ride, but we're out of seats."

"I'll call an Uber. Don't worry about us. Just get Marek home behind that barrier ward."

"Emma always worries. Right mother hen, is this one," Jono said. His words came out fond though, and Emma beamed at him.

Jono wrapped Emma up in a strong hug. She snaked her hand over his neck, discreetly scent-marking him when they parted ways. The pack scent would fade within hours, and no one would know she'd done it, because Jono wasn't going to be around other werecreatures for the rest of the night.

He gave Emma a crooked smile, and Patrick thought about what Jono had said in the café the other morning. How he'd left London without ever having a pack and been denied a chance at one here in New York City. How it looked as if Emma was more than willing to follow his orders instead of submitting to a god pack she didn't trust.

Patrick wondered how many other packs in the five boroughs were in her same predicament.

Emma waved goodbye and hurried down the pavement for

Marek's car. He and Jono watched her get in and waited until they'd driven off before Patrick unlocked his phone to call an Uber.

The sooner he got to the apartment, the less he'd feel as if he had a target on his back in the shape of Lucien's fangs.

11

PATRICK SLAPPED HIS HAND AGAINST THE DOORFRAME ON THE WAY
into the apartment, pushing his magic into the threshold, strength-
ening it as much as he could. The buzz of adrenaline had left him
somewhere downtown. A different sort of buzz hit his nerves
when Jono didn't hesitate to crowd him up against the door after
Patrick closed and locked it.

Patrick's head thumped against the door as he stared up into
Jono's face and the worry in those wolf-bright eyes. Without more
dangerous people taking up his attention, Patrick could focus
entirely on the other man. He remembered every second in that
warehouse when Jono was plastered against his back, those strong
arms refusing to give Patrick up to Lucien and Hermes when a
saner person would have.

Or maybe, just a less stubborn one.

"You need better backup," Jono said, his voice a quiet rumble
that went straight to Patrick's dick.

"You offering?" Patrick asked, unwilling to take the words back.

"I don't know why your agency doesn't give you a bloody partner. You need one to keep you from doing stupid shit."

"I don't—"

Whatever Patrick would've said, he forgot the words when Jono kissed him. Jono bypassed gentle and went straight to demanding, one hand framing Patrick's face to hold him still while Jono devoured him. Patrick let him, reaching out with greedy hands to grab at Jono's hips and urge him closer. Jono obliged in the best way possible.

He broke the kiss, warm hands groping Patrick's ass for a second or two before hauling Patrick into his arms with easy strength. Patrick wrapped his legs around Jono's waist, his hardening cock pressed against rock-solid abs. He dragged his hands through Jono's black hair, staring into blue eyes that weren't entirely human.

"Drop your shields," Jono said.

With anyone else, Patrick would have ignored the request, would have kept his shields up so no one could sense the damage in his soul and magic. Since Thursday night, he'd been making one exception after another for Jono.

What it all came down to was that Patrick *wanted*—had wanted whatever Jono offered to give him since Thursday night at the bar. He'd told himself one night, that was all he got, and here he was, going back on his own self-made promise.

At least he wouldn't owe anyone but himself over it.

Patrick knew he wouldn't get to stay beyond the length of the case, that Jono would just be a fond memory years down the line if Patrick survived that long. But for right now, he'd take one more night if that's what the Fates wanted to give him.

"Yeah, okay," Patrick said, chasing after Jono's mouth.

He dropped his shields, let them peel apart beneath his skin. The taint in his soul, in his magic, was something people usually flinched away from. Jono buried his face against Patrick's healed throat, licking a hot stripe up to his ear before biting down on the tender lobe there.

"I want to fuck you," Jono growled.

"Gods yes," Patrick groaned, tugging at Jono's hair. "I packed lube and condoms."

Jono lifted his head, staring at him. "You travel on business with those?"

Patrick rolled his eyes. "I was supposed to be on *vacation*. In *Maui*. Getting drunk and getting fucked."

Jono's smile was wicked, the heat in his bright eyes making Patrick press closer. "Could use the lube. Don't need the condoms, if you want."

The werevirus was sometimes classified as an STD, one most people didn't want. Werecreatures were immune to all other STDs because of it. Magic users had an immunity to the werevirus, but not anything else. Patrick was never going to turn furry, and the thought of letting Jono fuck him bare made his cock throb.

"The condoms stay in the suitcase," Patrick said.

Jono hauled him away from the front door, carrying him into the bedroom. Patrick busied himself with learning the shape of Jono's mouth more thoroughly. Jono didn't turn on the overhead light when they entered the bedroom, but he did turn on the bedside lamp after dropping Patrick on the bed. He bounced once before he got to work undoing the laces on his combat boots. He managed to get one off, but then Jono stripped out of his shirt and Patrick forgot what the hell he was trying to accomplish.

Shirtless, Jono's hard-cut abs and defined biceps were on full display. His skin was smooth and unmarked, and Patrick wanted to lick his way down Jono's chest the way some people craved dessert. Jono smirked at Patrick as he dug up the bottle of lube from the suitcase.

"Get your bloody kit off," Jono said.

Patrick yanked on the laces of his remaining boot. "Yeah."

It took him a little longer to get undressed than Jono. Patrick kept getting distracted by the utter unselfconsciousness Jono exuded once he was fully naked. Patrick's fingers fumbled at the straps and buckles holding his dagger in place once he got eyes on

Jono's cock. His mouth immediately watered at the sight of the half-hard length Jono was casually stroking. His cock was long and thick, black pubes trimmed down close to skin, and everything Patrick didn't think he'd get until this case was over.

He wanted Jono in him *now*.

Patrick pulled the coins from his pocket and left them in a pile on the nightstand before getting rid of his weapons and most of his clothes in record time. He only hesitated when he was about to take off his T-shirt. Sometimes, when he didn't want to deal with questions, he kept his shirt on during sex. Patrick knew Jono wouldn't care either way, which was what finally prompted him to pull it off. He didn't miss the way Jono's eyes went wide before narrowing as he stared at the mess of scars on Patrick's chest.

Jono stepped between Patrick's spread legs and went to his knees, tracing the scars on Patrick's body with hands and eyes alike, his touch gentle.

The entrance of the bullet wound he'd taken in the field years ago was low on his hip and to the side, a mere afterthought in the face of other, more prominent scars. The claw-mark scars were old, time and magic having faded the scar tissue from a vivid pink to pale white. They cut diagonally across his chest from the left collarbone down to the middle ribs on his right side. A second set of scars ran vertically over his sternum, the deeper, puckered edges there rough and numb from nerve damage. He couldn't feel the weight of his dog tags where they lay against the scars in some areas, but he knew they were there.

Patrick waited for the inevitable questions, but none came.

Instead, Jono leaned forward and pressed an openmouthed kiss to the center of the scars, the corner of his lips catching at the edge of the dog tags. Patrick shuddered at the touch, barely feeling it in spots, but he could feel Jono's hands on him, and he wanted more. Wanted Jono in him and around him, real and warm and not going anywhere, willing to let all the secrets carved into Patrick's body, in his mind, stay there, at least for tonight.

Patrick cradled Jono's head with his hands, tilting his head back for a kiss. Jono surged up to meet him halfway, the kiss just as demanding as before. Patrick let himself be manhandled farther onto the bed, the warmth of Jono's body spreading over him. Patrick arched up against that solid heat, feeling Jono scrape his fingers down his back and over a few more scars he carried there—faded lacerations and the pitted exit hole of the bullet wound.

Jono broke their latest kiss, Patrick's lips tingling as they parted. He licked his way down Patrick's throat with careful swipes of his tongue, teeth catching carefully against unmarked skin. "Wanted to fucking kill the bastard for touching you."

Patrick huffed out a soft laugh as he dragged his hands over Jono's back, feeling all that strength flex against his touch. "Which one?"

"*Both.*"

His answer had warmth spreading through Patrick's body, pooling low in his gut at the possessive tone in Jono's voice. Being wanted felt nice, even if it was just to get off. That's what he expected between them. Quick and hard and making him feel it.

Jono had other ideas.

When he pulled Jono's mouth back to his, the kiss was rough, the taste of Jono on his tongue not too dissimilar to the burst of recognition that skittered through his magic from time to time. Then it slowed, gentled, leaving his lips feeling bruised and raw, every nerve in his body buzzing like a live wire. When Patrick tried to demand more, Jono held him down, held him still, and kissed him soft and slow.

Patrick never did slow when he had sex with the men he'd hunted up in bars or through an app on shore leave while in the Mage Corps and days off between cases with the SOA. He picked up men to get fucked by, and nothing else. Patrick did friendships, not relationships, because both were dangerous to lose, but one more so than the other. Some part of him didn't want to know what he was missing, but it was difficult to ignore with Jono's hands on him.

Jono went at his own pace, and there was no hurrying him along. Patrick found he honestly didn't want to.

That sinfully hot mouth kissed its way down his scarred chest, hot hands running down his ribs. Patrick parted his legs even more, bending them at the knees as his toes curled into the duvet. Jono licked the tip of Patrick's cock before swallowing him down in one long glide. Patrick threw his head back with a groan, pushing against the bedframe with one hand while tangling his fingers of the other in Jono's hair.

"*Fuck*," he moaned, canting his hips upward, feeling his cock slide deep down Jono's willing throat. The faint scratch of beard burn on the skin of his inner thighs made him bite his lip.

It'd been so long since he'd gotten off with someone else, but Patrick couldn't recall a time when it'd been like this. Slow, methodical, guaranteed to drive him out of his fucking mind. Jono swallowed around his cock at a leisurely pace, bobbing his head, working Patrick over with a single-minded intensity that left Patrick a whimpering mess.

The heat low in his belly and the tightness in his balls had him tugging on Jono's hair a little frantically. "If you don't stop, I'm gonna come."

He'd be embarrassed at how little time it had taken for Jono to get him to this point, but the touch of another person was always more intimate than his own hand.

Jono pulled off with a hard drag of his tongue to the underside of Patrick's cock. He couldn't stifle the moan, watching as Jono finally lifted his head, a thin strand of saliva stretched between his tongue and the tip of Patrick's cock.

"That's the point," Jono told him.

Patrick drew in a shaky breath. "Yeah, well, it's been a while outside my own hand. For me."

"Good."

Patrick met Jono's heavy-lidded gaze. His wolf-bright eyes seemed to glow in the dim lamplight, reflecting the light back at the world. Patrick reached for him, cupping his jaw, palm curving around his spit-slick chin. The shadow of a beard Jono sported tickled his skin.

"I want you to fuck me," Patrick said quietly.

Jono blinked, turning his head into Patrick's touch to press a kiss to his palm. "I'm taking my time with you."

"You are the absolute *worst* at listening to orders. I want—"

Patrick broke off with a gasp as one long finger, slick with lube, pushed into his hole. Patrick bore down on the intrusion instinctively, lips parting on the exhale. Jono shifted on his knees, one hand pressing down on the bed for balance as he moved to kiss Patrick. His tongue stroked in deep, matching the motion of his finger as he thrust it in and out of Patrick's body.

Patrick wrapped his arms around Jono's neck, keeping him there, feeling almost too warm from the heat Jono was putting off and his own arousal that was coursing through his body.

"I'll get you there," Jono said against his lips as he pushed a second finger inside.

Patrick bit at Jono's bottom lip, arching up against him to get some friction on his own cock as Jono stretched him open. When Jono found Patrick's prostate, he couldn't quite hold back the cry that escaped his throat, burying his face against the curve of Jono's throat.

"You are *such* a fucking tease," he panted out, licking at the sweaty skin and tasting salt.

Jono's laughter rumbled in his chest. "You make it so easy."

Patrick dragged his fingers down Jono's back, blunt nails scraping over warm skin. "Are you calling me easy?"

A third finger pushed into his body, the sudden stretch nearly making Patrick swallow his tongue. The burn was almost too much, too soon, but it felt *good*. And Jono was careful with him in a way Patrick never got to experience.

"You don't strike me as a bloke who does easy," Jono murmured. "But I want to make this good for you."

"Pounding my ass into the bed would be the quickest way to get me off."

Jono pulled back, taking with him the warmth that seemed to live in his skin. "I said *good*, not quick."

He punctuated his words with two more hard thrusts of his fingers. Patrick twisted against Jono's hand with a whimper, biting his lip. He tipped his head back, swallowing thickly. When Jono wrapped a hand around his cock, Patrick couldn't help but thrust up into that frustratingly light touch, hips rolling back down onto Jono's fingers buried in his ass.

"You keep this up and I am going to come without your cock in me, and I *really* want your cock," Patrick told him.

Jono chuckled, the sound making Patrick's cock twitch. "Greedy."

He stretched his arms over his head, pressing his palms flat against the headboard, using the sturdiness of the bed to drive himself into Jono's touch. Jono smiled down at him, teeth just a shade sharper than usual in his mouth before they evened out. That hint of something preternatural didn't scare him away.

Patrick reached between his legs where Jono's hand was, curling his fingers around that strong wrist. "Don't tease."

He didn't get what Jono wanted to give him often, if ever—not like this. Not easy and warm and sweet in a way Patrick didn't think he deserved. But Jono thought he did, and Patrick was willing to let Jono believe he was worth that kindness, just for one night.

It wouldn't mean anything, in the end.

Jono pulled his fingers free and slid his hands up Patrick's thighs, pushing his legs farther apart. He lost his hold on the headboard and had to make do with the pillow when Jono finally guided his cock to Patrick's hole. The first push inside had him moaning, body stretching around the thick length seeking to fill him up.

Patrick nearly swallowed his tongue at the stretch. *"Yes."*

Inch by hard inch, Jono worked him open, lube making each slide in slick and easy. The feel of that hard cock inside him left Patrick breathless, unable to do anything but let Jono own him, just for one night. The slow thrusts were guaranteed to drive him mad even as his body made room for that thick, wonderful cock.

When Jono was finally buried to the hilt, throbbing deep inside him, Patrick sucked in a shaky breath, body aching from the fullness stretching him more than he was used to these days. Jono was thicker and longer than the guys he'd hooked up with in his past, filling him up so good. While Patrick wasn't complaining, he definitely needed a moment to let his body adjust.

"Fuck," Patrick groaned, pressing his knees against Jono's chest. "You feel so good in me."

Jono settled on top of him, his weight pressing Patrick down against the mattress, caging him in. Patrick had an idle thought that he could get free, could twist his body and flip them over, but he didn't want to lose this feeling of tenderness settling between them.

He unclenched his hands from the pillow, wrapping his arms around Jono's neck again. The shift of their bodies had Jono's cock gliding against his prostate, and Patrick squeezed his eyes shut, biting back a moan. A warm mouth covered his, and Patrick tasted himself on Jono's tongue.

"You need some looking after," Jono whispered against Patrick's mouth right before he rolled his hips and thrust in deep.

Patrick let out a shaky cry, nerves on fire as Jono did it again and again. He opened his eyes, finding Jono's face mere inches from his own, staring down at him with an intensity that made him want to hide. Instead, Patrick kissed him again, gasping at a particularly hard thrust that sent his own cock sliding between their bellies.

"Harder," Patrick moaned, moving his arms so he could clutch at Jono's shoulders with desperate hands. "Jono, *please*."

Jono sucked a kiss into the side of Patrick's neck, right over the spot Lucien had bruised. "No. I'll give you what you need. Trust me."

Patrick opened his mouth to say he didn't, but the words wouldn't come, blocked by the pleasure coursing through his body. Each hard thrust of Jono's cock hit his prostate, driving in slow and deep, filling him up. Jono lifted his head, stealing another kiss while he fucked Patrick with a focus that was almost too much to handle.

Jono dipped his head, nipping at Patrick's bottom lip. "You like my cock in you?"

Patrick let out a breathless little laugh that became a gasp on Jono's next thrust. "Do you even have to *ask*?"

Jono's smirk was far too self-satisfied for Patrick's liking. He clenched down around Jono's cock on the next thrust, liking the way those wolf-bright eyes darkened just a little with hot desire.

Patrick tangled one hand in Jono's hair, tugging him down into another kiss. His entire body felt charged, different from the way his magic made him feel. The heat in his belly was spreading, making him desperate for more, for whatever Jono wanted to give him.

"Make me come," Patrick panted, blinking sweat out of his eyes. "I want to come."

Jono snaked a hand between their bodies, wrapping warm fingers around Patrick's cock, and started to stroke him in time with his thrusts. Patrick made a strangled sound that wasn't any kind of language.

"Yeah, love," Jono said, his voice a deep thrum in Patrick's ear. "I'm not stopping you."

Patrick could feel his body reaching the edge, like lightning in his skin skittering over his nerves. Jono didn't speed up no matter how much Patrick pleaded for him to. That long, thick cock filled him up over and over at the same slow, relentless pace, dragging soft cries from his mouth that Jono drank down like fine whiskey.

Patrick came with Jono's hand on his cock, the other man grinding down into him without stopping. He buried his face against Jono's shoulder, fingers clenching and unclenching against the hard muscles of Jono's back as he shuddered through his orgasm. Patrick's cum was sticky between them, Jono still stroking his sensitive cock in loose fingers.

This time when Jono pulled back, he slid all the way out. Patrick watched with interest as Jono jacked his cock with a hard fist until he came with a groan, painting Patrick's thighs and spent cock with his cum.

"There's less messy ways to mark me," Patrick said.

Jono rubbed his cum into Patrick's skin, dipping his fingers down to stroke over his loose, sensitive hole. Patrick hissed a little at the touch but didn't move away. "Who said anything about marking you?"

Patrick arched an eyebrow, too sex-buzzed to really argue. "I'm not sleeping like this."

Jono got the hint and got up to grab a washcloth from the bathroom. He wiped up the mess he'd made of Patrick with gentle motions before tossing it on the floor. Then Jono crawled into bed next to Patrick and pulled him close. He was almost too warm for Patrick's liking, but he didn't push Jono away.

Patrick slept, wrapped up in Jono's arms.

He dreamed of ravens.

The fog rolled through his mind and the street of his childhood home in Salem, Massachusetts. It led him through the door of a place he could never go back to, into a basement full of blood and covered by a gray sky. The stairs leading down below were made of bone that cracked beneath his feet but never broke. Thunder echoed loudly in his ears. Patrick couldn't tell if it was his heart beating or the sound coming from hundreds of wings flapping through the sky above.

Red concentric circles and black radial lines filled the concrete floor of the basement, surrounding a figure who stood in the center of the pentagram. Bloodstained clothes hid the grievous wounds in the woman's body. The hooded cloak she wore was made with thousands of black feathers that rustled softly with every breath she took. Pale-skinned, with fingers stained red at the tips from blood and bare feet covered in grave dirt, she lifted her head, shadows peeling away from bone.

The features Patrick saw were that of a dead woman.

The voice coming out of his mother's mouth belonged to something else.

War does not rest, came the warning in twin echoes. *Neither do the dead.*

The shade of memory spread her hands, and feathers burst through skin and bone, folding into two shapes that matched the ones flying through the sky.

Glossy black wings and sharp black beaks. Talons that could rend a soul from a body. The pair of ravens stared at Patrick with black eyes that swallowed him whole, their attention like a knife through his heart.

War is owed what was stolen from her.

Thought and memory were dangerous things, and always would be.

Patrick woke up Sunday morning from the nightmare feeling as if he couldn't breathe, jackknifing up from the bed so hard he nearly bit through his tongue. The scream his lungs wanted to expel was locked behind his teeth, kept inside by old training.

"Patrick?"

Jono's quiet voice broke through the cold terror wrapped around Patrick's mind. He heaved out a shuddering breath, then another, struggling to hold the panic at bay. His skin was sweaty and clammy, and his hands shook from a buzz of adrenaline that hurt. His head felt as if someone had taken a pickaxe to his skull and was trying to excavate his brain.

Jono touched his shoulder and Patrick instinctively jerked away, cradling his head in his hands as he hunched over. *This* was the reason he always slept alone—his nightmares weren't pretty, and they didn't belong to anyone else but him.

"I need a shower," Patrick managed to get out, already scrambling out of bed.

He needed *space*, needed clarity, maybe someone else to live his life for him. All Patrick got after washing off the sour stench of terror was a cup of coffee pressed into his forced-steady hands and a careful kiss against the corner of his mouth.

When Jono pulled away, there were questions in his eyes, but he didn't ask them, the same way he hadn't asked them last night. He merely stroked his hand and wrist over the side of Patrick's throat in the same spot Emma had done to him on the street outside Ginnungagap.

Humans couldn't smell whatever it was werecreatures used to scent-mark those they considered pack. Patrick had half a thought to go back into the bathroom and shower Jono off him.

He didn't.

"Don't leave without me, yeah?" Jono said.

Patrick nodded slowly, and Jono moved past him for the bathroom. While Jono cleaned up, Patrick mentally pulled himself together. It wasn't enough the gods fucked with his life, they had to fuck with his mind as well.

He went back to the bedroom and retrieved his dagger, strapping it onto his right thigh before clipping his holster to his belt. The weapons went a long way toward steadying him. He hesitated before grabbing a handful of the Greek coins off the nightstand and shoving them into his pocket. Moving around reminded him that it'd been a while since he'd last had sex, but the discomfort was easily ignored.

"Ready?" Jono asked when he came out of the bathroom ten minutes later in clean clothes, sunglasses perched on his nose.

"Yeah," Patrick said.

Even to his own ears, it sounded like a lie.

They left the apartment and got picked up by an Uber that took them to the Upper East Side, close to where Marek's home was. The driver dropped them off in front of a seven-story mansion that had no less than twelve gargoyles crawling across its façade.

Patrick got out of the car, eyeing the gargoyle sitting over the double-door entrance to the home, munching on a pigeon. Stone wings arched over the gargoyle's body as it gnawed off the head of its lunch. The sound of its teeth coming together reminded Patrick of the crunch of gravel beneath a tire.

"Great," Patrick sighed. "Guard dogs."

"Think it's supposed to be a bat," Jono said.

"Whatever. Let's go."

Someone who owned the home must have warned the gargoyles they were coming, because the stone creatures didn't try to chase them away. Patrick rang the doorbell, making sure to stand off to the side on the porch so pigeon blood didn't fall onto his head.

He heard footsteps beyond the door, and moments later it was opened by a woman Patrick recognized from pictures in Casale's office.

"Uh, hello," Patrick said, staring at Angelina Casale. "I'm here to see Isadora Cirillo?"

Angelina arched an eyebrow as she opened the door wider. "Yes, she said you would be stopping by, Special Agent Collins. Please, come inside."

Angelina was a woman aging gracefully, her graying, light brown hair tied up to keep it off her neck in the New York summer heat. She was dressed in casual clothing and white leather loafers, and her soul's aura carried the power of a strong witch. The only jewelry she wore other than her wedding band and diamond engagement ring was a silver necklace that had a lotus-tipped staff pendant hanging from it. Patrick stared at the symbol and felt his stomach sink somewhere down to his feet.

Well, shit, he thought.

He locked down his shields, ignoring the sharp look Jono gave him as they crossed the heavy threshold stretched across the mansion. The power within that barrier set Patrick's teeth on edge. The uncomfortable feeling didn't fade until Angelina offered him the ritual of hospitality.

She reached for the small china plate holding fresh-baked bread and a small glass of wine, offering both to Patrick with a polite smile that didn't reach her eyes.

"Be welcome in my lady's home," Angelina said.

Patrick ripped off a piece of the bread and chewed fast, swallowing it down with a mouthful of wine. The invisible pressure bearing down on his shoulders eased as he took part in the ritual. Angelina offered Jono the same greeting, and he ate the bread and drank some of the wine.

"Thank you," Jono said politely, because his manners in some areas were better than Patrick's, or it was the British in him.

"You sent your son to guard Marek," Patrick said, not taking his eyes off Angelina.

"Yes, because my lady asked me to. Tyler is more than capable of handling himself in a fight, as he is an exceptionally strong sorcerer," Angelina replied. She put the bread and wine back down on the ornate side-table and curled her fingers at them in a beckoning gesture. "Come. The high priestess awaits your presence."

Isadora Cirillo might have been the Crescent Coven's supposed high priestess and a missing hedge fund manager's wife, but she was immortal to Patrick's senses when they finally reached the rooftop terrace. And wasn't that revelation a kick in the fucking teeth.

The muggy heat hadn't faded despite the heavily overcast sky, a far cry from the clear skies of yesterday. The change in weather was worrisome, especially with summer solstice two days away. A reactionary storm wasn't out of the question if things got worse. Nature reacted to powerful castings of magic by escalating natural phenomenon. Patrick only hoped a hurricane wasn't in the mix.

Central Park stretched out before them beyond the rooftop terrace walls, as did the New York City skyline in a view Patrick wouldn't be able to afford in three lifetimes. A round glass table beneath a wooden pergola covered in ivy was set with four place settings, two of which were already taken.

"My lady," Angelina said as they approached. "Your guests."

"Thank you, sister," Isadora said. She lifted her delicate porcelain teacup to her mouth, watching their approach with fathomless brown eyes. "You may leave us."

Angelina inclined her head in a gesture of respect before retreating. Patrick stayed standing in the sunlight, eyes flicking from Isadora to Hermes and back again. Isadora sipped at her tea, the porcelain coming away clean, her lipstick as perfect as ever. Her eyes never left Patrick's face. Hermes ignored them both and kept shoveling fried potatoes into his mouth.

Patrick cleared his throat. "Hera."

"Sit," the titular queen of the Greek gods ordered.

Patrick sat, because he liked his balls still attached, and Hera wasn't a goddess to be crossed. Jono took the seat opposite him with a blank look on his face, carefully pulling off his sunglasses and hanging them from the collar of his shirt.

Patrick didn't serve himself any food, despite the empty plate in front of him. Jono, after contemplating the abundance of breakfast choices on the table—from eggs to fruit to pastries—chose to follow Patrick's lead.

"It's rude not to break bread, Patrick," Hera told him.

"I broke bread for you already," he said.

"Guess the bacon is all mine," Hermes announced. The messenger god picked up the platter of bacon and used his fork to push the fried strips of meat onto his plate. "You're missing out, Pattycakes."

"I doubt that."

Hera set her teacup down on its saucer and leaned back in her chair. She had seemed older when they'd first arrived, but Patrick knew that form was a lie, because Hera was young again. No wrinkles tugged at the corners of her eyes, and the laugh lines around her mouth had smoothed out. Her thick brown hair was braided into a crown around her head, no longer carrying streaks of gray in it. Her rich brown eyes were ancient and otherworldly in a classically pretty face.

Her aura was blinding.

Patrick had to look away.

His thoughts tumbled through his mind, bits and pieces of knowledge slotting together to form a fraction of a whole. He remembered what Setsuna had said the day he'd touched down in New York City, how he'd been the only one she could send to handle this problem.

"You ordered Setsuna to give me this case," Patrick said.

Hera delicately spread cream cheese onto a piece of smoked salmon before stabbing the fish with her fork. "It is your job to fix your family's mess. They took my husband. I want him back."

Patrick tried not to flinch, but Hera saw right through him. The smile she gave him wasn't benevolent at all. The mere idea of Zeus in the hands of Ethan was a nightmare Patrick would like to wake up from.

This whole fucked-up mess was like the Thirty-Day War all over again, with immortals taken prisoner by human greed and the world at stake once more. Only this time the frontline was New York City, home to millions and millions of people, with no one the wiser about a spell being cast through murder to kill a god.

The scars on Patrick's chest ached at that quiet confirmation. The nightmare he'd woken from that morning was still fresh in his mind, but he wasn't sure the warning had been about Hera. She had no affiliation with war or the dead, and ravens had never flocked to her.

"Why did you stay?" Patrick asked, looking past the goddess, not at her. "If they're calling your power through sacrifices, why not leave?"

"Most of us have," Hermes explained. "We're the only ones left in the state."

Patrick couldn't decide if it was hubris that kept the two of them in Manhattan or stupidity. He wasn't going to ask.

"Not the only ones," Hera said darkly, taking another sip of her tea. "Hades was sighted in Manhattan early last week."

If he didn't think she'd strike him down and make it hurt, Patrick would get up from the table and leave.

"I have the coins Hermes gave me. I have the Fates giving me warnings instead of help," Patrick said.

"Not our Fates," Hera reminded him.

"Then maybe you should check that the Moirai still belong to you because the ones I'm dealing with can't see the future."

Hera took another bite of salmon, her teeth scraping over the metal prongs of the fork. She chewed carefully, attention still focused squarely on Patrick. "Perhaps if you did your job, their blindness would not be a problem."

"Murder isn't easy" was Patrick's flat reply.

There were icebergs in the Arctic warmer than Hera's voice when she spoke. "You're good at it. Be better."

Which was true, if you counted what he'd done in the Mage Corps and what he did for the SOA now. Killing for the gods was different.

They wanted him to destroy what was left of his past.

Hera reached for him, and Patrick made himself not flinch away. Strong fingers gripped his chin and forced Patrick to meet her eyes. The power he could see burning inside her nearly blinded him and made his eyes water.

"The Dominion Sect has hidden my husband from me, but I know he is still here, on this island. The murders are bound to Manhattan, and the island sits above the nexus. Ethan can do nothing without the nexus. It must be contained, so find a way to contain it and bring Zeus back to me."

Her touch burned, and Patrick couldn't move.

"Please don't hurt him, lady."

Jono's voice dropped between them like a rock, his hand settling on Patrick's shoulder with a heavy touch that anchored him. Patrick blinked, half-blinded from Hera's aura, colored spots dancing across his eyes.

Hera's perfectly manicured fingernails dug into his skin for another second or two before her touch eased off. She didn't let go, slanting a look up at where Jono now stood beside Patrick's chair.

"Wolf," she said warningly. "He does not belong to you."

"Think my Fates might argue that."

Patrick's vision cleared in time for him to see the calculating look that settled in Hera's eyes. "Ah. You are not of the god pack here."

"I'm not with any bloody pack." Jono's hand tightened on Patrick's shoulder, offering silent support. "But Patrick is mine and I'm his until this case is finished. That's what the Fates decreed if you want your husband back. Patrick can't do what needs to be done if you harm him."

Hera studied Jono with eyes that had lived through centuries, taking his measure. Patrick wanted to tell Jono to *shut up*, but Hera still had control of his mouth.

"Patrick hasn't done what needs to be done for years," Hera countered.

"He came when you called. That has to count for something, yeah?"

She let him go.

Patrick resisted the urge to rub his jaw because showing any kind of weakness in front of the gods was like giving up secrets one couldn't afford to lose. He ran his tongue over the back of his teeth and sat up straighter.

Jono never let go of him.

It felt as if it could become a habit, one Patrick wouldn't mind allowing.

Patrick cleared his throat. "Tell me how they took Zeus?"

"I've already discussed everything with the police," Hera said.

"I'm not the police. So humor me." Patrick paused before belatedly tacking on a quick "Please."

He'd read the missing person report back at the PCB, but he wanted to hear it from Hera himself. If she'd held anything back from the police, she might give up the information to him.

Hera leaned back in her chair and crossed her legs at the knees, the brightness of her aura dimming to something easier on the eyes. "He had a dinner meeting with a new client. He never came home. When I sent some of my followers to the restaurant, they found traces of magic and were told they had no reservation under the client's name."

"What name? That wasn't in the records I went through."

"Does it matter? The name was falsely given."

Patrick would have pressed for the name—it was still evidence in a way—but Hera didn't seem as if she cared to pass it along. She'd made up her mind it was useless, and there was no changing the mind of a goddess, especially not this one.

"You have your orders," Hera told him, waving her hand in a dismissive manner.

Hermes put down his fork and took a swig of orange juice before getting to his feet. "I'll walk them out."

Jono let his hand fall away as Patrick stood up and marched toward the rooftop terrace doors. Hermes overtook them easily, leading the way through the mansion to the ground floor and back outside. Once they crossed the threshold, Patrick took a deep breath, the weight on his chest lifting.

"That went rather well," Hermes said.

Patrick glared at him. "The hell it did."

"You're still alive, Pattycakes."

"Only because I'm useless to your kind *dead*."

"There are gods who would disagree with that."

"*Fuck* those gods."

Hermes wasn't put off by Patrick's attitude. "Hera is right. You need to stop running."

"If I was running, I wouldn't be here."

Hermes pulled a pair of sunglasses out of thin air and put them on his nose. "Standing your ground means nothing if you don't fight."

Patrick opened his mouth to argue when he was interrupted by his phone ringing. Pulling it out of his pocket, he checked the screen. He didn't recognize the number, but the area code was for New York City, so he answered it.

"Collins," he said.

"Got a call about another body. It's one of ours," Allison said. "Chinatown."

"Fuck. What's the address?"

Allison rattled it off. "Casale is leaving church and will meet us at the scene. Do you need a ride?"

"I'll catch a taxi."

"See you soon."

She hung up, and Patrick pulled his phone away from his ear. Jono ran both hands through his hair, interlocking his fingers together behind his head. "Tenth body, innit?"

Patrick nodded. "Two more days until summer solstice."

Two more bodies were needed for a complete zodiac of the signs representing the Greek gods. The clock was counting down to the longest day of the year when all hell might break loose again. Patrick was holding the line by sheer will alone if the ache in his soul was anything to go by.

"We are running out of time, so do your job," Hermes said before disappearing right before their eyes.

"And I thought my life before you came to town was interesting," Jono said, glancing at Patrick. "What's all this about your family?"

"What's all this about your Fates? Could've sworn Marek was the seer and not you," Patrick shot back, already opening up his Uber app.

Jono didn't answer, and Patrick grimaced down at his phone.

Guess I'm not the only one with secrets, he thought.

12

"How do the sacrifices work?" Jono asked as they hurried down the street.

Their Uber driver had let them off a block away from the crime scene due to the police presence. An open street where anyone could hear them really wasn't the place to talk about casework. "No fucking idea."

But Patrick could guess, and in the end, it wouldn't be pretty.

Chinatown was a densely packed neighborhood in Lower Manhattan full of locals, immigrants, and tourists alike. Middle of the day on Sunday, the markets were crowded with shoppers looking for fresh produce, seafood, and meat on offer, jockeying for the best prices and choicest cuts.

A police officer was redirecting traffic past Mott Street, but the street itself wasn't roped off to pedestrians yet. More police officers were huddled together halfway down the block. A storefront produce market and the stores on either side of it had been cordoned off while police dealt with the body in one of the apartments above. A crowd of curious onlookers and elderly Chinese shoppers were being held back by several officers. Patrick didn't see the ME's van yet, but CSU was on-site.

The first thing Patrick noticed as they closed in on the building was the hellish taint from black magic seeping into the street. The recognition burned against Patrick's weakened magic, the feel of the taint stronger than he remembered it being at the last two crime scenes.

Patrick frowned, dodging around a dolly someone had left unmanned on the sidewalk near a delivery van. "It's not contained in the apartment."

"What isn't?" Jono asked.

"The taint residue from the attack. It was only present where the bodies were for the last two murders. Now it's spread out across the street."

"I take it that's a bit out of the ordinary?"

"It's different. Means the MO has changed, and that's not good."

"Or maybe the cops were notified of the body earlier?"

Patrick shook his head. "What's been left of the spell doesn't work that way."

He dug out his badge as they approached the police line, flipping the thin wallet open to show the policeman on watch duty. They ducked under the police tape once the officer cleared them and headed for the apartment building.

Allison stepped through the entrance as they approached, squinting at them. "Glad to see you made it. We got a mess up there."

"You got a mess out here," Patrick told her. "The taint has spread to the street. You'll need to quarantine the area and get someone to scrub everyone's souls."

Allison gave him a surprised look. "The magic at the prior crime scenes has never done that before."

The taint had always been contained to the apartments where the sacrifices had died. This was more than fading residue or a spell gone wrong, because someone was still dead up there.

This, Patrick knew with grim certainty, was a distraction. One that still needed to be dealt with.

Patrick drew out his magic, wincing a little at the way it made his nerves burn. A tiny mageglobe spun into existence against the palm of his hand, the dull blue glow mostly hidden from sight. He formed the searching spell in his mind, casting it through the mageglobe to help better focus his magic.

He dropped his shields and expanded his awareness, the taint easier to sense this way. Patrick walked past Allison, following the pull of his magic toward the end of the block where more curious onlookers stood. Patrick's gaze skimmed over faces, barely taking a second for each one, until someone caught his eye.

Caught his magic.

Dark eyes in a thin face met his for a split second before the stranger ducked his head and ran off like hellhounds were nipping at his heels.

"I fucking hate it when they run," Patrick said to no one in particular.

He ran after the suspect, taking the most direct path he could. It meant dodging around the curious crowd, feet pounding against asphalt as Patrick followed the taint of hell trailing after the man on the run.

Patrick had cleared the crowd and had eyes on the guy when the hellish taint faded beneath a different sort of magic. The man reached the corner of the block before skidding to a halt long enough to thrust his arm in Patrick's direction and snarl out an incantation. The full-sleeve tattoo on his left arm seemed to move. The spiraling form of a serpent dragon exploded away from the man with a thunderous *boom* that rattled windows all around them.

The dragon filled the street in an instant, a monstrous creature of bright red and matte black, the heavy stylized lines of the tattoo disappearing beneath seemingly solid flesh and glistening fangs. It dug its claws into the street but left no damage behind as it advanced.

People screamed as the dragon opened its mouth in a roar that ripped through the air, the hint of fire in the back of its throat impossible to miss. Patrick ran right toward it, ignoring Jono's furious shout from close behind him.

Patrick had seen dragons before.

This wasn't a dragon.

It lacked the gravitas of those beings, the depth of age and shrewdness in the eyes. Patrick hadn't felt the subtle shift of power that came with the sloughing off of whatever skin they hid in before emerging whole and powerful in their original bodies. The physics involved in calculating the mass displacement always made Patrick's head hurt just thinking about it. The Old Man he once served under had made it look seamless.

Patrick ran into the dragon's gaping mouth before the flames burst forth, flinging a pair of mageglobes into the structure of the spell ahead of him. Raw magic exploded around him, ripping through the illusion and turning it into nothing but colored smoke that made his eyes and nose burn. Blinking the sting away, Patrick kept running, still following that thin presence of tainted magic mixed with the signature of a practitioner that felt like a sorcerer to his senses.

The illusion drifted away on a muggy breeze, nothing more than a fading smokescreen now. Patrick got clear and kept his eyes on the target when he wasn't scanning the buildings around them for any overwatch threats. Up ahead, the sorcerer had reached the next intersection and wasn't stopping; neither was the traffic. The guy ran across the street, heedless of the moving vehicles around him, and made it to the other side without getting run over.

Which was an utter fucking shame.

When Patrick made it to the intersection, the lights had already changed—but he raced into the street against a red light anyway.

Horns honked at him as the screech of brakes filled his ears. The shouts and swearing coming from the drivers were easily ignored.

The car that didn't stop demanded his full attention.

Patrick slammed his hands on the hood of the still-moving vehicle, twisting his body into the vault and swinging his legs over the front of the car. The driver finally hit the brakes when Patrick crossed his vision. The sudden lurch to stillness jerked his body as he slid across the hood with a grunt. Patrick didn't stick the landing on the other side, not wanting to risk breaking an ankle. He used his momentum to pitch himself forward, stumbling back into a speedy run.

"Federal agent! Stop where you are!" Patrick yelled. The order went ignored, not like he thought the guy would listen.

In the grand scheme of things, Patrick had done his legal duty with that warning.

The sorcerer was still running, and there were too many people between them for Patrick to safely use his magic. Patrick kept his eyes locked on the man and didn't miss when he took a sharp turn into a café where elderly Chinese men were reading the *Sing Tao*, drinking hot tea, and watching a taped singing show on the old television set bolted to the wall.

Patrick glimpsed it all in a flash as he ran through the front area of the café before slamming through the employee door in the back. It led to a cramped kitchen where one cook was helping another to her feet, having been knocked down by the man Patrick was chasing.

He went through the door that led to a dirty alley with his shields up and a mageglobe in hand, the strike spell burning at his fingertips. The narrow space was filled with black plastic bags of garbage spilling out of a nearby dumpster. The mouth of the alley was empty, but the fire escape rattled from quick footsteps. Patrick looked up right as the door went flying off its hinges from Jono's shove and crashed to the ground.

"You couldn't bloody *wait*?" Jono snarled.

Patrick pointed at the fire escape, magic burning across his skin. "Hold that thought."

He spun up a binding ward in his mageglobe and sent it careening upward through the gaps in the metal fire escape. The sorcerer tried to defend against it, but his magic dealt with illusions, and it couldn't hold up against a military grade spell. It technically wasn't legal to use against a civilian, but Patrick *had* told him to stop.

When Patrick's mageglobe crashed against the man's chest, bright ropes of magic wrapped around his body like webbing. He crashed down onto the stairs of the fire escape with a pained shout, down but not out.

"I need to get up there," Patrick said.

Jono shook his head before making a looping turn in the small space. He ran at the wall, kicking one foot out to hit the side of the dirty building and propel himself upward with preternatural strength. Jono grabbed the railing of the first landing one full story above them and easily hauled himself over. It took him less than thirty seconds to extend the ladder down to the ground so Patrick could climb up.

They ascended the zigzagging staircases together, with Patrick taking point. Three landings later they reached the suspect. The man was sprawled against the fire escape steps, bleeding from a deep cut on his jaw where he'd hit his face on a sharp edge when he fell. The binding ward held his magic in check along with his body. Patrick could feel the sorcerer fighting it, and the struggle was giving him a headache.

Patrick grabbed the guy by the collar of his shirt and belt, hauling him off the stairs. "When I say stop, I mean fucking *stop*, asshole."

"Fuck you!" the guy spit out.

"Want me to carry him down?" Jono asked.

"Nah, I got this."

Patrick shoved the sorcerer up against the railing, letting him dangle halfway over, head pointed at the ground. He could see tattoos on both arms rippling across the man's skin but unable to form any illusions.

"You want to explain what you were doing back there?" Patrick demanded.

The man was of Chinese descent, and while his full-sleeve tattoos were done in the traditional style, his accent was all New York. "*Fuck* you!"

"Not the answer I was looking for."

With a bit of help from his magic, Patrick shoved the guy over the edge and let gravity do its thing. Jono, for all his quick reflexes, didn't react fast enough, his hand coming down on empty air as the sorcerer fell with a high-pitched scream before being caught by Patrick's magic halfway to the ground.

"Are you *mental*?" Jono yelled at him in disbelief.

Patrick shrugged. "I'm gonna plead the Fifth on that."

Jono stared at him for a few more seconds before looking over the side of the railing at where the sorcerer hovered in the air, still screaming his fool head off.

"I want my lawyer, you crazy fuck!" the sorcerer yelled.

"I hate when they lawyer up."

"Absolutely mental," Jono decided before he started back down the fire escape.

"You say that like it's a bad thing," Patrick called after him.

They made it back down to the ground, and Patrick gestured sharply with one hand, magic sparking at his fingertips as he called the sorcerer back down to earth. Patrick wrinkled his nose at the smell of urine coming off the guy; he'd pissed his pants sometime during the free fall. He was in the process of adjusting the binding ward so the guy could walk when two uniformed officers approached the mouth of the alley.

"You got him?" the policewoman asked.

"This crazy fucker dropped me off the roof!" the sorcerer yelled.

The officers ignored him, too busy snapping a pair of hand-cuffs on him, which Patrick used to tie his binding ward to. The metal acted as a decent anchor to hold the spell. The binding ward was still active, even if the physical manifestations of magic had faded from the sorcerer's body. His tattoos and illusion-based magic had settled back into his skin, forced to dormancy by the binding ward.

The suspect protested loudly as he was hauled to the squad car parked in the middle of the street. The officers ignored the sorcer-er's continuous yelling about how Patrick was the one who should be arrested for attempted murder, not him.

Two more police cars—one unmarked—pulled up behind the squad car. Allison and Dwayne got out of their vehicle, hands hovering near their weapons. When they saw the problem had been contained, they approached Patrick and Jono rather than their fellow officers.

"Did you really drop him off the roof?" Dwayne asked.

"No," Patrick said with a straight face. "It was only a couple of stories."

"That's an excessive use of force charge right there that will bite us in the ass," Allison said. "Why did you chase him?"

"The taint from the crime scene was tied to him."

They looked over at where the officers were shoving the loudly swearing sorcerer into the back of their squad car. "That's a new development."

"Yeah, but it doesn't make any sense." Patrick stepped around them and approached the squad car holding the sorcerer. "He lawyered up already."

"But you have the bloke. That's good, right?" Jono asked.

"Only if the spell signatures match."

"You said the taint was tied to him?"

Patrick ignored the question. He nodded at the uniformed policewoman speaking into her radio before hauling open the side door of the police car. He braced an arm against the roof of the car and leaned down to look at the scowling suspect still struggling against the binding ward.

"You still want your lawyer?" Patrick asked.

"Fuck you," the man spit out.

"Original."

Patrick reached for the man, not caring that he ducked away. Patrick didn't need to touch him to read his aura. Tapping his magic, Patrick worked to isolate the taint in the sorcerer's soul. He was surprised at how easy it was to peel it out of the man's aura, as if the magic had no ties to the soul it was riding in, more a tangle of foreign power.

Which meant it wasn't his magic.

Patrick snuffed out the residual and moved back so he could close the door. "He's not the murderer. Accessory to it maybe, but he's not the one controlling the soultakers."

"Are you sure?" Allison asked.

"The taint from the crime scene was transposed onto his aura. It's not his, he's just carrying it."

"So why change tactics like this?" Dwayne wanted to know. "Why have someone remain at the scene? The person behind the murders has never broken their MO in six months. Why start now?"

"It's a question we can ask him, but interrogation will take hours," Patrick said slowly, mind shifting into overdrive.

Allison nodded. "We'll need to bring him back to the PCB immediately to get the process started. We won't even be able to talk to him without his lawyer present, and then we'll need to send him to Central Booking."

All that meant was they'd be holed up dealing with this new wrinkle in the case. They had a real live person to possibly get some answers from, but Patrick didn't believe anything viable would pan out. This was a glaringly obvious new lead, and in Patrick's experience, the obvious was merely a ploy.

Patrick craned his head around, catching Jono's eye. "Where's

Marek? He said something last night about Sage's birthday party going on today."

Jono frowned and dug out his phone. "I'll give him a ring."

"I'm going to need you guys to handle his processing," Patrick said to Dwayne and Allison, pointing at the sorcerer in the back of the squad car. "See if you can expedite it."

"Marek isn't picking up," Jono said tersely a few seconds later.

"Try Leon. I'll call Emma."

Patrick's phone just kept ringing before getting picked up by voicemail. He hung up without leaving a message. Jono didn't seem to have much luck either in reaching Leon.

Patrick put his phone away. "Dwayne? Allison? I need your car."

"Why?" Dwayne asked.

"Because mine got blown up, and I need to find Marek. Give me your keys."

"Why do you think Marek is in danger?"

"He's got a hefty amount of magic at his disposal, and a spell of this magnitude will need a large enough sacrifice at the end. Keys. *Now.*"

And because Marek, being a seer, had a direct tie to an immortal, which would give the spell an even bigger boost. Patrick didn't want to think about how messy things would get if Marek died on his watch.

"What if he's not home?" Allison said.

"We'll try his work and the bar. Does he have any other places he frequents?" Patrick asked Jono.

"He owns a mansion in the Hamptons," Jono said.

Patrick rounded on him. "Big enough to house a party?"

Jono nodded slowly. "Yeah."

"*Fuck.* I am chaining him to his goddamn apartment after this."

If Marek was in Long Island, the seer wouldn't have to be worried about dying by way of a soultaker's teeth and insatiable hunger. Patrick would kill the other man himself for not learning to stay fucking *put.*

Dwayne was on the phone to Casale about the latest situation they were all facing when an SUV braked to a halt behind their unmarked car. Patrick would've paid it no mind except the woman who got out from behind the steering wheel caught his attention like little else could.

Tall and lean, with her brown hair pulled back in a tight braid coiled at the base of her skull, the woman silently nodded at him. She wore black cargo pants tucked into combat boots, a fitted black T-shirt, and a tactical handgun holstered to her heavy-duty belt. Patrick could see nothing that would show any affiliation she might have with any agency. No badge, no name tag, no insignia— not that she needed any. After the missions they'd run together as combat mages in the Mage Corps, Patrick would know her face anywhere.

He'd ask what Special Agent Nadine Mulroney of the Preter- natural Intelligence Agency was doing here in New York City, but he already knew the answer.

Nadine was Setsuna's second call-in.

"Who's that?" Allison asked.

"Backup," Patrick said, already walking toward his ride. "Jono, you're coming with me. Allison, I don't need your car anymore, but I need you to send some of your people to Marek's Manhattan addresses. Call me with news on if he's there or not. Tell Casale I'll return when I can."

"Where are you going?"

"Long Island."

"You're gonna need an escort," Dwayne said after he hung up. He cupped his hands around his mouth and raised his voice. "Lee! You and your partner are taking Special Agent Collins to Long Island. Lights and sirens all the way."

The uniformed cop in question reached for his radio in antici- pation of giving dispatch an update. "Location?"

Patrick called out the address along with instructions for Lee to "Turn your lights and sirens off three miles out from the destination. I don't want to give away our position."

"Understood," Officer Lee replied.

"Collins," Nadine said in greeting once Patrick made it to the SUV.

"Mulroney," Patrick said. "Tell me you brought gear?"

"Back seat. Needs to be assembled."

"Jono, take the front." Patrick opened the side passenger door but paused before getting in. He raised an eyebrow at Nadine. "Weren't you supposed to be on vacation?"

"I was." She slid back behind the wheel and pulled her door shut. "Technically, I'm not even on loan."

Which meant Nadine was AWOL in the worst way possible and they couldn't rely on any backup from either of their agencies while in the field.

"Feels like old times," Patrick said before getting into the back seat and buckling up.

"Gods, I hope not," Nadine said as she put the SUV into reverse. "But this is you we're talking about, so I'm guessing we're all just fucked."

Patrick rolled his eyes, but he couldn't really argue with the truth.

13

"THESE HAVE THE SERIAL NUMBERS FILED OFF. DID YOU GET THEM from Lucien?"

Nadine took her eyes off the cop car clearing them a way through New York City streets to glance at Patrick in the rearview mirror. "Rifles aren't acceptable carry-on items for any airline, so what do you think?"

Patrick finished sliding home the magazine filled with spelled bullets for the M4A1 carbine he had assembled in the back seat. "I hate carbines. You think he'd pick a better rifle to sell."

"You're still fucking picky about what you carry even three years out of the Corps."

"Like you aren't," Patrick retorted. "Lucien said he was waiting for more shipments to arrive. I'm assuming they did if he's handing out weapons?"

"He still has a few more coming. These were appropriated from what he had on hand when he crossed the southern border on such short notice."

"What was he doing on this continent? Did the Middle East stop being lucrative or something?"

"You'd have to ask him."

"I'd rather not."

Patrick tucked the first carbine back into its transport case and put it on the seat beside him. He grabbed the second transport case and started to assemble the next weapon in less than a minute. The motions were practically muscle memory for him, so it was easy to do. He split up the extra magazine cartridges containing military grade spelled bullets between both weapons.

Nadine's borrowed gear was limited, but all of it was in excellent condition. Lucien's business might be exceptionally illegal, but no one ever complained about the products he sold on the black market. Those that did usually ended up dead.

She hadn't brought a uniform, but the Kevlar-lined tactical vest was similar to the kind they'd both worn in the military. Patrick had strapped on the set she'd brought for him over his clothes already, the weight of the gear familiar.

Patrick leaned back in his seat and scratched at his cheek. "Where were you when Setsuna pulled you this time?"

"Visiting my parents in Nice. I got the plane ticket back to the States under an alias. For all intents and purposes, I am still in Nice."

France was Nadine's home away from home. She'd been born in the United States but had largely grown up in Paris. Both her parents had worked for the State Department out of the Paris embassy for the majority of her childhood and teenage years. In some ways, she was culturally more French than American.

She'd joined the Mage Corps when she was nearly twenty-two after earning a degree in political science at the Paris Institute of Political Studies in three years. She was a few years older than Patrick but had earned the same sort of honorable discharge he had after the Thirty-Day War. Instead of transitioning into civilian life, Nadine had joined the PIA and opted to return to her adoptive country. She was based out of Paris now, working counterintelligence cases in Europe.

Patrick missed her. Nadine hadn't been part of his team back then, but they'd worked with her on and off for certain missions. She was a friend, and he didn't have very many of those these days.

"I need a sitrep," Nadine said.

Her hands in their fingerless gloves slid along the steering wheel as she took the long, curving exit off FDR Drive onto the Brooklyn Bridge at a fast speed. She was following their escort and the directions to the address Jono had plugged into his phone's GPS.

"What did Setsuna tell you?" Patrick asked.

"That you needed backup."

"What *else* did she tell you?"

Nadine sped up to make sure the asshole in the next lane over didn't try to cut her off. "That we have the Dominion Sect breathing down our necks again."

Patrick glared out the windshield at the cop car ahead of them. "Yeah."

"Should I be hearing this?" Jono asked from the front seat.

Nadine tilted her head in Jono's direction and didn't take her eyes off the road. "What's with the wolf?"

Patrick made a face. "The seer we're tracking down ordered Jono to stay with me."

"Immortals? Again?"

"When is it ever not immortals? Remember Cairo?"

"As if I could forget that battle."

"That's what we're up against, only they've fixed their mistakes."

The amount of swearing Nadine spit out in no less than three different languages was expected. "I should've taken the grenade launcher."

Before Patrick could ask why she hadn't, his phone rang. He saw Casale's name on the screen and answered it.

"Collins. Line and location are secure," Patrick said.

"I got a suspect on his way to the PCB, and you're not on-site. What the hell is going on?" Casale demanded.

"He's a distraction. MO doesn't fit and the magic at the crime scene doesn't belong to him. I'm tracking down Marek in case the Dominion Sect is targeting him right now."

"You still think he's who they ultimately want?"

"He's what will power their ultimate goal. A spell like the one they're killing for needs a large sacrifice at the end to anchor it. Marek technically has more magic than a mage, even though his power only translates into visions of the future."

"I was afraid you'd say that. I have officers going to his known locations here in Manhattan. I'll let you know if he's at any one of them or not. Where are you?"

"On I-278 about to hit I-495 on our way to the Hamptons."

"What's your final destination? I can call another department and have them send units over to the house."

"No more cops. This isn't a fight they need to be in the middle of."

"Collins—"

Patrick cut him off. "No. They won't be able to handle what I think we're heading into."

"You might have jurisdiction of the case, but it's still our job."

"And I'm telling you they can't handle it. Allied forces could barely hold the line against hell during the Thirty-Day War. How do you think your first responders will fare when they don't have the support the military did?"

"If you're so certain this case is turning into that mess, then maybe we should reach out to the military," Casale snapped.

"We have two days until summer solstice, and I'm going to do everything I can to stop it. I told you I needed a week, and my time isn't up yet."

"Sounds like it's getting close."

"And my job is to stop it, so let me do my fucking job."

"You can do what you have to, but I'm going to send officers to your location to handle the aftermath. You'll need representatives from the PCB on-site to deflect questions and handle the media."

"Fine. They can keep our escort company on the sidelines."

"They'll have instructions to maintain perimeter only."

"Great." Patrick hung up and peered out the windshield. They were heading east, the sky a dark wall of clouds rising over Brooklyn. "That looks ugly."

"Weather is a mess," Nadine agreed. "My flight in was turbulent for the last hour until we landed."

Patrick sighed. "I was hoping we wouldn't get a reactionary storm. Jono?"

"No one is answering," Jono said, phone pressed to his ear.

"Keep trying."

Nadine picked up speed to stay with their police escort as they raced down the highway. They'd both learned high-speed tactical driving while in the Mage Corps. Despite the growing traffic, Patrick had faith in Nadine's ability to get them to Marek's vacation home safely.

Silence fell between the three; the only sound in the SUV other than the hum of the engine was the faint ringing coming from Jono's phone as he tried to contact Marek. Patrick monitored their route on his own phone, watching the little arrow glide across the screen.

Ten minutes later Patrick got another phone call from Casale reporting that Marek wasn't in any of his known locations in Manhattan.

"It's the Hamptons," Patrick said after he hung up.

Nadine nodded silent confirmation and kept driving.

Hurry up and wait had never been his favorite way to pass the time, but even with a police escort, they could only move so fast. By the time they were five minutes out by Patrick's calculations, someone finally answered Jono's call.

"Marek? Marek!" Jono said in a relieved voice. "Fucking hell, mate. I've been ringing you like mad. Why didn't you—what do you mean am I coming to Sage's party? Bring a friend? Marek, wait, *what*? Hold on."

Jono covered the pickup on his phone with his hand and twisted around in his seat to look at Patrick. "Did you send SOA agents to guard Marek?"

A chill ran down Patrick's spine, and he leaned forward to grab Jono's phone. He put it to his ear even as he hand-signaled Nadine to *go faster*.

"Marek, listen to me. If Rachel Andrita is on-site, I want you to say great, can't wait to see you for the party. If she's not, and it's someone else, ask me to pick something up from the store," Patrick said.

Marek kept his voice steady and unaffected when he spoke. "Great, can't wait to see you guys at the party. The more the merrier."

"Emma and Leon, if you can hear me, corral your people and get Tyler to shield all of you right now. ETA five minutes. Tell him to hold his shield no matter what."

"We'll be waiting," Marek replied.

He hung up, and Patrick handed Jono back the phone. "Rachel Andrita is on-site with an unknown number of affiliates. We are to consider her hostile with a probable connection to the Dominion Sect."

"Isn't she SOA?" Jono asked.

"She stonewalled Casale for six months on this case and then demanded she have access to it after it got transferred to my division. Setsuna doesn't trust her."

"Setsuna needs to clean house quicker. A bullet to the head would work," Nadine said grimly.

"I'm not arguing that."

"Rachel is a witch?"

"Yes. Strictly civilian career tract, no military background. Whoever she brought with her to Marek's home could be military. She might have a mage with her if the Dominion Sect really is backing her."

Nadine smiled tightly. "Mage or not, I'd like to see them try to get through my shields."

Nadine was a combat mage whose magic leaned toward defensive rather than offensive. The shields she could build with her own magic while tapped into a ley line were nearly impenetrable. She had shielded entire forward operating bases for hours at a time from shelling by insurgents and demons while in the Mage Corps.

Patrick was glad to have her watching his six again.

"How's your magic?" she asked.

"It got partially eaten by a soultaker. I'm still not at full strength," Patrick told her before tapping Jono on the shoulder. "I need you to describe the house for us."

Jono started searching through the photos on his phone. "Can do you one better. Two-story mansion with direct beach access in the back. Gated entryway. Strong threshold, but nothing you lot can't get through, I'd wager."

Jono handed Patrick his phone again. The folder in question contained photos shot during a Fourth of July barbecue. In some of the outdoor shots, Patrick could make out the size of the house. His mind churned through several possible infiltration methods.

"Line of sight is clear if she put anyone with a long gun in the second-floor rooms facing the front. There are open areas on the side, but best ingress might be a frontal attack," Patrick said.

"I doubt they brought guns. That is never the first weapon civilian magic users go for in a fight. I'll hide our approach," Nadine said. "You sense anything yet, Collins?"

Patrick's magic was quiet in his soul, no hint of recognition of any type burning through it. "Not yet."

"Tell me when and what you feel the second you do."

"Copy that."

A couple of raindrops started to hit the windshield when their escort cut the lights and sirens off a mile out. Nadine sped up, overtaking their escort to take point the rest of the way. She braked to a hard halt a couple of houses down from Marek's and put the SUV into park before exiting the vehicle. She yanked open the side passenger door to grab her tactical gear, strapping it into place.

"Too bad you couldn't have borrowed some helmets," Patrick said as he scrambled out, M4A1 carbine in hand.

"You know Lucien. He thinks a head shot can't stop him."

Patrick snapped the assault rifle's carry strap to his vest to secure it to his body. He tucked the buttstock against his shoulder, finger resting over the trigger guard. Raindrops fell on his cheeks as he followed Nadine forward. The clouds out here were darker than back in Manhattan. Ocean salt hung heavy on the wind; he could practically taste it.

Officer Lee and his partner got out of their squad car, weapons drawn, but Patrick waved them back. "You two, stay put. No matter what you hear, don't come after us, got it?"

"Yeah," Officer Lee replied, eyeing their tactical gear. "Good luck."

Jono fell in beside Patrick, his sunglasses left behind in the SUV. "You need me to shift?"

If Jono had any experience in fighting magic users and demons in his other form, Patrick would say yes. But he didn't know Jono's capabilities, and he couldn't risk not knowing them in the field right now.

"Stay human," Patrick said. "And stay on our six."

Jono fell into step behind them. "Right."

A pale lavender mageglobe flared into existence near Nadine's left elbow, keeping pace with her as she ran. Patrick could feel her magic flowing around them, warm and clean in a stealth spell that quieted the sounds of their pounding feet and hid them from sight. She kept it up all the way to the front gate, where instead of picking the lock or shooting it off, she waved Jono toward the code box. Patrick stared through the ACOG scope of his rifle and cased the front of the home while Jono unlocked the gate.

"No overwatch that I can see, but they got a silence ward wrapped around the mansion," Patrick said.

"That I can sense," Nadine said.

The door lock buzzed open as Jono finished typing in the code. Patrick advanced with Nadine by his side, their weapons up and magic primed for immediate use. They were halfway across the freshly mowed lawn when recognition erupted through Patrick's magic, the same ugly sensation he'd felt at the bar, only multiplied.

"*Motherfucker*," Patrick growled, sprinting forward. "Soultakers are coming through the veil!"

"Raising a shield," Nadine replied.

She followed hot on his heels, wrapping a combat shield around them on the fly. It could hold up against a grenade dropped on it from the outside but was layered differently from within to allow for the firing of weapons without fear of ricochets. The shield moved with them, a malleable, invisible barrier.

They scrambled up the porch, crossing a threshold that felt choked off to Patrick's senses. The silence ward hastily drawn on the doorframe outside might have been the source, but the strength bolstering it burned in an ugly, familiar way.

He reached for the sigil, fingers hovering over the blackened lines before he made a fist. "Nadine."

"What?" she said in a low voice, already aiming at the door.

"Hera said Hades was sighted in Manhattan last week." Patrick turned his head to meet her gaze. "I think he's here."

"*Fuck* me. This day just keeps getting worse and worse."

Jono shook his head. "I thought dealing with Marek as one god's vessel was a headache. You win the prize, Pat."

"He's not a vessel," Nadine muttered right before she shot the lock off the door and kicked it open.

She advanced into an open foyer that led into a large living area with murder in her eyes. Patrick was right on her six, Jono close behind him. As soon as they crossed the threshold, Patrick could hear the screams coming from within the home.

Three people dressed for a day on the beach were writhing on the floor in agony, bodies twisted in half-shifted forms as a pair of sorcerers called forth their beasts. The two men looked up at their entrance, turning to ward off the unexpected threat, but it was too little, too late.

Sorcerers might have been on the stronger end of the magic spectrum, but they had nothing on a mage, and they definitely had nothing on a bullet to the heart. Patrick pulled the trigger, the first spelled bullet taking out the closest sorcerer in the chest, the second cutting through his head at an angle. Nadine took out the man's partner, and the ugly black spell circles glowing malevolently beneath the werecreatures disappeared.

The victims, members of Emma's Tempest pack, lay sprawled on the floor in their half-shifted state, alive but barely conscious. Patrick cased the area and saw no demonic threat, but the taint in his own magic was screaming a warning at him he knew better than to ignore.

"Jono, do you hear anyone else in the house?" Patrick asked as they moved forward, stepping over the three werecreatures and the bodies of the dead sorcerers.

"No," Jono got out tightly. "They're all outside."

Nadine wrapped a barrier ward around the werecreatures they left behind, encasing them in solid safety. "First group secure."

Patrick let his weapon lead the way forward, his magic a persistent warning buzz beneath his skin. They cleared every room between them and the broken french glass doors at the rear of the mansion leading to a backyard empty of the Tempest pack but not the enemy.

The man and woman stood between them and the path leading to the beach. Dressed in clothes that wouldn't be out of place in an office, with their magic meshed together to form a shield, the Dominion Sect acolytes seemed to be expecting them.

Patrick raised his voice. "Federal agent! Draw back your magic and stand down."

In response, the woman hurtled a bolt of raw magic at them that slammed into Nadine's shield. The attack exploded upon impact, but the shield never wavered.

"Guess that's a no," Nadine said.

Patrick took his hand off the barrel and called up a mageglobe, weaving the barrage spell through its shape. He waved two fingers in a single forward motion that sent the mageglobe streaking forward, passing harmlessly through Nadine's shield. The Dominion Sect acolytes didn't know what hit them until it was too late.

Military grade spells weren't supposed to be used against civilians. Patrick figured the SOA would probably give him a pass when it came to the Dominion Sect. The barrage spell ripped through the sorcerers' shield like so much paper. The blowback from the concussive force of the hit shattered the lower level windows of the mansion behind them. Torn-up grass, dirt, and body parts rained down around them.

A blackened crater now marred the backyard, but that was the least of their worries. Nadine modified her shield for mobility, and they quickly moved forward toward the beach, the rain beginning to come down harder. The curl of waves crashing to shore in the Atlantic were frothy whitecaps driven by strong winds.

Patrick smelled the sea, but he tasted hell.

His magic was frayed in his soul, but the Greek coins clicked quietly together in his pocket, and his dagger was within reach. The weapons didn't make him feel better about the situation.

They crested the wooden stairs leading to the beach. On the sand below were members of the Tempest pack huddled behind the rapidly fading shield Tyler could no longer hold up. Rachel's coordinated magical attack with other acolytes was moments away from breaking through Tyler's shield. Marek stood surrounded by Emma, Leon, and Sage, but werecreatures didn't have much hope against magic.

"Go time," Patrick said.

They had their roles in the field, and they didn't need to talk the details out. Nadine cut right, raising a barrier ward around the Tempest pack right as Tyler's shield collapsed. Rachel's attack rebounded off the shield, crashing back into a couple of witches who couldn't get out of the way fast enough. They were thrown off their feet, falling back down to earth meters away.

Patrick's feet sank into wet sand as he cleared the last step, blinking rain out of his eyes. Through his magic he could sense the suffocating presence of hell beginning to permeate their immediate area.

"The SOA might want you alive, but I'd be more than happy to put you in a grave, Rachel," Patrick yelled to be heard over the wind.

The soon-to-be former SAIC turned to face him, her face a mask of rage. "It's a shame you didn't die in your car."

"I've survived worse."

Nadine snorted as they kept advancing. "Understatement."

"Go guard the others and keep them safe. Soultakers in ten," Patrick warned. "Nine."

"Tapped into a ley line," Nadine replied. "Jono, with me. Eight."

"I'm staying with Patrick," Jono argued.

"Fucking hell, we told you to *listen*! Seven."

"Six. Just go, Mulroney," Patrick snapped. "Jono, don't get in my fucking way."

"I hope you're ready to die," Rachel spat out, the circle she stood within glowing brightly. Radial lines expanded outward, the structure of the spell not something a witch of her caliber could create.

Which meant someone else was casting through the veil.

Patrick ignored Rachel as Nadine split her shield between their two positions, keeping everyone safe. "Five."

He could feel it in his soul, the heavy weight of hell pulling at him. The world seemed to waver for a second, as if the rain coming down harder had blurred it out. The acolytes still standing were throwing whatever offensive magic they could at them, but nothing was getting through Nadine's shield.

At least, not yet.

"Four," Patrick counted down, Jono's voice joining in, the seconds pounding in his ears like drums. "Three."

The circle beneath Rachel's feet erupted in hellfire, but the witch didn't burn.

"Two."

Recognition screamed through Patrick's magic with soul-searing intensity, the taste of hell hot and bitter on his tongue.

"One."

The world seemed to tear around them, the veil ripping over the beach in the form of ragged fog given an eerie glow from the hellfire. It spilled over the sand, obscuring the immediate area.

It couldn't hide what crossed over.

A horde of soultakers pulled free of the veil, led by a god that made Patrick freeze in his tracks, heart pounding a mile a minute in his chest.

"If you'd like to take the seer's place on the sacrificial altar, then by all means, lie down and die, Patrick," Hades said.

The god's voice echoed in Patrick's ears in a way human voices never did. Hades stood within the lines of the circle, hellfire licking at his feet, untouched by the fury of the storm. He could have passed for a Wall Street tycoon if one ignored the unearthly power he exuded. The immortal wasn't charismatic so much as terrifying, despite the clean-cut image projected by the three-piece suit that was perfectly dry beneath the downpour. Hades was dark-haired, dark-eyed, and corpse-pale, all chilling malevolence in human disguise.

The Greek god of the Underworld still looked exactly the same as he had in that Salem basement all those years ago.

"Patrick," Jono said, breaking through the fear clawing at Patrick's mind. "Don't listen to him."

He drew in a shaky breath, readjusting his grip on his rifle. The hellfire bomb yesterday made sense now. Patrick should have remembered it was one of Hades' favorite little parlor tricks.

Hades smiled, the expression coloring in old nightmares in ways Patrick could have done without. Those dark eyes looked behind him at where Jono stood with a covetousness Patrick didn't appreciate at all.

"If not you, I'll take the wolf. I'd rather not go to war with the Norse gods just yet, but needs must. Either way, I will take a soul with me to hell today," Hades said.

The soultakers lunged forward, half the horde coming for Patrick while the rest went after the Tempest pack. Patrick repositioned his rifle against his shoulder and braced himself. He switched the M4A1 carbine over to fully automatic and held down the trigger. The loud release of bullets sounded like thunder in the air, echoed by Nadine's weapon. Her shields glimmered with a faint violet hue every time a bullet passed through them on the way to the enemy.

They aimed for the acolytes, because the soultakers weren't bothered at all by something as annoying as bullets. Three of the magic users were cut down, but none of them were Rachel.

Where's a fucking tank when you need one? Patrick thought a little frantically.

"I can shift and better protect you," Jono said, stepping up beside him.

"Don't even think about it," Patrick snarled.

Patrick might have been reckless with his own life, but like hell was he risking anyone under his protection.

"Would you stop being so bloody stubborn? I can *help* you."

"*You* can't do anything against a god except die. I am actively trying to prevent that from happening right now!"

"Maybe I can't," Jono conceded. "But my patron can."

Patrick's finger let up on his trigger for a fraction of a second at that confession. He clamped it back down again, getting close to needing to reload.

"Are you fucking kidding me?" Patrick ground out as the soultakers kept coming, mouth suddenly gone dry. "You didn't think that bit of information was important for me to know *before* now?"

No fucking wonder why the London god pack had exiled Jono and why Estelle and Youssef didn't want him around. Not every god pack had a patron these days. If the New York City god pack didn't have one and Jono did? Agreement be damned, but Jono would be well within his right to take over the New York City god pack.

Why Jono hadn't was a question for *after* they survived this fight.

The soultakers ran up against Nadine's shield and started to tear through her magic right as Patrick's rifle clicked empty. Patrick unclipped the strap from his tactical vest and thrust the weapon at Jono.

"Hold this and stay here," he ordered.

Patrick conjured up half a dozen mageglobes, pouring his magic into the barrage spell twisting through each one. Nadine couldn't hold her shields up forever against soultakers—no one could—and Patrick wasn't about to let her magic get drained to the breaking point.

He cast his mageglobes at the soultakers, his magic passing harmlessly through Nadine's shield. The second they were on the other side, two were immediately swallowed whole by the demons, and the rest detonated on Patrick's silent, willed command.

The resulting explosion sent a couple of soultakers and sand flying through the air. What magic didn't catch them off guard they ate. Patrick felt the metaphysical tearing in his soul like a heavy burn in chest.

It wasn't enough to stop him from walking through Nadine's shield, Jono's frantic yell whipped away by the wind that barreled into him from the Atlantic.

His magic had carved out a bit of space to stand in, and Patrick planted his feet in the wet sand, staring over the demons at Hades. He didn't reach for his dagger and instead pulled from his pocket the handful of Greek coins he'd left the apartment with that morning.

Lightning flashed directly overhead, illuminating the world in electric light. Thunder rolled across the beach and the waves lashing against the shore, drowning out the ear-piercing shrieks of the soultakers.

Hades' smile disappeared when Patrick raised his clenched fists, the coins already glowing.

"Where did you get those?" Hades demanded.

"You should quit pissing off your family," Patrick shot back.

The coins burned hot in his hand, and Patrick tossed them into the air. They hung suspended there for a moment, burning like miniature suns the soultakers couldn't seem to face. The feel of heavenly magic was a sharp juxtaposition against the ugly burn of hell currently suffocating the beach.

Patrick thrust one arm up and sent the coins skyward like shooting stars returning to space. They disappeared into the low-hanging clouds, bright flashes of sheet lightning turning the gray sky white in areas. Patrick blinked colored spots out of his eyes and thought about what Skuld had said in the filth of Ginnungagap.

Payment for the dead.

He wasn't dead, but it didn't matter. Nothing mattered in war except survival.

Patrick made a fist and yanked his arm down, as if he were

pulling down the sky. His magic burned weakly through his soul as he focused on the command to *strike*.

The borrowed magic from gods in the coins, guided by his own weakened magic, returned to Earth in the form of lightning.

Powerful bolts crashed down onto the beach with ground-shaking power. Patrick squeezed his eyes shut, but that wasn't enough to block out the searing brightness of the attack. Foreign power cascaded through his soul, tearing through scarred-over metaphysical channels that could no longer handle the overload.

Ozone burned hot in Patrick's nose when he screamed, every strand of hair standing on end as the lightning storm decimated the beach around him. The borrowed power of gods cut through him, and he had to let it because it was the only way any of them were getting out of this mess alive.

With an ear-popping *boom*, thunder rolled over the beach, vibrating though his body. Patrick stumbled forward, the world coming back in stages, looking more like an old photograph negative than sharp reality. He looked down at where sand used to be and only saw twisted white glass formed out of a lightning strike.

Gone were the soultakers, either burned down to ash that rain washed away or dragged into a retreat by Hades and what was left of the Dominion Sect acolytes. The borrowed power of gods had been enough to drive them back and cauterize the rip in the veil. How long before Hades returned was anyone's guess.

Patrick felt hollowed out, the world tilting badly. It took him a moment to realize it was him, not the horizon, as his legs gave out. He crashed to the ground, tasting blood, practically breathing it. His fingers skittered over hot glass, entire body shaking as he coughed.

Warm arms wrapped around his torso and hauled him upright. "Patrick!"

Jono's voice sounded far away through the ringing in his ears. Patrick closed his eyes, the sound of thunder nearly drowning everything out as he slumped against Jono.

"Hades?" Patrick managed to say, tongue thick in his mouth and not working right.

"Gone."

Pain threatened to rip open his chest, shock not enough to overcome it. Patrick reached for his magic and found a raw, gaping hole where it should have been in his damaged soul. He took a breath and let himself fall into darkness, somehow knowing Jono would catch him in the end.

14

Patrick went limp in Jono's arms, and he tried not to panic. He could hear Patrick's heart beating too fast for comfort, but the mage was alive. Blinking raindrops out of his eyes, Jono gathered Patrick into his arms and got to his feet.

Jono looked down at Patrick's too-pale face, head lolling against his shoulder. His dark red hair was plastered to his skull, the water running down his cheeks looking like tears. He felt too cold to Jono's heightened senses, and all Jono wanted to do right then was get Patrick somewhere safe.

Nadine ran across the blasted sand, and when she reached for Patrick, Jono couldn't help but take a step back. He didn't bother trying to choke back his growl.

She scowled. "Let me see him."

"He's cold. We need to get him out of the rain," Jono argued.

"And I need to do a field check, so hold still."

Jono allowed Nadine to do a brief check on Patrick, fighting against the instinct to find shelter. Emma and her pack were on high alert, keeping an eye on the damaged area of the beach they stood in. Leon had Tyler's arm slung over his shoulder. The sorcerer looked absolutely exhausted, but he was standing on his own two feet. That was a far cry from Patrick's condition.

Nadine pulled her hand away from Patrick, the violet glow at her fingertips fading away. "He's suffering from magical burnout. We need to go to ground."

"We can go to my apartment," Marek said.

Jono unclenched his teeth, anger riding his voice. "We wouldn't be in this bloody situation if you had just stayed *home* in the first place, Marek."

Hazel eyes washed out to a bright white, Marek's voice and eyes no longer his own. *"Our vessel came here because we told him to. This had to happen. This is the only way."*

"What way?" Nadine demanded. "Why have us do this?"

Fate had no further answers to give.

Marek blinked his eyes, the white disappearing. He shook his head hard, mouth twisting in pain and self-recrimination. "I'm sorry. I'm *sorry*. I didn't have a choice."

Sage took his hand in hers, giving it a comforting squeeze. "It's all right."

Jono held his tongue, knowing his anger wouldn't find the correct target right now. Skuld, or whichever of the Norns who controlled Marek's sight, had their reasons for drawing them out here. Jono had never been at the mercy of gods the way Marek was, and Patrick seemed to be, but he had a feeling that would change.

"We need to go," Nadine said.

"Where?" Jono asked.

Nadine ignored his question and went to retrieve Patrick's rifle where Jono had dropped it in the sand. "The wolf pack needs to get out of here and stay out of sight."

"The cops will need a statement," Sage said.

"They aren't getting one here." Nadine slung Patrick's rifle over her shoulder and jerked her head toward the stairs leading back to the property. "The seer can come with us."

Emma and Leon shared a single glance before Leon raised his voice. "Let's go. We're heading home."

Nadine headed up the stairs first, the way slippery. Jono was right behind her, Patrick deadweight in his arms. They passed through the destroyed backyard and entered the mansion. The werecreatures they'd left behind in the house earlier were no longer in half-shifted forms. Two were human while a third had fully shifted, the monstrous wolf growling at their approach from behind Nadine's shield.

"Shift, and head home," Emma snapped.

Nadine snapped her fingers, and the shields vanished. Jono followed her back outside into the rain. She immediately sprinted into a run and he easily kept up, holding Patrick tight in his arms. He could hear Emma, Marek, and Sage running behind him while everyone else started getting into the cars parked in the long driveway.

They ran for where they'd parked the SUV down the street. Jono could hear sirens off in the far distance, his enhanced hearing picking it up through the sound of the storm. "Cops."

"Not my problem," Nadine tossed over her shoulder.

Officer Lee and his partner had listened to Patrick's order and stayed in position. The two men were still alive. Officer Lee tried to flag them down for an explanation, but Nadine shook her head as she pelted past.

"We're leaving!" she yelled. "Do *not* follow us."

When they reached the SUV, Nadine hauled open the side door, and Jono carefully climbed into the far back seat with Patrick in his arms. He let Sage and Marek have the two middle seats while Emma claimed the front passenger seat.

"There's a field med-kit in the trunk," Nadine said to Jono before closing the car door. She hurried to the driver's side and got in, smacking her hand against the roof of the vehicle. Violet light flashed through the framework of the SUV.

Jono ignored everyone else in the car in favor of Patrick. He reached behind the back seat to the tiny trunk space and hauled over a gray rugged case with a red cross marked on it. He opened it and dug out an emergency foil blanket folded up inside a small plastic bag. Jono shoved it between his hip and the seat before he began stripping Patrick out of his soaked clothes. Patrick was cold in a way that Jono didn't like. Getting him warm would require body heat, and Jono had plenty to spare.

He got Patrick stripped down to his underwear, long, pale legs stretched over Jono's. His breath against Jono's neck was cool in a way it shouldn't be. Jono yanked off his own shirt and gathered Patrick close before tearing open the bag containing the emergency foil blanket. He shook it out over Patrick and tucked it around the both of them. He kept Patrick's dagger within easy reach. In the time he'd known Patrick, Jono had never seen the mage without it.

Jono wasn't paying anyone else any attention, too busy trying to rub warmth back into Patrick's arms under the blanket, when the SUV was hit.

The crackling boom of the explosion poured hellfire around the shape of the vehicle as Nadine fought to keep control. Jono braced himself and Patrick to keep them both from falling off the back seat.

"What the fuck?" he snarled.

The brakes squealed as they rocked to a hard halt, hellfire dripping off the SUV as Nadine's shield held strong against the attack.

"*Shit*," Nadine said with feeling.

Jono held Patrick tighter, squinting through the windshield at the person who had appeared a little ways down the street in front of the SUV. The man looked to be about his age, tall and well-built, with black concentric circles tattooed into the palms of his hands that were thrust their way. Blond hair was shaved close to his skull, revealing more rune tattoos inked into his skin there. The hate in his brown eyes made Jono's mouth curl.

"Who the fuck is that?" he demanded.

"Zachary Myers," Nadine said.

The name meant nothing to Jono, but he didn't like the stress he could hear in Nadine's voice. "Is this Zachary bloke going to be a problem?"

"Yeah."

"Can't you fight him?" Emma asked.

Nadine tightened her fingers around the steering wheel. "Maybe, but I don't have a strong affinity for offensive magic. Patrick would have a better shot."

"He's *unconscious*," Jono reminded her angrily. "He's already saved our arses once today, so maybe now it's your turn."

Nadine opened her mouth to argue, but before she got a word out, something slammed into where the mage stood and exploded with all the fury of a sun going nova. Jono squeezed his eyes shut and turned his face away, bright spots burning across his vision. The violet glare of Nadine's shield expanded outward from the frame of the SUV, rippling against the concussive force from the explosion.

"I definitely should've brought the grenade launcher," Nadine said, sounding wistful.

Jono's vision repaired itself in a few seconds. Blinking his eyes open, all he saw was a crater in the middle of the street where the magic user had stood, wispy fog twisting through the smoke.

"What was that?" Emma demanded.

"Military grade strike."

"Is he dead?" Marek asked, knuckling one eye.

Nadine shook her head and drew the shield back into the SUV again. "If only. That fucker doesn't die easily."

"Then where is he?"

Jono could see Nadine's eyes darting back and forth in the rearview mirror. "If there's no body, then it could have been an illusion. Either way, I should've known Ethan would have left a rearguard. That's my mistake. I'm sorry."

She conjured up a mageglobe, the violet sphere flickering above the steering wheel. Jono wasn't sure what spell she cast, but while he couldn't see it, he could sense her magic. Nadine's was cleaner than Patrick's by far; stronger, too.

"Anything?" Emma asked in a tense voice.

"No. I can't sense any magical threat in the vicinity," Nadine said.

Jono tightened his arms around Patrick as a motorcycle roared up beside the SUV, its driver and passenger both clad in black Kevlar-lined leather clothes and helmets with reflective face covers. The woman had a grenade launcher resting on her shoulder, red runes carved into the metal body of the weapon. Jono figured it wasn't a standard-issued kind of weapon.

Nadine hit a button to roll down her window a little bit. "I think we're in the clear, but keep an eye out. We'll follow you."

The driver nodded his head, the helmet bobbing up and down, before the motorcycle tore off again. Nadine slammed her foot down on the gas pedal and maneuvered the SUV around the crater.

"Are we taking Patrick to a hospital?" Marek asked.

"We can't risk it."

"Then I'll call Victoria to help him. She's a healer. Just tell me where she should meet us."

"Ginnungagap."

"Are you serious?" Jono growled.

Nadine glanced back at him in the rearview mirror. "You got a better idea?"

He didn't.

The drive back to Manhattan was taken up by Jono's worry for Patrick. Despite the foil blanket retaining his body heat to share it with Patrick, the younger man's skin was still cool to the touch. Jono didn't know anything about magical burnout, but he knew shock was never a good thing for the body. Jono listened to Patrick breathe, but he never woke up. He tucked Patrick's head under his chin, flattening a hand over the scars on his chest.

Please, Jono thought. *Please be all right.*

By the time they finally pulled down the small alley next to Ginnungagap, Jono was desperate to get Patrick the care he so obviously needed.

Sage hauled open the side door, still dressed in her bikini from the beach. She looked out of place, but the people walking by on the sidewalk at the mouth of the alleyway ignored them.

"Look-away ward," Nadine explained as she got out of the SUV. "No one will pay us any attention. Let's get Patrick inside."

The rain was still coming down, but Nadine cast a shield over Jono as he got out with Patrick in his arms, the dagger in its sheath dangling from one hand. Water sloughed off the invisible barrier, a kindness he nodded silent thanks for.

The motorcycle riders were already walking inside. Emma caught the door to keep it open, ushering everyone out of the storm. Jono stepped inside, that same chill as before from the other night making his shoulders tighten. Whatever magic was in this building, it wasn't a comfortable place to be.

Ginnungagap looked different. Most of the trash and debris had been cleared off to one side of the building. Heavy-duty crates were stacked against one cleared-out wall. Lights hanging from extension cords provided much-needed illumination. The place still didn't look clean, and Jono still wasn't certain this was the best place to bring Patrick.

The woman took off her motorcycle helmet, shaking out her black curls. Jono was unsurprised to see Carmen had been the one wielding the grenade launcher. Her glamour faded away, revealing the curled horns of her kind and eyes with their red pinprick pupils.

The driver made everyone's jaw drop except for Nadine's.

"Tell your Fates I don't appreciate their methods," Lucien said, staring at Marek.

"You're awake," Emma said faintly, eyes gone wide in her face.

"*How* are you awake and running around in sunlight? You're a vampire!"

"Daywalker," Jono said flatly. "Thought you lot were only legends?"

Jono wanted to punch the mocking smile right off Lucien's face. "Some stories are true, wolf."

"We got a witch coming by to check over Patrick. You can't be here when she arrives," Nadine said to Lucien.

Lucien slanted her a hard look. "You forget your place."

"I don't have time to argue, Lucien. We're two days away from summer solstice, that was *Zachary Myers* you tried to execute, and we need Patrick able to fight. The government doesn't know you're here and I'd like to keep rumors to a minimum. So please let us stay here, and just hide when the witch comes around so she doesn't see you."

Lucien's expression seemed carved from stone, and Jono wondered if they'd have to go back out into the storm. He didn't trust this building and the power it seemed to hold. Every instinct he had was yelling that it wasn't *safe*, but right now, Ginnungagap was their only hope to stay hidden, according to Nadine.

Patrick seemed to trust her. Jono supposed he'd have to trust Nadine as well, but he wasn't letting Patrick out of his sight.

"The old office area has a couch," Lucien finally said.

Nadine nodded. "Thank you."

Jono took that as permission given and made his way to the rear of the warehouse, where the previous owner had built out small, portable-like offices. His nose twitched at the smell of garbage, mold, and the buildup of dust in the warehouse. The place needed a thorough scrubbing and he didn't hold out much hope for a clean place to tend to Patrick.

Tiny sparks of light drifted ahead of him through the open door of the first office. Nadine's witchlights gave him more light to see by, brightening the space inside the main office. The sofa in question was broken-down and dirty, with holes chewed through by rats. Jono stopped in the doorway and looked over his shoulder at Emma.

"Call Leon. Tell him to bring a bed or sofa from your place," Jono ordered.

Emma peered around him at the garbage in the office and made a face. "On it. I'll tell him to bring us some clothes as well. I'll need to step outside to get signal."

"We'll be fine."

Jono turned around and headed back to the cleared area of the warehouse. Nadine gave him a questioning look upon his return.

"Not using the couch?" she asked.

"I wouldn't let a cat birth kittens on that thing. We're bringing our own furniture," he said.

"Should've asked first," Lucien said.

Jono leveled an unimpressed look at the vampire. "This might be your territory, but I don't trust your intentions toward Patrick."

"Still pissed I touched what you think is yours?"

"Keep your hands to yourself, or next time I'll rip them off." Jono smiled, fangs digging into his lips. "With my teeth."

Jono didn't care it was Lucien he was threatening. If the vampire threatened Patrick again, he'd do his best to rid the planet of the bastard. Lucien didn't seem impressed, but Jono didn't care. He might not have a pack, nor Lucien's reputation, but like fuck would he cower before the vampire.

"If you don't like the accommodations, you can leave," Carmen said with a disdainful sniff.

"Not with Ethan and Hades out there looking for us," Nadine said.

Carmen shook her head as she unzipped her formfitting Kevlar-lined leather jacket. "Hiding isn't going to stop them. It never has."

Sage touched Jono on the shoulder, and he looked over at her. Her face tipped upward so she could look him in the eyes. "Sit. You need to keep Patrick warm. I'll stand guard."

Jono's eyes flicked down to the artifact Sage wore, the turquoise pendant with its embedded fae magic bright against her tanned skin. It wouldn't stop her from shifting into her weretiger form, and Jono had seen her fight before. He trusted her to guard them until he could join the fight.

Nodding, Jono settled onto the floor in a cross-legged position, carefully repositioning Patrick so the foil blanket covered his cool body as much as possible. He couldn't tell if Patrick was getting warmer now that they were out of the storm, but he hoped so.

Nadine knelt beside him and touched one hand to the foil blanket, magic flowing from her fingertips into the material. Warmth grew around them as the heat charm settled into the foil blanket. Even through her magic he could smell the bitterness of Patrick's, faint as it was. The smell was part of his scent, and Jono took a deep breath, keeping it in his lungs.

"Ta, love," Jono grunted.

Nadine glanced at him. "It's not the first time Patrick has hit burnout. He'll be all right once we get him stabilized."

"I thought he couldn't tap a ley line? Did he try? Is that why he's like this?"

"He didn't tap a ley line. He can't. The coins were gifts from the gods." Nadine studied Jono with tired eyes. "The only things the gods have ever given Patrick are weapons. Somehow, I don't think you're any different."

Jono didn't know how to react to that statement. "There's more coins back at his flat. He didn't take all of them with us today."

"I'll go retrieve them."

"Patrick set a threshold around the place."

Nadine stood up, waving aside his words. "That won't be a problem. He always grants me access when he lays them down."

Some part of Jono—the wolf part that had taken years for him to be comfortable acknowledging—didn't like the thought of Nadine walking into his territory. It didn't matter that the flat wasn't his and that Patrick was only staying there temporarily.

Right now, that was Patrick's place of residence, his home, and Jono didn't want anyone he didn't know going into it.

Jono watched Nadine warily approach Lucien. He couldn't smell her fear, not with her shields up, but he could read the distrust in her body. Lucien seemed amused more than anything else, the uncaring attitude of an apex predator seeping through. Nadine might be a mage, but Lucien had tricks up his sleeves Jono would need to look out for.

Lucien put his motorcycle helmet back on and headed outside with Nadine. Emma darted inside before the door could close, wringing water out of her thick hair. She headed their way, leaving wet footprints behind her.

"Leon and the others made it back home. He'll be here as soon as he can, but he has to dodge the police," she said.

"Why are the police at our building?" Marek asked.

"Because we didn't know where you were. Casale sent his people to every address they had on file for you," Jono explained.

Most of his anger toward Marek had disappeared at the revelation the Fates had forced his hand today. What was left was directed solely at the gods currently fucking with everyone's lives.

Marek chewed on his bottom lip before sitting down beside Jono. Sage and Emma shifted positions, standing between them and Carmen, who seemed to find their situation *amusing* if the look on her face was anything to go by.

Jono itched to rip it off her face.

"I'm sorry this is happening," Marek said quietly.

Jono shook his head. "It's not your fault."

Marek reached out and tucked a corner of the foil blanket more securely around Patrick's body. "Feels like it is."

Jono was too on edge right now to soothe Marek's feelings. Most of his attention was reserved for Patrick, who still hadn't woken up. Jono bent his head, pressing his nose against now-dry red hair, breathing in the smell of rain and magic and the bitter notes of hell.

Jono's awareness of his patron god pulsed deep inside his own soul. He wasn't one for prayer, but Jono couldn't help the words he directed at Fenrir.

Please let Patrick be all right.

In the depths of his soul, Jono thought he felt an answering growl that echoed in his bones.

15

Patrick woke up slow, feeling like he'd come off the tail end of a weeklong bender. The pain in his body was a dull ache, seeping through sore muscles. His mouth was dry, teeth sticking to the inside of his cheeks, tongue glued to the roof of his mouth, and it tasted like something had died in it. He needed to piss—badly.

The hollow emptiness in his soul reminded him too much of the months after the Thirty-Day War. Days spent in the hospital and then rehab, his magic sucked dry and slow to return, only never to his original strength. His ability to tap into external magic had been forever damaged in the form of metaphysical scars lacerating his soul.

Some part of his brain knew he wasn't in the past, but fighting back the panic was hard, and reorienting was difficult. The first thing Patrick became solidly aware of was warmth. He was tucked close to a warm body, strong arms wrapped around his own. His nose was pressed to a hard chest, skin touching skin along his entire body. Patrick realized he was naked and weaponless, but the panic he knew he should feel wasn't coming.

A warm hand stroked down his back. "You awake?"

The deep voice rumbled through the chest his nose was pressed against. Patrick struggled to open his eyes but couldn't. Still, he knew that voice, even if it felt like it took forever to get his tongue to work.

"Jono?"

Cool air washed over his face as the blanket Patrick wasn't even aware of covering him was pulled down past his bare shoulders. He was rolled onto his back, one strong hand framing his face.

"I need you to open your eyes for me," Jono said, his breath ghosting over Patrick's mouth.

"Careful of his IV," a woman said.

Something tugged in the back of his hand, and the faint pinch from a needle made Patrick grimace. He took a breath and forced his eyes open, blurry vision filled by Jono's wolf-bright blue eyes. The astringent smell Patrick associated with a hospital wasn't present. In fact, it smelled like a garbage dump, despite the bed he was lying in.

"You with me?" Jono asked, pulling back a little.

Patrick blinked slowly, gaze drifting past Jono. He stared blearily up at a dirty warehouse ceiling. Dull sunlight cut through cracks in the boarded-up windows, giving the place a gray cast to it. The sound of rain hitting the roof was strangely muffled, and Patrick thought he could hear the drip of water from a leak some-where close by.

He dragged his hand out from beneath the blanket, pressing his thumb against the throbbing in his right temple. The IV tubing slid down his arm a little, the medical tape making his skin itch.

"Ginnungagap?" he asked, voice coming out raspy.

Jono ran his hand through Patrick's hair. "Yeah, Pat. Had to go to ground."

Patrick remembered the fight at the beach with a clarity that made him wince. As much as his aching head and body and drained soul made him want to pass out again, he didn't have that option.

"I need a sitrep," Patrick said.

"In a minute," an unfamiliar voice that brooked no argument said. "Let me check your vitals first."

A pretty face came into his line of sight. Thick black hair was tied back in a functional braid, her medium brown skin offset by pale blue scrubs with a pink-and-yellow flower pattern printed on them. The woman was very obviously a nurse and not one to give in to patients.

She gave him a friendly smile though, resting her hand on his forehead. "I'm Victoria Alvarez. I'm an RN witch at Mount Sinai."

Delicate magic scraped through Patrick's aura. He instinctively tried to raise his shields, but the absence of power made his stomach roil. Clenching his teeth, he breathed through his nose as he tried to get his stomach to settle.

"I have a tincture that will help get rid of the nausea and headache. I need you to sit up though," Victoria said.

Jono sat up, then helped Patrick to sit up. He hunched forward, the blanket pooling around his waist. "Didn't think Lucien had beds available here."

"He didn't," Nadine said as she approached. "Jono had Emma haul furniture here for you to sleep in."

Patrick lifted his head, watching as Nadine settled herself at the foot of the queen-sized bed. Victoria came back with a plastic bottle full of a dark green liquid. The drink looked like something sold in a health-nut smoothie store that only served organic everything and where a six-ounce glass cost twelve dollars.

"I know it doesn't taste great, but it'll help with your physical symptoms." Victoria quirked a tired, sad smile at him as she passed the bottle over. "I can't do anything about your soul."

"Didn't ask you to," Patrick muttered.

"Drink up."

Patrick made a face. In his experience, tinctures always tasted disgusting. He still chugged it down as fast as he could, coughing after the last mouthful was swallowed, hoping his stomach wouldn't rebel.

He handed the empty bottle back to Victoria before meeting Nadine's gaze. "Sitrep. And clothes. I need clothes."

"I'll get the bag," Jono said.

He got out of the bed, and Patrick couldn't stop himself from staring. Jono was naked, utterly unselfconscious about his body being on display. Patrick distantly felt it was unfair he couldn't really enjoy the sight, not with an audience. Exhibitionism had never been his thing even if werecreatures had no qualms about nudity within their packs.

Jono bent down and picked up a black duffel bag from the ground. Unzipping it, he pulled out a stack of clothes that he set beside Patrick before pulling out a set for himself. Patrick made a questioning sound in the back of his throat.

"I went back to your apartment and picked up some supplies. Emma and Leon brought stuff for Jono and the others staying here," Nadine explained.

"Who else is here?" Patrick asked.

Jono pulled on a pair of underwear, then yanked on his jeans, zipping them up. "Marek and Emma. Sage had to work today, and so did Leon."

Patrick rubbed gingerly at his face. "What day is it?"

"Monday. You were unconscious for almost twenty-four hours." Nadine shifted on the bed, digging into her front pocket and coming up with a familiar handful of gold. She poured the remaining Greek coins on the blanket between them. "I brought you these."

Patrick stared at the coins, not realizing he was grinding his teeth until Jono stroked his fingers against his jaw. Patrick blinked, gaze sliding toward Jono.

"You'll give yourself a headache that way," Jono said.

His words were enough to distract Patrick from trying to break his own teeth. Jono placed Patrick's dagger, still in its sheath and attached to its field straps, in his left hand. Patrick curled his fingers around the leather-encased weapon and took a shuddering breath. He looked up, meeting Jono's gaze, before turning his attention to Nadine.

"Tell me," he said.

Nadine settled her hands on her knees. "We're FUBAR. Ethan is definitely leading the charge, and he brought Zachary into the field with him. You know what that means."

He closed his eyes, hand tightening around his dagger. He didn't *want* to know what that meant, with those two men on the field, but he couldn't escape the truth staring him in the face.

Patrick couldn't escape his past.

"We got you and Marek out of the Hamptons and back to Manhattan with Lucien's help. I sent the sorcerer you had guarding Marek back to the PCB. I didn't want him to know where we were going."

Patrick opened his eyes when he felt Victoria touch the IV in the back of his hand. She expertly removed the tape and needle, pressing a gauze pad over the small hole it left behind.

"Keep pressure here," Victoria said.

Patrick cleared his throat. "Thanks, but I think you've done all you can. You should get going. How much do I owe you?"

"Marek pays my bills. You don't owe me anything."

She waved goodbye and walked away. Low voices caught his ear, and Patrick looked off to the side where Emma and Marek sat at a rickety card table some yards away. They spoke quickly with Victoria before the nurse left Ginnungagap, umbrella in hand.

Knowing that they'd been keeping watch was comforting in a way, but that they might have seen his scars left Patrick a little unsettled. He let go of his dagger and reached for his clothes. Getting dressed took some effort, but he had practice in working through damage like this. It wasn't easy, and it hurt, but Patrick had already spent too much time out of the fight.

"Your shields are down," Nadine said quietly.

Patrick dragged on one of the black T-shirts that had been in his suitcase. "My shields are fucked."

He could sense the emptiness where his shields used to sit, the anchor points of the wards fractured from heavenly power. Damaged magic or not, Patrick still had a job to do.

Patrick pulled on his underwear and then his jeans, not caring if anyone looked now that the scars on his chest were covered. He'd spent a good chunk of his life in the military where communal showers didn't allow for privacy. After yanking on his boots, he strapped his dagger into place.

He was thinking about getting to his feet when the entrance to Ginnungagap opened up and Carmen sauntered inside. She had a MacBook cradled in one arm and a large plastic bag filled with takeout hanging from her hand. Both were kept dry from the rain by the large umbrella she tossed aside.

"I see you're finally awake," Carmen said.

"Where's Lucien?" Patrick asked.

"Around" came the airy response as she shed her glamour. That otherworldly power filled her aura, pressing outward. Patrick could've done without the sexual energy though, especially since his shields were broken.

Carmen wore a leather miniskirt and thigh-high glossy black boots. The red halter top she had on matched the red pupils of her dark eyes. Patrick shook his head as he finally pushed himself to his feet, feeling a little light-headed. He watched as Carmen approached the card table where she dropped the bag of food and pointed at him.

"You're useless right now, so eat," she ordered.

Patrick ignored her. "You got a toilet around here, or do I just use the nearest wall?"

"Portable," Nadine said, pointing behind him.

Patrick looked over his shoulder at the large porta potty someone had hauled in. Walking on unsteady legs, he went to use it. The thing smelled like a sewer, but Patrick didn't care. He closed the door, undid his jeans, and aimed his dick at the dirty urinal until the pressure on his bladder eased.

At least Victoria didn't give me a catheter, he thought to himself. He fucking hated those things.

When Patrick finished, he washed his hands in the tiny plastic sink near the door. No paper towels were in the dispenser, so Patrick wiped his hands on his jeans before leaving. He was unsurprised to find Jono waiting for him right outside, despite the horrible smell.

Jono escorted him to where everyone was gathered around the card table. Someone had delivered metal folding chairs, and Patrick claimed one of them. His stomach growled at the smell of hamburgers, and fries but he knew he needed to work first.

"Where's my phone?" he asked.

Jono set it down on the table in front of him. It was nice not having to scramble around for everything on his own.

Don't get used to it, Patrick told himself.

His stay here in New York City was temporary. He only hoped he didn't end up in a grave at the end of the case.

Patrick powered on his cell phone and checked the time first. The clock on the display read 1512, and he was of the opinion someone should've woken him up sooner. He had no signal though, the magic in Ginnungagap's walls interfering with the nearest cell tower.

"Be right back," Patrick sighed as he got back to his feet.

"Eat first. Plan for war later," Jono said with a frown.

"You lose your lunch that way."

Patrick headed for the entrance, picking up Carmen's discarded umbrella along the way. Hauling open the door that led to the alley, Patrick opened the umbrella and stepped outside into the downpour. The threshold wrapped around the building grated against his soul, and he hissed at the discomfort. A couple of seconds later, Jono and Nadine joined him outside. Jono took the umbrella from him and hefted it higher, giving them all room to huddle underneath it. Nadine cast a shield around them to help keep out the rain and the wind.

As Patrick's cell phone reconnected to the nearest tower, it began to vibrate with numerous notifications. He had nearly fifty missed calls, about as many text messages, and it looked like his voicemail was full. Patrick didn't bother with any of the messages.

"Have you been in contact with Setsuna?" Patrick asked Nadine.

"We're dark. I don't know her burner number," she said, crossing her arms over her chest.

Patrick went through the usual protocol of calling Setsuna on her burner phone. On the last call into the number, he switched it to speaker. He doubted the werewolves around him would keep their ears to themselves, but Nadine needed to hear what was being said.

The line picked up on the second ring. Patrick knew Setsuna wouldn't have picked up at all if she wasn't in a secure location.

"Status?" Setsuna asked in a low voice.

"Alive. Not functional. I have my backup, and the immortals want me to fight. We're a day away from the Dominion Sect's latest attempt at stealing a godhead. They have Zeus."

"There's a warrant out for Rachel's arrest."

"So she's officially labeled Dominion Sect now? You find any evidence to make your charges stick this time?"

"We're working on it."

"I would work on a bullet to the head over an arrest if you find her. She's working with Ethan, after all. The murders paired with the soultakers and a missing immortal? Hermes was right. New York City is a sacrificial altar."

Nadine leaned closer to the speaker pickup and raised her voice. "Zachary Myers was on the field in the Hamptons. So was Hades. If Zachary is helping Ethan cast the spell like last time, we're going to need someone who can counter high-level blood magic. They should be a mage, but tell them not to tap a ley line.

When I tapped one yesterday, I noticed the currents were wilder than they should be. Have you had any reports on the stability of the nexus below New York City?"

"Nothing recent. Nothing I would trust, at this juncture," Setsuna replied.

"You need to get someone down here to check, someone you *trust*. I'd do it, but if the nexus and ley lines leading into it are compromised, then I'm going to need to save my strength to help build breakwaters in the ley lines later."

"If the nexus is compromised, then it's already too late." Patrick rubbed at his face tiredly. The dull ache in his body was fading faster than it would if he hadn't taken Victoria's tincture, but she couldn't cure exhaustion. "We can't trust the nexus will remain stable. They've had six months to fuck around with it under Rachel's watch."

"She's a witch though. How would she be able to do that without anyone noticing?" Jono wanted to know.

Nadine shrugged. "The SOA has mages on its payroll. I wouldn't be surprised to find some of them were dirty."

"You speak as if we're the only agency that has been infiltrated" was Setsuna's flat response.

"We didn't call to argue about which agency is cleaner. The SOA and the PIA will both lose under that criteria," Patrick said.

Setsuna steered the conversation back on track. "What is your status, Collins?"

"If you're asking if I can pull off the same stunt as last time, let's go with no. It doesn't help that we don't have the military as backup."

"It may come down to that in the end. A pity we can't pull them in now."

"You can't call in the military on a *what-if* basis," Nadine muttered.

Patrick rolled his eyes. "I'm sure the governor of New York will *love* needing to send in the National Guard for a federal agency's fuckup."

"Your attitude isn't helping this situation any," Setsuna said.

"Ask me if I fucking care." The line went quiet, neither side speaking up. Patrick sighed heavily and pinched the bridge of his nose. "In case anyone hasn't thought about it yet, because I doubt Rachel had clearance to enter the base, you need to do an audit of the Repository."

Setsuna's voice was cold when she spoke again. "I'm aware of that. An audit is already being implemented."

The Repository was housed in a highly classified remote detachment of Edwards Air Force Base known by its vernacular name of Area 51. The Department of the Preternatural, the Supernatural Operations Agency, and the Preternatural Intelligence Agency all had equal control over the Repository. It held magical and supernatural relics of the past and newly made ones from modern times, all of them drawn from one myth or another.

Every country on Earth had an equivalent of the United States' Repository. A build-up of magical weapons and artifacts had happened during the two World Wars and ramped up during the Cold War. Weapons of high magical strength were usually under the express control of governments. No one ever really knew what items each country had under their control. That information was always highly classified, but it didn't stop people from trying to infiltrate the heavily guarded locations across the world.

It certainly hadn't stopped Ethan and the Dominion Sect during the Thirty-Day War. It wasn't until months after that fight that someone even thought to check the Repository in the United States for any discrepancies. Patrick had heard rumors of missing items, though he didn't know for sure what they were.

By law, Patrick's dagger should have been confiscated and listed in the United States' Repository since it was made by gods. Since receiving it, Patrick had played the weapon off as nothing more than a well-crafted artifact but nothing truly out of the ordinary. Outside of Setsuna, Nadine, and a handful of others he trusted, no one knew about the dagger's true origins. He knew if it had been placed in the Repository after the Thirty-Day War, then it would be in Ethan's hands by now.

"Send whatever backup you can trust to help us hold the line. Put them in touch with Chief Giovanni Casale. We'll handle the frontal attack," Patrick said.

If Setsuna was going to argue, no one heard what she had to say. Patrick ended the call with her and then dialed Casale, putting it back on speaker again. Casale picked up almost immediately.

"Where the hell have you been?" Casale said.

"Out," Patrick replied.

"In more ways than one," Nadine said under her breath.

Casale didn't seem to hear her. "You didn't answer my question."

Patrick leaned tiredly into Jono's warmth and didn't shake off the arm the taller man wrapped around his waist. He steadfastly ignored the raised eyebrow Nadine directed his way.

"You sound like you've missed me."

Casale blew out a heavy breath, the pickup turning it into a quick crackle of static. "Like a nail through my skull. I need answers."

"We had to go to ground. I hear Rachel has a warrant out for her arrest. Does she have her face slapped on a Most Wanted poster yet? Please tell me she does."

Nadine rolled her eyes. "Have there been any more murders?"

"Who are you?" Casale snapped.

"Backup," Patrick replied. "Let's not use names. She's doing me a favor by being here, but it's not technically legal."

"Collins—"

Patrick cut him off. "Look, Casale. I got Marek out of the mess on the beach, and believe me, he and I are going to have words about that. Arguing about what's already happened won't get us anywhere. We have a day, maybe less, until whatever spell is being cast will go off. Summer solstice is tomorrow. I need a sitrep, Casale. I need it *now*."

Casale was quiet for half a minute before he spoke again. "You told Tyler to hold his own against a group of mercenary magic users."

"I told him I was on the way."

"You're lucky my son knows what the hell he's doing when it comes to wards, or we wouldn't be talking."

"Your son had a good teacher," Nadine said. Coming from her, it was high praise. Casale didn't see it that way.

"His mother" was Casale's short reply. "Incidentally, she wanted me to tell you the reactionary storm is getting worse. Her high priestess has tasked the Crescent Coven with warning all magic users in the five boroughs to stay behind their wards and thresholds for the next two days."

Patrick made a face, wondering about Hera's generosity to mortals she didn't much care about. Her coven worshipped her, and she drew her power from their prayers, but it was nothing compared to what it once was. Gods needed religion to regain their strength and power. All they had now were stories in books, and some didn't even have that.

"Probably a good idea. We think the nexus is compromised."

Casale's job, coupled with him being married to a high-ranking witch, gave him enough of an understanding to know just how exceptionally fucked the situation was in relation to that statement.

"*Fuck*," Casale bit out. "What are you doing about it?"

"Director Abuku is sending someone to monitor it. She'll be reassigning SOA special agents to help with the problem."

"Considering it's your agency that royally fucked things up, I'm not inclined to trust whoever she sends our way."

"She sent me," Patrick said. "Am I suddenly not good enough for you now?"

"I never said I didn't trust you. I said I don't trust your agency."

"That's nice. Remember that week you gave me? It's not over yet. I need to get to work."

"I need updates."

"I'll call you."

Patrick hung up and tightened his grip on his phone. Nadine studied him with tired eyes, but it was Emma who spoke up first from where she stood inside the warehouse, propping open the heavy door with one foot.

"Are you done? Food is getting cold," Emma said.

As if right on cue, Patrick's stomach growled. Jono's hand on his hip tightened.

"Come on," Jono said, pulling him along as Nadine took down her shield. "Let's get you fed."

The wind chased them back inside Ginnungagap, the threshold making Patrick grit his teeth when they crossed over it. Jono somehow seemed to know something was off judging by the questioning look he gave Patrick.

"What's wrong?" Jono asked.

"What isn't wrong?" Patrick countered.

Marek had set out the food Carmen had delivered, the food boxes holding hamburgers and fries ready for anyone to claim. He was holding a hamburger in one hand and typing away with the other, his MacBook hooked up to a portable generator. Patrick didn't know where Carmen had disappeared to.

Patrick frowned at the setup. "Didn't think we got signal in here."

"We don't. I used a hotspot off my phone outside to download some stuff earlier. I'm working offline," Marek said, not looking up.

Jono pulled a folding chair back and gestured at it. "Sit. Eat."

For once, Patrick listened without arguing and sat down.

"Can your director be trusted to do the right thing?" Emma asked as she settled onto a metal folding chair.

Patrick opened the takeout container and popped a fry into his mouth. "Yes, but it's her methods that are questionable."

"Personal experience, I take it?"

"And then some." Patrick hesitated but opted for a bit of truth that Emma and Jono could smell. "I was Setsuna's ward for nine years. She means well, but it's more a means to an end for her."

"Can she fight against this Zachary bloke or send someone who can?" Jono asked.

"That was supposed to be my job."

"You've done enough, mate."

Patrick picked the top off his hamburger to get rid of the pickles. "It's never enough."

"Why?"

He suddenly wasn't hungry, but it felt like all the times in the field when he knew he needed to eat, needed to choke down some calories, but didn't want to. Patrick picked up his hamburger and took a bite, chewing slowly.

"What do you know about this?" Marek asked, directing his question to Nadine.

She shook her head. "It's not my story to tell."

Marek finally looked up, staring at Patrick. "You know who is behind the murders."

The statement fell between everyone like a rock. The hamburger suddenly tasted like rancid meat in Patrick's mouth. He had to force himself to swallow it down. "I didn't know for sure. Not until yesterday."

"Seriously?"

"I've seen this shit before, but living through it once doesn't count as evidence. We need proof that ties the perpetrators to the murders, and right now we don't have anything solid that will stand up in court beyond a reasonable doubt."

"So who wants us dead?"

Patrick thought about keeping his mouth shut, but too many

lives were on the line right now. He couldn't keep quiet in the face of those who were god-touched like he was.

"Ethan Greene."

Marek stopped typing. "I thought...rumor said he died at the end of the Thirty-Day War."

Patrick smiled grimly. "Rumors lie."

He should know. Patrick had started one or two of those rumors when he'd given his official report to the brass while holed up in a field hospital.

"If he's behind the murders, what makes you think you can stop him? And why wasn't Ethan identified for the public?" Emma wanted to know.

"Who here missed the fact that I got assigned this case last Thursday? The SOA didn't have solid evidence because Rachel was stonewalling. We still don't have any evidence that will link Ethan to the murders."

Marek started typing again. "Ethan was a former SOA special agent. Rachel tried to kill us on the beach. Your agency has a problem."

"You aren't the first one who's pointed that out," Patrick said irritably.

Nadine sighed. "The Dominion Sect is nearly impossible to weed out. Sometimes, in the grand scheme of things, it's better to keep your enemies closer."

"Is this the same Ethan we talked about over breakfast with Hera?" Jono said with a frown.

Nadine nearly choked on a fry. "Really? You broke bread with that bitch?"

"Not by choice," Patrick muttered.

Jono's gaze never wavered, but Patrick couldn't see any trace of judgment in his eyes. "She mentioned your family."

"Ethan isn't just the enemy," Carmen said as the succubus sauntered past the table. Her heels clicked loudly on the dirty cement floor as she headed for the door, phone in hand.

"Carmen," Patrick bit out warningly.

"You may as well come clean. Your father is the reason you owe a soul debt to the immortals and are in this position in the first place."

Patrick resolutely kept his eyes trained on his food, heart pounding in his chest so hard he wasn't sure he could take another bite. Jono's hand settled on the back of his neck, startling him badly. Those long fingers squeezed his neck gently, and Patrick glanced at Jono, feeling pinned to the chair by those bright eyes.

"You don't have to talk about it," Jono said in a low voice.

"If Ethan is—" Emma argued.

Jono shook his head, his eyes never leaving Patrick's. "Shut it, Em."

Surprisingly, she listened. Emma let out an irritated huff, but kept quiet. Jono reached over and nudged at Patrick's takeout box. "Eat. You need the calories."

The sound of the warehouse side door opening again had Patrick looking over his shoulder. Lucien stepped inside, pulling off his motorcycle helmet. Carmen greeted him with a kiss that wouldn't have looked out of place on a porn set. Lucien broke the kiss and started walking their way, his black eyes finding Patrick's.

"You're finally awake," Lucien said.

Patrick made a face. "You sound so disappointed by that fact."

Lucien's regard was never friendly, and Patrick was all too aware of what had happened the last time they were in the same place. Jono let go of Patrick and stood up, putting himself between the two of them. Patrick had to lean to the side in order to watch their interaction.

"Keep your distance," Jono warned.

"Or what?" Lucien said with a smirk. "This is not your territory."

"Ginnungagap? Maybe not. But who's to say it can't be?"

"Is that a challenge, wolf?"

"More like a warning. You aren't the only one mixing it up with gods."

Lucien studied Jono with unblinking eyes, the stillness of his body when not speaking creepy. "Ah. You actually hear your kind's patrons. You'd be one of the few these days."

"It's why they're both targets," Patrick said, turning around to pick up his hamburger again. "Him and Marek."

"A wolf and a useless seer. They'd be better off dead."

"Hey, now. I like living," Marek protested. "I've been working hard all morning to keep doing that."

Patrick blindly reached behind him to grab for Jono's hand, tugging the other man back to his vacant seat. "By doing what?"

"Trying to come up with a plan. Nadine has been helping." Marek searched for the last fry in his takeout box and ate it. "Skuld said she wasn't the only Fate looking for a way to win. So did Hades. I'm pretty sure their conflicting futures localizing around you are why I can't see a way out of this mess. Which means anything goes, really."

"Is it too late to eat my gun?" Patrick asked no one in particular.

Nadine kicked him in the ankle. "Have you been talking to your therapist?"

"Have you?"

"Bloody hell," Jono muttered under his breath.

Marek turned his MacBook around so everyone could see the screen. "I made a map of where all the murders happened because Nadine asked me to. Pretty sure I got the correct locations."

Patrick wiped his hands on a paper napkin before reaching for the computer and dragging it closer. The downloaded map of Manhattan had little black X marks dotting the island. He checked the placements against his memory of the case files and ended up adjusting one or two of them.

"Crude circle," Patrick said, tracing his finger through each murder location. "Hermes said the City itself was an altar. Ethan could've chosen to kill in any of the five boroughs, but he stayed in Manhattan."

Carmen picked up the remaining Greek coins from the bed, then walked over and dumped them on the table. "We saw what you called down onto the beach. Is there any power left inside these ones?"

Patrick picked up a coin and rolled it between his thumb and forefinger. He might have been drained dry of magic, but he could still sense the power inside that innocuous bit of gold. He looked at the map of Manhattan, eyes tracing the edges of the island where it met blue water.

They had ten coins left, and Patrick separated them out in pairs before marking the cardinal points on the map and drawing lines between them. The intersecting point was in Central Park.

"We need to contain the spell and choke off the nexus. We can use the coins to build a circle around Manhattan. The rivers will give us a natural barrier that can help shore up the borrowed magic," he said slowly.

"You think that's where the last sacrifice will happen?" Nadine asked, tapping at the spot in Central Park.

"I can guess, but nothing is certain where Ethan is concerned."

"It's a shame you didn't kill him in Cairo like you were supposed to," Lucien said bitingly. "I have shipments arriving today. We'll have enough weapons to maybe dent a soultaker or two, but that's only if the spell happens at night and my people can join the fight."

"Youssef and Estelle still don't want us or any other pack to have anything to do with you," Emma said. The frustrated tone in her voice was a clear *you have got to be fucking kidding me* sort. "That's an order I'm not following. You'll have my pack for the fight, Patrick. Twenty werewolves and one weretiger."

"And me," Marek piped up.

"No" came a chorus of voices around the table.

Marek scowled, opening his mouth to argue. Emma promptly clamped her hand over his mouth.

"You're staying here," she told him firmly. "We've run around on the whims of your visions enough this week. I need to know you're safe, and right now, Ginnungagap is the safest place you can be."

Jono stared at Patrick with defiant eyes. "I'm not staying here. Where you go, I go."

"Ethan is after you, and I have nothing left of my magic to keep you safe," Patrick argued.

"All the more reason for me to stay with you. That's what the Fates wanted, innit?"

"You're a target, Jono."

"Pot, kettle."

"They'd sacrifice you to power the spell. They want me dead because I can break it," Patrick said, breathing harshly through his nose. "Ethan is…he's my father by blood. I can break any spell he creates *because* of that connection. Your only recourse would be to die, and I don't want that on my conscience."

Forcing the words out felt like a confession of his sins, but there was no absolution given in the silence that followed. Jono only looked at Patrick with an unreadable expression on his face before he leaned forward.

"I'm not letting you do this alone," Jono told him, enunciating every word.

Then Jono kissed him, his words a vow that could've been binding if Patrick had any magic left to make it so. Except he didn't, but he wondered if it even mattered considering Jono's own connection to a god.

"We'll figure it out," Jono promised when he pulled away.

Patrick swallowed tightly, nodding a little at his words.

They had to, because if they didn't, New York City would end up how the Middle East once was—a place ravaged by hell.

16

"I can't believe Lucien smuggled a tank across the border on such short notice," Patrick said as he pried open another crate.

Packed carefully inside was another spelled M32 MGL grenade launcher. Patrick ran a finger across the runes etched into the metal, watching as they flared up briefly at his touch. He grimaced at the scrape of the magic against the gaping emptiness in his soul, but the runes reacting to touch proved the spell was intact.

"It's not military grade," Nadine grunted as she set down a second crate near the first. "Lucien left Irena in Texas when they came over the border. She had orders to retrieve a Lenco BearCat G3. The police in some small town in West Texas weren't using it."

Patrick looked across the warehouse at the shiny assault vehicle currently being equipped for a fight by several vampires. He caught sight of Irena's blonde head as the vampire conferred with Einar over a crate.

Irena was taller than Lucien even in the flat boots she wore and the youngest vampire he'd turned. Her age hadn't stopped her from becoming one of his cruelest. Lucien had pulled Irena out of a sex-trafficking ring in Eastern Europe decades ago. Ashanti had told him the story once, how Lucien stuck around in some city long enough for Irena to murder all the local men who'd paid for her unwilling services in front of her pimp. Then Irena killed him slowly under Lucien's guidance. Since then, Irena had been his most creative interrogator.

The story had been a lesson when he was younger, but all Patrick really took away from it was don't mess with Lucien's vampires. Unfortunately, they crossed paths more often than he liked these days.

Patrick closed the lid of the current crate and moved onto the one Nadine had carried over. It was smaller but still heavy, containing boxes of spelled bullets. He counted how many boxes were inside and matched the number to the list of supplies Lucien had given him. Lucien was only willing to allocate so much of his product to the fight ahead. The rest he intended to sell.

What they might lack in weaponry and artifacts, they made up for in brute strength. Emma and Leon had called in their pack hours ago, giving them Ginnungagap's location and orders to take a roundabout way to the warehouse. Most of them had arrived before sunset, while Lucien's vampires had come after. None of the Tempest pack were thrilled about working with vampires, but no one had argued. Their presence said a lot about how they felt where the New York City god pack was concerned.

Speaking of god packs, Patrick mused.

His attention returned to Jono, who was carrying two heavy crates their way without breaking a sweat. Jono hadn't strayed far from Patrick's side, especially when Lucien was present. It made Patrick feel safe, and that wasn't something he experienced often.

"You're drooling," Nadine said.

"Liar," Patrick said.

She just smirked at him before moving on to her next task. Jono set his crates down next to the others. Patrick watched the way his biceps flexed and then belatedly realized that his attraction was coming through his scent when Jono smirked at him. Patrick missed having his shields. Hell, he missed having his *magic*, but it would take days for it to fill his soul again.

Right now, they didn't have time to wait.

He absently trailed his hand along the dagger strapped to his thigh. At least he still had borrowed magic to rely on.

"Too bad we can't take a kip," Jono teased, jerking a thumb over his shoulder at the bed Patrick had woken up in earlier that afternoon.

"In that bed? With this audience? Hell no," Patrick said.

"Suppose you're right." Jono ran a hand over the top of a crate. "How does the SOA feel about you palling around with Lucien? Him being a wanted fugitive and all."

"Outside of the director, no one in the SOA is aware I know Lucien. Less than ten other people know about him, and more than half that number belongs to my old team in the Mage Corps. They all know how to keep a secret. Nadine and another PIA special agent out on the West Coast are the only other people who know, and I trust them."

Jono rested his hip against the stack of crates and crossed his arms over his chest. "Were you lot all military?"

"Yeah."

"No one will hear a word out of me."

Patrick may have only known Jono for less than a week, but something told him the older man knew how to keep a promise. "I'd rather the SOA didn't know anything about you at all."

Jono raised one eyebrow. "Not keen on you hanging around with werecreatures?"

"Dealing with the supernatural and preternatural is part of the job. I don't want the SOA to know about you because we're still digging up Dominion Sect double agents within our ranks."

"I'm not the one who needs looking after," Jono said after a moment. "Pretty sure that's you."

Patrick sighed heavily and scratched the back of his head.

"Normally my cases don't have so many immortals running around."

"Most people don't have any running about because they don't believe in them anymore."

Patrick looked Jono in the eye when he said, "We're not most people."

Jono nodded slowly. "No, we aren't."

"So you'll agree that since you're a target you'll keep Marek company here tonight?"

"Now I know you're taking the piss," Jono said, stepping closer. "Thought we had this plan of yours already sorted?"

"The plan consists of not dying. You'd accomplish that a lot better if you would—"

"I'm not leaving you."

The conviction in Jono's voice stopped Patrick's argument cold. His mouth snapped shut, teeth clacking together. He didn't know what to say in the face of Jono's refusal to walk away. All he could think about was the way he'd lived his own life, bound by the needs of the gods he was indebted to, and what it had cost him over the years.

"Don't let the Fates take control of your life, Jono. Marek doesn't have a choice, but you do," Patrick said quietly.

Jono reached out and trailed his fingers along the edge of Patrick's jaw, his touch warm, like it always was. "Guess we're just gonna have to murder the fuck out of the Dominion Sect bastards together, then, won't we?"

While Patrick could get behind that any day, he knew war was never easy. "You know our chances are shit, right?"

"Can't be much worse than waking up in hospital after a bad car crash with the werevirus running through your veins."

"Didn't take you for an optimist."

"I can be with the right motivation."

The filthy look Jono shot him made Patrick wish they were alone in his apartment with nothing to do tonight but fuck. Except there was a plan in the works that involved saving a city, and time wasn't on their side. They needed to choke off the nexus, deny whatever mages the Dominion Sect put in the field an external power source, get to the center of the spell, and break it apart.

In other words, Patrick needed to stop thinking with his dick and start using his brain.

"Let's get the go-bags put together," he said.

The go-bags full of stolen weaponry were for Lucien's vampires to use. The Tempest pack would shift into their animal forms once everyone was in position in Central Park tomorrow. The only problem was they didn't know *when* Ethan would begin casting the spell. If it happened in daylight, Lucien's vampires would be no help at all in the fight.

The NYPD was on alert, and the PCB had been notified that Central Park was the likely spell location. Patrick had argued with Casale about blocking access to the park. All that open green space was easier to fight in than an apartment building. It had taken pulling the federal card, but Patrick had gotten Casale to agree that they didn't want the Dominion Sect to go to ground any more than they already had.

Patrick didn't know what they'd find at the center of the spell, but he could guess. If it was anything like in Cairo, it wasn't going to be pretty, and they'd need space to maneuver.

Patrick checked the time on his phone, glad to see he was getting signal again. Lucien had finally done something with an artifact that allowed radiofrequency waves to pass through the threshold surrounding Ginnungagap unhindered. The connection was weak, but they had one again. Right now, they needed to get the coins set before midnight hit and summer solstice began.

"Three hours," Patrick said. "Maybe the go-bags can wait."

He retrieved his black leather jacket from the duffel bag on the card table. It'd been buried at the bottom of his suitcase in the apartment, but Nadine had found it and brought it along with her. One of the first things he'd bought after joining the SOA, the weight of the jacket was comforting. Patrick hadn't been wearing it recently due to the hot weather, but he always traveled with it.

The charms set into the jacket—heat and cold and durability— made him wince when he pulled it on. Without his shields, everything that had to do with magic felt a little rough on his soul.

It didn't take long to gather the others in the middle of the warehouse. Emma, Leon, Sage, and Marek peeled away from their pack. Carmen and Lucien weren't ones to be left out, and Jono was a shadow Patrick couldn't shake if he tried.

"The coins need to be set at the cardinal points before midnight. It doesn't matter that some of you don't have magic," Patrick said as he dug the coins out of his pocket.

"You sure about that?" Emma asked as she extended her hand.

Patrick handed out a pair of coins each to Nadine and Lucien, Emma and Leon, and Carmen and Sage. He kept four for himself, two for the cardinal point and two he'd carry with him into the fight.

"The gods on our side have a stake in this fight, and they can't afford to lose. The coins carry some of the Greek pantheon's magic, so odds are they'll work how we need them to."

"You hope," Nadine said as she pocketed her coins. "We'll take the west cardinal point."

"South," Carmen said.

Leon shrugged. "East, I guess."

"I'm texting you all the coordinates so you can plug it into your GPS apps on your phones," Marek said as he approached, staring intently at his own.

Phones beeped one after the other with incoming texts. Patrick checked their coordinates and the route they'd need to take. Their designated area north of here was the farthest away.

"Marek, can we borrow your car?" Jono asked.

"Sure." Marek pulled his keys from his pocket and removed just the car key, keeping the rest. He tossed it to Jono. "Don't scratch it."

"Cheers."

Nadine shrugged into her lightweight waterproof jacket and zipped it all the way to her throat. "Let's go."

Patrick zipped up his own leather jacket as everyone headed for the door. Lucien's vampires would keep working under Einar's guidance, and the rest of the Tempest pack would follow Marek's orders.

The moment Lucien pushed open the door, the howling wind nearly slammed it shut again. Patrick ducked his head against the pounding rain coming down sideways when he finally stepped outside. He looked up at the sky out of reflex when lightning flashed through the storm clouds, followed by the rumble of thunder.

"Bit wet out," Jono said. He grabbed Patrick's hand in his and started for the mouth of the alleyway. "I'll show you where Marek parked."

None of them wanted to be out in this weather, so everyone made a run for their respective vehicles. Patrick followed Jono's lead, the two of them racing down the sidewalk for half a block until they reached Marek's car.

"I'm driving," Patrick said.

"You know how to drive manual?" Jono asked as he tossed Patrick the small set of keys.

"If I didn't, you'd be driving. I don't think Marek would appreciate me stripping the gears."

"Hope he doesn't whinge about the water damage to his seats."

"He's rich. He can afford the fix."

They got inside the relative dryness of the vehicle. Patrick started the engine and the Maserati rumbled to life. He waited just long enough for Jono to buckle up before pulling into the street.

The Greek coins in his pocket clinked together every time Patrick pressed down on the clutch, navigating through saturated Manhattan streets. The window wipers were going at full speed, but the rain was coming down so hard it was still difficult to see anything. Patrick had to concentrate on the road as he followed the GPS map on his phone for the NY 9A North onramp.

Despite how late it was and the ferocity of the storm, there were still people out on the roads. Most of the vehicles seemed to be taxis or ride-share workers. Sane people knew not to be out on a night like this. He was merging onto the West Side Highway when Jono broke the silence between them.

"All the reports about Ethan's children said they'd gone missing and were presumed dead like his wife."

Patrick gripped the steering wheel so hard his knuckles went white. He didn't want to have this conversation. Unfortunately, he couldn't throw himself out of a moving vehicle to escape it.

"Reports lie," Patrick said.

"I can see that." Jono glanced at him. "The immortals say you owe them a soul debt. Is Ethan why?"

Patrick thought of the lies he'd lived over the years, the background Setsuna had never let him forget since he was eight years old.

"Setsuna changed my last name in a closed federal court hearing and sealed the files when I was a kid. She gave me a new identity and took me on as her ward because it was the only way to keep me safe back then. The public thinks I'm dead. The files show me alive."

Jono's voice was quiet, a murmur barely heard over the rain pounding on the car roof. "And your twin sister?"

Patrick reflexively pressed his foot harder on the gas pedal, holding on tight to the steering wheel and the gear shift. "What do you think?"

The police had only found one body in his family's home in Salem—his mother's. Hannah Greene, his twin sister, had disappeared, a missing person presumed dead and relegated to a cold case that still haunted the detectives who'd covered the crime. At the time, the sacrificial murder of a loving mother and the assumed deaths of her twin eight-year-old children had rocked Salem's magical community to its core.

Ethan, the prime murder suspect, had gone on the run and disappeared, only to show up years later on grainy CCTV footage in Europe, making a new life as a mercenary. Over the years, every shred of evidence that proved Ethan was alive had never confirmed the same fate for Hannah.

As for Patrick?

The sins of the father were owed by the son in the eyes of the immortals.

"These gods," Jono said quietly. "They aren't as powerful as they used to be."

"They're still powerful enough. People still worship them. Why do you think Hera formed that coven of hers?" Patrick switched lanes to get out from behind the added spray of water coming from a truck's tires. "Gods will always have power we mortals never will. It's why Ethan does what he does."

Greed was his father's defining feature and always would be.

Headlights and taillights refracted through the rain. Jono didn't ask any more questions, but he did reach over and settle his hand over Patrick's on the gear shift. Patrick let out a long, slow, deep breath at the touch, though the tension in his shoulders only got worse.

He drove them north, wishing for a cigarette or a goddamn drink to settle his mind. It took close to thirty minutes even without a lot of traffic on the road to reach Exit 17, fighting the wind for the entire drive. Patrick veered right, gliding onto Riverside Drive, most of Manhattan's bridges behind them. He took a left on Seaman Avenue, driving between red-bricked buildings on either side of the street.

Patrick followed the route on the GPS all the way to where Seaman Avenue intersected with West 218th Street. He turned left and managed to drive only one block before coming to a stop. The car's headlights illuminated the large boulders placed between short metal pillars to keep cars out of the park.

"Be right back," Jono said.

He got out of the car and jogged toward the closest pair of boulders through the rain. Patrick watched through the downpour as Jono easily picked up each boulder and tossed them to the side, clearing the way.

"Okay, that was hot," Patrick said, knowing Jono could probably hear him.

Jono returned to the car and raised an eyebrow at Patrick. "Hefting rocks about turns you on?"

Patrick took his foot off the brake and pressed down on the gas and clutch, shifting gears. "You know exactly what turned me on about that, and it wasn't the rocks. Don't fish for compliments."

He drove them onto a bumpy road, the asphalt broken and pitted in places. They ended up at a roundabout situated on a wedge of land jutting into the choppy water. Inwood Hill Park sat on the northernmost tip of Manhattan, a little spot of green with eddies of magic flowing beneath its surface. Ley lines snaked beneath it in metaphysical rivers of power that fed through to the nexus behind them. The park was dark, empty of people, the reactionary storm having driven everyone away.

Patrick parked against the curve of the roundabout. Off to the side was an empty baseball field, the tall stadium-style lights dark against the stormy sky. Rain pounded against the car roof and streamed down the windshield in a waterfall that blurred out the world. Patrick knew the reactionary storm would only grow worse as the hours ticked down. He didn't want to think about the damage the five boroughs would sustain when hit by something resembling a strong tropical storm or a low-category hurricane that wouldn't move on.

He took the key out of the ignition and opened the car door. "Let's go."

Jono followed him into the storm once more, the two of them

trudging across muddy grass that sucked at their feet. They walked parallel to the baseball field, heading for the line of trees at land's end; the park one last, crushing bit of nature that sprouted defiantly in one of the world's most human of cities.

Patrick could see lights from the buildings across the choppy water shining through the trees. Patrick ducked his head against the wind shrieking over the park, leaning into it as he walked. His leather jacket kept his upper body mostly dry due to the charms laid onto it, but rain still slipped between the collar and his neck.

They made it to the pathway circling the jut of land before passing through the copse of trees. Jono had to duck a little under some of the branches until they cleared the tree line and came upon the rocky shore. The low-lying water before them churned violently from the storm.

"This the spot?" Jono yelled over the sound of the wind.

"North enough," Patrick yelled back.

The lightning-edged storm sparked blue and white in the cloud-heavy night sky, thunder a sound Patrick could feel in his bones. The earth itself seemed to vibrate from the sound. He slipped two of the four coins out of his front pocket and stared down at them. They glittered in the dark; tiny, rough-hewn circles of gold that burned with an amount of magic Patrick would have to be dead not to feel.

The coins weren't from this world, but like the ruins in Greece that let their gods still be remembered, they were a pathway of sorts. A foothold. For Patrick, they would be nothing but a possibility for some breathing room.

Patrick drew his arm back and threw the coins into the water, putting all his strength into the motion. They spun through the air like tiny meteorites before crashing into the water below, sinking to muddy depths.

The water began to swirl around where the coins had sunk, drawing in like a whirlpool, its center a softly glowing twist of magic. They watched the light grow brighter before the whirlpool swallowed it up.

Something trembled from deep below. Patrick felt it, on the very edge of his awareness, something powerful settling into place. He hoped the formation of the barrier ward wouldn't catch Ethan's attention, but he wasn't going to hold his breath.

Patrick would pray if he thought it would do them any good, but he'd long since discovered that prayers were nothing more than wasted breath, and begging never helped anyone.

Jono bent his head so he could speak directly in Patrick's ear. "Will it work?"

"I don't know."

"Did it work in Cairo? At the end?"

"We didn't do this in Cairo."

Their defenses had been different, tied to what the military could offer, spearheaded by the Mage Corps and its foreign allied equivalents, and all their worn-out magic users. In the end, Patrick's team had been the only group to reach ground zero of the sacrificial spell. He had been the only one able to cross it, and that only by the grace of gods and his own misbegotten blood ties.

Jono grabbed his hand, pulling Patrick away from the water's edge and back onto the muddy firmament of the island. "C'mon, mate. We're done here."

They stumbled back under the trees in the dark, Jono leading the way with preternatural sure-footedness. With the rain coming down relentlessly, Patrick would have to wait until they were back in the car to text the others of their success so his phone didn't become waterlogged.

He never got the chance.

Patrick felt the burn of recognition like a knife sliding between his ribs. He choked on a cry, stumbling sideways into Jono, who immediately caught him before he face-planted in the mud. Bitterness filled his mouth, filled his lungs. Patrick got his feet under him and his hand on his dagger right as a hulking beast slid out of the veil in front of them.

Three pairs of coal-red eyes glowed through the dark, the smell of sulfur thick in the air. The deep, rumbling growls that ripped through the air didn't sound like they belonged to any animal on Earth.

"Stay behind me," Jono snarled, moving to get in front.

Patrick ripped his dagger out of its sheath, magic crawling across the black blade, as he stepped to the side to get clear line of sight. "I don't fucking think so. They're after *you*."

The beast roared, its voice crashing through the air louder than thunder. Its charge forward made the earth shake, and Patrick couldn't get out of the way in time. Something solid and powerful clipped him in the side, violently jarring his entire body. He was thrown by the force of the hit, crashing to the ground hard enough to punch the air from his lungs.

"*Patrick!*"

He spit mud out of his mouth, hand still clenched around the hilt of his dagger, heavenly magic twisting around his fingers. "Jono! Run!"

Somehow, he knew Jono wouldn't listen.

Hellfire sparked into existence, burning bright, cradled in a human hand. It dripped from fingers unaffected by its heat, pooling on the muddy ground before bursting outward in a long snaking line that encircled the area they were in. Even the fury of the storm couldn't snuff it out.

In the light the hellfire cast, Patrick could finally see the shape of the creature before him—the snakelike tail whipping back and forth over its three heads. Thick legs that ended in monstrous claws supported a barrel-chested body that shouldn't have been capable of the agility it had. Blackened teeth dripped thick saliva in three wide mouths.

Cerberus was a nightmare made real.

"Fuck," Patrick said as he scrambled to his feet, ignoring the pain in his body. "*Fuck.*"

Cerberus' three heads snapped at the air before it let out another howl. Patrick knew better than to take his eyes off the threat, but he wasn't the target—Jono was. He looked away, catching sight of Jono and the rapid change the other man was going through.

Jono's human body broke itself apart before reforming into a monstrous wolf, magic twisting through his DNA. Clothes ripped apart as his body expanded. Blood sprayed through the air, whipped away by the wind. Bones snapped, ripping through skin, as his limbs reshaped themselves in seconds. Muscles twisted and stretched into a new shape, fur sprouting in thick patches before flowing over newly formed skin.

New joints snapped his limbs into place, their position articulated differently from normal wolves to give Jono more strength to grip and rend. His spine popped and locked into place with a violent motion. His head was shaped like a wolf's but with a heavier jaw and thicker skull, long fangs sliding free of his lips.

Jono was frightening in this shape, as most werecreatures were, a shade of the animal the werevirus drew inspiration from. But his eyes were still the same wolf-bright blue, the human intelligence in them tempered by a viciousness driven by animalistic ferocity.

Jono put himself between Cerberus and Patrick with a challenging snarl the thunder couldn't drown out.

"Those coins weren't yours to use. Hermes had no right to give them to you," Hades said as the hellfire he commanded grew brighter.

Patrick's ribs ached from the hit and the fall, but he never lost his grip on the dagger. He might not have his magic, but the blade he wielded was more than powerful enough to replace it.

"Hera sanctioned it since you betrayed your family *again*," Patrick spat out. "What have you done with Zeus?"

"I'll tell you if you will trade yourself for my brother. A life for a life, what do you say?" When Patrick didn't answer, Hades snapped his fingers. "I didn't think so."

The hellfire rose higher around them, trapping them inside a circle of hellish heat. Patrick couldn't tell if it was rain or sweat sliding down his neck beneath his leather jacket.

"Is Ethan still promising you Macaria's life? Are you still believing his lies?"

"You, of all people, don't get to say my daughter's name," Hades snarled.

Patrick took a step forward, heavenly magic twisting around his arm. "Don't try to lay your guilt at my feet."

"I wanted to survive. I wanted to be *remembered*. There are different paths forward, and not every Fate is on heaven's side. You and the wolf were never supposed to meet." Hades smiled, the expression a slow, vicious promise as he twisted his wrist, all five fingers spread, palm pushing outward. "*Va.*"

Hades words rang through Patrick's head, freezing him where he stood for one agonizing moment.

It was enough for the god to gain the upper hand.

As if Hades' insult was an order, Cerberus surged forward with a threefold roar that nearly made Patrick's ears pop. Jono met the hellbeast's charge with an answering snarl as he launched himself at the three-headed immortal.

"*No!*" Patrick yelled, unable to hold him back, to protect him. "Jono!"

Jono and Cerberus tore into each other with a ferocity that could only lead to death. Even as they fought, Hades was walking toward Patrick with a promise of murder in his dark eyes.

Patrick had no magic, no weapon save the gods-made dagger in his hand. As much as he wanted to save Jono from the wrath of a god, his odds weren't good when he couldn't even save himself.

So someone else did the saving for him.

The wall of hellfire had nearly reached Patrick when the flames suddenly went up in smoke. Slim arms coiled around his torso from behind, two slender hands pressing hard over the scars carved into his chest. The rich smell of flowers and fresh, earthy grass filled his nose, spilling into his lungs.

It tasted of spring.

Hades rocked to a halt, one hand lifting in what might have been supplication in anyone else but him. Patrick could see the hurt and deep anger that suffused Hades' face, the way the immortal's eyes went wide with both betrayal and a love that bordered precariously close to hate.

"My love, don't do this," Hades said, sounding almost desperate.

The smoke turned into fog, blocking out the world as it pulled Patrick under. Those impossibly strong arms caught him as he fell, Hades' shout and Jono's snarl of pain fading away.

"I have you," Persephone whispered into his ear in the ethereal space of the veil.

Which was true, in every way that mattered.

The Greek goddess and queen of the Underworld owned his soul debt, after all.

17

PAIN WAS A COMPANION JONO HAD BECOME USED TO SINCE HE WAS seventeen.

Over the years, he'd never quite gotten used to the god riding his soul.

The beast broken forth from his bones was a familiar shape he'd learned to find comfort in. Jono snarled weakly against the binding wards holding him down in the center of a pentagram. The expensive wooden floor beneath him had been ruined where his claws could reach, but it wasn't enough to break himself free.

Be still.

The voice that echoed through Jono's mind came from a distance, carrying a roughness to it that sounded how teeth biting into flesh felt. Jono could only obey, the connection in his soul that tied him to his patron tightening like a bowstring. Fenrir's presence filled his body, filled his soul, as the immortal stared through Jono's wolf eyes.

They were in someone's living room, all the furniture removed to make space for the outline of the spell painted on the hardwood floor. Thirteen concentric circles extended away from the pentagram, five supporting radial lines slicing through each one of the star's points. Magic flowed through the lines, heavy and powerful, keeping Jono trapped in one place.

Fucking Dominion Sect, Jono mused darkly to himself.

He could feel the slithering, ropy twists of his intestines twitching outside his body between his belly and the floor. The savage wound to the underside of his body had occurred when Jono had tried to get to Patrick. One of Cerberus' claws had caught him midlunge, eviscerating him with an agonizing swipe before Jono could reach the mage.

Jono didn't remember much after that aside from the feel of Cerberus' teeth at his throat, the threat impossible to miss. In his half-conscious state, unable to shift, Jono hadn't been in any condition to fight back.

Cerberus had dragged Jono through the veil after Hades, mud and blood and his own organs trailing behind him. Werecreatures were capable of rapid healing, but to heal a wound like this required a full shift back to human. The binding ward wrapped around Jono's damaged wolf body prevented him from shifting. The blood loss left him woozier than he would've liked, but at least some healing was happening on the inside.

If he could just *shift,* then he'd feel better about his chances of surviving.

Jono's ears pricked forward as he felt vibrations through the floor, indicating the arrival of people. Someone had set a silence ward around the living room. He couldn't hear anything beyond the walls, which meant people wouldn't hear him screaming.

Lovely, Jono thought.

He lifted his head, tongue sliding out of his mouth to lick his nose, watching as Ethan Greene entered the living room with a cadre of magic users. Ethan was as tall as his son, but a bit stockier. Where Jono expected red hair, Ethan sported a dark blond quiff going a bit gray with a close-shaved beard to match. His rugged, tanned face spoke of years out in the sun, the wrinkles at the corners of his green eyes carved deep.

Jono had seen those same eyes in Patrick's face, dark with passion or light with sarcastic humor. *He must get his hair from his mum.*

Ethan stepped over the lines of the concentric circles and came to stand in the space between two points of the pentagram. Feet splayed wide, hands on his hips, Ethan looked down his nose at Jono with a thoughtful expression on his face that made Jono snarl.

He'd honestly expected brashness from a man of Ethan's reputation, but Jono supposed one didn't have ambitions like the mage did without being a calculating bastard.

Ethan lifted one hand, flattening his palm outward in Jono's direction. A sickly, red-orange mageglobe twisted into existence against his hand. *"Change."*

Jono would have liked to believe he could withstand the magical command that tugged at his soul, but he had a vested interest in shifting for his own reasons. So he didn't fight the black magic pulling at the werevirus that ran through his veins.

The initial break of the shift was white-hot agony that cascaded through his body before his central nervous system switched off the pain. Jono could feel his body changing from wolf back to human, but his brain processed it at a distance.

In moments, Jono found himself kneeling naked in the center of the pentagram, panting for breath, his body whole once more. Sweat slid down his skin, the exertion from the forced change making him feel a little light-headed. He fought to lift his head, the binding ward still twisted around his body and keeping him in place.

He blinked hard, thinking for one second it was Patrick standing beside Ethan. Then his vision steadied, and he could only stare uneasily at the woman who looked back at him with Patrick's eyes.

Hannah Greene was shorter than her twin brother, skinny in an unhealthy way that spoke of overuse of magic and not enough nourishment. She looked starved of life, and Jono's mouth curled at the scent of her—a rancid bitterness that was nothing like the taint of Patrick's magic. Hannah smelled like death underneath the ozone burn emanating from her aura.

Jono knew what that particular charged scent meant now. Having seen Marek during his visions and being in Patrick's presence since Thursday night, Jono could recognize the presence of a god even if all he saw was insanity in the depths of Hannah's dead-eyed gaze.

Jono wondered, staring at Patrick's twin, what their lives would have looked like if Ethan hadn't been such a fucking awful father. But none of them could change the past, only live the future it created.

"It seems the Moirai failed me," Ethan said, breaking the silence. "You crossed paths with my son after all."

Jono swallowed dryly, wishing for some water to unstick his throat. "I don't know what the bloody hell you're on about."

"There are very few god packs in existence who are truly guided by the patrons their kind once worshipped. Are you going to insist you know nothing of the god that resonates in your soul?"

Jono tilted his head and attempted to shrug beneath the binding ward. "I'm an atheist."

Ethan smiled thinly. "I sincerely doubt that."

Jono watched in horror as Ethan pulled magic out of Hannah's soul rather than his own, the near-celestial brightness shining through her pale skin. He poured it into the circles of the pentagram, the lines a flash-fire of magic that flowed outward before slamming back to the center like a tsunami.

The wave of magic hit Jono with all the force of a lorry. All the air was punched out of his lungs, and he couldn't find breath enough to scream. Ugly tendrils of magic pierced his skin, reaching for his soul without care for his own well-being. That foreign touch spread through the very essence of who Jono was and refused to leave.

Deep inside, Jono felt his soul rip at the edges, the pain of it worse than the first moment of the preternatural shift, when his nerves still worked.

Then the tugging stopped, his soul held fast to his body by the ephemeral teeth and claws of a god.

"Yes, I think you'll be of more use to me than the seer when it comes to killing Zeus," Ethan decided with a covetous look in his eyes.

He stepped closer, mindful of the circles and lines of the pentagram, until he stood in the center with Jono. Ethan's shiny wingtips came into view, and Jono watched as the older man crouched down in front of him. Strong fingers gripped his chin and shoved his head back, forcing Jono to look Ethan in the eyes.

"This isn't your war. You should never have come to these shores," Ethan said.

Somehow, Jono didn't think the words were directed at him.

"Wasn't my war before this week. It is now," Jono said with a snarl more reminiscent of his wolf. "I'll fight you until my last bloody breath."

Jono expected the blow that punched through him like a silver bullet, foreign magic slicing across his naked body once again. The pentagram turned molten with reddish-orange power when Ethan's magic crashed through the circles for a second time. Jono locked his scream behind his teeth, cracking a molar or two in his struggle to not give in.

Swearing, Jono glared at Ethan through the haze of magic between them, forcing back the pain with long practice.

"Then it will be my absolute pleasure to break you," Ethan said silkily as he stood up.

Jono *laughed*, baring his flat human teeth at the whole bloody lot of them. "Brilliant. You sodding well do that. Good *fucking* luck."

Because Jono knew something they didn't, even with their magic keeping him bound—his body would break before his word.

Ethan wouldn't get all of Jono, but he'd get pieces, and Jono could live with that.

Jono had a lifetime of experience in tearing himself apart. *Before* as the lad from Tottenham who'd tried to fit in with any numerous groups of people and never quite could. *After* as a were-wolf with no pack to call home and still yearning to belong.

Maybe all those years of hardship were just practice for this moment. He had no doubt Ethan would try to break him. For all the trauma Jono had endured in his life, in the end, he knew he wasn't up to surviving the level of torture he could see promised in Ethan's eyes.

Not alone, at least.

Fenrir's growl in his mind made Jono shiver, fingers digging into the grooves his claws had made in the hardwood floor earlier.

They cannot have you, the immortal promised.

Fenrir's regard was a blessing, or maybe a curse. Jono couldn't decide which when Ethan pulled a long silver stake from the inside pocket of his suit jacket, a chemical sheen glistening at the point. The smell of aconite and silver hit Jono's nose, and he had to force aside the panic clawing at the back of his mind.

He couldn't force back the scream when Ethan drove the stake through his left shoulder. The acidic burn of aconite seared Jono from the inside out like fire, skin and muscle ripping beneath the sharp point of the stake. Pain tripped his nerves in a way the shift from human to wolf never did, and he couldn't stop the tears that gathered in the corner of his eyes from falling.

"You are not the predator here," Ethan said as he ground the stake through Jono's shoulder. "You never will be again."

In Jono's mind, Fenrir *howled*, but there was nothing the god could do as aconite ravaged his system. Between the silver stake, aconite poisoning, and magic, Jono's ability to change forms was lost to him. Warm blood flowed out of the wound, dripping down his chest and arm. The wound throbbed in time with every heart-beat, the metal grating against tissue and bone, the aconite burn a painful heat deep inside.

Unclenching his jaw, Jono sucked in a ragged breath, never taking his eyes off Ethan and the magic sliding into the shape of a mageglobe between them once more. Behind the mage, Hannah's broken soul that somehow carried the power of an immortal began to shine through her skin with a sickening light. Around him, the acolytes started to pray in a language Jono wasn't familiar with.

This was a nightmare he couldn't escape.

In the end, the only thing Jono would get to choose out of this whole fucked-up situation was *when* he would break. Because Ethan would break him—that's what men like him did—but Jono would get to *choose*, and that was a win they could never take from him.

Running out the clock to summer solstice was the only chance he had at seeing Patrick again because Jono refused to believe the other man was gone. If he paid that price in blood, then so be it.

I'm not dying here, Jono thought fiercely.

If there was one lesson Jono had learned on the streets of London as a child that had followed him through the years, it was this: you didn't get to keep the things you wouldn't fight for.

18

PATRICK'S FEET CONNECTED WITH THE GROUND, AND HIS KNEES took the impact hard. Persephone kept him upright as they came out onto the dark banks of a river flowing beneath a gray sky. The wind howled over the water and across the gray wasteland that surrounded them. It chilled him worse than his mostly soaked clothes. Not even Persephone's warm touch could drive the cold away.

The goddess pulled away and circled around to face him. Patrick's fuzzy memory of her sharpened into focus. Persephone hadn't changed at all, not in the years since he'd seen her when he was a child. Immortals never aged, not really, but that didn't stop him from trying to find some differences in her face, some hint of the years he'd lived reflected back at him. But the immortal was as ageless and untouched as she had been when she'd saved him from dying beneath his father's hands all those years ago.

In hindsight, it hadn't been much of a rescue.

Patrick flashed back to that night in Salem, to the dark, bloody basement Persephone had pulled him out of. The memory only lasted the length of a heartbeat, but it felt like a lifetime.

He took a step toward her, ignoring the aches in his body from Cerberus' hit. "Take me back right the fuck now. I can't leave Jono behind. He's supposed to *stay* with me."

Persephone arched one dark eyebrow. "I am aware of what the Norns decreed, but I could not reach the wolf through Cerberus."

"*Bullshit.* That mutt would've listened to you."

She shrugged in the face of his anger. The wind tugged at the T-shirt she wore, the ragged threads of her denim cutoff shorts fluttering in the air. She wore sandals, but unlike Patrick, her feet weren't sinking into the wet ground. Persephone's golden-brown skin seemed to glow against the darkness surrounding them, as if she were the only bright spot in the realm of the dead.

Freckles dotted the bridge of her nose and cheeks, her curly, dark brown hair like a halo around her face. She didn't seem bothered at all by the wind or the bone-deep chill that called this place home.

"You are who I wish to speak with, and only you," Persephone said.

Patrick tried to still the rabbit-fast beating of his heart, but the rage and fear he felt wasn't dying down anytime soon. "Take me *back.*"

"In due time."

Which was a fucking riot of a joke because immortals had more time to spare than anyone. Patrick was stuck here behind the veil in the Greek Underworld where time ran slower than it did on Earth. Depending on the plane, time could also run faster, as in Underhill. Either way, Patrick couldn't afford to lose even a single second. The quicker he got this reunion over with, the sooner he could get back to the mortal plane and the fight waiting for him.

The quicker he'd get back to Jono.

"Just let me go back. *Please.*"

"I see you still desire the same thing as when you were here as a child. Do you think this time you will find something different on the mortal plane when you return?"

Patrick flinched, thinking of Jono, thinking bleakly, *Don't be dead. Please don't be dead.*

He'd begged for the same result when it came to his twin sister years ago. Only when he came out of the veil into Ashanti's waiting arms in Washington, DC, his life in Salem was forever lost to him.

"You don't care about what I think, Persephone. Say what you want to say so I can get out of here."

Persephone's gaze was heavy-lidded and knowing. "My husband has always been a single-minded bastard. I love him, I always will, but I do not appreciate him attempting to do to me what he allowed to happen to his daughter. Zeus will not forgive him this time."

"It wasn't just your husband last time."

"And it is not him alone now."

Patrick chewed on his bottom lip until he tasted blood. Persephone's statement was all the confirmation he needed to know that when he made it back through the veil, Ethan would be waiting for him.

And so would Hannah.

Persephone settled her hands on her hips, cocking her head to the side as she studied him. "I will not apologize for saving you."

"I was *eight*," Patrick bit out. "I was *dying*."

"I healed you."

He let out a bitter laugh. "You offered life to a dying child, but you never said you would *own* me when I begged for your help. That's not healing, Persephone. That's enslavement."

"Your father and his ilk stole Macaria's godhead when they had no right to take what they can never own."

"Owning me won't bring her back as she was."

Persephone stepped closer and pressed her hands to his chest, right over the scars. "Who better to stop your father than his own son? The magic the Dominion Sect covets is old, Patrick. It is primordial. It is *ours*, but they use it against us when they can find us. So we will use you to break the ones perpetuating this blasphemy through blood."

"Killing one won't stop them all. There is no stopping a group like that by taking out a single person, even if that person comes from a founding family."

"Your father is attempting to turn himself into a god who will head up a new pantheon, build a new myth, and rule over a new hell. He failed in Salem with Macaria. He nearly succeeded in Cairo with Ra. He tries again in New York City with Zeus. Ethan is too prideful to ever share that glory with someone else."

Deep down, Patrick knew she was right. Ethan had always been ambitious during his years rising in the ranks of the SOA until his true allegiance was brought to light. That ambition had proven useful to the Dominion Sect.

It took a mix of blood magic, necromancy, and soultakers to carve a godhead from an immortal's body and soul. The essence of a god was too powerful for mortals to carry alone, but Ethan had been determined to try. Both Patrick and Hannah were supposed to die for their father's ambitions the same way their mother had.

Except he hadn't died because Persephone had found him and stolen him away to the Underworld. Her interference had broken the spell his father had sought to complete, taking Patrick's soul and blood out of the sacrificial circle. In the end, Macaria's godhead had been transferred into Hannah's soul instead of Ethan's, and his twin was now forever bound to their father. The feedback loop between their souls and the siphoning off of her power to Dominion Sect acolytes kept Hannah's body from dying. As for Macaria, she wasn't dead and gone, but she might as well be in the eyes of the Greek pantheon.

When it came down to it, Patrick had never truly escaped that basement. Part of him was still standing in a grave.

"Then maybe you gods should get rid of the problem yourselves," Patrick finally said, shoving old memories aside.

"Your father has immortal allies the same way you do."

"Ethan is not my father, and you are no ally."

Persephone gave him a derisive look, her gold-brown eyes burning straight through him. "That is what you take away from this conversation? Half his blood runs through your veins."

Patrick took a step back, putting distance between them. Pebbles shifted around his feet, and the wind snaked its way beneath his jacket, icy and sharp. "A father is more than blood. You immortals never seem to understand that."

"We understand family and the trials that come with them far more than you mortals do."

Persephone reached for him again, her fingers brushing against his cold cheek before he turned his face away. Looking out over the River Styx, Patrick could just make out a hazy, bobbing light coming closer out of the gloom.

"You wanted the arms of your mother when you were a child bleeding at my feet. You wanted kindness," Persephone said with all the gentleness of an iron brand searing skin. "Nothing in war is ever kind, Patrick."

He squeezed his eyes shut, taking in a steadying breath. She spoke a truth he'd lived through but which never got any easier to accept. Patrick knew what death looked like on the battlefield, delivered by his own hands or others. He knew how this fight he'd been sacrificed to as a child had colored his life and bled into his nightmares over the years. Patrick had begged Persephone to save him from the mortal wounds Ethan had inflicted on him. He hadn't known what he was giving up back then.

He knew now.

A debt was owed and owned. Patrick would not pay that price again.

"Look at me."

The powerful command in her voice snaked its way through his mind, and Patrick could only obey. He opened his eyes, turning to face Persephone once again. She didn't speak, not at first, the expression on her beautiful face unreadable.

"Your shields are damaged. The wards I set in your bones need resetting," she finally said.

"Blame the coins Hermes gave me. They wrecked my magic."

Her magic had kept him hidden so he could stay alive through the years. The anchor points she'd carved into bone helped confine the taint in his magic and his aura to his body, leaving no trace as he traveled through the world. Her foundation for his shields had never been easy to carry.

Persephone placed her hand over his scarred heart, her touch warm in this cold place. "Remember to breathe."

Magic burned through Patrick's body like a flash-fire, and he choked on a scream. His knees went out from under him as molten heat twisted through every last bone in his body. He could feel Persephone's magic branding him deep inside, the pain of the casting something Patrick had forgotten.

He could've done without the reminder.

Persephone rebuilt the foundation she'd laid into his body once before, and Patrick could only breathe through the agony. When it was over, he felt light-headed and hollowed out, every movement of his body a painful reminder of the debt he carried. The throbbing in every inch of his body and brain was worse than the hit from Cerberus.

She pulled Patrick to his feet with strong hands, holding him steady with a care that would be more meaningful if it was directed at his own well-being.

He knew it wasn't.

"What will you ask of me this time to leave these shores, I wonder?" Persephone mused as she brushed back his dark red hair.

Patrick licked his lips, mouth dry and tasting of coppery blood. "I ask nothing. I'll pay my own way."

The hull of Charon's boat wedged itself against the shoreline nearby, the brackish waters of the River Styx splashing against the old gray bones that made up the vessel's shape. The prow of the boat was formed with skeletal hands, thin finger bones curled together, as if climbing out of the dark waters. At the top of the prow sat an old skull gripped by bony hands, a soft, eerie glow floating behind broken teeth and within dark eye sockets.

The ferryman was shrouded in ragged black robes, cowl pulled low over his face, casting him in shadow. Charon's gnarled hands and bony fingers held an ancient wooden pole topped with a human skull. It, too, held light within the empty eye sockets and gaping jaws. The skin of the immortal's hands was gray and pulled taut over his bones, almost desiccated in appearance.

Persephone rose up on her tiptoes, cupping the back of Patrick's head to pull him down within reach. She pressed her lips to his forehead, the gentle touch a benediction he wanted no part of.

"Fight for us. Return Macaria to me. Do your duty and you may yet find your freedom," she murmured. "You may yet find peace."

Peace was a gift this war had yet to offer. Patrick couldn't accept what no one else had.

He walked away from Persephone and the tricky, slippery promises immortals always offered in exchange for a life.

Patrick pulled out the second to last Greek coin rattling around in his pocket and slipped it between his teeth. He held it there, tasting metal on his tongue as he splashed through brackish water and climbed into Charon's boat. He sat down on the bone bench, staring at the ferryman with defiant eyes.

One bony hand lifted off the pole to reach for him. Icy fingers brushed against his lips when they pried the payment from Patrick's teeth. The ferryman brought the coin to his own mouth, shrouded in shadow, and swallowed the payment whole.

Patrick didn't look back as Charon gripped the pole and separated his boat from the shore with a strong push. They glided forward over the depths of the River Styx, Charon ferrying him to the other side. Fog rose up to white out the world so completely Patrick could barely make out the ferryman after a while. Fog clung to the boat and his wet clothes, sliding into his lungs with every breath he took.

Only when the boat hit against the opposite shore, rocking him on the bench, did Patrick feel like he could breathe again. Charon made a wide gesture with one arm, one finger uncurling to point beyond the boat. Patrick clambered over the side and splashed into the calf-deep water. His combat boots felt waterlogged as he trudged out of the River Styx and into the edges of the veil.

Three strides got him past the water's edge. Two more strides and Charon disappeared. All that surrounded Patrick was thick gray fog that went on forever. He couldn't orient himself at all, and panic began to settle in his chest.

Then long fingers wrapped around his wrist, dragging him forward up the sudden sloping ground and into an iron jungle.

"This way," Hermes called out.

Rain melted the fog away, pounding down on Patrick's head and shoulders as they stumbled into the middle of Times Square. The wind hit him hard enough to drive him back a step on the famous meridian. The illuminated red staircase was behind them, empty of tourists. Patrick tried to blink his vision clear, but the bright lights of the famous intersection made his vision worse.

The usual crowds had disappeared in the face of the reactionary storm, leaving behind strangely empty streets only a handful of taxis braved. Some of the stores and chain restaurants were open, but many more were shuttered against the vicious weather.

Patrick looked up at the night sky and the black clouds hanging low and angry over New York City. "Tell me it's still Monday night."

"You went across the veil. You know I can't tell you that," Hermes said, his faded dyed blue curls pressed flat against his skull from the downpour. Unlike Hades, he didn't seem to care if he got drenched or not. "It's summer solstice."

Which meant Patrick had lost a day, because it was Tuesday

night and he didn't know what had happened in the last twenty-four hours.

He didn't know if Jono was still alive, and Patrick desperately needed that answer to be *yes*.

"Where is everyone?"

Hermes smiled grimly. "Where do you think?"

A faint tremble ran through the ground. North of them, bright above the jagged skyline, Patrick could just make out an orange glow that seemed to flicker like a pulsar star. Patrick didn't need his magic to know what was coming. He grabbed Hermes, barely getting the warning out in time as a powerful wave of magic rolled over Manhattan.

"Shield!" Patrick yelled.

Hermes might not have a coven worshipping him into a shadow of what he once was, but he was still a god. He still had magic at his command. Hermes raised a hand, eyes sparking gold as he formed a shield between them and the metaphysical power crashing through Manhattan.

Hell-tainted magic broke over them in a hit that seemed to freeze time. The rain stilled in its fall, trillions of drops just hovering in the air around Times Square, refracting the neon lights around them like crystal. In the clouds above, lightning crawled to an unimaginable stillness. It lasted only for an instant before the magic was sucked after the leading edge of the wave, causing the rain to fall back down to earth again with a roar.

That wasn't the only thing that came down.

The air crackled with static, the sharp smell of ozone burning hot all around them. Patrick instinctively ducked as a massive bolt of lightning cut through the sky toward the earth. It struck the famous tower of screens behind them with enough force the ground shook. Thunder nearly deafened Patrick as crackling blue light exploded away from the ruined electronics, glass shards flying through the air like shrapnel.

The wind spun metal and glass through the air with frightening force. Patrick spared a single glance over his shoulder at the now-darkened and damaged tower of screens. An ugly black scorch mark three stories tall was seared down the front of the wall of electronics. Whatever electrical fire might have started from the strike sputtered out in the deluge from the storm.

Hermes' shield held steady against the onslaught. He dragged his attention away from the sky to meet Patrick's gaze. "It's starting."

"No fucking shit," Patrick snapped. "I need to get to Central Park."

Hermes rolled his eyes. "I am aware of that, Pattycakes."

The immortal dropped his shield; rain and wind once more hit Patrick. He squinted through the rain, movement coming down Broadway catching his eye. The motorcyclist was driving at unsafe speeds for the weather, but they didn't seem to care about that or the actual street lanes.

The motorcycle jumped the curb and braked to a stop on the cement meridian moments later, tires spinning against the slick ground as the back wheel spun around in an arc. With one foot on the ground, the driver kept their balance and the motorcycle under control as it slid in a semicircle.

The driver straightened up, helmet on but visor up. It would be impossible to see anything in this weather through the tinted, hard plastic polymer. Nadine's keen brown eyes stared at them through the opening.

"Marek said you would be back. Now gear up and let's go," she said.

Nadine tossed Patrick the duffel bag secured to the seat behind her. It hit the wet ground between them with a heavy thud. Patrick knelt with a pained grunt, the lingering ache from Cerberus' hit and Persephone's painful touch stiffening his body, but he was good at working through pain.

He pulled out a tactical vest and hard helmet, along with one of the M4A1 carbines they'd put together back at Ginnungagap, as well as two extra magazines. Patrick pulled everything on in record time before slinging himself across the back of the motorcycle. He wrapped his arms around Nadine's waist and settled his boots on the footrests.

"I need a sitrep!" he yelled over the sound of the storm.

"Later!"

Nadine revved the engine and twisted her hands on the handles before the motorcycle shot forward with a skidding lurch, water spinning off its wheels. Patrick looked back only once, unsurprised to see Hermes had disappeared.

Patrick faced forward and concentrated on keeping his balance in tune with Nadine's as she sped down Broadway, heading for Central Park. She didn't care about traffic laws and drove through intersections and down the opposite lanes whenever she had to get around what vehicles were still on the road. The closer they got to Central Park, the more crowded the streets became with first responders and the media.

Nadine veered sharply to the right, directing the motorcycle up onto the sidewalk to drive down it for the last two blocks, angling northwest. She revved the engine constantly, warning people out of her way, but no one wearing an NYPD uniform tried to stop her. A minute later she drove off the sidewalk and cut through a thin gap in the crowd of police clad in riot gear gathered in Columbus Circle. She aimed the motorcycle for a cluster of people standing outside a Mobile Command vehicle set-up in the street.

Patrick's teeth clacked together when she braked to a halt. He scanned the faces turning their way, finally seeing a familiar one. Casale stepped forward, a tall Indian woman Patrick knew on sight if not personally right by the chief's side. Whereas Casale was in uniform beneath an NYPD rain slicker, the woman was in civilian clothes with an SOA jacket zipped to her throat. Her dark hair was tied back in a tight braid, dark brown eyes calm and cool, despite the situation.

"Where the *hell* have you been?" Casale demanded.

"Doesn't matter. I need a sitrep," Patrick said.

SOA Deputy Director Priya Kohli stepped forward, handing Patrick a waterproof earwig and radio set. "Special Agent Collins."

Patrick nodded, resisting the urge to salute. "Ma'am."

"Channel One is command. Channel Two is general operations. You and Special Agent Mulroney have access to Channel One and override authorization."

He took the miniscule radio and clipped it to the front of his tactical vest before slipping the earwig into his left ear. He switched it on and listened to the general channel before tapping the radio to switch to the command channel.

"Special Agent Collins to command. Confirm connection, over," he said.

It was on the tip of Patrick's tongue to switch his designation to the call sign he'd used in the military. Except this wasn't a military operation, and his military record was a whole lot of classified.

The line crackled in his ear before someone responded with "This is command confirming connection, over."

"Copy, command." Patrick focused on Priya now that he was in radio contact with those in charge. "Surprised to see you here, ma'am."

"Director Abuku sent me to assess and shield the nexus and to liaise with the PCB in your continued absence," Priya replied.

"Who did you bring with you?"

"Half the Rapid Response Division out of DC who could be spared have been pulled for this situation. All agents are on the ground around Central Park, but we can't get through the barrier ward."

She pointed at the line of trees and greenery making up the edge of Central Park that now resided behind a glimmer of dark red-orange light Patrick could only see if he looked out of the corner of his eye.

"Our team is in position," Nadine said as she took off her motorcycle helmet. She handed it to the nearest SOA agent, who exchanged it for a hard helmet that Nadine secured with practiced fingers. "We managed to get them inside before the barrier ward closed off all access."

Which meant Lucien, his Night Court, and the Tempest pack were inside Central Park with no magic user at hand and only spelled weapons and artifacts to fight with. Patrick knew that wouldn't be enough, not against Ethan.

"Who is on the ground with you?" Casale wanted to know.

"Werewolves and vampires. All friendly. Radio your people not to shoot them," Patrick replied.

"Vampires? Are you serious? I know they can't be from the Night Courts here because Tremaine doesn't care about anyone but himself, and none of the other vampires who claim territory in New York City will cross him."

"The undead can't feed off demons. They have as much incentive to keep hell off the mortal plane as we do."

"How did you pull them in?"

Patrick went with the best lie he had. "Their leader is a criminal informant of mine."

"Jesus." Casale pried his radio off his belt. "I'll pass the word on."

Patrick nodded before asking the question he'd been wanting an answer to since crossing the veil. "Where's Jono?"

Nadine finished speaking into her comms to the SOA agents about not shooting the friendlies before saying, "I was hoping he'd be with you."

Patrick's stomach twisted, and he shook his head. "We were ambushed while setting the coins at the north cardinal point."

He couldn't elaborate on how or by whom, not with everyone listening in, but Nadine could read between the lines. She bit her lip, eyes searching out his. "We found Marek's car at Inwood Hill Park, but no signs of either of you until Marek told me to head to Times Square."

The thought of Ethan having Jono within reach for even a minute was enough to make him feel ill. A day was too much.

Please don't let me be too late, he thought.

Patrick looked at Priya. "Are you shielding the nexus right now?"

Priya hadn't gone into the military, but that didn't change the fact she was a powerful mage with an affinity for defensive magic. "I have mages creating breakwaters in the ley lines, but whoever is behind this spell has majority control of the nexus. I'm doing what I can."

"The barrier shield linked to the cardinal points is holding," Nadine said.

One good thing in this mess wasn't enough to erase the bad.

"The Dominion Sect will be calling up soultakers. You'll want ESU to cover any possible exit out of the park in case any of those fuckers get past us. No matter what happens, you keep your people out of the park," Patrick ordered Casale.

Casale scowled. "We should be in there stopping this."

"If you inundate the park with police, you're just asking for a mess of friendly fire. This has been a federal investigation since you brought the SOA on board, which means SOA agents are the only ones going in. They have the training and the magic to handle the threat."

He hoped. Honestly, Patrick would be far happier calling in an air strike right about now, but something told him the public wouldn't appreciate that plan of action.

"I'll hold some of our mages in reserve to help monitor the nexus and prepare for the worst. The rest of our agents will follow you into the fight," Priya said.

"Let's hope the worst doesn't happen." Patrick never took his eyes off Casale. "You gave me a week, remember? It hasn't been a week yet. I promised you I'd leave this city still standing after everything was over. I'm keeping that promise, Casale."

Lightning cut across the sky above, thunder rumbling through the air. Casale let out a heavy breath. The rain fell from the brim of Casale's police-issued cap like a waterfall. "I'm holding you to that."

Patrick nodded and wrapped his arms around Nadine's waist again. "Let's go, Mulroney."

"That shield won't break. We've tried everything," Priya warned.

The last Greek coin in Patrick's pocket and the heavens-backed dagger strapped to his thigh were the only warm points on his body. He dug out the coin, holding it tightly in his fist.

"Not everything."

"Next time we're calling in a tank. Maybe your old team," Nadine said as she revved the motorcycle's engine and kicked them forward. "I wouldn't be averse to some heavy ordnance right now."

"You and me both," Patrick shouted over the wind.

She drove them toward Central Park, picking up speed as they followed the curve of the roundabout to the corner entrance. The crowd of police officers flashed by in a blur, backlit by the red-and-blue lights flashing in the streets behind their ranks. Patrick felt the coin burning against his skin, magic seeping out from between his fingers until it looked like he was holding a fiery star.

Nadine straightened out and pointed them at the barrier ward surrounding Central Park, never wavering from her path. Patrick reared back and put all his strength into the throw. The last Greek coin streaked through the air, trailing heavenly magic behind it. When it hit the barrier ward mere seconds before they did, the explosion sent broken, molten bits of magic flying everywhere.

Nadine shielded them from the backwash of the barrier ward's disintegration, the damage spreading out like a sizzling domino effect. The burn of recognition seared Patrick's soul now that nothing stood between them and Central Park. He swallowed hard against the bitterness in the back of his throat, hell the only thing he could sense around them in the urban greenery.

"Ready?" Nadine yelled over her shoulder.

"Ready," Patrick yelled back, because he had no other choice.

He never did.

His soul debt was always going to be do or die.

19

Nadine drove up the West Drive, aiming for the North Meadow. That's where the pull of hellish magic was strongest. It scraped through Patrick's soul, the rawness of where his own magic once resided a stinging pain that translated to physical aches.

With the barrier ward down, Patrick could make out the distinctive sound of explosions ripping through the air beneath the roar of the storm. He braced his weapon against his side, the body of the M4A1 carbine angled outward in case he had to shoot. Nadine wasn't slowing down, the single headlight of the motorcycle cutting through the darkness. All the streetlamps were burned out, the only light around them coming from the flash of lightning above and the thousands of illuminated windows in the buildings ringing Central Park.

They passed SOA agents who had crossed the barrier ward to hold defensive positions at the outer perimeter. Still others were running toward the fight. He could hear the chatter of everyone getting into position through his comms and tuned them out.

It took Nadine less than two minutes to traverse three-quarters of the park at top speed. She leaned right when they came to an area of the road with multiple pathways branching off in different directions. They took a path that ran adjacent to the 97th Street Transverse, wheels never losing traction.

Nadine slowed her speed as the trees thinned out, the North Meadow coming into view, the area lit up by hellish magic. Patrick took in the sight with a grim twist of his mouth.

The metal fence surrounding the grass and baseball fields had been destroyed in areas. Fiery red-orange spellwork spanned the grass in intricate lines and large concentric circles. The structure of the spell rose into the air by way of ten pillars of light that burned a clean, pure white. One space stood dark and empty, missing a pillar, while the last was filled by the solid shape of an unmoving man. In the center, nearly hidden by the glow from the spell, Patrick could just make out the kneeling form of a person.

A spell like this always required a final sacrifice on-site. His fingers tightened on the grip of his weapon as desperate hope bloomed in Patrick's chest.

Jono could still be alive—but not for too much longer.

"Let's get in the field, Mulroney!" Patrick shouted.

Scattered around the large sacrificial spell were Dominion Sect acolytes battling it out with vampires, werecreatures, and a handful of SOA agents who had finally reached the scene. The ground was pitted with small craters from spelled grenades and not a few bodies. Patrick hoped none of the dead belonged to their side.

Halfway between their position and the spellwork sat Lucien's stolen BearCat like a hulking bulwark of safety. The armored vehicle had been fully outfitted with military grade weaponry sometime during Patrick's absence from the mortal plane. Shield wards had been set into its metal framework, providing much-needed cover in the open area. Vampires were wielding assault weapons as well as artifacts against the magic users allied with the Dominion Sect on the front line.

"I'm going to owe him so many offensive spells for this," Patrick said.

"He's already called in an order of defensive wards from me."

"Worth it if we survive this."

Nadine braked to a slick halt on the pathway, the wheels sending small waves of water into the air. They scrambled off the motorcycle, weapons in hand. Nadine took point, keeping her shield wrapped around them while Patrick fell behind to cover her six. They cut through two engaged groups on either side of them, Nadine's shield taking the brunt of a wayward attack.

Patrick scanned their surroundings, on heightened alert. Hell was the overriding sensation he could feel, and that could really only mean one thing aside from Ethan's magic.

Demons had entered the fray.

They were running past one of the muddy baseball fields when something moved through the trees on the little hill behind them, a shadow within a shadow. Patrick twisted around on his feet as they ran, angling his weapon behind them. His night vision was shit with all the magic being thrown around, but the threat wasn't a figment of his imagination.

"Soultakers on our six," he said loudly to Nadine.

"Copy that," she said. "I'll notify command of the sighting."

Patrick tuned her out on the comms and braced his rifle against his shoulder. The staggered rush of hunched-over bodies coming their way was an unholy problem of the worst kind. The six soul-takers separated, moving in different directions. Two headed their way and Patrick started shooting, aiming a spray of automatic fire at the demons. The spelled bullets wouldn't make a dent in their thick skin, but he just needed to hold them back long enough for Nadine and him to get behind the defensive lines where Lucien's vampires were.

Vampires had no souls and couldn't be fed upon by soultakers. In the final push through Cairo during the Thirty-Day War, those in command of magic users had relied on an uneasy alliance with several Night Courts to help defend against hell. It's why, even though they hated each other, Patrick was glad Lucien had come.

A flash of orange in the darkness snagged Patrick's attention. He took his finger off the trigger when his brain clocked the figure as *friendly*. The soultakers managed a couple more strides forward before Sage burst out of the tree line on four legs and streaked across the grass, a blur of orange and black, followed by three werewolves. In her weretiger form, she was a hulking, monstrous beast, larger than a wild tiger normally would be. Her size meant taking down the two soultakers at once was possible.

Sage slammed into the soultaker closest to her before leaping onto the back of the second one, driving it to the ground. The werewolves traveling with her focused on the demon she left for them. Her wide jaws wrapped around the back of its ugly, bulbous head. She bit down with inhuman strength and got a good grip. With a muffled snarl, Sage wrenched her own head up, the weight of her shifted form keeping the demon on the ground. She tore the soultaker's head off with preternatural strength, the demon's body going limp beneath her own.

Werecreatures could rip a soultaker limb from limb—Patrick had seen it happen before—they just had to be mindful of their souls. Nadine must have passed that warning along while he'd been in the Underworld.

With a disgusted growl, Sage flung the head aside. Some of the soultakers who'd been going after the nearest SOA agents started to regroup to deal with the werecreatures.

"That's one way to kill them," Nadine said.

"Remind me to never piss her off."

They turned their backs on the fight Sage and the others had well in hand. Nadine and Patrick double-timed it to Lucien's position, passing harmlessly through the wide shield wrapped around the BearCat.

Lucien didn't stop reloading his M32 MGL grenade launcher as they approached, black eyes looking right at them. "You're late."

"I was in hell," Patrick retorted.

"You think we aren't?"

Patrick peered around the side of the BearCat at the sacrificial spellwork and the Dominion Sect magic users doing their damnedest to tear through Nadine's shield. "Veil isn't torn yet, so I'll go with no."

"Ethan is preparing to sacrifice your wolf, so maybe you'll change your answer in a few minutes."

Patrick's gaze went unerringly to the hunched-over figure he could see kneeling in the center of that hellish circle some distance away. His heart skipped a painful beat in his chest. "Jono is alive?"

"For a given definition of alive," Carmen said as she jumped off the roof of the BearCat. She carried an assault rifle and a machete, but both were her secondary weapons. Desire and mental persuasion were known to drive men and women mad on the battlefields when incubi and succubi deigned to fight.

Patrick just hoped Carmen pointed her powers *away* from their side.

"I need to get to Jono."

"Ethan's circle is warded by Zachary's blood magic."

"That's a bad habit they picked up during the Thirty-Day War." Patrick braced his weapon against his chest and pulled his dagger free of its sheath. Countless silvery words floated up from the depths of the matte-black blade, the magic of gods warm and steady in his hands. "I'm sure I can help break it."

"Maybe you should wait until we have more SOA agents to back us up. Your magic isn't replenished, and my specialty is defense, remember?" Nadine said.

Carmen made a face. "You had to call in the feds."

"My vampires will be leaving the field without being arrested when this over. If any of your people try to stop mine, they won't live to see dawn," Lucien said coolly as he hiked the grenade launcher onto one shoulder.

Patrick waved off the threat in his voice. "Sure, sure. I told them you were my CI, but I didn't use your name. Try and keep your face covered, and make a run for it when the fight is over."

"Your planning skills still leave plenty to be desired."

Lucien walked right up to the edge of the shield and pressed the barrel of the grenade launcher through Nadine's magic. The hole opened up from the inside, sealing around the weapon. Lucien took aim and fired, the spelled-ballistic cutting through the enemy when it exploded in the midst of a group of Dominion Sect witches attempting to join their magic together.

Their bolstered shield broke apart beneath the strike spell layered over the ordnance, the same way their bodies did in the explosion.

"I don't think the City is going to appreciate your attempt at relandscaping," Patrick said.

"Do your fucking job before I rip out your throat."

Easier said than done, despite their last-minute planning. They had breakwaters set into ley lines, a shield powered by magic borrowed from gods around Manhattan island, and New York City's finest waiting to play cavalry on the streets outside Central Park. All of that would be meaningless if Ethan succeeded in murdering Jono and stealing Zeus' godhead.

"Cover me," Patrick ordered.

Nadine twisted her fingers in the air, a violet mageglobe spinning into shape against her palm. "I'll wrap you in stealth with a shield and get you as far as I can."

Tendrils of magic flowed over Patrick's body, wrapping him in a muffled cloud. As in the Hamptons, it would quiet sound and hide him from sight, but with other mages in the field that knew what to look for, it wouldn't hold for long.

"I'll notify you when I reach the spellwork so you can drop your shield." Patrick hefted up his dagger, the dark blade shining with magic. "I don't want you caught in any backwash."

"Understood."

The shield rippled, providing just enough give in one spot for

Patrick to pass through it without jeopardizing the structure of it. Nadine shored it up once he was clear, and Patrick started running. Around him spells were being flung with reckless abandon by both sides, magic crackling through the air. Soultakers were having a feast, even with vampires and werewolves acting as shock troops against that hellish assault.

Patrick kept his eyes on the spellwork and the handful of people standing within its circles. He had to dodge and weave his way through what had become a war zone in the middle of Central Park. Rather than take a direct approach, Patrick peeled off at an angle to get out of range of his side's firepower.

Magic was all well and good in a fight, but when paired with military weapons, the upgrade was deadlier. Another one of Lucien's grenades exploded off to his left, hitting against the shield that encased the spellwork. For a second, the shield became visible as Zachary's magic reacted to the hit. Patrick noted its position and kept running.

He was halfway to the outermost circle of the spellwork when the rapidly pulsating magic reached another peak. Patrick dove for the muddy ground, his rifle sliding through the muck. His head and body throbbed from the impact—Persephone's wards still hurt—but he ignored the pain. Nadine's shields followed him down, settling close as the air became static-charged.

Like before, in Times Square, the magic erupted outward in a rolling wave of power, intent on crashing over Manhattan. This close to the epicenter, the explosion burned Patrick's eyes even through his eyelids. His ears popped, body gone near-weightless in the wake of the explosion, even behind Nadine's shields.

That's a lot of power, Patrick thought bleakly.

But it took a lot of power to kill a god.

The world went silent for a long, painful moment before sound rushed back like a sonic boom. Patrick coughed against the internal pressure, scrambling back to his feet with jerky motions.

His body ached, and the fight right now wasn't helping the pain any.

The insidious glow of Ethan's magic filled his eyes. What powered this spell was blood and souls, the stolen lives of decent, innocent people who had died terrible deaths. As in Salem and Cairo, those souls would act as a bridge for the godhead to travel— if Ethan succeeded in prying it out of Zeus' soul.

Something Patrick had learned in the ensuing years, and which Ethan must have realized at some point as well, was that it took a god to kill a god.

Marek had the Norns.

Jono had his own patron, whoever that might be.

And Ethan had Jono imprisoned at the center of the sacrificial circle.

He'd failed all the times before this because Ethan carried no godhead in his soul, was no more a modern god than the myths who walked Earth in all their faded glory. His only success, if one could call it that—and Patrick never would—was he'd stolen Macaria's godhead through sheer gods-be-damned luck. It only cost him the lives of his wife and daughter. Clara was dead, but Hannah was his power source these days, held in check by the prayers of the Dominion Sect. Ethan wasn't a god, but he could almost wield power like one when needed.

All Patrick had was a gods-gifted dagger and a stubbornness that had been a thorn in everyone's side since he was a child.

Weapons firing on either side of his position drew attention away from his location. Soultakers could sense magic in any form though, and a couple of the demons peeled away from protecting the shield, heading straight for Patrick.

Patrick got eyes on them right as a grenade exploded in their midst, knocking the demons to the ground. The ground shook from the impact, a spray of mud and chunks of grass rising into the air. Unfortunately, the demons seemed to be in one piece when the smoke cleared.

"Shit," Patrick muttered under his breath.

Nadine's stealth spell hadn't been stripped by the magical buildup. Patrick was still unseen, but that was about to change. With a burst of speed, Patrick covered the distance between himself and the pillar of light in front of him. Magic spilled in sparks from the dagger he held, guiding him past magical landmines Dominion Sect magic users had set in the meadow. The traps were intricate and dense, becoming nearly unsurpassable in front of Zachary's shield.

Patrick rocked to a halt, his muddy boots mere centimeters from the defensive magic in the ground protecting Ethan's shot at godhood. He tapped his radio, accessing Channel One.

"Mulroney, drop your shield."

Nadine's magic disintegrated around him. Wind and rain instantly buffeted his body now that her shield was no longer protecting him. Patrick could feel the heat of Ethan's magic even through the storm, hell a rancid taste in his mouth.

The shadow of a hand pressed against the inside of the pillar that stood on a radial line. The afterimage of a face came into view, mouth open in a soundless scream. The pretty face of a college student who would never fulfill her dreams stared out at him with horror in the remnants of her soul, most of her essence gone into the structure of the sacrificial spellwork.

Mud sucked at his feet, boots sinking into the earth. The storm raging above the City was like a monster. Here, at ground zero, there was no calm to be found. Only the roaring protest of Mother Nature as she railed against the upending of a balance at risk all over again. The fight was familiar, except for how it wasn't.

This time, Patrick wasn't standing in the ruins of a war-torn city. He wasn't grieving the teacher who had taught him how to survive what the immortals demanded of him. Unlike before, Patrick knew what waited for him at the center.

Patrick stared hard at the soul trapped inside that prison as he flipped the dagger in his hand, getting a better grip. It wasn't made to be thrown, but Patrick was out of options right now. He drew back his arm and snapped it forward, putting all his strength behind the throw, the blade disappearing beneath a fiery white light.

The dagger spun through the air and sliced through Zachary's shield with a piercing sound that made Patrick want to cover his ears. Glittering cracks fractured the air in front of him, the damage from the hit cascading through the defensive wards and offensive spells layered on the ground around it.

Past the shield was the pillar, and the dagger didn't stop.

"Shit!" Patrick yelled as he went to his knees and wrapped an arm over his head.

The dagger crashed through the pillar, and the column of magic dimmed, as did the radial line it stood on. Between one heartbeat and the next, it *shattered*.

White-hot light exploded outward, the raging wind catching most of the burning magical sparks and flinging them into the sky. The pushback from the explosion knocked Patrick over, hands sliding through the mud as he searched for purchase. He blinked rain out of his eyes, watching as the imprisoned soul found freedom. It twisted free of the anchoring magic, ghostly arms reaching skyward, the shape of who she once was dissipating into the storm.

The ground underneath him heaved as the magic powering the spellwork jolted from losing an anchor point, spinning unevenly through the pattern of the pentagram and circles. The radial line went black, dead, no more magic running through it.

A hand thrust itself past Patrick's face, grabbing him by the collar of his jacket. "On your feet."

Carmen hauled Patrick up with preternatural strength, the succubus covered in mud, holding her machete etched with runes in the other hand. She raised the machete, the sharp edge of the blade facing a nearby witch who'd turned their way. With a shout, the witch released an attack that spiraled through the air. Like a rock that waves crashed over, the magic set into the machete's blade forced the attack aside. Flailing tendrils of magic stung Carmen's arm, but the succubus didn't seem bothered by the burning welts that showed up on her skin. They'd heal soon enough.

"Mulroney's wards?" Patrick asked, spitting out mud.

"She's still useful," Carmen said with a sniff. Then she shoved him toward the sacrificial spellwork. "Get moving."

Patrick nearly fell on his knees again but managed to stay upright. He could see his dagger shining in the mud between the outermost circle and the next. Breaking a complicated spell like this without his dagger in hand would be impossible. With Carmen watching his six, Patrick made a run for the gods-given weapon, feet sliding in the mud.

A wall of fire exploded out of thin air right as his fingers wrapped around the hilt. Patrick brought the dagger up in a wide arc, heavenly fire following in its wake. The gods-backed magic crashed against the spell aimed his way, breaking it apart. As the magic-driven flames died to nothing beneath the rain, Patrick got eyes on his attacker.

Rachel planted herself in the space between two concentric circles, one hand raised and carrying an athame. The silver blade glowed a sickly green from her magic. The former SOA Special Agent in Charge looked thinned out in the ghastly light surrounding them. Shadows stood out starkly under her eyes, anger twisting her face into an ugly expression. Patrick knew a thing or two about rage and how sometimes it was the only thing that could fuel a body.

He grabbed for his rifle hanging from his tactical vest, bracing the butt of it against his shoulder. The weapon was difficult to wield one-handed but not impossible to use. He pulled the trigger and held it down, hoping Rachel's shields were shit.

They weren't.

The spelled bullets ricocheted off her defenses, and Patrick groaned. "Betrayal isn't how you do your civic duty!"

"You can't stop us," Rachel yelled, taking a step forward. Her athame trailed bright lines of magic in its wake as she drew a pentagram in the air before her. It wasn't a mageglobe, but her magic's focus was still obvious.

"Are you going to *monologue* at me?" Patrick asked incredulously. "I don't got time for that bullshit."

In answer, Rachel threw a bolt of raw magic that careened away from her pentagram focus. The attack was nothing like what a mage could produce, but without his magic, it was more than enough to wound him. While Patrick didn't have his old team watching his six, he had a decent replacement.

"On your six," Nadine snarled over his comms. "Duck!"

Patrick fell to his knees, keeping his dagger pointed at Rachel even as Nadine raised a shield around him. The attack exploded against the shield, violet light rippling around him. Patrick sucked in a deep breath, wincing at the sharp spike of pain in his ribs. It didn't stop him from getting his feet back underneath him. He took a couple of steps back to the darkened radial line in the spellwork, Nadine's shield following him.

Ethan's magic pulsated wildly all around them. Patrick had damaged the spellwork just enough that the outermost circle was no longer stable. Even as he watched, the pillars slid down their radial lines to the next circle. The spellwork shifted, compensating for the damage. Patrick's attention drifted toward the center where Dominion Sect acolytes surrounded Jono's kneeling form.

He needed to be *there*, not dealing with Rachel.

An arm brushed against his, and Patrick wrenched his gaze away from his target. Nadine nodded at him, weapon braced against her shoulder as she sighted down the barrel at Rachel. Her mageglobe cast a washed-out violet glow across her face, expression calm despite the crazed fighting happening around them.

"Dead or alive?" Nadine asked calmly.

"Alive," Patrick ground out. Movement out of the corner of his eye tugged at his attention, at his soul, but he didn't look. Not yet. "We'll need answers."

"Acknowledged." Brown eyes slid his way for a single instance, Nadine's head tilting in the direction of the spellwork and the threat coming their way. "Your sister is the enemy now. Remember that, Collins."

"I know."

She nodded and advanced toward Rachel, who didn't seem all that thrilled with facing off against a mage of Nadine's caliber. Nadine dropped her shield from around Patrick as she sought to take down the witch. The rain returned, soaking him once again. Patrick slowly turned, the fight a distant noise all around him as he faced his past.

Walking down the blackened radial line, long red hair whipped away from her face by the wind, came his twin sister.

Hannah's arms were held out to her side, hands moving through the air in undulating motions, as if she were skimming them over objects no one else could see. Her aura was broken wide open and shone like a dying star, washing out her skin with power her mortal body could barely contain. A body that was too thin, too broken, too *human*.

She might carry Macaria's godhead in her soul, chained by prayers, but she was no god.

Patrick swallowed thickly, a fine tremble running through his hand that held the dagger. "Hannah."

Despite being fraternal twins, they still shared certain traits: the same hair from their mother, the same eyes of their father. That was where the similarities ended. Where Patrick had lived a life under Setsuna's distant care and Ashanti's critical teachings, Hannah had only ever known the hell their father had put her through. Patrick couldn't even begin to understand the life she'd lived that put such insanity into her green eyes.

In Cairo, Patrick had grieved for her, tried to reason with her, but there was no reasoning with madness. He knew that now. For so long, Patrick only had the ghost of her in his head, memories he couldn't forget of a night that separated them forever. That horror had never left him, and it never would.

The hardest lesson Patrick had ever learned was the day he realized he had to give Hannah up as lost if he was going to survive their father's cruel ambition.

Patrick knew now there was no saving those who could not be saved.

But it still hurt.

"You can't hope to stand against us," Hannah said.

Her voice reminded Patrick of Marek's when the seer's patron shared his body. Powerful, inhuman, but with a thread of the person whose body it was underneath. An echo of humanity that had yet to be snuffed out.

Magic seeped out of her aura, writhing around her body. Hannah's magic and the godhead residing in her soul had long since become Ethan's to control. She lived only for their father, and it was his words coming out of her mouth, his will calling magic through her soul.

Patrick's twin sister was a living, breathing nightmare of a nexus.

Nothing more than a weapon.

"Hannah, please don't make me go through you," Patrick said, incapable of not begging. He couldn't tell if the wetness in his eyes was rain or tears.

They should have grown up together. They should have been family. Instead, they were two pawns on opposite sides of a war driven by beliefs that weren't theirs.

Three years ago Patrick hadn't done enough in Cairo. He'd been too shell-shocked by his sister's survival and his father's attempt at harnessing a second godhead in the midst of hell on earth to do more than survive.

Patrick would always mourn what might have been when it

came to his family. But this was where the grieving stopped. Tonight, he would pay his respects to the ghosts of all the things that made him and *fight*.

The magical attack Hannah levied at him blasted through where he'd stood. But Patrick was already moving, diving toward the next active concentric circle of the spellwork. He tumbled head over heels, mud sliding down his jacket and squelching against his skin as he rolled into the hell-tainted magic.

It seared through the damaged parts of his soul deep enough he thought he'd puke. Choking back bile, Patrick sliced the dagger through the earth and the circle of magic within reach. The backlash of the disruption tossed Patrick through the air toward the center of the spellwork instead of out of it. The throw caused him to miss dying beneath his sister's second attack by a fraction of a second.

Patrick hit the ground hard, air punching out of his lungs with a heavy exhale. Ethan's magic fluctuated all around him as Patrick forced himself to his feet. Hannah wrenched her arm around in a semicircle, screaming wordlessly as magic guided by Ethan lashed toward Patrick in a sickening bolt of power that made the air crackle and burn.

Patrick spun on his feet, the weight of the carbine dangling from his tactical vest nearly pulling him off balance. He raised the dagger to counter the attack, gritting his teeth against the heat that burned through his fingers.

The dagger point lit up like a star, a literal spiderweb of magic flaring out around him. The makeshift shield held back Hannah's attack, hellish fire curling against the gods-created defense a mere arm's length away.

For one moment, Patrick thought he might have stood a chance.

The bullet slamming into his left thigh disabused him of that thought.

The familiar flash-fire agony of hot metal parting flesh ripped through him. Patrick yelled in pain as his left leg collapsed beneath him. He went down hard on one knee, swearing harshly. He let go of his carbine and pressed his hand against the exit wound in his thigh, not caring about the filth he was probably contaminating the wound with. Bright red blood welled up between his fingers, the flow steady but not the death sentence quickness of a nicked femoral artery.

Patrick looked over his shoulder and blinked dazedly through the rain at where Hades stood between two concentric inner circles, a semiautomatic pistol gripped in one hand. Even as Patrick watched, Hades shifted the angle of the handgun, aiming for Patrick's head.

"You will die here tonight as you should have when you were a child," Hades promised.

Hades pulled the trigger, and Patrick knew there was no escaping that bullet.

Halfway between them, the bullet transformed into flower petals, the delicate plants ripped apart by the wind. Patrick's breath caught in his throat, and all he smelled was spring.

"No," Persephone said as she stepped out of the veil to stand between Patrick and Hades. "He will not."

A hand wrapped around his other wrist, and Patrick's attention jerked to where Hermes stood behind him, a grim smile on the immortal's face. "This is certainly one way to stop running, Pattycakes."

Hermes peeled the spiderweb shield off the point of the dagger, pressed his hands to the golden strands, and poured his magic into reflecting Hannah's attack back at her. She was propelled backward by the blast, crashing outside the spellwork to land near a couple of soultakers.

"You shouldn't be here," Patrick said, clenching his teeth against the pain.

Hermes shrugged, helping Patrick to stand. "Here or elsewhere, your father's power calls to us."

"Then get the fuck out of the goddamn spellwork."

Hermes watched as Hannah picked herself up off the muddy ground, power a sickening fire around her body. "I'll keep her distracted."

"Don't get yourself killed."

"Worried?" Hermes smiled, a brief flash of mirth in hell. "Don't be. Hera has her coven praying for me."

What little strength their prayers would give Hermes probably wouldn't be enough to face off against Hannah.

"I don't get paid enough for this," Patrick said, mostly to himself.

"I don't know. I think I compensated you just fine." Hermes unhooked the carbine from Patrick's vest and easily hefted it in one hand. "I'm going to borrow this."

Hermes ran off to fight, heaven's light shining in his other hand, a brighter, cleaner burn than what poured out of Hannah's soul. Patrick wrenched himself around to face the center of the spellwork, unsurprised to see that Hades had yet to pull the trigger.

"Do not take his side, Persephone," Hades pleaded.

"What would you have me do? Take yours?" she demanded.

"Yes, because it is the only way we will survive. The Dominion Sect will pray for us."

"Is that what they promised you when they stole Macaria's godhead?"

The weapon Hades held wavered before falling as he dropped his arm back down to his side. The god's expression twisted. If he was human, Patrick would think Hades was grieving.

"They wanted *you*," Hades said, his deep voice catching on the word. "I could not give them my heart."

Persephone clenched her hands into fists. "So instead you gave them mine? Macaria may not be of my blood and essence, but I was her mother in all the ways that mattered. I would have rather you sacrificed me instead of her."

She made a sweeping gesture with her arm, and the force she let loose knocked Hades off his feet. The god flew through the air and slammed back to earth outside the sacrificial circle. Persephone looked at Patrick, the fury in her gold-brown eyes tempered by regret.

"Stop Ethan before we lose Zeus the same way we lost Macaria," she ordered.

Then Persephone strode toward her husband with all the life-affirming power of spring held in one clenched fist.

On his own, Patrick staggered toward the center of the spell-work, leaving the immortals to battle it out on their own for once. He had other things to worry about, like the fact that Ethan was close to ripping open the veil despite the damage done to the spell-work. Hell on earth would be more than enough of a distraction for Ethan to strip Zeus of his godhead.

Between the few acolytes left in the center, Patrick could see Jono's battered, naked body where he was bound to the spellwork. A binding ward kept Jono from escaping while the silver stakes driven through each shoulder kept him from shifting. The skin ripped open around the spikes looked burned and infected. Behind him stood a soultaker, ugly maw open near his skull, the scene reminiscent of the vision Marek had seen last week.

"*Motherfucker*," Patrick snarled.

Those fever-bright wolf eyes unerringly searched out Patrick. Jono spoke, but Patrick couldn't hear what he said. The shape his lips formed could have been his name. Patrick crossed another circle, getting closer.

He almost made it, but almost didn't count in war.

Patrick crossed the innermost circle that connected the points of the pentagram when magic slammed into him from behind, knocking him forward. The only reason the hit didn't kill him was due to the durability charm set into his leather jacket. The charm burned out beneath the onslaught, but it lasted long enough to save Patrick's life. He hit the ground hard with his shoulder, rolling with the motion to save his neck.

Patrick came to a stop, head spinning, still holding tight to his dagger. He rolled onto his side with a groan, getting an elbow beneath him as he tried to sit up. He missed seeing the boot that slammed into his face, but he definitely felt it.

Patrick pitched sideways, falling down into mud all over again with rain pouring into his eyes. Blackness ate away at the edge of his vision, mingling with the storm. His jaw throbbed from the kick, blood filling his mouth. He turned his head to the side, watching blearily as his past came back to haunt him.

Ethan looked exactly how he always did in Patrick's nightmares. The sickening glow of his magic, bolstered by Macaria's godhead, pulsed through his father's aura. Patrick tried to move, to roll over, to *get the fuck away*, but his brain wasn't working. Fear choked the breath from his lungs, and blood loss left him feeling dizzy.

Beneath all of that—the pain, the panic, the desperation—was the realization that this was not how he wanted it to end. He didn't want to see another city ravaged by hell, or for Jono to end up like Hannah. Patrick didn't want to lose any more of himself than he had already given to this war. He'd offered up all he was willing to since he was eight years old, and it stopped *now*.

Lightning flashed through the sky above, shocking the air and illuminating the night. The clouds looked like a living thing writhing above New York City, beginning to spin in a way Patrick was all too familiar with. The veil was growing thinner, and they were running out of time. The damaged sacrificial spellwork thrummed with renewed vigor, but it felt wrong, as if the magic it contained was spinning out of control.

Ethan stared down at Patrick with the distance of a man who had never cared about his family, had only cared about the power they could ultimately give him. A wife whose pure soul was enough to help trap a forgotten immortal. A daughter he had bound himself to for life to further his own needs.

And a son who didn't know how to fucking lie down and die.

"I have no use for you. I never did," Ethan told him. Magic dripped like fire from his hands as he reached for Patrick's heart to try to tear it out all over again.

"You keep trying for godhood," Patrick spat out as he raised both hands over his chest, the dagger gleaming with magic-wrought prayers. "And you keep failing because you aren't fucking *worthy*."

He sliced the dagger over the meat of his palm, cutting deep. Blood coursed down his hand and wrist, a waterfall of red that he slammed down onto the line of the hexagon making up the center of the pentagram. The impact rang like a bell in his head, a deafening sound that blocked everything else out.

Blood called to blood, and Patrick only had one command.

"*Break!*" he snarled, pouring all his will into the word.

He had no magic left, only what borrowed strength the dagger could give him. It was enough to crack the outline of the pentagram, the center of the spellwork breaking into pieces.

"No!" Ethan roared, forced to pour his magic into the spellwork rather than Patrick's body, struggling to keep it together.

Patrick rolled away, digging deep for a strength that had gotten him through his life. He got his hands and one knee underneath him and started to crawl. Pieces of the pentagram floated in the air, strands of magic struggling to realign the shape of it. But the magic was too wild, the foundation too unstable, for it to be pieced back together quickly and correctly.

The acolytes at the center of the spellwork screamed as they died, their magic and souls sucked into the spell by Ethan's need. The air felt heavy around him, pressure coming from above where the sky broke open from the backlash, the tear in the veil an ugly hole between all the hells and the mortal plane.

The pillars of light burned out one by one save for where Zeus stood, still tied to the spellwork, an anchor that needed to be set free. Patrick kept his focus on Jono, eyes flickering to the soultaker that could only follow its hunger.

That gaping maw split wide, all its jagged teeth glinting in the glow of magic. Desperation gave Patrick the push he needed to lunge at Jono and the demon intent on ripping out the other man's soul.

The dagger cut through the soultaker's skull with ease, but not before those sharp teeth sank into Jono's shoulder. His scream filled Patrick's ears, blood pouring down his torso. The black blade of the dagger turned white, heavenly fire burning through the soultaker's body like an inferno. The demon turned to ash that mingled with the rain, dirty rivulets of water running down Jono's torso, mixing with his blood.

The binding ward fell apart beneath the cut of the dagger. Patrick panted for breath, the crash of thunder directly above causing him to look up. A hellish red glow spread through the sky, and all he could sense in his damaged soul was hell.

"You must close it."

His eyes snapped to Jono's pale face, the voice of a god falling between them. Jono's accent was gone, replaced by a different one that sounded like teeth ripping through bone.

"I can't," Patrick said desperately. "Closing a rift requires a nexus."

He didn't have that reach anymore, didn't have the ability to channel external magic. Three years since that loss and his soul wound had never felt so crippling.

"You must."

Patrick frantically shook his head as he pulled the silver stakes out of Jono's shoulders one at a time. The wounds didn't immediately close, the blackened chemical burns at the edges telling Patrick aconite was probably involved. Jono was still tied to the spell that Ethan was holding together, Zeus' godhead a prize his father would do anything to gain—even if it meant letting hell reign on earth once more.

"Patrick." Jono's voice this time, without the ringing other-worldliness of a god in his tone. "This is where I'm meant to be."

Here, in the middle of a maelstrom, a god pack alpha werewolf with ties to an immortal. Someone the Fates had thrown into Patrick's path without giving either of them a choice in the matter.

"Jono," Patrick said, his voice breaking on the other man's name.

The magic all around them began to reform, the spellwork piecing itself together beneath Ethan's focused will, backed by the Dominion Sect who served him.

They were running out of time.

"*Save us.*"

Patrick touched his bloody hand to Jono's face, smearing red across too-cold skin, and pressed a hard kiss to cold lips. "Tell your god he fucking sucks at guiding you."

Then he grabbed Jono's right hand in his left, pressed it to the muddy ground, and drove his dagger through both their hands.

Pain ripped through Patrick's arm, fingertips going numb. Magic exploded away from their joined hands, the dagger impossible to see within the star-bright glow. Patrick knew he screamed, but he couldn't hear his own voice over the scalding rush of raw power pouring through his soul. It cut deep, ripping through metaphysical scars, and Patrick was certain the only reason his soul wasn't torn out of his body was due to Persephone's wards set in his bones.

The scarred channels of his soul broke open as something else —*someone* else—filled the space. Patrick stared into Jono's strangely calm eyes as the magic set in the dagger tied their souls together through blood.

Exactly how Ethan had bound Hannah to him.

Like father, like son.

That sickening realization had Patrick reeling backward, but he couldn't escape what was happening. All he could do was live through it, the bright wash of awareness he hadn't felt in years pouring through him by way of Jono. Through Jono's soul, Patrick could sense the nexus—filled with wild magic—far beneath the earth.

He could *reach* it.

Jono's soul, bound to his, acted like a safety break for his magic. Patrick could feel how the connection between them could help him channel power without either of them burning out—Patrick because he was a mage with crippled magic and Jono because of a god's favor.

Patrick fumbled for the dagger, weak fingers pulling it free. His mouth opened on a silent scream, pain lancing up his arm from the self-inflicted stab wound. Blood pooled in the wound it left behind before spilling between his fingers. Everything around him had taken on a new hue, and the colors spun sickeningly when Jono shoved him to the ground.

The shock-wave spell rolled over them but the leading edge of the attack broke against Jono's shifting form, the magic between them dispelling it. He shouldn't have been able to shift, not with aconite poisoning running through his veins, but Jono was a god pack alpha werewolf with ties to a god. He had reservoirs of strength few other werecreatures possessed.

Man changed to beast with a sickening crunch of bone and splitting of skin above Patrick's body. One large paw the size of his head sank into the muddy ground near his ribs. Jono was so big in his wolf-form that he mostly blocked the rain from soaking Patrick's body. That monstrous wolf head swung down toward him after the change, bright blue eyes meeting his.

Patrick lifted his bleeding hand and gently touched Jono's cold snout. His shaking fingers slipped between sharp teeth. Magic crackled between them, the pull of the nexus impossible to resist through both their souls.

So Patrick didn't.

He closed his eyes, reaching through Jono's soul for something he hadn't thought he'd ever touch again. Patrick's soul stretched itself thin, but Jono's kept him anchored as he sought to replenish his drained magic with the reservoir of power that lived beneath New York City.

It roiled far below the surface, destabilized by Ethan's interference. Patrick could sense how the ley lines had been choked off from it, breakwaters initiated in those rivers of magic by SOA mages. The nexus itself was still viable, despite everything happening around them.

Patrick breathed in, and when he exhaled out, it was like being struck by lightning.

Magic poured through him—deep, wild magic that he bent to his will. Drawing on skills he'd left by the wayside when he never thought he'd have this again, Patrick manipulated the raw magic into something akin to a reverse lightning bolt. He opened his eyes and raised his other arm toward the sky, staring past the brightly burning dagger in his hand at the fury of hell twisting through the storm.

Patrick framed the spell in his mind, the same one he'd used in Cairo. He could see it forming in the world around him, the pattern crystal clear and sharp.

"*Close.*"

Magic exploded through them, guided by Patrick's focused will. His spine arched, shoulders and heels pressing down into the mud as power crashed through the spellwork with devastating results. It raced through their souls and found release through the dagger, heaven's fire guiding magic into the sky.

It hit the clouds, sinking into their black depths. The rain seemed to flow upward, into the sky, before falling back down to earth. The sonic boom of magic gone nova exploded in the sky, shining like the sun at high noon for one searing instant that momentarily blinded Patrick.

He blinked, colored spots dancing across his eyes before

coalescing into stars in the night sky. A perfect circle had formed within the storm clouds above Central Park, the rain falling around them at the edges like a waterfall.

The veil had sealed shut, but what had come through while it was open would need to be dealt with in the future.

Patrick's arm dropped to the ground, grip loosening on his now-quiescent dagger. His fingers slid free of Jono's teeth as the werewolf collapsed to the empty ground beside him. The radial lines and circles of the sacrificial spellwork had shattered into a million glowing pieces that were fading away all around them.

At the head of the radial line once pointing true north, Zeus shook himself free of the magic that had bound him. His precisely tailored suit was ruined by the storm, graying hair wet and curling around a stern face. The king of the Greek gods looked unsettlingly human in that moment, which proved how close Ethan had come to succeeding this time around.

The god approached where Patrick and Jono lay with measured steps. Patrick watched him come—too numb, too cold, too drunk on magic to care about immortals and their games anymore.

Zeus knelt in the muck of an urban battlefield and touched a finger to Patrick's forehead.

"Sleep," Zeus said, his voice like the rumble of thunder in the storm high above.

Patrick closed his eyes and slept, but couldn't escape his nightmares. They followed him relentlessly into his dreams.

20

LOSING TIME NEVER STOPPED BEING DISORIENTING.

Patrick opened his eyes to the white walls and ceiling of a private hospital room, the steady sound of machines monitoring his vitals filling his ears. The pinch of a needle stung the back of his hand, and he blearily looked down at where two IV lines were each connected to a vein. The hospital gown was itchy and rough. The heart rate monitor clipped to the end of his right index finger was annoying.

The bed was positioned so he was half sitting up. Patrick gazed around the empty hospital room, noticing the large window off to his right that looked out onto a nurse's desk. He could see two armed SOA agents standing guard outside his room.

His left thigh hurt, but not as badly as he thought it should. He dragged the thin blanket aside and poked at the bandage wrapped around his leg. Either he'd been unconscious longer than he thought, or someone had added a healer to the mix of doctors overseeing his care. Patrick assumed it was the latter. A healer could tend to the body, but they couldn't do anything about the state of his soul.

His left hand was lightly bandaged, and ached, but no longer felt as if it were on fire. When Patrick flexed his fingers, they all responded, a clear sign he'd escaped nerve damage. Patrick pressed his other hand over the scars on his chest, trying to calm his breathing. He could feel his magic again, a quiet flicker deep in his soul as it slowly returned, but that wasn't all he could feel.

Jono, he thought bleakly.

Patrick shied away from the ties that bound his soul to another person, the illegality of the act threatening to make him sick. He used his trickle of magic to reset his personal shields using the anchors carved into his bones. They did nothing to block out Patrick's awareness of Jono.

"Fuck," he said, dragging a hand through his hair.

"I see you're finally awake."

Patrick's head snapped up, watching as Nadine walked into the hospital room. She looked tired, one hand holding a little paper cup of shitty hospital coffee. She approached his bedside on quiet feet, eyeing him critically. Dark circles showed beneath her eyes even through her makeup. Her shoulders were slumped with exhaustion, but she still managed a tired smile for him.

"Where am I?" Patrick asked in a rough voice. His mouth was dry and tasted disgusting. He needed about a gallon of Listerine to fix that, or a shot of whiskey. He'd take either right about now. "What day is it?"

Nadine grabbed the water pitcher off the rolling bedside table and poured him a glass. Patrick took it from her gratefully.

"Bellevue. It's Thursday afternoon. You've been out for quite a while," she said.

Patrick eyed the whiteboard bolted to the wall opposite the foot of his bed. The name of his current nurse was written in washable ink, as well as a coded list of his current treatment that might as well have been written in a foreign language for all he understood it.

He swallowed slowly, shivering at the memory of the fight in

Central Park. "Tell me what happened."

Nadine dragged the uncomfortable-looking hospital chair closer to his bed. She sat down, never letting go of her coffee. "I'm sure you noticed the guards."

"I'm not handcuffed."

"You're not under arrest. They're for your protection. Not all of the Dominion Sect magic users were caught."

He could guess who was missing. "Ethan and Hannah escaped."

"Yes. Hades took them through the veil."

Patrick let his head fall back against the pillow. "You realize no security guard in the world would be able to stop them if they really wanted to get in here?"

Nadine smiled grimly. "I shielded the room. Besides, Ethan will probably lay low for a while now that the public knows he's alive."

"Did any of his people survive that fight?"

"Rachel did. Outside of Ethan's escape, her arrest is all anyone is talking about on the news."

"You didn't kill her?"

Nadine arched an eyebrow. "You asked me not to."

Patrick shrugged tiredly. "If your finger accidentally slipped on the trigger, I wouldn't have blamed you."

"Believe me, I thought about it, but your director is going to need a scapegoat when the dust finally settles."

"What do you mean?"

"That Congress isn't appreciative of my decision to keep Rachel in her position when I first had my suspicions about her loyalty. They fail to realize a belief isn't probable cause, much less solid evidence," a familiar voice replied.

Patrick stared at where SOA Director Setsuna Abuku stood in the doorway to his hospital room. The fifty-one-year-old woman packed a wealth of power in her aura despite only being a witch. Her sheer presence was enough to draw anyone's attention when she stepped into a room.

On the petite side, with jet-black hair cut into a blunt bob around a thin, barely wrinkled face, the SOA director wore a precisely tailored business suit. She held a tote bag in one hand and a rosewood cane in the other. The cane had intricately carved steps twisting upward to the image of a Shinto shrine at the top. Delicate kanji were written over every step, the prayers a quiet hum to Patrick's senses.

Setsuna let the door close behind her and tapped it with her cane, warding the room for silence. Static flowed over the walls and ceiling and floor, shrouding them in a bubble of privacy.

"There are rumors already about a congressional hearing," Nadine added.

Patrick made a face. "Great. What I wouldn't give to be back in the military so the brass could deal with the mess and leave me out of it."

His after-action reports regarding the Thirty-Day War were highly classified and he had gladly let the chain of command handle the scrutiny of the public once the fighting was over. Unfortunately, Patrick didn't think he'd be able to get out of testifying before Congress about what happened this week if they subpoenaed him.

"I may have to reach out to the Joint Chiefs regarding this issue. We'll see," Setsuna said.

Nadine took a sip of her coffee and made a face at whatever she tasted. "We have Rachel to take the fall. That should be helpful to a degree."

Patrick snorted. "Until the Dominion Sect decides she's better off dead in order to keep their secrets."

"She is under twenty-four-hour watch at a classified location," Setsuna said.

"Running black sites on domestic soil again, are we?" Patrick asked caustically.

Setsuna leveled a flat look his way. "The SOA does no such thing."

Patrick rolled his eyes, letting her stick to whatever story she wanted to tell. He'd claim deniability by way of unconsciousness all the way to the courts in that area. "When can I leave?"

"You still need to be debriefed."

"That isn't an answer."

"You're recovering from a gunshot wound in your thigh, a stab wound to your hand, severe bruising, and magical backlash on top of magical burnout," Nadine pointed out.

"I can negotiate with the doctor or just AMA my way out."

"They're doctors. We don't negotiate with medical personnel like that."

"AMA it is."

Nadine picked his cell phone off the table and waved it at him. It had survived the fight in Central Park with only a slightly cracked screen, which was impressive. "I have a text from Smooth Dog who insists you'll try to pull that stunt and to handcuff you to the bed as a preventative measure."

"Kinky, but he knows that's not my kind of kink. Give me my phone."

Nadine handed it over. She knew his passcode for the same reason he knew hers. Patrick wasn't surprised she'd been monitoring his phone while he'd been out of it. Patrick unlocked the phone and stared down at the text messages from his old team captain. Smooth Dog was a call sign Captain Gerard Breckenridge would never live down as long as Patrick was alive to tease him mercilessly about it.

The text conversation between Gerard and Nadine was from ten hours ago, the glut of messages spanning roughly thirty minutes.

"Huh," he muttered. "Guess they're no longer running dark."

That didn't necessarily mean his old team was accessible, or they'd have tried to call. Most likely Gerard had bribed someone to give him clearance to use his personal cell phone and get a signal boost.

Patrick tapped back into the general queue of text conversations and hit Marek's next. He didn't get past reading the latest one.

EVERYONE SAFE. JONO'S WITH US.

Seeing Jono's name reminded Patrick of all the problems this case had spawned for him personally and how he wasn't remotely ready to process any of it. His VA therapist would probably have something to say about that, but Patrick was all for keeping his head in the sand for a little while longer.

He dropped his phone on the bed, sighing heavily. "Did we lose anyone?"

"We have more critically injured than dead, but yes. We lost some agents. They died making sure soultakers didn't escape Central Park. When the spellwork blew, the overload took the demons apart since they were tied to it," Setsuna said.

"Anyone I know?"

Because nearly all of the SOA agents in the field Tuesday night had been from the Rapid Response Division. Patrick didn't have a permanent partner, but he'd worked with a few of them over the years when their cases crossed paths and he'd been brought in as backup on others.

"Maybe. I'll get you a list."

As if she didn't already know the names of the dead, which meant he'd probably known one or more of the agents who died. "Okay."

"They'll all be awarded posthumous commendations for bravery in the line of duty."

And funerals with all the pomp and circumstance the agency could muster beneath the glare of media cameras. Patrick knew Setsuna wouldn't be above using their deaths to engender sympathy toward the SOA and the danger its agents operated under. Patrick hated politics with a passion, but he knew how the game was played.

"What about Lucien?"

"Sticking around," Nadine said. "Whether for a few days or a few weeks, he won't say."

"And you?"

Nadine's mouth curved into a slight, lopsided smile. "I am being formally reprimanded for agreeing to liaise without permission while on vacation, without the proper paperwork done up, and for not informing my superiors of my intentions or the threat at hand. The PIA will also be giving me a commendation for bravery in the field."

Patrick laughed a little. "Of course they will."

Setsuna cleared her throat. "Special Agent Mulroney, I'd like to speak with Patrick alone."

Nadine got to her feet without argument. "I'll go find the doctor and let her know you're awake, Patrick."

She left the room, the silence ward reforming after she was gone. Setsuna approached the bed and set her tote bag on the chair Nadine had vacated. She withdrew his dagger from it, and Patrick didn't realize how tense he'd been until he got eyes on it again. Setsuna passed the dagger over, and he practically snatched it out of her hand.

"Thanks," he said.

Setsuna folded both hands over the top of her cane, her fingers curling over the gates of the Shinto shrine. "What did you do in that circle?"

"I'm not talking about it with you."

"Then shall I make an educated guess? Because your soul reaches for another when it never has before."

"I *know*."

The sound of his heart rate monitor beeping louder caused Patrick to rip the electrodes off his chest to silence the damn thing. He glared at Setsuna, clenching his jaw so hard his teeth ached. He knew *exactly* what he'd done to Jono and just how illegal that action was.

Souls were supposed to be off-limits.

Patrick had strived for his entire life to never become like his father, and that had all changed on summer solstice. He'd done the unthinkable, and he didn't know how to *fix* it—because the bond tying his soul to Jono's felt permanent.

Setsuna regarded him with an unreadable look in her brown eyes before she nodded, more to herself than to him. "I set a forgetting spell on the healers and witches who are responsible for your care. Your actions regarding this particular problem will be kept out of all official reports. That won't stop Mr. de Vere from needing to be interviewed."

Patrick bit his tongue at that admission. Her actions, as illegal as they were, didn't make him feel any better. But they would keep him safe, whether he liked it or not. As for Jono...well, Patrick doubted he'd have to remind Jono to keep his secrets.

"The SAIC position here in New York City will be filled on an interim basis for eventual permanent placement by the Assistant SAIC out of California," Setsuna continued.

"I take it you can't trust the one here?"

"The entire upper management in the New York City office is under investigation. The office in California is clean of any hidden threats."

Patrick had to think hard for a few seconds on why that was before he remembered who headed up the SAIC post in San Francisco. "Maybe you should put a witch with an affinity for mind magic in every office."

Former Major Veronika Federova was years out of service with the Caster Corps within the US Department of the Preternatural. Her penchant for doing everything by the book and *knowing* when people were lying, even through shields, meant the ranks below her operating out west were clean. Patrick knew she wouldn't like giving up her Assistant SAIC, but whoever was transferred to New York from that office would be trustworthy.

"It will be a tough sell to make the general public trust our office here again. A transparent investigation will go a long way toward helping with that."

Patrick eyed her dubiously. "You hate transparency."

"Sometimes it is required and necessary," Setsuna said with all the distaste of a person stepping in dog shit.

"Good luck with that."

"You'll want to keep some of that luck for yourself. I'm transferring you here to New York City."

"*What?*"

Setsuna didn't seem bothered by his anger. "You helped save this city, and that's goodwill I refuse to give up. The Rapid Response Division here lost a couple of agents in the fight. You're more than capable of taking over one of their spots."

"No."

"This isn't negotiable, Patrick. The transfer paperwork has already been drawn up."

Patrick knew this was an order he couldn't argue against. His contracted government job was one of the few barriers between himself and the demands levied by immortals. He wasn't keen on giving up that defense, even if it meant he bowed to the demands of what the SOA needed from him instead.

A tiny voice in the back of his mind pointed out that staying in New York City meant staying with Jono.

Patrick ignored that voice.

"You could have at least asked," Patrick said angrily.

"You'll have a month to get all your affairs in order in DC and move out here. I'll even give you time to take your vacation."

"It's a little late for bribes, and the agency better reimburse me for the vacation I had to cancel."

Setsuna tapped the point of her cane against the floor, her gaze never leaving his. Patrick thought she might reach out to try to comfort him, except she didn't. He didn't know why, in that moment, he wanted her to. Setsuna had taken over guardianship of him when he was a kid and relinquished it when he turned seventeen and joined the Mage Corps. She'd provided almost a decade of year-round boarding schools away at an Academy and an apartment shared with her in Washington, DC, during holiday breaks that never felt like home.

She cared for him but had never seemed to care *about* him.

For once, Patrick wished she would.

"I'll expect your report by the end of the weekend. I believe Chief Casale would prefer it earlier, but take your time. I will handle everything else," Setsuna told him quietly. "Goodbye, Patrick."

Patrick didn't watch her leave. Nadine came into the room with the doctor a minute later. "I'm leaving," he said.

"I would advise against that," the doctor replied.

"Advise away. It's not going to change me walking out that door today."

"Can you give us a minute?" Nadine asked the doctor, flashing her a polite smile.

The doctor left, but not before giving Patrick a stern look, which he ignored. Nadine went to his bedside again and reached out to card her fingers through his dirty red hair. "You still have mud in your hair. Guess the sponge bath didn't get rid of it all."

"I can take a shower back at the apartment."

"Stay another day, Patrick. You need the rest."

"Nadine—"

"One more day. Then I'll escort you out of here no matter what the doctor says. Whatever you think you need to do, it can wait." She paused, settling her hand on his shoulder and looking him in the eye. "Jono can wait."

Patrick closed his eyes and let out a frustrated sigh. "I hate hospitals."

"We all hate hospitals. Now don't bite the poor doctor's head off when she comes back in."

Nadine left to go fetch his doctor once again. Turned out modern medicine and a witch's brew could cut his healing time in half, but it wasn't a cure. The soft tissue damage in his left thigh was weeks ahead in the healing process, but the muscle there was still delicate. He'd scar and need a couple of weeks of physical therapy, but the doctor believed he'd regain full range of motion in the leg.

The stab wound in his left hand had healed up as well, but the skin there was still delicate. The bandage was to hold the last salve treatment in place, and the RN witch promised the marks in his skin would fade in a couple of months.

No one mentioned the mess of his soul, Setsuna's forgetting spell keeping his secret.

Nadine left not long after the doctor, off to deal with whatever needed to be handled right now. Patrick grabbed the remote off the side table, turned on the television, and switched it to a news channel. He needed to get caught up on things.

It turned out when you broke up a high-level sacrificial spell-work by way of magical overload, it really did a number on the grass.

The North Meadow in Central Park was nothing but mud surrounding craters made from grenades and offensive spells. The baseball fields were absolutely ruined for the rest of summer, and the park itself had been closed off to the public for the next week at the very least. A dozen talking heads across half that many channels were busy discussing what had happened and getting a lot of facts wrong as they did so.

The spin is going to be ugly, Patrick thought to himself a couple of hours later.

"You shouldn't be watching that. It'll just piss you off."

Patrick jerked his head around as Casale stepped into his hospital room. He cleared his throat, muting the television. "Needed to get information somehow. What are you doing here?"

Casale eyed him critically as he came closer. "I wanted to see how you were doing."

"Did you come by before now?"

"I did, but you were still unconscious. Got a call from your director that you were awake."

"I don't have my report ready."

"While I'd be happy if you did, I'm not here for that." Casale pulled a flat white envelope out of his inner suit pocket and handed it to Patrick. "This is for you."

Patrick took it and slid his thumb under the flap to open it. He stared in confusion down at the small stack of money stuffed inside. "Is this a bribe? Are you bribing me? Wait a minute. Shouldn't I be the one bribing you to keep the press at bay?"

Casale let out a dry chuckle. "It's not a bribe. Ramirez and Guthrie wanted me to give that to you. Apparently you won the pot I know nothing about. Figured you'd earned it."

It took a moment before Patrick remembered what Casale was talking about. He didn't bother to hide his grin. "I won the pot."

"Of which I know nothing about," Casale stressed.

Patrick stuffed the envelope under the blanket and waved at the only chair in the room. "Take a seat. I can't promise I'll be great company right now, but it's not like I'm going anywhere today."

"What about tomorrow?"

"Oh, you're good. But no, it's still today, so I'm stuck eating hospital food for one more night."

Maybe he could bribe the nurses to order him a pizza. With cash on hand, that was a possibility now.

"You sure leaving medical care so soon is a good idea?"

"I'll be fine, Casale. I've had worse and kept working."

"That's not exactly a ringing endorsement of your decision-making skills when it comes to your health."

Casale sat back in the chair a little. His suit was slightly wrinkled in places and damp at the shoulders. Patrick glanced out the window that faced the street, seeing rain still coming down, but nowhere near as violently as it had during summer solstice. Right now it was more of a lazy shower.

"Our weather witches on staff say the reactionary storm will disappear by tomorrow night," Casale said.

"That's good." Patrick was absolutely terrible with weather

328

magic. He didn't have an affinity for it at all. He figured out what the weather would be like on a day-to-day basis by checking an app on his phone rather than communing with nature. "Means I can take a smoke break outside when it finally stops."

Casale's mouth twitched a little. "I should warn you the media has camped outside the hospital. Might want to wait on that smoke break."

Patrick scowled. "Fucking media. The press are like cock-roaches."

"Worse, on occasion."

"Yeah, well, I'll get Nadine to cast a look-away ward when we make our great escape." He scratched at where the medical tape had been adhered to on his arm. No matter what brand was used, it always made his skin itch. "Are all your people accounted for?"

"Yes. We didn't lose anyone, though I hear your agency did."

"Hazard of the job."

"From what I understand, this particular job almost cost you your life."

"Well, it didn't."

Casale got to his feet and extended his hand. "Get some rest. I'll keep in touch with you and your director as we close out the cases on our end."

Patrick shook Casale's hand firmly. "I'll have my report done by Sunday night at the latest. Director Abuku will have to sign off on it before it goes to you for your records."

"I'll keep a look-out for it."

Casale left with a final wave goodbye. Patrick picked up the remote control and unmuted the television. He shifted on the bed, trying to get comfortable. The pain in his leg was a hazy sort of ache, numbed by drugs, despite the forced healing medical profes-sionals had put him through. He tugged the blanket aside and hiked up the hospital gown a little, poking at the bandage again.

"You probably shouldn't touch that."

Patrick had his dagger out and pointed at Hermes before he

HAILEY TURNER

even registered moving. The messenger god rolled his eyes from behind the gigantic vase of white flowers he carried. He was dressed in wet, skinny black jean shorts that fell to his knees, a waterproof cycling jacket, and cycling shoes. A waterproof messenger bag was slung over one shoulder, and his black bike helmet had silver wings painted on the sides.

"Seriously?" Patrick asked. "You're a bike messenger when you're not annoying the fuck out of me?"

Hermes smirked at him and deposited the vase on the rolling side table, taking a moment to adjust the bunches of small white flowers. "Today I am."

"What do you want?"

Hermes leaned his hip against the bedside railing, taking in Patrick's less than stellar state. "What do you think? I've come to give you a message."

Patrick eyed the flowers, in no mood to accept any more gifts from the gods. "Any chance I can reject it?"

"It's customary to bring the invalid flowers. Hera thought you'd like them. They're cliff roses. Native to Greece." Hermes cocked his head to the side, rainwater dripping off his helmet onto the bed. "Manhattan now sports four bushes of the flowers on land at the cardinal points."

"A simple thank-you would've sufficed, but your kind doesn't know the meaning of that phrase."

Hermes laughed. He snapped his fingers and a single gold coin spun into existence in the air. It fell onto the bed between Patrick's knees.

"The fight isn't over. That is your message."

Patrick blinked. When he opened his eyes again, Hermes was gone.

"Fuck my life," he muttered.

Patrick pressed the call button for the nurse, figuring they'd like the flowers more than he would.

He kept the coin.

21

THE RAIN WAS NOTHING MORE THAN A LIGHT DRIZZLE FRIDAY morning when Patrick finally escaped the confines of Bellevue.

Dressed in actual clothes rather than a hospital gown, Patrick ignored the disapproving frown of his doctor and signed himself out against medical advice. Nadine hustled him out of Bellevue under a look-away ward and a stealth spell, keeping them hidden from any prying eyes.

"Where are we going?" Patrick asked, zipping up his leather jacket despite the muggy weather. Nadine had reset the durability charm in his jacket, and he liked the comfort that provided right now.

"Your apartment," Nadine said.

His fingers brushed against the hilt of his dagger as they walked, and all Patrick could think about was Jono. Part of him wanted to ask Nadine to drive to Marek's home on the Upper East Side so he could come face-to-face with his worst mistake. The rest of him wanted to run, but that was no longer an option.

It never really had been.

Nadine had traded in her rental SUV for a nondescript car

taken from the PIA's motor pool. Patrick got in the front passenger seat and buckled up, staring tiredly out the windshield.

"Here," Nadine said, handing him the coffee thermos sitting in the cup holder between their seats. "Don't say I never did anything for you."

"You've done more than enough, and you know it." Patrick took the thermos and thumbed it open. The smell of whiskey-tinged coffee reached his nose, and he sighed happily. "Thanks."

"Figured you could use some liquid courage," Nadine said as she pulled into the street.

Patrick froze with the thermos against his mouth. "What's that supposed to mean?"

"Take a wild guess."

Suddenly the coffee made his stomach churn.

The thing about having friends was that sometimes they wouldn't let him wallow in his guilt. He should've known Nadine wouldn't indulge his vices without an ulterior motive.

The drive to his apartment didn't take that long. Patrick wished it could have lasted forever.

"Can I request a ride to the airport instead?" Patrick asked when she finally stopped in front of the apartment building.

"No." When Nadine looked at him, all he saw was encouragement in her eyes. "He doesn't blame you."

Patrick shook his head. "He should."

Patrick got out and let the door slam shut behind him. Nadine drove off without a backward glance. He ducked his head against the drizzle still coming down and pulled his keys out of his jacket pocket. He'd lost his original set during the fight and these were his second, reissued set. He'd have to return them soon, because no way was he staying in this place permanently.

Patrick made it to the apartment and was unsurprised when the door opened before he could stick his key into the lock. He held on to the key tight enough it left an imprint against his palm as he stared at the man who'd occupied nearly all of his thoughts since waking up after the fight.

Jono stood framed in the doorway, alive and in one piece, even if it was all a lie. Jono's soul no longer belonged only to him, and Patrick would never forgive himself for doing that. Patrick drank in the sight of him, noticing the dark circles under Jono's eyes, the beard growth that needed a good shave, and the exhaustion in every line of his body.

"Hi," Patrick croaked out.

Jono stared at him, wolf-bright eyes drifting up and down his body. "Shouldn't you be in hospital still?"

"I hate hospitals. I signed myself out."

Jono huffed out a tired sigh, running a hand through his messy black hair. He looked like he hadn't slept in days. "Of course you did."

Jono pushed the door open and stepped aside. Patrick walked past him, shoulders hunched, waiting for a blow that never came. He followed Jono into the living room and shrugged out of his leather jacket, hanging it off the back of a dining room chair.

"Have you been staying here?" Patrick asked.

"I've been staying at Marek's. I came here this morning because Nadine told me to meet her. Guess I know why now."

"How is Marek? And Emma? What about her pack?"

"They're all right. Marek is in a bit of a tiff with Youssef and Estelle. They weren't pleased about the Tempest pack fighting on summer solstice." He paused, staring at Patrick with tired eyes. "They're angrier at me for being at the center of the entire cock-up."

Patrick was aware that maybe, admittedly, he wasn't ready for this conversation. But hiding would only push off the inevitable because here, now, this was where he faced his mistakes. To not make amends would be criminal.

Swallowing against the sudden dryness in his mouth, Patrick forced himself to look Jono in the eye. "I'm sorry."

"You don't have anything to be sorry about, Pat."

The soulbond they shared now said otherwise, and always would.

Patrick could see how Jono's soul bled through his aura now, like he had magic when he didn't. The lack of wounds on his body was nothing compared to what Patrick had done to Jono's soul without permission.

His whiskey-laced coffee wanted to crawl back up his throat. "This is my fault."

Jono shook his head and sat down on the couch, picking up his mug of tea from the coffee table. He gestured for Patrick to take a seat beside him. "You have a thing for misplaced guilt, don't you? All of the bollocks that happened on summer solstice? It wasn't your fault."

Patrick sat down, mindful of his left leg. Even with a witch's brew pushing his healing weeks into the future, his leg was still sore. "You don't know that."

"I know that you weren't the one who hurt me."

Patrick instinctively reached for him at that admission but froze when Jono flinched, spilling hot tea over the side of his mug. Jono grimaced and set it down on the coffee table, wiping his hands clean on his jeans. Patrick stared at him, stomach twisting.

"Oh," he said woodenly, thinking back to the day he'd lost while past the veil. "What did Ethan do to you?"

Jono wouldn't look at him. "Doesn't matter."

"Jono—"

"No, mate. That's not on you."

Patrick clenched his teeth, his chest tightening. "Except for how it is."

More than anyone else in the world, Patrick owed Jono a truth he hadn't given voice to since he was a child. Patrick scrubbed a hand over his face and slowly dropped his shields. Without them, Jono was a shining beacon beside him that Patrick would never be able to walk away from.

"I'm not very good at talking about my problems. Even my therapist doesn't know what I'm going to tell you. It'd probably help with my therapy if I *could* tell him, but he can't know," Patrick confessed.

Jono's scrutiny was difficult for Patrick to face, so he didn't. He looked at the wall, his hands, the floor—anywhere but at Jono. It made it easier to find the words, but they still hurt.

"I was born in Salem, Massachusetts," Patrick said quietly. "My mom's side of the family is originally from there. She was a witch, a healer, who belonged to the Salem Coven."

The Salem Coven was the only group of witches who practiced in that city these days. Everyone in that coven were descendants of those who had survived the Salem Witch Trials. They were one of the oldest covens in the country and the most powerful, a tight-knit group of extended family.

Patrick hadn't set foot in Salem in twenty-one years.

"My mother was Clara Patterson. She would've been the Salem Coven's high priestess one day. If she had lived." Patrick picked at a thread on his jeans, dredging up memories he'd buried long ago. "She married Ethan when she was eighteen. She gave birth to my twin sister, Hannah, and me when she was nineteen. Eight years later he murdered her in the basement of our home."

Patrick swallowed thickly, but kept talking. "Ethan wasn't around much. He spent most of his time at the SOA head offices in DC than in Salem, or in the field. I think his absence took a toll on my mom. I remember they fought a lot near the end, always over us. But it didn't matter because my mom was always going to lose against the Dominion Sect."

"Why?"

"Because Ethan's family is one of the three that helped found the Dominion Sect. It's why Ethan believes he deserves to be a god. It's why he only ever saw his wife and kids as a means to an end."

Patrick shook his head, trying to shake off the memory of that long-ago night when his world was destroyed. The past he came from was one he'd resigned himself to never fully outrunning.

"I saw your sister," Jono said quietly. "She was there where they kept me before taking me to Central Park. She wasn't...right."

"She's carried a stolen godhead in her soul for over two decades. There's nothing left of my twin sister." The words hurt, but they were true. Patrick scraped a hand through his hair, hunching his shoulders. "I was told when I was a teenager that the Dominion Sect had found Macaria at Harvard. They lured her to Salem for the Halloween festival. Ethan sacrificed us to the spell that was supposed to transfer Macaria's godhead to him. I don't know how Persephone found us, but she did. It was still too late to matter."

"You're alive."

Patrick tilted his head back, staring at the ceiling as mirthless laughter escaped his mouth. "Yeah. I'm alive. No thanks to Persephone. She broke me free of the spell and brought me to the Underworld. She left Hannah behind."

He pressed a hand to his scars, chest suddenly aching. The phantom pains made Patrick dig his fingers into the scar tissue he could feel beneath the T-shirt. He startled badly when Jono pulled his hand away, strong fingers looping around his wrist. Patrick looked at him, his breath coming quicker than was comfortable.

"You didn't get those scars during your time in the Mage Corps, did you?" Jono asked.

Patrick slowly shook his head. "Ethan had soultakers helping with the spell. One of the demons kept trying to claw out my heart. Both our hearts. The last thing I remember is Hannah screaming for me to help her when Persephone arrived."

"The immortal saved you."

Patrick's mouth twisted in a hateful smile. "She didn't save me. She enslaved me. Persephone owns my soul debt."

Jono blinked in surprise. "Oh."

"I tried to convince Persephone to go back and save Hannah,

but I was bleeding out in the Underworld and she asked me if I wanted her to save me. I said yes. I was eight and didn't know any better, so I said *yes*. Yes to her healing me. Yes to me owing her my life and soul. To owing her and her kind a debt."

"Because of what Ethan did to Macaria?"

Patrick nodded tiredly. "The Greek pantheon wants Macaria back. When Ethan is dead and she is returned to them, they'll let me go. My soul debt will be paid in full."

It was an impossible task that got harder and harder to complete with every year Patrick put behind him.

"Ethan isn't a god, even with her under his control."

"No, he's not, because the spell went wrong and she got trapped in my sister. Back then, Macaria wasn't worshipped and was mostly forgotten. She didn't have the worship recognition most of the other gods did at the time. Ethan was able to bind them together and…" Patrick's voice trailed off, and he tried to pull free of Jono's grip. Jono wouldn't let him, instead sliding their hands together and holding on tight.

"And?" Jono coaxed.

"He's still searching for a godhead. He went after Ra during the Thirty-Day War."

"Reports on that war only focused on all the hells."

"Yeah, well, hell makes a great distraction. People aren't looking for the creation of a new god when they have literal hell on earth to worry about." Patrick chewed on his bottom lip and shrugged. "I had a chance during that war to kill him. We were in Cairo, and I had Ethan in my sights and in my magic, but Hannah got in the way."

Patrick lost himself in that memory, the scene in his mind vivid and surreal, almost like a waking dream. A wounded Ethan on his knees as the spellwork broke apart around them, the dagger in one hand and his rifle in the other, when Hannah came between them. The shock of seeing her alive had robbed Patrick of his focus and the upper hand.

He should have killed her that day. He could have.

He didn't.

"I thought she'd died in that basement all those years ago. When I saw her, I thought maybe there was something left of her for me to save. I couldn't kill her to get to Ethan. I begged her to get out of the way, but she wouldn't move. Looking back, I know there wasn't anything left of my twin, but it was impossible to understand that at the time."

"You can't blame yourself for that," Jono said.

"Easier said than done," Patrick replied, trying not to sound so bitter. "Ethan destroyed what was left of the nexus below Cairo through Hannah's soul before escaping. I took the brunt of that backlash to try to save my team. I'm Ethan's son by blood, so I could access the spellwork, but it cost me."

"Were you able to save them?"

"Not all of them, and I lost my ability to tap ley lines and nexuses because of my efforts."

Patrick looked away, eyes dry, because he'd already had his breakdown over finding his twin sister alive and losing members of the Hellraisers three years ago. He'd done his damnedest to climb into the bottom of a bottle and drown his nightmares after that fight. He'd buried too many people, folded too many flags taken from caskets, watched as the brothers-in-arms he couldn't save were lowered into the green hills of Arlington.

He still left quarters on their headstones every year around Memorial Day.

"Ethan tied Hannah to him so he could access Macaria's godhead like a nexus. He siphons off the power in the godhead to his acolytes within the Dominion Sect to keep Hannah alive as its vessel. But he never intended for things to be like this. Ethan wants to be a god. He wants power. He wanted it to be him."

Jono squeezed his hand. "You are nothing like Ethan."

"Except for how I am, and I never wanted to be like him, Jono. I'm so fucking sorry."

"There's nothing to forgive."

"I bound your *soul* to mine," Patrick said, his voice tight, panic making him bite out the words at a quick pace. "I bound you, Jono, and that's a death sentence in this country. In *any* country."

Deep down, part of him reveled in being able to tap a nexus again, even if it was through Jono's soul. Patrick felt whole again in a way he hadn't in years.

It just came at the cost of Jono's freedom and autonomy.

"Look at me, Patrick. Please."

Patrick shook his head, trying to tug his hand free of Jono's grip. Jono wouldn't let him go. Strong fingers curled over his chin, forcing Patrick's head around. He found himself staring into Jono's eyes and seeing none of the hate he expected, none of the anger.

"Can you undo it?" Jono asked.

"No," Patrick answered truthfully. "It wasn't my magic that bound our souls together."

"Can someone else?"

Patrick hesitated, thinking of his only friend living on the West Coast. Spencer Bailey was a mage whose magic was *technically* classified in the family of necromancy, but the government had issued him a pardon to live when he was a child. Spencer was a soulbreaker, but he used his magic to exorcise demons and send the dead to rest; he didn't raise them. Patrick didn't know if what tied him and Jono together was something that could be broken, but if anyone had a chance at succeeding, then it would be Spencer.

"Maybe."

Jono's thumb skimmed over his cheek in slow strokes. "It can wait."

"It really can't. I won't use you like how Ethan uses Hannah. For fuck's sake, I just said—"

"I know what you said," Jono interrupted. "But it's okay, love."

Patrick stared at him in disbelief, digging his fingers into the back of Jono's hand. "*How* is this okay?"

"Because the Fates gave me to you," Jono said slowly. "I think that's why Marek brought me here. For you."

Patrick swallowed thickly, the motion making his ears pop. "Who do you serve?"

Jono tipped his head to the side, as if he were listening to something Patrick couldn't hear. "Fenrir guides me. He'd guide my pack if I had one."

Patrick closed his eyes, taking a steadying breath. Jono was meant to be a weapon, a way for the gods to give back what Patrick had lost over the years. To level the playing field between Patrick's crippled magic and Ethan's slowly decaying hold on Macaria's godhead.

The gods had stolen a life the same way Ethan had, and Patrick wondered if this was a punishment or the only way forward through the lonely dark of this fight.

Knowing the gods, it was probably both.

"My usual answer to what Fate wants is a middle finger or a bullet," Patrick muttered, opening his eyes again.

Jono's mouth quirked into a soft smile. "Bit mercurial, are we?"

Patrick lifted his free hand to Jono's mouth, pressing his fingers over dry, chapped lips. "You like me that way."

"Yeah, Pat. I do."

"I hate that nickname."

Jono smiled against his finger, slow and warm. "No, you don't."

Patrick owned so little of himself these days, and names were currency in their own right. But Patrick hadn't bothered to hide the lie he'd just spoken. "You're right. I don't. Not when you're the one using it."

Jono tugged his hand aside and closed the distance between them. The first touch of their lips meeting was soft, a gentle exploration that was as easy as breathing. Then Jono tilted his head, slipped his tongue past Patrick's teeth, and kissed him until it hurt. Patrick let him, drawing him closer, feeling that connection between their souls burning at the edge of his awareness.

"I'll be your weapon if you'll be my pack," Jono whispered against his lips, echoing Patrick's thoughts.

After everything they'd gone through—everything that had changed between them at the hands of the gods—Patrick could deny Jono nothing. He would fight to his last breath to keep Jono safe from any further machinations the gods might throw their way, no matter how fruitless his efforts might be.

For Jono, he would do anything.

"Okay," Patrick said, leaning into Jono's touch, craving it. "We'll figure this out."

Jono hauled Patrick onto his lap, mindful of his left leg. He was warm and solid beneath Patrick, his skin unmarked thanks to the werevirus running through his veins.

"Do you think you can do what you did in Central Park with your magic again?" Jono asked.

Patrick ran his fingers through Jono's hair before cupping the back of his skull. "Yes, but I won't."

"You should never hold back in a fight."

"I've lived without that part of me for years already. Hurting you just to tap a ley line isn't something I'm willing to do."

"Doesn't hurt," Jono said, staring at him with those bright eyes of his.

Patrick leaned forward to kiss him. "You're such a fucking liar and I don't even need enhanced senses to know that."

Patrick kissed away Jono's argument, drowning in the taste of him. Jono's hands stroked down his back to grab him by the hips and pull him closer. Patrick didn't know if the desperate need for closeness was driven by their newly bound souls or the exuberant realization that they'd survived the fight. Whatever drove them, it was a far cry better than searching for the bottom in a bottle of alcohol.

Only when his lungs ached with the need to breathe did Patrick tear his mouth from Jono's, pressing their foreheads together.

"What happens now?" Jono asked into the quiet between them.

Patrick sighed, leaning backward a little and trying to ignore how uncomfortable his jeans were getting. "I'm being transferred to the New York City field office here, so you won't have to move."

Jono slid his hands beneath Patrick's T-shirt, rucking it up a little as he sought out skin. "Bet Youssef and Estelle will be thrilled about that."

"Do they have immortal patrons?"

Jono shrugged. "Maybe? Don't really know. I'm not part of their god pack."

"Great. That's all we need," Patrick muttered. "A fucking civil war in the werecreature community."

Jono nipped at his mouth, stealing another kiss. "When does the transfer happen?"

"Setsuna gave me a month for the move. She even offered me a vacation."

"So you're not moving because of me?"

"I didn't tell Setsuna about you."

Jono eyed him thoughtfully. "But she knows?"

"About our bond? She suspects, but she made sure no one else would find out," Patrick said carefully. "If someone discovers what I did to you, I will go to jail, Jono. I will be charged with destroying the essence of your soul, and that's a capital crime right up there with murder."

A soul, like a life, was sacred. The law was very clear on that, and as often as Patrick had bent the law to finish a case, he'd never outright broken it like this before.

"I've spent the past thirteen years without a pack. No one is taking you away from me," Jono growled.

"I don't know anything about how to be pack."

"Neither do I. We'll figure it out."

Patrick looped his arms around Jono's shoulders, drawing him forward. Jono went willingly, pressing his forehead to Patrick's chest, right over the scars. He let out a shuddering sigh that made Patrick hold him tighter.

"I can't sleep," Jono said in a slow voice. "I'm so tired, but all I see is…"

He trailed off, but Patrick knew what lived in that silence. He knew the way nightmares could steal everything from a person—their sleep, their dreams, their sense of peace. Trying to go through the motions of acting normal after trauma would only make a person crazy over time. If there was anything years of one-on-one and group therapy had shown Patrick, it was that normal was relative, and you lived every day one day at a time.

He shifted, pulling away from Jono just long enough to get them both lying down on the couch. Jono wrapped his arms around Patrick's torso, their legs tangling together. Patrick settled his chin on the top of Jono's head, listening to him breathe.

Between them, the soulbond drew ever tighter.

It should have scared him, but if Jono was okay with it, then Patrick would learn to be as well.

What was one more debt, after all?

22

"YOU OWE ME A VACATION."

Patrick laughed in Nadine's face. "I owe myself one first."

"Should've taken your director's offer to add it onto your moving timeline and costs."

"Maybe."

Nadine rifled through her purse, triple-checking that she had the appropriate documents in hand that would get her Browning 9mm through security. LaGuardia was crowded with returning business flyers on a Tuesday night. No one even looked twice at their goodbye in the terminal.

Setsuna had kept Nadine's identity locked down at the request of the PIA in the aftermath. She was having a harder time keeping Patrick out of the spotlight, but that was the nature of the job.

Nadine's carry-on luggage was a hardback case well-worn from travel, the handle sticking up in the locked position. The dove gray jacket of her pantsuit paired nicely with the pale pink blouse underneath. Her heels looked like they could murder a man, and Patrick's feet ached just looking at them.

She'd dressed for a fight today in the face of several long meetings in New York City. Marek had bought her a couple new power suits to get her through the next few days as a thank-you for her help during the mess last week. Patrick didn't envy the poor bastard back at the PIA headquarters in Washington, DC, tasked with Nadine's in-person debrief tomorrow. She'd eat them alive.

Finding everything in order, Nadine settled her purse straps on her shoulder and tucked a bit of her loose brown hair behind an ear, papers and PIA badge in hand. "Call me when you make it to DC. I should still be stateside. We'll get dinner."

"This weekend, maybe. I need to pack up my apartment and call one of the vetted movers the agency uses."

"You take a look at any apartments here yet?"

Patrick made a face. "I'm going to be spending half of my paycheck on rent alone. Let me mourn my bank account a little longer."

"Soon as you pick a place, send me your address. I'll mail you a housewarming gift from Paris."

"Better be alcohol."

"It'll be something."

Nadine reached out to adjust the collar of his button-down shirt. They'd both dressed up a little today in the face of meetings with city officials, NYPD brass, and the upper echelons of the SOA. Setsuna had returned to DC days ago but Priya was still in New York City helping the new SAIC get settled in the midst of the fallout from the case. Patrick didn't envy Henry Ng that job at all.

Patrick looked at the departures board and checked the time. "You should get going. Security looks like it's a mess, and you need to get your weapon cleared through."

"I still have time." Nadine smiled at him before leaning forward to kiss the air on either side of his cheeks. "Watch your back."

"You too."

"Good luck with your wolf."

Patrick had to bite down on his denial that Jono wasn't his

wolf, because at this point, arguing was futile. "Thank you. For everything."

She gave him a quick little salute and winked. "What are friends for?"

"Safe travels."

Nadine inclined her head in silent acknowledgment before grabbing the handle of her luggage and walking off. She didn't look back, and he didn't expect her to. That's not how their friendship worked. If they needed each other, they would be there for each other, no questions asked. Patrick crossed his arms over his chest and watched her leave.

The itch between his shoulder blades intensified.

"She is a fine warrior," a deep voice that echoed like thunder said from behind him.

"Nadine saved a lot of lives overseas," Patrick replied as he turned around. "She still does."

"Loyalty is an admirable trait."

Zeus stood in the midst of the airport crowd wearing a bespoke suit that probably cost at least five figures. The immortal looked better than he had during summer solstice, bound to a spellwork that came too close to undoing his godhead. Tall and broad-shouldered, with deeply tanned skin and black hair that glinted with strands of silver, Zeus' presence burned against Patrick's newly replenished magic, even through his shields.

The moment they locked eyes, the world froze, time coming to an impossible standstill. Patrick kept his heartbeat steady as he felt himself get pulled into the orbit of the immortal's powerful, primordial magic.

Zeus was nothing like Hermes, with his quicksilver trickery. Nor was he like Persephone, with her deep connection to the earth and her ties to hell brought about by the magic inside six small pomegranate seeds. No, Zeus was nothing like the rest of the gods in his pantheon. His magic was as fierce and unpredictable as a storm, and just as destructive. The all-consuming power shining in his aura should have burned Patrick to his core, but it didn't.

He had Hera to thank for that.

The goddess stood beside her husband, passport in hand and dark sunglasses perched on her aquiline nose. One hand curled over the crook of Zeus' elbow in a possessive manner, as if she knew how close she had come to losing him and didn't want to let him go.

"Patrick," Hera said. "Did you enjoy the flowers I sent you?"

"Pretty sure the nurses did," he said.

"They were meant for you."

"I don't like gifts from gods."

"You seem to like the wolf just fine," Zeus said.

Anger resonated in Patrick's soul as he took those words to be a threat. "He wasn't supposed to be anyone's to give."

"The Norse do what they like," Hera said derisively. "As do we all."

He didn't want to talk about Jono with them. He'd prefer they kept their distance from the werewolf, but Patrick had a feeling that was wishful thinking at this point. "Leaving the country?"

"Taking a much-needed break," Zeus replied.

The news had briefly reported on Malcolm Cirillo's disappearance and reappearance, with supposedly no memory of where he'd been, before dropping the story in favor of the sacrificial murders. Sensationalism sold way better than a missing rich guy these days. Patrick had a feeling Hera might have cast a little magic, with the help of her coven, to get the local media to look the other way. In the grand scheme of things, he was fine with the news missing the link between the two stories. He had a feeling Zeus and Hera were as well.

"If you're leaving, you didn't need to tell me goodbye. Your kind doesn't ever come around unless you want something," Patrick said.

"We already have you."

"Because Persephone couldn't let me die."

"We are not ones to cast aside a weapon when we find one," Hera replied coolly.

"Takes a real shitty person to think a child should be turned into a weapon."

Zeus raised an eyebrow. "We immortals have a different view of worth. We always have."

He didn't sound condescending; he didn't sneer the words. Zeus spoke as if what he said was a factual truth, nothing more and nothing less. The god either didn't care, or wasn't aware, of how his words scraped Patrick raw somewhere deep inside, where the child he used to be still screamed in horror at what he'd witnessed and the adult he'd grown into mourned what he'd become.

"Must be hard," Patrick said tightly. "Surviving the way you do. All of you too old to change, too set in your ways, and then you wonder why the world forgot about you over the years. You wonder why you need to beg what few followers you can find to pray for your lives."

Zeus' mouth ticked ever so slightly downward at the corners. "We have never been forgotten."

"You just got relegated to a footnote in someone else's story, give or take a millennia or two. See, that's the thing about myths. They aren't men and they aren't legends. At their core, you're just a bunch of tragedies and cautionary tales. You don't grow old when you're a myth, but that just means you don't know how to let things go and die."

Zeus' gray-blue eyes filled with the fury of a storm that would never die. When the god finally deigned to respond, his words felt like a warning, like a calm before a storm rising high on the horizon.

"I see Persephone chose the right twin all those years ago."

Patrick raised his chin in silent defiance, clenching his hands into fists. "I would've preferred she let us both die."

Hera chuckled, the sound grating in Patrick's ears. "There is power in bloodlines, and in twins. You know that, Patrick. You know where you come from. We gods had an opportunity, and we took it. That is why Persephone took you."

"You know what Ashanti told me once?" Patrick said, thinking about the mother of all vampires and her implacable will. The way she refused to let him remain ignorant of his lot in life. "Immortality isn't living. It's merely surviving."

Something ugly and dangerous flashed across Zeus' eyes, like a lightning strike before he spoke. "Far be it from me to speak unkindly of the dead."

Ashanti might be dead, but her children and her teachings lived on. Patrick might carry a blade made by heavenly power, but he carried the taint of hell in his soul and Ashanti's words in his mind.

A weapon, no matter its shape, is still a weapon. So use it.

He and Jono would do all that they could to wield themselves before they let the gods control their lives.

In the end, it might kill them, but they'd die on their own terms.

Patrick blinked, and in that split second, Zeus and Hera disappeared. The world snapped back into motion, the noise of the crowd rushing back to fill his ears. Patrick shook his head to clear it and walked toward the exit.

"Fucking immortals," he muttered under his breath.

Patrick made his way to the borrowed car from the SOA motor pool and drove back to Manhattan. It took over an hour for him to arrive at Tempest in evening traffic and an extra fifteen minutes after that to find a parking spot. He finally found one three blocks away. Locking the car, Patrick stepped onto the sidewalk, dodging a couple of tourists.

With the reactionary storm long since blown away, summer heat had returned with a vengeance. The muggy weather didn't dissipate with sunset and Patrick's button-down felt a little too warm, even with the sleeves rolled up to his elbows. The tie he'd worn to his meetings had been tossed in the back seat the moment his day was over.

He waved hello at the bouncer when he arrived at the bar. Tempest had fully recovered from the attack the other week, the crowds having returned to fill up the space. Gone was the unease and fear from the first soultaker attack, replaced by laughter, loud conversation, and music. The glances thrown Patrick's way this time were curious and respectful rather than hostile. People slid out of his way before he could even get out an *excuse me* as he made his way up to the bar proper.

The small group of people who were slowly creeping their way into the friends category, whether Patrick liked it or not, were waiting for him. Emma and Sage sat on two of the stools, a third empty between them, while Marek and Leon leaned in around them to chat with Jono, who was working on their drinks.

Patrick watched as Jono lifted his head, eyes searching out his own in the crowded bar. Whether by scent or heartbeat or through their soulbond, Jono could always find him. Patrick stepped closer, and Emma reached back without looking to grab his arm. She hauled him over to the empty stool, never once stopping to argue with Marek about a work-related project. Whatever their conversation was about had Jono rolling his eyes and sharing a commiserating look with Sage.

Patrick settled himself on the stool, leaning his elbows against the edge of the bar as he looked at Sage. "Do I want to know what they're arguing about?'

Sage didn't look up from reading work email on her phone, her glass of wine hovering near her mouth. Marek had a hand pressed to her lower back and her body was canted toward his. "It's all code."

"Crypto work?"

"No. Code as in coding. They've been arguing about a new update to PreterWorld since they got here."

"I thought we weren't going to talk about work tonight? I was promised a night of drinking."

"I'm cutting you off at two drinks. You drove here and you fly tomorrow," Jono reminded him.

Patrick drummed his fingers against the bar counter. "I can always move my flight back."

Jono vigorously shook the drink shaker, and Patrick let himself get distracted by his muscular arms. "I will kick you out of bed and drive you there myself. Pick your first drink."

"My usual."

It felt strange that he had a usual here. Patrick had never had a local bar where he could go to drink that wasn't near a base and catered to soldiers. He rarely hung out at the ones near his soon-to-be old apartment in Washington, DC, preferring the privacy of his home over any public space. That was changing, if only because Emma was adamant he not keep his distance, no matter what the New York City god pack preferred.

Patrick wondered if her opinion of him would change if she knew what he'd done to Jono. He and Jono were keeping what had happened to them a secret, and would for as long as they could. Patrick wasn't sure how their soulbond would affect their lives going forward, but the less people who knew about it the safer they would be. Their little two-person pack wasn't official, though they'd opted to share that news with Emma, Leon, Marek, and Sage, who'd only been happy for them.

If—when—the New York City god pack found out that Jono had formed a pack inside their territory, there would be hell to pay, but they'd pay it later.

Marek moved around Sage to stand between where Patrick and Emma sat when Jono set the glass of Macallan 15 Year Old whiskey in front of Patrick. He pointed at the glass. "Put your wallet away. That's on the house."

Patrick picked up the glass and tilted it in Marek's direction in a silent toast before taking a sip. "Thanks."

Jono set a salt-rimmed glass in front of Emma, the thin layer of fluffy egg white foam on top already slowly dissolving. "Patrick is right. Stop chatting about work, Em."

Emma rolled her eyes and clamped her hand over Marek's mouth before he could protest. "Fine."

"Where's my drink?" was Marek's muffled question.

Jono handed an IPA to Leon and a shot of Bulliet to Marek. His own drink was a double pour of Redbreast, which he clacked against Patrick's glass. "Cheers, mate."

The rest of the group moved to join the casual toast, laughing through the "Cheers!" and Leon's loud *"Salud!"*

They didn't down their drinks after the gesture except for Jono, who set aside the empty shot glass in a dirty dish bin. He moved down the bar a little to take care of a couple of drink requests. Patrick watched him work, eyes lingering on his ass and biceps. Jono's presence was a frisson Patrick couldn't ignore, and he didn't want to.

Emma nudged him in the side, drawing his attention away from Jono. She quirked an eyebrow at him. "Everything okay?"

"Yeah. Just thinking."

"Don't think too hard. Tonight's supposed to be fun."

"Been a while since I've had any of that," Patrick admitted.

"So you didn't take the vacation time?" Marek asked.

"I'll take it later. Probably around the holidays. I need to get settled here first."

Sage finally looked away from her phone. "Any idea where you want to stay? I can recommend a good broker if you need one."

Patrick couldn't take over the lease of the apartment he'd been staying in, and truthfully he didn't want to. If Patrick was going to call this city home for the foreseeable future, he damn well was going to stay somewhere he liked.

"We're working on it."

"We, is it?" Leon asked, raising an eyebrow at Jono. "You breaking your lease early?"

"Not that it's any of your business, but yes," Jono retorted, measuring out a shot of vodka.

"Don't break your lease," Marek said as he moved closer to Sage again in order to wrap an arm around her waist. "You have another six months on it, right? I'm sure we can sublet it to someone in the community."

"I'll let you figure out the logistics for that."

The conversation moved on from apartment hunting to figuring out everyone's schedule for the monthly pack dinner at Marek and Sage's place.

"You're coming whether you like it or not," Leon told him.

"I can't cook," Patrick protested. "I never really learned how."

"Seriously?" Emma asked.

"I went to a boarding school for magic users and then joined the military. When do you think I would have had time to learn to cook?"

"The past three years you've been out?" Marek said with a teasing grin.

Patrick shook his head. "Anything other than A-rations is crap and my stomach is still recovering from mess food. I'm making up for lost meals by eating as much takeout as possible."

"For *three years*?"

"I am determined to try every state's version of comfort food at least once. If I can expense it to the agency, so much the better."

Leon laughed, smacking him on the shoulder. "Our tax dollars at work."

"Damn straight."

"Bring a couple bottles of alcohol. We'll still let you through the door, no hospitality ceremony needed this time around," Sage told him.

"What about Jono?"

"Oh, will you make your roast, Jono?" Emma asked, perking up.

"I'll pick up a Crack Pie instead," Jono called out from the far side of the bar. "But only one. You lot can sort out who gets some of it this time."

Emma grinned. "That's almost better than your roast."

"Crack Pie?" Patrick asked.

"Only the most ridiculously sweet pie full of gooey butter and sugar you'll ever have. You'll like it," Sage said.

She downed the rest of her red wine and scooted the empty glass across the bar. Jono came over after finishing his round of orders to check on their drinks and set about making them new ones. He was in the middle of pouring Patrick a second glass of whiskey and talking with Marek about his schedule at the bar for the next week when Patrick's phone rang.

He pulled it out of his pocket, blinking down at the long string of numbers on the screen. He accepted the call and pressed the phone to his ear. "Special Agent Collins. Line and location are not secure."

"Soultakers," a familiar voice said over a staticky long-distance satphone connection. "I had to learn your dumb ass was fighting fucking soultakers from the goddamn news, Collins?"

Patrick froze, eyes going wide as he recognized the voice. "Oh, shit."

Captain Gerard Breckenridge, commanding officer of the Hellraisers, snorted derisively over the phone. "Oh, shit, he says."

"What do you mean, *oh, shit?*" someone else yelled in the background of the call, sounding an awful lot like Sergeant Keith Pearson, the team's demolitions specialist. "That's not a fucking answer."

"Not much of an answer, but I'll take an explanation any day now, Collins."

Patrick winced, aware he had drawn the full attention of the others, with Jono going so far as to pause in pouring his whiskey. Patrick made a desperate gesture at Jono to keep going.

"Mulroney kept you updated," Patrick said, knowing it wasn't much of an excuse.

"Only because she had access to your cell phone and could answer my texts for the thirty minutes I managed to wrangle permission to use my personal phone," Gerard retorted. "Had to get in contact with the Old Man and cash in a favor for that call."

Patrick's wince got deeper. Goddamn dragons and their hoards. "You didn't have to give up a favor for me."

"I got plenty to spare. Mulroney mentioned you had vampires in the field. I *told* you never to call—"

"What part of the line is *not* secure did you not hear?" Patrick interrupted.

"Where the hell are you that it's not secure?"

"In a bar."

"In a bar" came the flat reply. "Please tell me you aren't drinking with no one to watch your six after the shit show that just happened."

"I'm not alone, but it's a werecreature bar, so watch your goddamn words, sir."

Gerard made a questioning sound in the back of his throat. "I still don't hear you denying you took that bastard into the field with you."

Patrick snatched his glass of whiskey off the counter and swallowed it down in one quick gulp, staring up at the ceiling with a full on *oh god, why* look on his face. "I wasn't the one who called him."

"I see." Gerard sighed in aggravation. "I'm going to have words with your director for pulling that asshole in. What the hell was she thinking?"

"I had a team—"

"Like hell are goddamn *vampires* a goddamn *team*—"

"I didn't say it was them, I said I had a team. If you'd been available I would've called, but you've been dark for two damn months already—"

"Who backed you up?" Gerard cut in. "Just tell me it's someone who knows your heart attack-inducing, near-suicidal habits in the field like I do. Mulroney doesn't count because she's just as fucking crazy as you are sometimes."

"I never gave you a heart attack," Patrick muttered.

"My stress levels when you were on my team say otherwise. Now answer my question."

Patrick sighed. "Mulroney handled defense. The rest were civilian werecreatures before SOA agents got on the scene. It was a fucking mess, but it got handled."

Gerard was silent for long enough Patrick wondered if the connection had broken. Field calls weren't always reliable. He pulled the phone away from his ear to make sure the call was still live.

Jono eyed him curiously. "All right?"

Patrick nodded before putting the phone back to his ear. "You there?"

"Civilians," Gerard said, sounding annoyed in the way Patrick remembered from years in the field when his captain was *done with this shit* and ready to wreak havoc. The half-fae were rather good at that. "You had civilians backing you up. That's just un-fucking-believable."

"They held their own, and everything got handled."

"Oh, I'm well aware of what you mean when you say *handled*." Gerard pitched his voice into a mockery of Patrick's when he said, "No, everything's fine, Captain, I'm not bleeding out from a bullet hole in my side—"

"That was *one time* and I wasn't bleeding out, so respectfully, fuck off, sir. I made it to the exfil on my own two feet."

Gerard's voice turned far too contemplative for Patrick's liking. "You know what? We're due back stateside after the next mission. Me and a few of the boys are going to take some R & R and come for a visit to check out this so-called team of yours. We'll make sure you can still find your ass with both hands after three years of being a civilian."

"I'm sorry, which one of us in this conversation is wearing rail-road tracks?"

Keith erupted into laughter in the background of the call, his words coming through the line a little muffled. "He's got you there, Smooth Dog."

Gerard ignored him. "We're visiting, and you're paying the bar tab when we do."

Patrick groaned, well aware of how much his old team could drink. "Fine."

"Listen, we have to go. Keep your head up, Collins. Don't get dead."

"Right back at you." The call cut out, and Patrick dropped his phone on the bar counter. He stared at Jono for a long moment before saying, "Hand me the bottle of whiskey. Another shot isn't going to cut it."

Jono picked up the bottle of whiskey but didn't hand it over. "Was that your old captain?"

"I know you didn't keep your ears to yourself, so I'm not even going to bother answering your question."

Jono poured him another glass, despite his earlier protests about Patrick's limit. "Sounds like a decent bloke. Wouldn't mind meeting him."

Patrick made an inarticulate sound of affronted rage in the back of his throat. Emma laughed at him and knocked her fist against his shoulder. "Let us know when they come out. They can drink here."

Patrick curled his hand around the glass of whiskey like it might save him. "Hell no. I'd never survive that meeting."

Judging by the unimpressed looks everyone shot him, they didn't care.

"Traitors," he muttered darkly, taking a sip of whiskey. "You're taking Gerard's side and you don't even know him."

"Someone needs to be on your side, and he sounds like he has been," Jono retorted.

Patrick couldn't really argue with that statement. "Yeah. I guess."

Jono rolled his eyes and leaned across the bar counter, his fingers sliding beneath the collar of Patrick's shirt to hook around the dog tags. He pulled on them firmly, drawing Patrick forward into a quick, hard kiss that didn't go unnoticed by anyone in the bar, judging by the catcalls erupting around them.

"All right, all right, do your job, Jono. You can do Patrick later," Marek called out over the noise of the bar.

Patrick sat back on his stool, then reached around a hunched-over and laughing Sage to smack Marek upside the head.

"Ow!" Marek exclaimed in a faux wounded voice. "What was that for?"

"Every time you wouldn't stay put the other week and I couldn't throttle you."

"That's it. I'm not getting your next round."

"He's not drinking another round," Jono reminded everyone.

Patrick sighed and resolved to make his final glass of whiskey last the rest of the night. "At least the company is good for once."

Jono smiled at him from the other side of the bar, and it warmed Patrick better than the whiskey on his tongue.

JONO STOOD WITH HIS ARMS CROSSED OVER HIS CHEST IN THE baggage claim at LaGuardia's Terminal B, eyes hidden behind his sunglasses. The smell of so many people coming from so many places, packed in a tight area, made his nose twitch. Jono could've stayed in the car, but he was too impatient right now. He checked his mobile one more time, but Patrick hadn't texted since saying he'd landed and responding with a smiley face emoji when Jono had replied he was waiting in the baggage claim.

Jono had picked a spot that was out of the way of people arriving to claim their luggage but still had a good view. No one looked twice at him if he didn't count the toddler a weary mother was trying to keep occupied. Jono ignored the kid in favor of keeping an eye on the shifting crowd, perking up when he caught sight of a familiar face.

In a sea of people, Patrick's dark red hair stood out, and Jono felt his shoulders ease as he finally got eyes on the mage. Three weeks of separation had hurt in a way they hadn't anticipated, the soulbond still too new for distance to be easy. The soulbond was settling, the awareness of it burying itself deep beneath his wolf, but Jono knew he'd always be aware of Patrick to some degree from here on out.

"Hey," Patrick said with a tired smile. "You could've picked me up curbside and saved some money."

"Shut it. You're worth way more than a parking ticket."

Jono closed the distance between them and gave Patrick a welcoming kiss that lingered longer than was probably polite for public. Jono didn't care, just happy to have Patrick within sight again. Texts, phone calls, and FaceTime couldn't compete with being able to reach out and touch. Having the only member of his pack away had left Jono snappish and irritable, to the point Emma had sent him home early from the bar a few nights over the last week.

When he pulled back, Jono made sure to drag his hand over the side of Patrick's throat, discreetly scent-marking him. Most people wouldn't recognize the touch for what it truly meant, but it settled something deep inside him. The raised eyebrow from Patrick told him he wasn't being subtle, but Jono didn't care.

Patrick hiked the worn-looking, probably military-issued camouflage rucksack higher on his shoulders and nodded at the baggage carousel. "I came with two other bags."

"Hope that's the last of it."

"Should be. You handled everything else."

Jono nodded, remembering the numerous walk-throughs of dozens of flats Patrick had him do with the help of a broker. Sage's suggestion had been a witch who hadn't blinked at Jono's eyes and could easily interpret the magical requirements Patrick threw at her over the phone that Jono had no clue what he was on about.

In the end, after seven days of nonstop searching, Patrick had signed the lease with Jono for the top-floor flat of a five-story Chelsea townhouse. The townhouse was older than most of the other places on the list, but the two-bedroom flat was surprisingly spacious and had gone through a recent renovation. The small, private garden space at the rear of the building shared by all the tenants had been a perk Jono doubted they'd use much, but it was nice to have.

Jono had been living in Manhattan long enough to know it was a steal. Patrick's job as an SOA special agent could've tipped their chances either way, but they'd lucked out and beat out other potential renters. Jono had handled the moving trucks full of Patrick's things around being interviewed by police out of the PCB about what had happened during summer solstice.

Jono had claimed not to remember much of his time with Ethan only because he hadn't wanted to relive that torture just yet. Aside from that, he didn't know where the Dominion Sect had held him captive, nor did he know the identities of the acolytes he'd seen.

Right now, all Jono cared about was the man who'd come home to him. Patrick had managed to condense all his meetings into three weeks rather than four since he'd had Jono helping with some of the moving issues. That was one week sooner than they'd initially thought, and Jono couldn't wait to get Patrick alone.

The luggage came out surprisingly quick, and Jono picked out Patrick's by scent. He hauled both off the conveyer belt and started for the exit.

"I need to buy a car," Patrick said as they stepped outside into muggy July heat. The afternoon sun was bright overhead in a cloudless sky. "I'm gonna hate driving in this city."

"Marek is letting us borrow one of his for now. It's what I drove to pick you up."

"The Maserati?"

Jono snorted. "If only."

The Lexus was perfectly serviceable for their needs, and Jono hadn't argued the choice. He chucked the luggage in the boot when they reached the vehicle and got behind the wheel.

"Will Marek kill me if I smoke?" Patrick asked once they were on the road.

Jono frowned. "Probably, but you really shouldn't smoke."

Patrick slouched in the seat and tipped his head back. "It's stress relief. DC was shitty."

"How?"

Patrick shrugged. "The agency is getting raked over the congressional coals. It never looks good when double agents are unearthed in the government. Setsuna's holding on to her job, but who knows if she'll keep it."

"And you?" Jono wanted to know.

"I've submitted my official report, but there's a chance I'll have to testify in a closed hearing before the House Committee on Oversight."

Jono wasn't well versed in how the United States government functioned, but that didn't sound good to him. "Does that mean you're in trouble?"

"Just means I've got too many eyes looking my way. We'll need to be careful."

"All right."

"I still want a cigarette."

Jono didn't care for the smell of nicotine, but he'd deal with it until he could convince Patrick to break that habit. He reached over and settled his hand high on Patrick's thigh, fingers stroking lightly. "Think I can distract you from that craving."

"Huh." Patrick spread his legs a little and Jono took a deep breath, smelling arousal beneath the underlying bitterness in his scent. Even after weeks apart, he still smelled good. "You might be onto something."

The drive back into Manhattan was excruciating, not just because of traffic. Patrick was *right there*, and Jono couldn't do anything about that until they made it to their new home. It took almost an hour for them to finally arrive there. Jono found a parking spot on the street a block and a half away on the side that wouldn't have street cleaning tomorrow.

They got out and Jono grabbed the luggage again, waving off Patrick's attempt to take one. "This way."

Jono led Patrick home, his mood lightening with every step that brought them closer to the front door. The townhouse itself had a brown façade and stairs leading up to the entrance. Nearly every window facing the street had an air-conditioning unit set into it. Jono didn't mind the heat as much as most people, but he'd turned the air-conditioning on that morning for Patrick.

"Keys are in my pocket," Jono said as they reached the front landing.

Patrick took that as the invitation it was to step closer and slide his hand into Jono's front pocket. They stared at each other through their sunglasses as Patrick did his very best to drag his fingers alongside Jono's clothed cock while searching for the keys. The touch made his cock harden a little in anticipation.

"Where's my set?" Patrick asked when he finally pulled his hand free, keys dangling from his fingers.

Jono's jeans were definitely too tight now. "Upstairs."

"Lead the way."

Jono lowered the handles of the heavy luggage and picked up each one as if they weighed nothing. Patrick opened the door for him, and they stepped inside the tiny entranceway. Jono ignored the door to the first-floor tenant and started up the stairs to the right, bypassing three more landings until they reached the fifth floor.

Their entranceway at the top landing was small, made more crowded by both of them and the luggage. Patrick tossed Jono the keys, and he unlocked the door. Shouldering it open, Jono carried the luggage inside and deposited them near the wall.

Patrick didn't immediately enter, standing just beyond the front door with both hands on the doorframe. He stared down at the floor with a look of concentration on his face, pale blue light flickering at his fingertips. Jono expected to feel something through the soulbond as Patrick cast magic, but he didn't.

Guess it's only when he needs to tap a ley line that I'll feel it, Jono thought.

They'd talked a little about what happened before Patrick left for Washington, DC, three weeks ago. Figuring out the extent of the soulbond was going to happen through trial and error. It wasn't something either of them could flaunt in public, and Patrick was reluctant to even try channeling his magic through Jono's soul still.

Jono was adamant that they work on it. In a fight, Jono needed to know what to expect when magic rushed through his soul. He needed to know how to handle it. The only way to do so was to experience it firsthand.

For now, Jono could wait.

"Okay, threshold is set," Patrick said, finally stepping inside and taking off his sunglasses. "The broker was right. This place has strong anchor points."

Jono watched as Patrick took in the flat in person for the first time. The door opened up on the long open-plan living area. The living room was to the left, the blinds over the windows facing the street pulled high to let in the sunlight. The kitchen was located off to their right, with an island separating it from the dining area. The windows there overlooked the garden out back.

Directly across the way from the front door was a tiny hallway leading to the master bedroom and its private bathroom, as well as the smaller room and second hallway bathroom. Most of the furniture was Patrick's, but a few new items had been purchased from a local department store, and Jono had brought over one or two of his own pieces. The sofa was new, as was the king-sized bed Jono had been sleeping alone in for too long. The flat had only smelled like him for the past week and a half since officially moving in, and Jono was determined to fix that today.

He closed the distance between them, wrapping his arms around Patrick from behind. Jono dragged one hand down Patrick's chest to cup his dick with strong fingers. Patrick let out a hiss, arching into the touch in a delightful way.

Jono ran his nose against the arched line of Patrick's neck up to his ear, breathing in the scent of him. "There's a brand-new bed I've been wanting to break in."

Patrick raised an arm to tangle his fingers in Jono's hair as he turned his head for a kiss. "Yeah?"

Jono slanted his mouth over Patrick's, kissing him with a need he wasn't ashamed of. His hardening cock pressed against the top curve of Patrick's ass, and Jono couldn't wait to bury himself in the other man.

"Bedroom," Jono growled.

"You'll have to stop trying to get me off right here if you want us to get *there*," Patrick said, grinding back against Jono.

Jono turned Patrick around and easily hauled the leaner man over one shoulder. The undignified yelp Patrick let out had him chuckling.

"I will *kill you* if you don't put me down," Patrick snarled.

Jono smacked him on the arse, giving him a bit of a squeeze. "Promises, promises."

The fact that Patrick didn't struggle to get down made Jono smirk as he headed for the master bedroom. The large space had a mix of mismatched furniture in it, but the bed was the only thing that mattered. Jono hadn't made it that morning, so he got a fistful of the duvet and yanked the bedding off before tossing Patrick onto the mattress. He bounced a little upon landing, face flushed from arousal and a bit of embarrassment.

"You ever do that again where anyone can see and you're sleeping on the couch," Patrick told him, already yanking at the laces on his combat boots.

"Doubtful," Jono said as he pulled his T-shirt off.

Patrick's fingers faltered for a second as he took in Jono's bare chest, eyes darkening. "You think I wouldn't ban you from the bedroom?"

"Bed is half-mine."

Patrick kicked off his shoes and started to unbuckle the thigh straps holding his dagger in place. "Shut up and strip."

Jono laughed, already undoing his belt buckle. "Bossy. We're a pack, love. You don't get to be a dictator."

"I do if it means you're going to fuck me."

Put like that, Jono hurried up and got naked. By the time he'd stripped out of all his clothes, Patrick was just getting around to undoing his jeans. Jono helped pull them off along with his underwear with swift tugs. Then he went to his knees in front of Patrick, following the musky scent of arousal to Patrick's cock.

"Gods," Patrick groaned when Jono took him in his mouth. "*Jono.*"

Patrick's voice trailed off in a hitched sigh that washed over Jono's ears. Jono sucked hard at the head of his cock before swallowing down more of him. The dark red hue of his pubic hair was shaved close to his skin, and Jono dragged his thumb down Patrick's balls, tugging at them in a teasing manner.

Patrick's legs pressed against Jono's shoulders in reaction to the touch. Jono pulled off far enough to lick at the precum leaking from the slit, tongue curling around the sensitive head. Callused fingers tangled in his hair and gave it a good tug. Jono stroked Patrick's cock with firm fingers as he looked up refusing to stop touching him.

Face flushed, eyes wide, Patrick looked as if he wouldn't mind Jono having his wicked way with the mage.

Jono intended to do exactly that.

"Get up here," Patrick all but begged.

That was an order Jono didn't mind obeying. With one last suck to the tip of Patrick's cock, Jono got to his feet as Patrick moved further onto the bed, unconsciously licking his lips. Jono stroked his own cock as he dug up a brand-new bottle of lube from the nightstand, well aware of how Patrick couldn't seem to look away.

Jono took pride in his body in both forms, and he enjoyed the greedy way Patrick reached for him when he crawled closer. His skin didn't carry the roadmap of scars that Patrick's did, and

Jono resolved to trace the memories scattered over pale skin at a later date. Right now, Jono wasn't in the mood to go slow. Giving in to Patrick's need today was the only thing Jono wanted to do.

Patrick liked it hard and fast, wanting to get off as quickly as possible. Teaching him to go slow was a work in progress, and Jono didn't mind showing him how good it could be. But after three weeks of separation, if he didn't get his cock in Patrick's arse, he'd bloody well maim someone.

"Missed you," Patrick groaned against his mouth as Jono settled between his thighs. "Fuck, I don't remember missing anyone like I missed you."

"Yeah," Jono muttered as he opened up the bottle of lube with one hand. "Hated having you gone."

Maybe it was the soulbond making them feel this way, but Jono wasn't so sure. Patrick had caught his eye from the very first second they saw each other. Attraction had simmered between them since the first night they'd had sex. Relationships and packs had been built on less. He'd seen it for himself in London and here in New York City.

People had killed for less.

He had killed for less, and Jono knew Patrick would never judge him for it.

Jono would fight for Patrick, and he knew Patrick would do the same for him. It might not be love, but loyalty and affection were still powerful in their own right.

The sex was definitely a plus.

Jono coated his fingers in lube before wrapping them around both their cocks. Patrick bit his lip and groaned, thrusting up into the tight circle of Jono's fingers. The flush on his face had moved down his neck and chest, nipples dusky and hard. Jono couldn't help himself and leaned down to suck one into his mouth.

"You're killing me here, Jono," Patrick moaned, his hand settling on the back of Jono's skull to keep him there.

He chuckled against warm skin, biting at the sensitive nub between his teeth. "What a way to go, love."

Patrick laughed, the sound hitching in his throat when Jono gently pinched the tip of his cock. "Fuck me. *Please.*"

Jono gave one last stroke to both their cocks before sitting up and reaching for the lube again. Patrick shifted against the bed, pushing himself to a sitting position. He crawled into Jono's lap with a heated look in his green eyes, legs splayed wide over Jono's thighs.

"Like this," Patrick said, rising up on his knees a little. "Show me what you got."

Jono dragged a hand over one of his ass cheeks, opening Patrick up so he could push one finger inside that tight, clenching heat. Patrick shuddered against him, pressing their mouths together for a kiss that was all teeth and tongue as they fought for control. Jono stroked his free hand up Patrick's back to get a good grip on his hair and pull his head back. Keeping him in one place, Jono kissed him absolutely breathless.

Patrick gasped against his lips when Jono pushed a second finger into him, rising up before sinking down onto Jono's fingers.

"Couldn't stop thinking about you on the flight here," Patrick murmured, digging his hands into Jono's shoulders.

"I'm not on shift tonight," Jono said as he curled his fingers, searching for that sweet spot. "Could christen the sofa if you want. Maybe the wall. Dining table is a bit too dodgy—think we'd break it."

Patrick laughed, the sound breaking on a moan as Jono found his prostate and rubbed at it. "Are you calling me *cheap?*"

Their cocks rubbed between their bodies as Patrick rocked against him, riding his fingers. The ache in his own cock was starting to get distracting. "You aren't skint, but your taste is."

Patrick laughed, his entire body shaking with it. Jono stretched his fingers against the clench of muscles and smiled against the warm curve of Patrick's neck and shoulder. He breathed in deep, Patrick's scent bitter and sharp in his nose.

He was the best thing Jono had smelled in a long, long time.

"You are," Patrick said, still laughing. "You're calling me *cheap*! I work for the government, what did you expect?"

"Sod the government," Jono muttered as he pulled his fingers free.

He grabbed Patrick by the waist, urging him higher. Warm hands framed his face, and Patrick kissed him with a focused intensity Jono relished. He carefully guided Patrick down onto his hard cock, groaning as the fat tip pushed inside. The resistance gave way with a shallow thrust as more of his cock slid inside with a little pressure. Patrick moaned, biting at his bottom lip. Jono spread his legs, forcing Patrick's wider.

He pushed up into that heat with quick, forceful thrusts that opened Patrick up inch by thick inch. Jono had always been pleased at how long and thick his cock was, the way he knew his partners enjoyed taking it. Patrick was no different, the soft, hitched breaths that caught in the back of his throat with every inch Jono worked inside him impossible for Jono to ignore. Fingernails scraped over his skin, the quick irritation fading in seconds as Jono stared into Patrick's eyes.

Jono fit one hand to Patrick's hip, flattening his other against the space between sharp shoulder blades on that scarred back. Patrick leaned back into his touch, eyes half-lidded, tongue peeking out from between wet lips as Jono pulled him all the way down onto his hard, aching cock.

The sound that came out of Patrick's mouth was wordless, needy, his fingers digging bruises into Jono's shoulder. Jono bottomed out with a growl, cock throbbing deep inside Patrick, exactly where he wanted to be. He could feel Patrick clench weakly around him, the tightness something Jono had to breathe through. He reached around to trace his fingers around where they were joined, rubbing warm fingertips around the tautly stretched skin of Patrick's hole.

The way Patrick shuddered brought a smile to Jono's face.

"If you don't move," Patrick gasped, hips rolling shallowly to get away from Jono's touch. It only served to shift Jono's cock inside him, making him moan.

"You'll what?" Jono asked, as he readjusted his grip on Patrick's body, sliding the mage off his cock a little.

"I'll—"

Whatever he would have said was forgotten at the first hard snap of Jono's hips, cock driving in deep. Patrick cried out, pushing back down onto Jono's cock even as he thrust up again. Jono got both hands on Patrick's ass and pulled him up off his cock again, keeping him there. It gave Jono room to thrust into him, cock dragging against his prostate. Patrick twisted in his arms, swearing as he tried to sink down and was unable to. Jono held him in place with strong hands, hole stretched wide around his cock, the long glide in wet and a little less tight now.

"Going to take you like this. Going to *own* you," Jono growled as he sped up the motion of his hips. "You want that?"

Patrick answered through a messy, uncoordinated kiss. "*Yes.*"

Jono hiked him up higher, just a little, holding him there with easy strength so Jono could fuck him as hard as he liked, as hard as he dared. The sound of skin slapping together filled the bedroom, sweat making their bodies slippery as they held on to each other. Patrick's breathless little whines were like music to Jono's ears, and he chased the sound with his mouth.

Patrick's cock was trapped between their bodies, the friction and the pounding Jono was giving his arse all it took to eventually tip him over the edge. Patrick came with a cry, head tipped back, cum painting both their chests. His body shook in Jono's arms, tightening around his cock in an exhilarating way. He grunted, shifting position and slowing down a little through the sudden resistance.

"C'mon, don't stop," Patrick said, tugging at his hair. "You know you want your cum on me."

Jono swore, biting at Patrick's scarred collarbone with gentle teeth at those words. "Fuck, I want to *wreck* you."

"Yeah, yeah, you should."

Jono took that as permission given and leaned forward, guiding Patrick down to the bed again. He didn't pull out, just twisted his hips so that when Patrick's back touched the mattress, Jono was driving back into his hole. Patrick groaned, his hands on Jono's shoulders, pulling him closer.

Without needing to hold Patrick up, Jono could focus on getting off in the best way possible. Fucking Patrick was like coming home, his body open and willing beneath Jono, hands greedy with touch. Jono couldn't last much longer, not with the way Patrick was looking at him, as if Jono was the only one he could ever want.

Jono came with a shout, grinding into Patrick for a few short thrusts before he pulled out all the way and stroked his cock with a hard fist. Cum spattered over Patrick's balls and the delicate skin beneath them, dripping down to his loose hole.

Spent, Jono reached between Patrick's legs to rub his cum into too-sensitive skin, mingling their scents together in that intimate spot. Patrick twitched a little at the touch, knees pressing against Jono's sides.

"You're cleaning me up," Patrick said lazily, breathing a little hard, skin flushed red in the afternoon light from sex.

Jono smiled at him, slow and full of promise as he teased Patrick's hole before pushing a bit of cum back inside him. He let his fingers stay there, keeping Patrick open to his touch.

"Later. We still have a sofa to desecrate."

Patrick's laughter filled the bedroom, easy and rich, his smile all Jono could see. The soulbond was an indescribable thing tying him to this man, and it should have frightened him, but it didn't.

This, right here, was what Marek had promised Jono three years ago when the seer had pulled him out of London.

Pack, Jono thought as Patrick reached for him, drawing him down into a lingering kiss.

Home.

INDEX

Short descriptions of words, acronyms and phrases used in the story that weren't readily explained in text. Included as well are character names.

Abuku, Setsuna: Witch. Director who oversees and leads the Supernatural Operations Agency.

Academy: K-12 school that teaches magic to practitioners of all affinities and designations. All provide boarding options to students.

Ares: Immortal. Greek god of war.

Artemis: Immortal. Greek goddess of the hunt, forests and hills, the moon, and archery.

Ashanti: Immortal. Goddess and mother of all vampires. Takes the shape of an Asanbosam vampire out of West African myths.

Beacot, Sage: Weretiger. A Diné lawyer who works for the fae law firm Gentry & Thyme.

Carmen: Succubus. First known recorded appearance was in Venice, Italy.

Casale, Giovanni: Human. Chief of the NYPD's Preternatural Crimes Bureau.

Caster Corps: Military branch under the purview of the US Department of the Preternatural. Accepts all types of magic practitioners except mages.

Cerberus: Immortal. Hound of Hades and guards the gates of the Underworld.

Charon: Immortal. Ferryman of the Greek Underworld.

Citadel: United States military academy for magic users. Located in Maryland. All Academies across the nation feed into the Citadel. Mages get automatic inclusion. All other kinds of magic users need recommendations.

Collins, Patrick: Mage. Former combat mage with the Mage Corps, currently an SOA special agent. Has a tainted soul and crippled magic. Is technically a mage in name only due to a soul wound.

DCPI: Office of the Deputy Commissioner, Public Information. Part of the NYPD, this office is responsible for working with local, national, and international media organizations to provide the most accurate and timely information to the public regarding news of ongoing cases.

de Vere, Jonothon: God pack werewolf. Originally from London, England, currently resides in New York City. Is an independent alpha within the werecreature community and belongs to no pack.

Dionysus: Immortal. Greek god of the vine, grape harvest, winemaking, wine, ritual madness, religious ecstasy, and theatre.

Dire: A rank held only within a god pack. The moniker is taken from the dire wolf, but has been shortened to account for different werecreature species. Essentially a rank held by a loyal pack member who helps enforce the alphas' orders.

Dominion Sect: A shadowy terrorist group consisting of mundane humans, rogue magic users, immortals aligned with the hells, and other preternatural creatures intent on destroying the veil between worlds so that hell and its denizens can reign on earth. Some members are attempting to steal godheads in order to ensure their hold on power in the new world they hope to create.

ESU: NYPD Emergency Service Unit. The unit is part of the NYPD Special Operations Bureau. They are trained and equipped to perform tactical and technical rescue duty for other NYPD departments.

Fenrir: Immortal. Wolf in the Norse pantheon. Patron to a god pack.

FOB: Forward Operating Base. A forward military position that supports tactical operations.

Ginnungagap: Primordial void. Belongs to the Norse myths.

Godhead: Primordial power belonging to immortals that gives them life. The strength of their power can be altered by worship, or lack thereof.

God pack: A pack of werecreatures infected with the god strain of the werevirus. They act as spokespeople for hidden werecreature packs in their territory. They are supported by monetary tithes from the packs under their protection. Very few retain a connection to their animal-god patrons.

Greene, Ethan: Mage. Was a double-agent formally employed by the SOA. Is currently a mercenary and allied with the Dominion Sect.

Greene, Hannah: Mage. Currently a vessel. Spiritually deceased.

Hades: Immortal. Greek god of the dead and the Underworld.

Hera: Immortal. Greek goddess of women and titular queen of the Greek pantheon.

Hermes: Immortal. Greek messenger god and god of trade, thieves, travelers, sports, athletes, border crossings, and guide to the Underworld

Hernandez, Leon: Werewolf. Partner to Emma Zhang and co-leader of the Tempest pack.

Kavanaugh, Nicholas: God pack werewolf. Dire of the New York City god pack.

Khan, Youssef: God pack werewolf. Alpha of the New York City god pack.

Ley lines: Metaphysical rivers of powers that drain into nexuses.

Lucien: Master vampire. Was a soldier in William the Conqueror's army before being turned by Ashanti. Currently a weapons and magic trafficker. Is wanted by many governments.

Macaria: Immortal. Greek goddess of the blessed death and Hades' daughter.

Mage: Highest rank of magic users and the only practitioners who can tap external power from ley lines and nexuses.

Mage Corps: Military branch under the purview of the US Department of the Preternatural. Accepts only mages.

Magic: Emanating from and powered by a person's soul. Roughly one-quarter of the world's population has magic. Strength varies, with different titles being bestowed depending on a person's magical reach. Casting is divided into defensive wards and offensive spells.

Moirai: Immortals. Greek Fates.

Mulroney, Nadine: Mage. Works counterintelligence for the PIA. Is fluent in French and based out of Paris, France.

Necromancer: A magic user who can be of any rank. Their magic has an affinity for the dead, allowing them to raise the dead, control zombies, and manipulate the lingering souls of the deceased. Their kind of magic is heavily restricted in use in the United States and in most countries.

Necromancy: A family of magic that deals with the dead, usually involving blood magic and sacrifices. Predominately illegal or restricted in most countries.

Nexus: Metaphysical lake of power beneath the earth. Usually located in sacred areas or beneath major cities.

Night Court: Vampire group that oversees claimed territory. Headed by a single master vampire. Several Night Courts can exist in the same major city.

Norns: Immortals. Norse Fates.

Persephone: Immortal. Greek goddess of the Underworld and springtime.

PCB: Preternatural Crimes Bureau. A PCB is usually found only in the police departments of major metropolitan areas in the United States. The PCB in New York City is headed up by a Bureau Chief. The five Detective Boroughs within the NYPD all field detectives specializing in preternatural crimes through the PCB. The PCB has jurisdiction throughout the five boroughs and its own detachment of cops that work in homicide, narcotics, major crimes, and CSU. The PCB is one of the least manned departments in the NYPD due to the type of cases it handles.

PIA: Preternatural Intelligence Agency. PIA is a national-level foreign intelligence organization overseen by the Secretary of Defense directly through the USDI. The PIA's intelligence operations extend beyond the zones of combat, and approximately half of its employees serve overseas at hundreds of locations and US Embassies in many countries. The agency specializes in collection and analysis of preternatural-source intelligence, both overt and clandestine, while also handling American military-diplomatic relations abroad. The agency has no law enforcement authority. (Equivalent to CIA)

Preternatural Infantry: Military branch under the purview of the US Department of the Preternatural. Accepts only those with a preternatural or supernatural background, i.e. werecreatures, vampires, cryptids, etc.

Railroad tracks: Military slang for a captain's ranks, which is two vertical bars.

SERE: Survival, Evasion, Resistance, and Escape. A military program that provides US military personnel, Department of Defense civilians, private military contractors, and other at-risk agents and personnel with training on how to evade the enemy, survive and resist the enemy if captured, and to escape.

Shields: Ward. Defensive magic used for protection on a large or small scale.

Skuld: Immortal. Goddess of fate and one of the Norns.

Spells: Offensive magic.

SOA: Supernatural Operations Agency. SOA is the domestic intelligence and security service of the United States that focuses on magical and preternatural crimes and terrorism. Employs human, preternatural and magically affiliated people to field positions for domestic defense. (Equivalent to FBI)

Sorcerer/Sorceress: Second-highest rank of magic users and moderately more common than mages but are outnumbered by witches and wizards.

Soulbond: A binding of two or more souls to tie people together for magical needs. Illegal under the laws of all governments.

Taylor, Marek: Seer. CEO of PreterWorld, a social media platform geared toward the preternatural and supernatural community. His patrons are the Norns.

Threshold: Ward. Applied to a hearth and home for protection to keep out negative magic, spirits, and demons.

US Department of the Preternatural: Employs all manner of magically affiliated and preternatural people for military service. Active duty combat mages are seconded to the Army, Navy, Air Force, and Marines and are required to go through BTC and joint training.

Veil: The metaphysical barrier between Earth/mundane plane and other worlds/dimensions/planes, such as Faerie, versions of hell and heaven derived from myths.

Walker, Estelle: God pack werewolf. Alpha of the New York City god pack.

Wards: Defensive magic.

Warlock: Most common rank of magic users. On par with witches.

Werecreatures: Humans who are infected with the werevirus.

Can change form into various animalistic shapes. Werecreatures are either infected later on in life or are born with the disease.

Werevirus: An incurable disease that makes those who are infected change into monstrous beasts. Created by an ancient Roman mage, the werevirus was one of the first recorded instances of magically created biological warfare introduced into society. People are born with the werevirus or become infected through intercourse or blood. Two strains exist: a normal strain and a god strain. The god strain has stronger magical properties which can cause the infected to be susceptible to an immortal patron.

Witch: Most common rank of magic users. On par with warlocks.

Wizard: Second most common rank of magic users.

Zeus: Immortal. Greek god of thunder and titular king of the Greek pantheon.

Zhang, Emma: Werewolf. Alpha of the Tempest pack.

AUTHOR'S NOTES

This story has been a labor of love for many, many years. It's the book of my heart, and I am immensely happy I finally get to share it. But the heart of this story truly belongs to Nora, who spent years reading the many versions it went through. Who pestered me for more, who never let me forget it was there, and who talked me through every major detail no matter where she was in the country or the world. This story would not exist without her input and for loving it almost more than I do.

To the best beta reader in the entire world, that prize belongs to Leslie Copeland. Seriously, what would I do without you? It's not even fathomable. You make the little moments shine. So incredibly glad I can call you a friend.

To Lily Morton, who has become an invaluable friend. You're also one of the best alpha readers out there, who made sure I didn't go the Dick Van Dyke route. Your friendship means the world to me and I can't wait for the day we're in the same city together!

To Sheena J. Himes for the fresh eyes and your willingness to take time out of your busy summer to do an alpha read for me.

Your help was immensely appreciated and I can't thank you enough. You're amazing.

To May Archer, another amazing alpha reader and friend who helped immensely with making sure I didn't mess up some of the tinier details! Salt bae of my heart, never leave me.

To Bear, for all your help and accepting the numerous texts I send you without complaint! Your encouragement knows no bounds, and I adore you for it.

Last but not least, to my readers. Thank you so much for enjoying the worlds I get to write about, so that I can write more. You guys are amazing and I wouldn't get to do this without you.

I took liberties with police work and federal agencies in this story. I don't work in either field, and I tried to blend both into the world I created as best as possible. Any mistakes belong to me.

I would be thrilled and grateful if you would consider reviewing *A Ferry of Bones & Gold* on Amazon or Goodreads. I appreciate all honest reviews, positive or negative. Reviews definitely help my books get seen, so thank you!

Cover design by AngstyG.
Professional Beta Reading by Leslie Copeland:
lcopelandwrites@gmail.com
Edited by Sandra at One Love Editing
Proofing by Lori Parks: lp.nerdproblems@gmail.com

CONNECT WITH HAILEY

Keep up with my book news by signing up for my newsletter and get the free Soulbound prequel short story *Down A Twisted Path* and several free Metahuman Files short stories while you're at it.

Join the reader group on Facebook: Hailey's Hellions

Visit Hailey's website: www.HaileyTurner.com

Like Hailey's author page on Facebook

OTHER WORKS BY HAILEY TURNER

M/M Science Fiction Military Romance:

Captain Jamie Callahan, son of a wealthy senator and socialite mother, is a survivor.

Staff Sergeant Kyle Brannigan, a Special Forces operative, is a man with secrets.

Alpha Team, the Metahuman Defense Force's top-ranked field team, is where the two collide and their lives will never be the same.

Metahuman Files
01 – In the Wreckage
02 – In the Ruins
03 – In the Shadows
04 – In The Blood
05 – In The Requiem

A Metahuman Files: Classified Novella
01 – Out of the Ashes
02 – New Horizons

M/M Urban Fantasy
Soulbound
A Ferry of Bones & Gold - 1
All Souls Near & Nigh - 2

Thanks for reading!

SOULBOUND 2 SNEAK PEAK

Special Agent Patrick Collins winced as he clattered down the stairs of the Brooklyn Bridge-City Hall/Chambers Street subway entrance, the motion jarring his still-healing nose. The medical tape slapped over the bridge of it itched his skin, but he refrained from scratching at the annoyance.

The passage down into the subway was packed with people from a delayed rush hour commute on a Wednesday night. Despite the crowd, everyone got out of his way when Patrick said, "Federal agent, coming through."

Patrick's Supernatural Operations Agency badge hung from his neck, and his semiautomatic HK USP 9mm tactical pistol was holstered on his right hip. The gods-made dagger he never went anywhere without was securely strapped to his right thigh. Patrick had opted to leave his jacket with the agency lettering across the back in his car. August in New York City was too fucking hot to wear anything but short sleeves.

Patrick had been upstate dealing with an incursion of Redcaps for the past week. He'd been looking forward to going home once he landed at LaGuardia. One call from Special Agent in Charge

Henry Ng before he even deplaned and he'd been assigned an emergency case with the NYPD's Preternatural Crimes Bureau. It was a familiar song and dance he was too tired to perform but didn't have a choice.

He raked a hand through his dark red hair as he made it to the fare gates and kept moving past the officer on guard duty. No one tried to stop him.

At least this case is local.

Since June, Patrick had called New York City home. The transfer from the national office to a field office had taken some getting used to. The majority of the cases he handled now came out of New York state, though he still got sent out on national ones if the need was great enough. Media focus aside, Patrick was enjoying how less chaotic his job was lately.

Nothing about a dead body ruining a rush hour subway commute was enjoyable though.

Detective Specialist Dwayne Guthrie waved Patrick over once he made it to the subway platform. "About damn time, Collins."

"Would've been here sooner, but traffic was terrible," Patrick said.

"Maybe you should look into getting some lights and sirens put into your car. Or convince the mayor he needs a better outreach program for troubled youth so shit like this doesn't happen and we all get a night off for once. The dumbasses who sneak into the tunnels to tag turf keep getting eaten and it's annoying."

Patrick jerked his thumb over his shoulder. "There were signs up by the gates. No feeding the trolls."

Dwayne rolled his eyes. "Do you think any of the fools selling shit on the corner actually read? And what happened to your face?"

Patrick made an aborted motion to touch his face, his healing nose and bruised green eyes throbbing a little. "Went face-first into a tree. I took a potion before I got on the plane. I'll be fine."

A witch's brew was better than painkillers some days. The accelerated healing it could produce meant the swelling had gone down enough that Patrick could see out of both eyes, and the cartilage in his nose would mend straight in a couple of days rather than weeks. His head was still sore, not to mention the rest of his body, but ignoring the discomfort was second nature at this point.

Patrick gazed around the crowded center platform of the station. Several uniformed police officers were keeping the area near them clear, but no trains were running on their side of the platform. Patrick tugged at the collar of his T-shirt, feeling sweat trickle down his spine. Summer in the city was a swamp-like hell of high heat and high humidity, especially down in the subway.

"Where's the body?" Patrick asked.

"In the Old City Hall subway station," Dwayne replied.

"You've confirmed it's not a suicide?"

Dwayne nodded as he headed toward the end of the platform where a set of gated stairs were located, guarded by an officer. "You'll see why. A train operator spotted the body when his train looped around. Victim wasn't found on the tracks, but the MTA is holding the 6 line until we're done processing the area for evidence. We've been waiting on you."

"Bet the commuters aren't happy about that."

"Not my problem."

Patrick followed Dwayne off the platform and onto the subway tracks. The tunnel itself was dark, so Patrick called up a couple of witchlights to guide their way. Pale blue sparks erupted from his fingertips as he pushed magic out of his damaged soul, the illumination bouncing ahead of them. Casting the spell was harder than usual, but he chalked that up to the location.

Patrick grimaced at the feel of the wards that lined the tunnel walls. Subways were built through swaths of the veil, which meant their construction had been done by both mundane and magical means. The magic protecting the subway system was old, extensive, and powerful, with the anchor points of the wards radiating out from Grand Central Terminal. The wards made casting magic difficult, but an innocuous spell to conjure light was doable.

Minutes later, Patrick's witchlights merged with the brightness put out by portable floodlights, and he let his magic fade away. He and Dwayne came out of the dark tunnel into a station that made it feel as if they were stepping back in time. The vaulted ceiling with its leaded glass skylights and chandeliers were part of a bygone era that seemed out of place in today's modern world.

The body on the platform ruined the retro atmosphere.

Patrick lowered his personal shields, trying to get a read on the area, but his magic recognized no discernable threat. Members of the PCB's Crime Scene Unit were diligently working on collecting evidence while PCB officers kept watch. Patrick spotted Dwayne's partner, Detective Specialist Allison Ramirez, almost immediately. She waved them over, frowning at Patrick once they got closer.

"I know the chief requested federal help for this, but I didn't think we'd get to work with you again so soon," Allison said. "You look like you went a couple of rounds in the boxing ring and lost."

Patrick shrugged. "Actually, I won. What do we got?"

This was only the second time Patrick had been assigned to take over a case from the PCB. June had been a clusterfuck of epic proportions, but he'd come away from it having earned a little of Bureau Chief Giovanni Casale's respect. The people under his command were less antagonistic when dealing with Patrick this time around, which he appreciated. Usually local police didn't much like it when federal agencies took over their cases.

Allison gestured at the body. "Victim's state in death is similar to the murders in June, but they don't seem related. No heavenly signs sliced on his eyes. Body was chewed on for dinner though. Considering the amount of demonic cases the PCB has wedged in its pipeline, I'm inclined to add this one to the list."

"The wards down here should've prevented any demonic incursion. Any magic user on the MTA's payroll should know what to look for when it comes to damage while checking the lines."

"Maybe they missed something."

"It's possible. Sometimes the damage doesn't show right away and you get holes later on. The London Underground had a basilisk incursion about thirty years ago. Things ate their way through a weakened section at a switch point. Made a meal out of the morning commute."

"I read about that. Not a fun way to start your morning."

New York City had seen an increase in demon activity ever since the veil had torn over Central Park. Patrick had closed the hole between worlds at the end of that fight, but demons and monsters had still slipped through. It was possible the subway wards had taken some unnoticed damage.

Since June, the homicide rate had gone up in the city, faith in the SOA's ability to handle the problem was in the gutters, and Patrick was still the House Committee on Supernatural Oversight's favorite whipping boy at the moment.

Thinking about politics made Patrick want to drink.

The kid lying dead on the subway platform was never going to learn the joys of the legal drinking age. He was your typical troublemaker because it was usually troublemakers who decided to ruin public property. Cans of spray paint were scattered over the platform, each one tagged with an evidence number. Strangely enough, there wasn't any graffiti on the walls.

"Maybe it's a dump job," Patrick said.

"Hard to dump a body in the subway, especially in this spot. Access isn't easy on tracks with trains running, even for MTA workers," Dwayne pointed out.

Patrick approached the body and the woman crouched down taking notes on a clipboard. He was mindful of the numbered evidence tags in the area and made sure not to knock any over. "We have a time of death yet?"

"Sometime this morning, but it has to be verified back at the lab," the woman said. Her jacket had Medical Examiner written across the back, and her brown hair was twisted into a messy bun at the base of her neck. The identification dangling around her neck had her photo ID and the name Catherine Margolin printed on it beneath the medical examiner's logo.

"No chance of getting a more accurate time frame?"

Catherine shook her head, looking up at him. "Wards in the tunnel are messing with my equipment. Think you can stop the interference?"

Patrick pulled out a pair of black nitrile gloves from her work case. "No. Anchored protective wards on this scale aren't something you mess with. Besides, I don't really have an affinity for defensive magic."

"Then you're stuck waiting until I get back to the morgue for a more precise answer."

Magic users made up a quarter of the world's population, but everyone born with magic had a different affinity. Patrick excelled in offensive spells, and the damage done to his soul as a child meant he was better at recognizing threats from all the hells than most other magic users. That unwanted talent had come in handy throughout his nine years in the Mage Corps under the US Department of the Preternatural, and the past three with the SOA, usually at the expense of his health.

Crouching down, Patrick frowned at the corpse. "Trains were running during his time of death and all day today. The body would've been seen before now. It has to be a dump job."

Catherine waved her pen in the general vicinity of the crime scene. "Killed here or somewhere else, no one saw the victim until the train operator spotted the body. You'd be surprised at the things people don't see."

"No, I wouldn't. You already got your pictures?"

"Lots. Feel free to poke around. The PCB is starting to bag up evidence. We were waiting on you before we bagged the body."

The victim was missing the left arm up to the elbow, and the left leg was barely hanging on at the knee. The right arm lay mangled about a meter away, as if tossed there. The tears weren't clean, nor did they have the pulverized look to them that would've indicated being run over by a train before being laid out on the platform.

His head looked strangely misshapen until Patrick realized it wasn't damage, but most likely the body caught in the middle of a shift. He prodded at the stiff, cold lips, managing to get a look at the too-sharp, large teeth in the corpse's mouth.

"Werecreature," Patrick said.

Catherine nodded, still taking down notes. "Yeah. We're going to need to bring a hazmat crew down here to clean up the crime scene. Judging by his eye color, he's not god pack, so we can rule out that strain of the werevirus."

"Can't rule out dealing with the god pack."

Patrick wished he could.

The two strains of the werevirus had segregated the werecreature community into packs that were able to hide their status and god packs who couldn't. Those infected with the god strain of the werevirus were visual scapegoats for society, and the New York City god pack was hostile to anyone who didn't share their disease.

In the past, god packs used to have a connection to their animal-god patrons, but those were a rarity these days. The only god pack alpha Patrick knew of with a patron was a man the Fates had thrown at him without either of their consents.

Jonothon de Vere was an ex-pat Englishman, exiled from the London god pack and refused acceptance by the New York City god pack when he emigrated three years ago. The attraction between them upon first meeting two months ago had been purely physical. What Patrick felt for Jono now went deeper, though he wasn't sure if he could trust his own emotions in that area.

At the end of the fight in June, Patrick had unwittingly bound their souls together through the magic buried in the gods-given dagger he carried. The soulbond enabled Patrick to once again tap ley lines and nexuses by virtue of his newfound ability to channel his magic through Jono's soul. He'd spent three years since the Thirty-Day War carrying a soul wound that prevented him from accessing such an integral part of his magic. Having that ability back was life altering. That it came at the expense of Jono's autonomy meant Patrick had yet to do anything with his returned strength.

The soulbond was illegal, despite the accidental creation of it. Messing with a person's soul was a capital crime in the United States. Patrick couldn't ask for help in breaking the soulbond without being arrested, so he and Jono had agreed to keep it a secret, the same way they'd kept their newly formed pack a secret from the New York City god pack.

It was a good thing Patrick knew how to keep his mouth shut.

But like any good federal agent, he was adept at speaking for the dead and getting justice for the crimes committed against them.

The skin around the teenager's throat was mottled with bruises that lined a strip of burn scars too uniform to be anything but intentional. Werecreatures were severely allergic to silver, and aconite poisoning could be lethal. Patrick traced his gloved fingers over the burn area, measuring the space with his fingers.

It was just wide enough for the shape of a collar, which spoke of enslavement of some kind.

"He put up a fight," Catherine said.

"Against who is the question," Patrick said.

"Werecreatures have enhanced strength. Whatever killed him would've had to have been stronger."

"A silver bullet to the heart is just as lethal as a fight for dominance. He's got bruises, and werecreatures can heal those in seconds."

"Then he was killed before the bruises could disappear and before he could fully shift." Catherine pointed at the arm lying some distance from them. "His hands have defensive wounds. He didn't die easy."

"Nothing about his state in death suggests that. I'm going to need to know the werevirus strain he was infected with to figure out what pack he came from."

"I can type him once we get the body to the morgue and get you that confirmation tonight."

"Appreciate it."

"If you want to talk to the dead, we can call in the necromancer."

"I doubt a judge would sign off on a Resurrection Order for a murdered werecreature."

Necromancy was illegal in most countries. Calling back a soul gone to rest in order to raise the dead was anathema in most cultures. There were exceptions. Sometimes the government allowed a necromancer to work with strict government supervision, usually at the federal level or with a Preternatural Crimes Bureau in a major metropolitan area. Getting a Resurrection Order out of the courts was damned difficult most days.

All they had was a body and no motive. Setting aside society's inherent biases toward werecreatures, no judge would rubber stamp an order with that little evidence in hand.

Patrick lifted up some of the stiff jean fabric out of the way to get a better look at the cavity ripped into the left thigh. The femur bone was intact, but the femoral artery had damage to it reminiscent of bite marks. The only creatures Patrick knew of who liked blood as much as flesh were vampires.

"He had to have bled out somewhere else before getting dumped here," Patrick said thoughtfully. That was a headache he really didn't want to deal with.

Patrick's experience with vampires and their Night Courts was unique in a way he could've done without. He hadn't crossed paths with any of the Night Courts that claimed the five boroughs as their territory since transferring here. Looked like that was going to change.

In the grand scheme of things, vampires were still better than dealing with his father and twin sister. Their toxic family reunion back in June could've gone worse, but only if Patrick had put a gun to his own head and pulled the trigger.

Patrick straightened up, wincing as his bruised muscles pulled from the motion. The witch's brew could only heal so much. "Anything else I should know about?"

"Ramirez has the evidence I pulled out of the vic's pocket," Catherine said. She put her notepad into its metal carrying case and tucked it under one arm as she stood. "You might want to take a look at it."

"Allison?" Patrick called out as he stripped off his nitrile gloves and deposited them in the biohazard bin. "What was the guy carrying?"

Allison pointed at where evidence bags were laid out on the platform, hastily marked with a Sharpie pen. "Over there."

When Patrick got close enough to see, it wasn't what he was expecting. The first bag carried a handful of white pills, some broken and a few others whole. The intact pills each had a tiny red-black dot staining the center of each one, and Patrick frowned, poking at them through the plastic.

"Is this what I think it is?"

Allison nodded as she came over. "If you're thinking shine, then most likely. The drugs still need to be tested and verified."

Patrick rubbed at his mouth, staring hard at the pills in the evidence bag. Shine was a drug that had been around for hundreds of years through various iterations. Its origin stemmed from vampires, though historians couldn't agree on which Night Court first created and introduced it to their human servants.

These days the demand for shine meant most of it was lab synthesized. Its popularity came and went, but it looked like the city was having another love affair with the drug. The pills showing up this summer were cause for alarm though. Patrick had read a memo the SOA had sent out about them back in May.

The stuff hitting the streets right now was the real deal. Made with true vampire blood and all its supernatural properties, shine was a potent drug that offered a euphoric, sexual high to those who took it. Highly addictive, it allowed mundane humans the ability to see a person's aura, the bright shine of a person's soul that only magic users could sometimes see. Mundane human eyes weren't meant to process a sight like that, and they craved darkness—any kind of blindness really—while high.

Vampires had no souls and were more than willing to comfort an addict in the throes of addiction and withdrawal. The drug running through an addict's veins didn't affect them, merely gave the blood a different flavor.

Shine was how some Night Courts enslaved their human servants. Addiction could happen on the first hit, and the list of industrial chemicals that made up the drug could literally rot a person's brain. Bartering sex and blood to stave off some of the harsher effects of the drug wasn't a great trade-off. Most people in their right mind didn't want to be owned by a vampire, but addicts never made rational decisions.

Some mundane humans liked dancing with the darker aspects of the preternatural world. Magic users who took shine never handled the drug well and almost always ended up on a bad trip. They could already see a person's aura; shine stripped away their safeguards and could tip their magic dangerously out of control. Patrick, despite using cigarettes and alcohol as a crutch to get through his adult life, had never gone down the black hole of hard drugs.

As for werecreatures? Patrick knew the god pack had treaties with the Night Courts here marking off territory. The only way to get shine was through street gang dealers or directly from the source. Werecreatures shouldn't be working for vampires or buying from them, except he had a dead kid that said otherwise, amongst other things.

Patrick dropped the evidence bag onto the platform and reached for the second one that held a small figurine. Made out of white plastic, the skeleton reaper was shrouded in a hooded robe, carrying a scythe in one hand and a globe in the other. Despite the wards down here, Patrick could sense traces of black magic emanating from the figurine.

"This is an artifact," Patrick said, weighing it in his hand. Artifacts, portable objects capable of holding magic that nonmagic users could wield, felt heavier than they looked.

"Not surprised, considering what it is. Any idol of Santa Muerte is usually handled by a witch in this city. Our evidence bags are lightly warded, so anyone transporting it should be safe enough," Dwayne said as he approached.

Patrick was familiar with the religion that had sprung out of Mexico over the last few decades or so and spread through North and South America. It made him uneasy, but not for reasons most people would assume. Worship was a powerful tool for any god or goddess in the modern age, but he didn't much care for those who presided over the dead.

Patrick carefully set the sealed figurine down on the platform. "I doubt the kid worshipped Santa Muerte. Possibility of him being either a dealer or a junkie isn't something we can discount. The toxicology report is going to take weeks to confirm."

"The drugs could've been planted," Dwayne said, staring at the body. "Kid is African American. There's no love lost between black and Mexican gangs. Werecreature aside, he wouldn't be part of *any* Mexican gang unless he was killed out of retaliation or for an initiation. If that's the case, I don't know why he ended up down here and not in his own turf as a warning."

"Something to look into," Patrick said as he got to his feet.

"You may want to talk to someone in Narcotics and the Gang

Unit. They have a better handle on the shine problem than we do, even if they haven't tracked it to the source yet," Allison said.

Dwayne snorted. "Good luck with that. The DEA has been trying for years. Everyone knows the Omacatl Cartel has a monopoly on shine in the five boroughs, and every gang member the DEA has managed to arrest hasn't confessed to any alliance with vampires. Been that way for decades. I doubt it'll change anytime soon."

"Killing a werecreature goes against the treaties the Night Courts have with the god pack here though," Patrick pointed out. "That's an angle we need to figure out."

"We're always looking for hard evidence to pin on the blood-sucking bastards. Maybe we'll get lucky with this case." Dwayne cocked an eyebrow at him. "You can be our lucky charm."

Patrick made a face. "Like last time? No, thanks. I'll let you handle the transport of the body and evidence to your morgue. The sooner we get the autopsy report, the sooner we'll have some answers."

"Not handling it at the federal level?" Allison asked.

"I *am* the federal level, but I think everyone will feel a lot better if it all stays within the PCB."

He might hate politics, but Patrick could play the game when required. The SOA didn't have a stellar reputation at the moment, especially here. The PCB, on the other hand, was viewed far more favorably in the public eye right now. Patrick would prefer to work with the PCB rather than work out of the SOA field office, which would cut down on communication issues. His individual efforts with the PCB back in June had gone over a lot better than the SOA as a whole in media polls.

Besides, Patrick didn't have an assigned partner, and he'd learned over the years that relying on local help tended to smooth things over.

"You heading back to the PCB with us?" Dwayne wanted to know.

Patrick shook his head. "I'm going to run down the werecreature angle."

"I don't envy you talking to the god pack alphas at all."

Patrick shrugged and said nothing. Estelle Walker and Youssef Khan were the god pack alphas of New York City, but they weren't who Patrick was going to talk to.

Click for your copy of All Souls Near & Nigh now!

CPSIA information can be obtained
at www.ICGtesting.com
Printed in the USA
LVHW090836130222
710917LV00004B/146